THE KILL

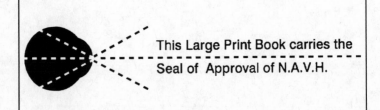

This Large Print Book carries the
Seal of Approval of N.A.V.H.

THE KILL

JANE CASEY

THORNDIKE PRESS
A part of Gale, Cengage Learning

GALE
CENGAGE Learning·

Farmington Hills, Mich • San Francisco • New York • Waterville, Maine
Meriden, Conn • Mason, Ohio • Chicago

GALE
CENGAGE Learning·

Thorndike Press® Large Print Crime Scene.
The text of this Large Print edition is unabridged.
Other aspects of the book may vary from the original edition.
Set in 16 pt. Plantin.

LIBRARY OF CONGRESS CATALOGING-IN-PUBLICATION DATA

Casey, Jane (Jane E.)
  The kill / by Jane Casey. -- Large print edition.
    pages cm. -- (Thorndike Press large print crime scene)
    ISBN 978-1-4104-8382-9 (hardcover) -- ISBN 1-4104-8382-7 (hardcover)
    1. Women detectives--England--London--Fiction. 2. Police--Crimes against--Fiction. 3. Murder--Investigation--Fiction. 4. Large type books.
  I. Title.
  PR6103.A847K55 2015b
  823'.92--dc23
                                                    2015028976

Published in 2015 by arrangement with St. Martin's Press, LLC

Printed in Mexico
1 2 3 4 5 6 7 19 18 17 16 15

For Mary Brennan,
with love and thanks

GLOSSARY OF POLICE TERMINOLOGY

Cell site analysis: a method of establishing where a mobile phone was when it made or received a call, by reference to the mast (or "cell site") that connected the phone to the network.

CPS: Crown Prosecution Service; responsible for assessing the evidence gathered during police investigations and deciding what, if any, offense a suspect should be charged with. Also responsible for the prosecution of defendants in the criminal courts.

CRB: Criminal Records Bureau; responsible for carrying out criminal records checks on those wishing to work in sensitive fields.

DPS: Department of Professional Standards (officially the "Directorate of Professionalism"); unit of the Metropolitan Police responsible for investigating allegations of misconduct against officers and civilian staff.

IPCC: Independent Police Complaints Commission; responsible for overseeing or conducting investigations into incidents where there may be police misconduct.

MIT team: Murder Investigation Team; operational units of the Met's Homicide and Major Crime Command; responsible for the investigation of murder, manslaughter, and attempted murder, as well as other serious and complex incidents. Each MIT has about thirty members and is led by a senior detective.

PC: Police Constable; the lowest rank in the British police.

PCSO: Police Community Support Officer; uniformed civilian staff employed to provide an additional uniformed presence and gather intelligence at a local level.

PM: Postmortem examination; medical examination of a body intended to establish, among other things, a cause of death.

Public order offense: an offense contrary to one of the Public Order Acts involving offensive behavior in public places, including serious public disorder.

QC: Queen's Counsel; a senior barrister with a high degree of experience and professional competence, instructed to prosecute and defend in the most serious criminal cases.

Response Officer: uniformed police officer attached to a team that responds to 999 calls from the public.

SNT: Safer Neighborhoods Team; a local police unit covering one local government ward, typically consisting of one uniformed sergeant, several PCs, and a number of PCSOs.

SOCO: Scenes of Crime Officer; civilian police staff who gather forensic evidence. Officially known as Forensic Practitioners in the Metropolitan Police.

Specials: Special Constables; volunteer police officers who have the same powers as full-time officers but are unpaid.

TSG: Territorial Support Group; uniformed unit mainly tasked with preventing and responding to incidents of public disorder. TSG units are routinely used to support local officers dealing with large-scale violence.

Warrant card: photocard identifying the holder as a police officer.

Richmond Park

The cold was like a living thing. It had sunk its teeth through the layers of clothing Megan wore, sliding through her skin to get to her bones. They ached. They hurt even more than the muscle cramping in her calf. She pulled her sleeves down over her hands and tucked her arms under her body. Slowly, she let her head sink down too, so her face was pillowed on the grass. She wanted to sleep so much. Her eyes kept closing. Maybe it would be easier to stay awake if she paid attention to the sounds of the night: Hugh's breathing beside her, the wind in the trees, a rustle in the undergrowth, the music of the stars . . .

"See that?"

The voice was little more than a whisper but it stabbed through the lovely, soft darkness that had wrapped around Megan like a blanket.

"Hm?" She jerked her head up and looked

11

keenly into the night at absolutely nothing.

"Ten o'clock."

It took her a second to work out what Hugh meant, and by the time she'd looked where she was supposed to, there was nothing to see. Beside her, Hugh's leg twitched in what she guessed was irritation.

"What was it?"

"Great big sow. Lovely lady."

"I missed it."

"Shh. She might be back."

Megan rubbed her eyes and peered at the featureless undergrowth again. All she needed was one flash of black and white, one sighting that she could take home like a trophy to prove that she'd been right to spend Saturday night sprawled in the mud in Richmond Park. She couldn't shake the unworthy thought that she'd missed *The X Factor* for this. Bloody Ruby would have watched it, hours ago, curled up on the sofa in their flat. Ruby, who'd be asleep now. Ruby, who'd suggested she was only going out looking for badgers with Hugh because she fancied him. Megan had thought he was cute, but in an abstract, on-the-television-and-therefore-attractive way. She wouldn't even kiss him, never mind anything more. Even the thought made Megan gag a little, but she turned it into a cough, just in case

12

Hugh asked her what was wrong. She was no good at lying and she didn't want to hurt his feelings. That good deed earned her a glare from Hugh, and a twitch that made his beard move in a very disconcerting way. Badgers were shy, he'd told her. They had to be quiet and still. With the two of them there, they'd be lucky to see anything at all.

And now she'd missed the only thing to happen for hours. Who knew when Hugh would give up?

The silence settled around them again. Megan made herself concentrate. She would make the best of this. She would see a beautiful badger in the wild, and have an experience to remember forever, and she would never, ever do this again.

The bang was shatteringly loud. It echoed around them and rolled out across the dark open spaces below, and as it faded Megan wasn't altogether sure she hadn't imagined it, until the second one came a moment later.

"What the eff was that?" Hugh abandoned any attempt to be stealthy, sitting up, bristling with outrage. He was still too conscious of his image to do anything as uncouth as proper swearing, Megan noted. Minor television personalities did not swear.

"It sounded like a gun," she said timidly.

"It can't have been. Must have been a car backfiring."

"I don't think it was a car."

"Must have been." Hugh was older than Megan by at least ten years, and he didn't like it when she offered opinions, she'd noticed. He liked it when she listened to him and agreed with what he was saying. But she knew what she'd heard.

"We should call the police."

"Don't be ridiculous."

"I'm not being ridiculous." But she let her phone slide back into her pocket anyway, recalling that there was no signal where they were. "Look, I don't like it. Let's go." She stood up, assuming that adventures in badger-watching were over for the night since Hugh was practically shouting.

"Get down!" He grabbed her leg, just above her knee.

"If it was a car, it doesn't matter if I stand up."

Cowardice fought a battle with superiority and won. "All right. You might be right. It might have been a gun. So stop drawing attention to yourself."

"They weren't shooting at us."

"How do you know?" She could see the whites of his eyes gleaming in the darkness. "They could be extremists. People who hate animal-lovers like us."

"Now that really is ridiculous." Megan began to walk away, taking long strides to get through the tangled grass. A flurry of movement behind her was Hugh, rushing to catch up.

"Meg! Wait!"

Megan absolutely, one hundred percent loathed being called "Meg." She went faster, concentrating on where she put her feet rather than the swearing and fussing behind her.

"Megan! Get down! There's a car!"

The road skirted the bumpy hillside where Hugh had said there was a badgers' sett, where they had waited for hours. She crouched and watched the car pass below them. It was just a shape, little more than a shadow, driving without lights. Its engine seemed noisy in the stillness of the night. Beside her, Hugh was trying to hide in the grass. The tiny spark of attraction flared and died forever.

"It's okay, Hugh. They've gone."

"Christ . . . I mean, crikey . . ."

She gave him a minute to recover himself. "Let's get back to the car park."

"I'm going to call the police."

"Okay. Good idea." *It was a good idea five minutes ago when I suggested it, too.* Megan hoped he was on a different network, but in the blue light of the phone's screen, Hugh's face was grim.

"Damn. No signal."

He hurried past her, not waiting to see if she was following. She stuck her hands in her pockets and trudged after him, trying to remember the car and whether she'd seen anything of the driver, or if there'd been a passenger. The police would want to know. If it was connected with the shooting.

If there had even *been* a shooting.

They were following a different route back, she realized after a while, across the flank of the hill.

"Why are we going this way?"

"This is the quickest way," Hugh threw over his shoulder, not stopping. "And I don't want to walk along the road in case they come back."

Megan considered the long, winding walk they had taken at the start of their expedition, over uneven ground that required a lot of arm-holding and hands-on guiding to navigate. She'd wondered about it, but she hadn't minded. She minded now, now that she was cold and her feet were wet from the dew and fear prickled across her skin like an electrical charge. She didn't think they had been targeted, or even noticed, but she didn't like being out there in the dark when something strange was going on.

Woodland crowned the top of the hill. Megan was glad that Hugh didn't lead them through it — the trees grew close together and the darkness under the canopy seemed impenetrable. Going around the edge wasn't much less hazardous. Hugh tripped over a log half-hidden in the grass.

"Sh— sugar."

He was concentrating on watching where he was going when Megan exclaimed, "Look."

"What is it?"

"Another car."

Hugh was crouching before she'd finished saying the second word. "It's a trap. It must be. An ambush. They pretended they were leaving so we'd show ourselves." He pulled his phone out of his pocket and checked it again, with the same result. Twisting around to look at her, he snapped, "For God's sake, Meg, get low and stay low."

"This one is parked," Megan pointed out.

It was parked in an odd place, though. There was a small service road that branched off the main one. It wasn't open to the public — Megan had noticed the signs earlier, on her way past. The car was parked under the trees, pointing into the darkness, and from the road it would have been more or less invisible. From where Megan was standing she could see the back windows and the boot, but that was only because her eyes were used to the lack of light. She couldn't have said why but she was drawn toward it.

"Where are you going? Come back!"

Megan was getting used to ignoring Hugh's hissed orders. She kept going, bending to peer inside the car, but the darkness was total. She was within twenty yards of it when she stopped.

"What is it?" Hugh had followed, staying well back.

"The windscreen is shattered."

"Maybe they crashed."

"I don't think so." She took a few more steps, getting closer. "I think —"

It was like one of those pictures that plays with perception, where a flock of birds turns into a crowd of people. One minute there was a car, familiar and unthreatening despite the broken glass. Then she looked again. Once she'd seen the blood, she couldn't see anything else.

"What? Meg, what's wrong?"

The Megan who had agreed, giggling, to go badger-watching with Hugh would have whirled around to bury her face in his chest.

That Megan would have let him take charge. That Megan would have sobbed out her horror and upset and would have been glad to be comforted.

That Megan was gone, maybe forever. The new Megan turned to Hugh. Her voice was calm, when she spoke. Cold, even. The distress was there, somewhere, but hidden by a strange kind of composure.

"We do need to call the police. We should hurry."

"What is it?"

"I think what we heard *were* shots." She paused for a second. "I think we heard a murder."

CHAPTER ONE

Afterward, everyone agreed on one thing: she was a beautiful bride. Christine Bell was always pretty, but on her wedding day she glowed with happiness. A cynic might have said the glow was something to do with the small bump under the forgiving folds of her empire-line wedding dress. *I* might have said it, but I was having a day off from cynicism. Even though I was allergic to public displays of affection, I let Rob hold my hand as Christine walked past us up the aisle. She beamed as she clung to her father's arm, taking her time about getting to the altar although the organist was thundering through "Here Comes the Bride" as if it was a race to the finish.

Leaning out, I could see Ben Dornton as he turned around to watch her walking toward him and the mixture of love, awe, and hope on his face jolted me out of my usual composure. Ben was a detective sergeant on my team. Balding and thin, he was not my idea of a romantic hero, even in a pearl-gray morning suit, but there was something unguarded and honest in his expression that brought tears to my eyes. I squeezed Rob's hand as I swallowed the lump in my throat and blinked furiously, afraid to rub my eyes in case I smudged my mascara. He didn't look at me but I could see the corners of his mouth twitching and knew why: a five-pound bet outside the church that I would cry before Christine made it to the altar.

Which reminded me about the other party to that particular bet. I leaned forward to see across the aisle, to the box pew where DI Josh Derwent was standing on his own, order of service in hand, glowering at me. He shook his head slowly, disgusted. He'd thought I could hang on until the vows before I wept. Not for the first time, I'd let him down.

And since I'd bet both of them I wouldn't cry at all, I'd let myself down too.

I didn't care. I shrugged at Derwent and went digging in my bag for a tissue. There were plenty of other people in the congregation who were sobbing happily too: most of Christine's family, including her father, and lots of my colleagues' girlfriends who were obviously imagining the day it would be their turn. The two bridesmaids, still pink from their walk to the altar, were dabbing at their eyes. And why not cry? It was a beautiful day, and Christine was a beautiful bride, and the two of them couldn't have been happier to be getting married. There was a baby on the way, it was true, but this wasn't a shotgun wedding. They had got engaged months before the bride got pregnant. Christine was a civilian analyst in our office, and liked to confide in me for no reason that I could see, so I had been party to the long, tearful discussions in the ladies' loo about whether it was better to postpone the wedding until after the baby had arrived or whether she should just get on with it. My vote had been firmly for getting on with it. There was a limit to how many times I could feign interest in swatches of material for bridesmaids' dresses or wedding favors or accent colors for decorating the chairs at the reception.

Besides, I was looking forward to the wedding. I had a dress I wanted to wear that would just about do for a September wedding. Midnight-blue, narrow, and strapless, it was a world away from my usual work clothes. Rob had booked time off from work so we could go together, and I'd never been to the part of Somerset where the bride's family lived. The wedding was in a tiny thirteenth-century church in the middle of a postcard-perfect village. The church was currently crammed with rather a lot of the Met's finest, but you could still admire the rood screen if that was your thing, and the carving on the pulpit, and the marble monuments to local worthies from centuries ago. Afterward the reception would be across the road, in a marquee in the garden of the bride's aunt's house. We were staying in one of the local pubs, where they had romantic rooms with low beams and wide, soft beds, and a roll-top bath by the window. I had booked to stay an extra night, so Rob and I could be alone together. In almost two years we'd never gone away anywhere on holidays. A trip to the country, even if it was just for the weekend, made a nice change.

The only problem was that I couldn't drink any of the French wine that Ben had traveled across the Channel to buy — cases and cases of it, since he knew his colleagues well enough to cater for a big night. Derwent had driven some of it down from London in his car, and Rob had gone to help him unload it while we hung around before the wedding.

"Not that there's much point since I won't be able to have any." Derwent dumped a box by the marquee and went back to get another one.

"Are you on call? So's Maeve." Rob was moving much more slowly than Derwent, not being in the least bothered about the inspector's compulsion to prove himself quicker and stronger than any other man. Tall and broad-shouldered, Rob looked extremely handsome in his best suit. As if he knew what I was thinking, he winked at me before he disappeared inside the marquee. I guessed he was going to put the case behind the bar, where it was needed, rather than leaving it outside. Derwent was on his third case by now, piling them up. I sat on the wall and watched the two of them, amused.

"It's typical." Derwent glared at me. "And I'll be watching you, Kerrigan. No sneaking a glass of fizz."

"Just to toast the happy couple."

He pointed at me. "Not a drop."

"I wouldn't," I protested. "I know the rules. Besides, the boss is going to be there. I wouldn't dare." The boss was Superintendent Charles Godley, one of the Met's stars, who was handsome and talented and expected the best from his team. We investigated murders. The most complex and sensitive ones came to us, which was flattering, but it meant that we couldn't shut down for the weekend. Everyone was invited to the wedding but some of us had to stay sober, ready to rush back to London if we were needed. Rob had been one of us, once upon a time. He knew the score. Given the choice, he would have been happy to be on call too, I felt.

But we wouldn't be needed. I closed my eyes and tilted my face up so the sunshine could warm it. The weather was perfect. Everything would be perfect.

Derwent nudged my foot with the toe of his shoe. "Wake up."

"I'm not asleep," I said, not opening my eyes. "Why are you bothering me?"

"There's no one else to talk to."

"Why didn't you bring a date? Couldn't you find anyone?"

"Of course I could have found someone. I wanted to come on my own."

"Why?"

"I have my reasons."

Something in his voice made me open my eyes. I shaded them with my hand so I could look at him. "Do I want to know what those reasons are?"

A grin. "Probably not."

"Tell me anyway."

"Maybe later." He looked past me and raised a hand. "There's Ben. Poor fucker. He looks as if he's going to spew."

"He's probably nervous."

"Nervous that Christine won't turn up. It's a good thing he got her pregnant. She's a long way out of his league."

"She's completely in love with him," I said, my voice sharp. "She'll be there because she wants to marry Dornton."

A slow headshake. "That was quality minge."

I shuddered. "Congratulations. That is absolutely the most offensive way you could have said you found Christine attractive."

"Do you reckon?" Derwent leaned back, hands in his pockets, thinking. "I bet I can come up with something more offensive than that."

"Please don't bother." I stood up.

"Aw. I was enjoying the view."

"What view?"

The grin again. "You should always wear skirts like that. With a slit, I mean."

I had forgotten about the slit. It ran up as far as my thigh, and when I sat down, most of my left leg was on display. I blushed, which was annoying. "Not exactly ideal for work."

"No. Not with stockings, anyway." The grin had got wider. "Lace tops, too. Nice."

"What are you two talking about?" Rob had finished moving the boxes from Derwent's car, as well as the ones Derwent had abandoned outside the marquee. Now he strolled across the grass to stand beside me. He slung an arm around my shoulders and pulled me toward him so he could drop a kiss on my cheek. I knew my face was hot.

"I was just saying what a lucky man you are," Derwent said smoothly.

"You won't get any arguments from me." Rob's arm tightened around me for just a second and I didn't duck away. Having him there was like emotional body armor, which I badly needed when Derwent was around.

I twisted to see the church, where there was a growing crowd centered on Dornton. "Let's go and talk to the others."

Derwent had come with us, but diluted by lots of other people he wasn't as bad. The conversation had been distinctly less personal, at least until Rob and he had started placing bets on whether I'd cry or not.

I looked across the aisle again, to where Derwent was sitting, somber in dark-gray. He looked more like he was at a funeral than a wedding, I thought. Coming into autumn he was at his leanest, with two marathons done for the year and another lined up before winter. His jawline was sharply cut, his cheeks slightly hollow, and to me he looked hungry, but possibly not for food. He was sitting quite still, his attention directed somewhere other than the couple standing at the front of the church, exchanging their vows with tremulous sincerity. I followed the line of his gaze to see where he was looking and I was not in the least surprised to find that he was staring at the prettier of the two bridesmaids. Nor was I all that surprised that she was staring back. He looked all right, from a distance. It was only when you got talking to him that you realized he was the last man on earth you should tangle with.

I just hoped she'd have the sense to run away.

It was after the dinner (excellent), the speeches (long), and the bride and groom's first dance (awkward but tender) that Derwent came for me. I was sitting beside Rob, my back to the rolled-up side of the marquee. I was enjoying myself in a mild way but I hadn't said much all evening. I was missing Liv, my friend and colleague, who was recovering from a nasty injury and had been off work for almost a year. She was traveling with her girlfriend, and had sent good wishes. I would have preferred to have her there. A light breeze from the garden sighed across my skin, but it was hot in the marquee and I didn't need or want my jacket. Rob had taken off his too, and his tie, and rolled up his sleeves. His hair was a little bit rumpled and I watched him laughing at one of Chris Pettifer's jokes, the lines lengthening around his eyes in a way that made my heart turn over. True to my word, I hadn't had a drop to drink but I felt not quite sober, all the same, when I looked at Rob. I wanted to lean against him and whisper in his ear. I wanted to tangle my fingers in his hair and kiss him. I wanted to press my body against him. I wanted to draw him into the dark garden and be alone with him. I settled for dropping a hand on his long, lean thigh, feeling the muscles move under my palm as he registered the contact and knew just what it meant.

Derwent's voice shattered my reverie. "Can I borrow your bird?"

"Depends," Rob said. "Why do you want her?"

"Just a dance."

I looked up at Derwent, unsmiling in his suit. He was as immaculate as he'd been eight hours earlier. So much for the party mood.

"I'm not dancing," I said.

"Why not?"

"I hate dancing when I'm sober." It was true. I felt too self-conscious. I was too tall to be inconspicuous on a dance floor.

"I'll look after you." Derwent held out a hand to me. "Come on."

"Go on." Rob nudged me, as if I wanted his encouragement. "I don't mind."

"I do," I said.

"Don't be such a misery-guts," Derwent snapped. "Just come and dance with me. It won't take long."

Something in the way he said it made me suspicious. "Why? What's your game?"

He leaned down so he could lower his voice. The music was loud enough that he didn't really need to murmur. All the same, I could see the need for caution when he said, "I need you to make Beth jealous."

"Beth?"

"The bridesmaid."

"Which one is Beth?"

"Does it matter?" Derwent demanded. Then he relented. "The fit one. Dark hair. Nice tits. Not the one who looks like an ironing board in a frock."

31

"Good choice," Rob said. "Good luck, mate."

"No luck required. Just Kerrigan."

I was glaring at Rob, who had given no sign of even noticing the bridesmaids, let alone of having assessed their chests.

"What?" he said, blinking at me, all innocence.

"Nothing." I looked up at Derwent who tilted his head to one side.

"Please?"

I really wanted to say no. I'd felt sorry for Derwent earlier, though, coming to the wedding on his own. He looked lonely. I was pretty sure he *was* lonely. And I was so completely happy with Rob I couldn't take away his chance to feel the same way.

"Go on, Maeve," Rob said. "Have fun."

I stood up and it took Rob a second to follow my face all the way up. He squinted slightly as he tried to focus and I wondered just exactly how drunk he was. To Derwent, I said, "One dance. But I want you to know I don't approve of you playing mind games with the poor girl. If you like her, just tell her that."

"Yeah, because that always works." Derwent rolled his eyes.

I opened my mouth to reply and stopped, as Rob's hand slid inside the slit in my skirt and ran up the back of my leg. When he slipped his fingers between my legs so he could stroke the soft skin at the top of my thigh, I thought, *Oh.* That *drunk.*

I looked up and saw Derwent grinning at me. He knew exactly what Rob was doing, I realized, and I stepped away from my boyfriend so I was out of range.

"Do I have your permission to do what I like with her?" Derwent asked Rob.

"You have my permission to try. But don't blame me if she hurts you."

"Can you stop talking to Rob as if he owns me?" I grabbed Derwent's arm and marched him toward the dance floor, where the band was halfway through "That's Amore."

"When I'm dancing with someone who's taken, I like to get everything agreed in advance so I don't get thumped. He's a big lad, your bloke."

"So are you."

"I still wouldn't want to fight him."

"Well, I wouldn't want to ruin Ben and Christine's wedding with a brawl, so behave yourself."

Derwent shook his head. "That's not going to work."

He took hold of me and took charge, spinning me around so I was breathless and laughing after a couple of minutes. It turned out that Derwent was surprisingly good at dancing, despite the slight limp he'd acquired a few months earlier when he was injured in the line of duty. I was almost disappointed when the song ended. He stood beside me, though, and made no move toward the edge of the dance floor.

"They look happy," I said, watching Ben and Christine kiss in the middle of the dance floor as people applauded them.

"It'll be you next."

"Not next," I said. "But maybe someday." I looked across at Rob, who was watching us, a half-smile on his face. His eyes were still slightly unfocused but I had the feeling he was paying more attention than a casual onlooker might have thought.

"That's commitment," Derwent said.

"It is for me."

"I wasn't taking the piss. He's lucky."

"Oh." I was wrong-footed and, for once, speechless.

"How's the self-esteem today, Kerrigan?"

That was more like Derwent. I glowered. "Fine. I'm not used to you being nice, that's all."

"Saying it as I see it, that's all. Nothing nice about it." He waited a beat. "You're lucky too, though. He puts up with you which is more than ninety-nine point nine percent of men would bother to do."

Ugh. "If you want to find a girlfriend, do you really think the best way is by dancing with me?"

He pulled me toward him. "I'm not looking for a girlfriend tonight, Kerrigan. I'm looking for a shag. Weddings are all about shagging. And making Beth jealous is the last thing I need to do to tip her over the edge."

"You old romantic."

"I am romantic. I love weddings." The band played the first few chords of "Can't Help Falling in Love with You." The singer was no Elvis but he gave it his best shot, crooning into his microphone with his eyes closed. Derwent pulled me so close to him the buttons on his jacket dug into my stomach. "I've got a system. Scope out the talent during the ceremony. Choose your target. Make contact with her before the meal. Watch her during the meal, so you can see if she's eating." He leaned even closer so his lips were almost brushing my ear. "Desire kills all other appetites. If she's eating, forget it. If she can't eat, you're in."

"Did Beth eat?"

"Not that I saw. And I was watching." He sounded infinitely smug.

"I still don't know why you're mauling

me and not her." I could hear the irritation in my voice and Derwent wouldn't have missed it. He skimmed his left hand down so it was resting on the curve of my bottom.

"Because she thinks she's missed her chance and she'll be so grateful to be wrong."

"What are you doing?" I wriggled, trying to get away.

"Dancing with you. Settle down and enjoy it, Kerrigan. For the next two minutes, you're mine."

He was too strong for me to be able to put any air between us. I felt his breath on my neck, his heartbeating much slower than mine, his hand warm on my skin through the thin material of my dress. His chest pressed against mine and my bodice slid a vital quarter of an inch lower. His hips moved against me, in time to the music, and I found I couldn't quite catch my breath. His attention was focused on my cleavage but as I leaned back, trying to get some space, he stared straight into my eyes, and that was somehow more intimate than anything else. I couldn't look away, until he did, and then I took a few moments to find my voice.

"Take your hand off my arse, sir."

The grin. "Fifty-six seconds. I'm impressed."

"Move it," I ordered.

"On a normal bird, that would be your waist."

"The fact that I'm taller than average is not a reason for you to grope me."

He let go of me altogether and stepped back, laughing. "I wondered what it would take to make you angry."

"Sorry to ruin your game."

"You didn't." Derwent's eyes were narrow with amusement. "Beth left when we started dancing to this song. She's been gone pretty much the whole time."

My face was flaming. "So that was you having fun."

"Oh come on, Kerrigan. You enjoyed it too."

I turned away from him and stalked through the marquee, then out the other side without speaking to anyone. The sign for the ladies pointed toward a trailer with three cubicles in it and a bank of mirrors and sinks on the other side. I rattled up the steps of the trailer, moving fast, as if I was home free once I got inside. Derwent would follow me if he felt like it. The sanctity of the ladies' loo meant nothing to him. But why would he follow me? He'd had his fun.

He spent his whole life trying to get a re-action from people, the more outraged the better, and I'd played right into his hands. I needed to be alone, just to get my composure back, but of course I wasn't alone.

Standing at the sink, arms folded, was Beth the bridesmaid. The other bridesmaid was leaning on the counter beside her. The two of them broke off their conversation to glare at me, which settled what they'd been talking about. I took my time checking my appearance in the mirror before I shut myself in a cubicle. I wasn't going to be intimidated by two twenty-four-year-olds in flamingo-pink satin. I stared at myself, noting that my cheeks were flushed, my eyes bright with upset. At least my hair, straightened for the wedding, was under control for once.

I shut the door and sat down on the closed loo, my hands to my face. My heart was still pounding. I took a few deep breaths of chemical-sweet air. I couldn't even work out what I was feeling: a hell-brew of embarrassment, shame, and anger. It wasn't just that I was mortified about being felt up in front of my colleagues and my boyfriend. I couldn't bear the fact that I had responded to Derwent on some base, biological level, far below logic and reason. Outside, the conversation was continuing in whispers and stifled giggles. Irritation, I found, was a lot better than humiliation. I counted to twenty, then unlocked the door.

"Was there something you wanted to ask me?" I said to Beth.

She looked terrified. "No."

Her friend was bolder. "What are you doing with Josh? He likes Beth."

"Yes, he does."

"And you were hanging around with that fit dark-haired bloke earlier. Isn't he your boyfriend?"

"Yes, he is."

For a split-second, the bridesmaid who was not Beth looked disappointed that Rob wasn't single. *As if,* I thought, abandoning the moral high ground.

"Well, why were you all over Josh? How do you know him? Or don't you?"

"I work with him."

"No you don't," Beth said. "He's a police officer. He investigates murders."

"So do I."

She looked surprised. "Seriously?"

"I'm a detective constable."

I watched the two of them stare at me, checking out the shoes and the legs and the very fitted dress that was cut to make the most of my chest and the least of my waist.

"I think, even if I was a police officer, I'd be ashamed to be that much of a slut in public while my boyfriend was watching." Plain bridesmaid's tone was biting.

God, I hated the word *slut*. I was tempted to snap back, but I took hold of my temper. There was one way to neutralize Derwent, at least for the rest of the evening, assuming he was right and the lady was willing.

"I was just dancing," I said. "And Josh really likes Beth. Beth, do you like Josh?"

She nodded.

"Then go and find him. Put us all out of our misery."

I'd have warned her to be careful but there didn't seem to be much point. I left her checking her makeup as her friend redid her hair, shoving in hairpins with thin-lipped concentration. It had to be hard to be the not-pretty bridesmaid, even if Beth's reward was a short liaison with my DI.

I walked down the steps to the path that led back to the marquee, not hurrying this time. Light spilled out of the tent across the grass, and the band had gone up-tempo again with "Walking on Sunshine." Gales of laughter rang out and a woman screamed, then cackled loudly. I wished I felt more like partying. I wished I could have a drink and forget the previous twenty minutes had ever happened.

My eyes were getting used to the darkness. Glancing to my right, I saw a figure standing motionless under a tree. Derwent.

As I got close enough to see his face I faltered and stopped. It was his expression — dark, undisguised desire. I could tell what he wanted and how he wanted it: a willing partner bent over a car bonnet, right there and then. No preamble. No romance. Just sex.

And I was scared. Not of him, but of what I might do. There was a reckless, hand-in-the-fire, jump-in-the-river part of me that I kept hidden, but it still existed. I wasn't to be trusted with my own happiness. I hadn't wanted to fall in love with Rob because I knew I would wreck it, somehow. Derwent was the ultimate bad idea, on every level. And I loved Rob.

I knew, though, that if Derwent said my name then, I might be tempted to go to him.

All of this flashed through my mind like a wildfire in the space of a half-second, before I realized he was looking past me, to where Beth was stepping down from the trailer on to the gravel path. I don't even think Derwent had noticed me break my stride.

I walked on, into the brightly lit marquee,

where everyone was flushed from the heat of dancing and the good French wine. Nothing about my appearance would make me stand out to anyone, even though my face was flaming. I tacked sideways, away from where Rob was sitting, knowing that his very inconvenient habit of reading my mind would be too dangerous to risk. I was heading for the bar and a glass of water. I had to recover something like self-possession before I went back to him.

"Maeve."

I jumped about a mile. "Sir."

Godley smiled down at me, tall and film-star handsome as ever. "You can call me Charles. We're off duty."

"I don't actually think I can," I said truthfully and he laughed.

"Give it another couple of years of working with me and you'll be calling me far worse things than my name. Look at Josh. He has absolutely no respect for me."

I flinched a little at the sound of Derwent's name, and Godley saw it. He frowned, then asked, "Are you having a good time?"

"Of course." I smiled at him. "I was just going to get a drink. Water, I mean."

"I could do with a refill too." He stood back to let me go first, following me to the bar where I waited for the bar staff to notice us. And waited. And waited.

"If you don't mind, I could try," Godley said in my ear.

"Be my guest." I swapped places with him. Instantly, two of the girls dropped what they were doing to rush over and take his order. While we waited for the drinks a heavy-set middle-aged man blundered up to the bar and cannoned into me. With tremendous courtesy Godley put his arm around me to move me out of range. For the second time that night, I was aware of getting a completely undeserved glare from other women because of who I was with.

Which reminded me. As I took my glass from Godley, I asked, "Is Serena here? I haven't seen her."

His expression darkened. "She isn't here. I came alone."

"You and Derwent both did. You should have been each other's dates."

"I've seen what Josh does to his dates. No thanks."

I wondered if Godley had seen what Derwent had done to me. He had moved on, though.

"I should tell you, Maeve . . . Serena and I are getting divorced."

"What? Why?" I realized it was none of

43

my business as soon as I asked. "I mean, I'm sorry. Sorry to hear that."

Godley grimaced. "It's been coming for a while. Sometimes things go too far and you can't find a way back to where you used to be."

"I'm sorry," I said again.

Godley was about to say something else but his expression changed and he reached into the inside pocket of his jacket to get his phone, which was vibrating from an incoming call. He handed me his glass so he could hold the phone and jam the other hand against his ear. I moved a few steps away to give him some privacy, even though his side of the conversation was monosyllabic. Minutes passed and I edged further away, thinking I should find myself someone else to talk to rather than hang around waiting for the boss to remember I was there. He had tucked the phone between his shoulder and his ear so he could scrawl notes on a paper napkin, writing fast, his expression grim. I watched, not sure how I could help or if I should try.

Godley turned around then, looking for me, and I knew it was bad, whatever he was hearing. He snapped his fingers to get me to come closer and shielded the phone so the person on the other end couldn't hear what he was saying. "Go and get Derwent. Right now."

I went. I dumped the glasses on a nearby table and hurried out to the sweet-smelling garden, going as fast as I could though my heels were slowing me down on the gravel path. After a few steps I slid my shoes off and ran on the grass instead, heading for the car park.

The area where the cars were parked was deserted and badly lit, but I could see straightaway I'd been wrong about the car bonnet. No one was even near Derwent's car, let alone sprawled across it. I slowed down, looking around. I'd been so sure . . .

As I got closer, I realized I wasn't as wrong as all that. They were in the back seat.

Without my shoes I was completely silent. I moved around to the window closest to Derwent's head, and I used the heel of the shoe I was carrying to rap on the glass, hard. His head came up fast and I saw him swearing as he reached over to open the door. Beth was frantically trying to readjust her dress, tugging the top half up and the bottom half down.

"What the fuck, Kerrigan?"

"We've got a call." For Beth's benefit, because Derwent already knew, I added, "We have to go."

45

CHAPTER TWO

"It goes without saying that I'm sorry for spoiling your evening." Godley looked around the small circle of his team, the five of us who had been pulled out of the party to stand and wait for our orders. We were standing a little way from the marquee, on a paved area beside a small pond. Frogs chirped in the darkness. I checked the time: after one and there was no sign of the wedding reception winding down.

Godley went on: "We've been asked to investigate the murder of a police officer."

There was an intake of breath from most of us, but no actual surprise. If we were being brought in to investigate in the middle of the night when we were miles from London, it had to be something serious and complicated. That was Godley's remit after all.

"Who?" Derwent demanded.

"A sergeant who works out of Isleworth.

Terence Hammond is his name. Have any of you come across him?"

Five heads shook in unison.

"Good. That's a help." Godley took a paper napkin out of his pocket and checked the notes he'd taken earlier. "He was forty-two. Married, with two children. He was shot in the chest."

"On duty?" Chris Pettifer this time, barrel-chested and gravel-voiced.

"He was coming off duty. On his way home, around a quarter to one."

"While he was driving?" I asked.

"No. He'd stopped his car in Richmond Park. His home address is on the Kingston side of the park. I assume he used the park as a shortcut to get home."

"But why did he stop?" I asked.

"No idea. He was in a side road near the Pen Ponds car park." Godley read out the GPS location so we could find it. Richmond Park was the biggest area of open ground in London, a diamond-shaped wilderness that sprawled for more than 2,500 acres. I'd worked smaller crime scenes.

Godley went on: "I don't know any more than that, except that he was found almost immediately, so we can be fairly sure about the timings. His family still hasn't been informed. This came straight to us because

47

of his job."

"Are you sure there's a connection? Was he killed because he was a copper?" Derwent asked. His face was watchful, his concentration total. I found it hard to imagine he had been up to his elbows in a bridesmaid minutes before. His gaze flicked to me for a second and I cut my eyes away from him, staring at Godley as if I had to memorize every detail of his appearance.

"Not sure of anything yet. I'm not even sure of the details. That's why we need to get there. I don't like getting everything secondhand." Godley looked around at us, the light from the marquee throwing half of his face into shadow. "Does everyone have a way to get to the scene from here?"

"I'm all right," Chris said, and Dave Kemp nodded too. Chris was divorced and Dave had come on his own, just like Derwent. I wondered if he'd had his eye on Beth too. Dave was young and good-looking in a boyish way. Blue eyes, fair hair, and a ready smile would give him a shot with most girls. He hadn't had a chance, once Derwent decided he wanted Beth. Dave was just too safe. I shivered as the breeze sighed across the garden, rustling leaves around us.

"I'll need a lift," Colin Vale said. "I'll be in even worse trouble with the wife if I take the car."

"You can come with me," Godley said. "Maeve?"

"Oh. I should probably get a lift too." I hadn't even thought about how Rob was going to get back to London, but of course I wouldn't be back before he needed to leave. He'd cancel the second night in the hotel. He was practical about these things. He wouldn't mind as much as I did.

"She can come with me," Derwent said, as if he was conferring a tremendous honor on me.

"There's room in my car," Godley said after a couple of seconds, and I realized everyone was staring at me. I should have said thank you immediately. I should have been more guarded about my expression.

"No, that's fine. Thank you, sir," I said to Derwent, who glowered back at me. He wasn't placated. He didn't know the meaning of the word.

"All right. Drive carefully, everyone. It's late and he's already dead. They're preserving the scene until we get there so I don't want anyone to break the speed limit. And for God's sake stop if you need to get coffee. It's going to be a long night." Godley nodded to Colin and the two of them set off toward the sleek black Mercedes that was Godley's pride and joy. I wished I was going with them. Chris and Dave followed, heads down, hands in their pockets. It wasn't how any of us had wanted the night to end.

"Do you need to say good-bye to your bloke?" Derwent asked.

"I should," I said.

"Be quick." He was already walking away and I hurried to catch up. "You'll need to get changed too."

"I was planning to."

"Can't crawl around a crime scene looking like that."

"I'd already come to that conclusion myself."

"So hurry up." Derwent kept walking, away from the marquee, and I watched him go for a second before I remembered what I had to do.

Rob was standing up when I went to find him. He'd sobered up somehow, and I could see from the other side of the dance floor that he was fully aware of what was going on.

"Bad luck."

"I'm sorry," I said. "There's nothing I can do."

"I understand. Is it bad?"

"Police officer."

He frowned. "On duty?"

"He'd just come off late turn. He was on his way home." Which reminded me. "I'll leave you the car, okay? Can you pack for me?"

"No problem."

I leaned in and kissed him, but briefly. "I'll see you back in London."

"Fine," Rob said, his mind obviously elsewhere. "Is Derwent driving you?"

I wondered why he was asking. "Yes. He offered."

Rob picked up my hand and kissed the palm. "I'll miss you. Be careful, Maeve, all right?"

I couldn't tell if it was my guilty conscience or his gift for mind reading that made me think he wasn't talking about road safety. Not that I needed telling. That moment with Derwent earlier had been like looking through a doorway into a dark room. Like every heroine in a horror film, I'd been tempted to go in. And every horror film I'd ever seen proved that that would have been a bad idea. At least, and thank God, he hadn't actually been thinking that way about me. The awkwardness was all on my side, and if I could hide it well enough, no one need ever know.

■ ■ ■ ■

Traveling at that hour of the morning, the traffic was light. There was nothing moving on the little country roads that tracked through farmland and forest until we reached the main road, nothing except an occasional rabbit or fox streaking across the tarmac, a blur in Derwent's headlights. I caught my breath at one near miss and it was all too audible in the silent car. Derwent's hands tightened on the wheel.

"Just so you know, if the choice is between going into the ditch and running over a rabbit, it's going to be rabbit jam."

"Fine."

"They get plenty of warning. You must be able to hear the engine from a mile away at this time of night. If they're stupid enough to run out in front of the car, it's their problem."

"I didn't say anything."

"No. You didn't."

Silence settled on the car again. I was thinking about whether I had remembered to pick up everything I needed from the little hotel room with its smooth unused bed. I'd changed at lightning speed, leaving my dress in a heap on the floor with my heels as I struggled into the trouser suit I'd brought with me. Footwear was a problem; I hadn't brought much that was suitable for scrambling around in the woods. I'd pulled on the boots I usually wore with trouser suits, hoping they would survive, wishing I had wellies. Mindful of the chill in the early morning air, I wore a thin jumper under my suit jacket. I'd brushed my teeth and scrubbed at the makeup that had settled under my eyes so I looked a little bit less like I'd been partying when the call came. I'd picked up my bag, which I'd left ready to go, complete with notebook, pen, gloves, torch, and radio. Then I let myself out of the room and locked it. I hurried as quietly as I could through the dark up-and-down corridors that ran through the mismatched old buildings that made up the hotel. Then down the creaking stairs to the front door, where Derwent's car sat with the engine running. I'd paused to hide the key in a flower pot where Rob could find it, then ran to the car. Five minutes, no more than that, and Derwent had still been frowning when I opened the passenger door and got in.

"Leave your stuff on the back seat," was his only comment, as I arranged my jacket across my lap and tucked my bag into the foot well.

"I'd rather not."

That got me a raised eyebrow first and a wolfish grin second as he worked out why I didn't want anything belonging to me anywhere near the back of his car. I didn't smile back.

So, silence. Derwent whistled under his breath, a habit that always annoyed me, and I looked out of the window. He kept the car moving at a steady hundred wherever he could and I hoped we wouldn't attract any bored traffic officers. It wasn't that we'd get in trouble; it was just that it would hold us up. I wanted to get there quickly, but not because I was feeling particularly keen to find out what had happened to Terence Hammond. I wanted to get out of the fast-moving metal box where I was trapped with a man I — what? Disliked? I certainly felt uneasy around him. The Met didn't believe in partnering up its detectives; it was pure chance that I ended up working with Derwent so often. Chance and a suspicion I had that Godley liked me to work with the inspector, believing, despite much evidence to the contrary, that I was a good influence on him.

The A303 merged with the M3 and Derwent took up his rightful position in the fast lane. I didn't dare look at the speedometer. Rob drove fast too, but I always knew he was in control of what he was doing. With Derwent, I had no idea if he was being careful or not. I wasn't going to challenge him about the speed he was doing because it would only make him go faster, so I sat completely still and hoped he was concentrating.

After a few miles, without warning, Derwent swooped from lane three to lane one in a single move. No indicator, but then there were no other cars on the road. I felt the seatbelt press against my sternum as we slowed.

"What are you doing?"

"Stopping."

"Why?"

"I need a piss."

We'd passed a sign for services a little way back. Now another flashed by: one mile to go. Derwent eased off the accelerator some more. I checked the time and bit my lip.

"Sorry. I didn't realize you were in a rush. You took long enough about getting changed." His voice was soft but I didn't make the mistake of thinking that meant he wasn't angry.

"It took me five minutes."

"More than that."

"No."

"Are you arguing with me?"

I didn't answer.

The car park was almost deserted, with just a few cars dotted here and there. Derwent parked in the space beside the one reserved for police cars, right in front of the main building, making a point that he could have used the dedicated space but he chose not to. I'd already opened my door before he turned off the engine, desperate to get out and stretch my legs. When Derwent got out, he didn't even look at me. He locked the car and walked away, into the building, and I had no idea if he was planning on leaving immediately or if he needed a longer break. I followed, leaving him plenty of space.

The services were always bleak, but especially so at that time in the morning. Most of the shops and catering concessions were closed but one of the coffee shops was open.

Derwent was in and out of the gents in record time. He headed for the counter and I came to stand next to him while a yawning teenager sold him coffee.

"And a chicken sandwich."

"Is that breakfast?" I asked, and got no answer. He paid and took it to one of the tables, sitting down, which I took as a clue that we'd be there for a while. I got coffee for myself. I had no appetite for food. My stomach ached and so did my jaw. I had been clenching it, I realized.

I sat down and watched Derwent picking the meat out of his sandwich. "No bread?"

"Carbs," he said, as if it was a complete answer. He drank some coffee and swore, then picked it up and strode back to the counter.

"If I wanted to wait fifteen fucking minutes to be able to drink my coffee, I'd ask for it to be extra hot."

"Sorry," the teenager mumbled. His fingers trembled slightly as he took the cup and poured a little away, then filled it up with cold water.

"That's better." Derwent came back and sat down. "How's yours?"

Too hot. Undrinkable. "Fine." I glanced across at the counter, where the teenager was wiping down the coffee machine with his back to us. His ears were red. "Was that necessary?"

"What?"

"Did you have to be so unpleasant? I know you're in a bad mood, but —"

"*You're in* a bad mood."

"I'm not the one who just swore at a poor

57

kid doing a shitty, badly paid job in the middle of the night."

"What the fuck is your problem, Kerrigan?"

"You should apologize."

Derwent's eyebrows went up. "To him?"

"Of course."

"Not to you."

"Why would you need to apologize to me?"

"I have no idea but I know when I'm getting the silent treatment."

I shook my head. "I'm not talking to you because you're in the kind of mood where you're going to use anything I say as target practice."

"Bullshit."

"It's true." I sipped my coffee, managing not to wince as it scorched my mouth.

"You're the one who's pissed off with me," Derwent said.

"And why would that be?" I traced a pattern on the lid of my cup. The coffee was cold compared to the rage that was making it hard for me to see straight. My voice was level, though. "Maybe because I work very hard to be seen as more than a token female on the team, and I've proved myself time and time again. And despite all of that, you thought it was okay to feel me up in front of all our colleagues."

"Oh, buy a sense of humor. It was a joke."

"To you, maybe."

"It was nothing. It was a couple of minutes of dancing. No one was watching."

"Everyone was watching."

He waved a hand, brushing the objection aside since he knew it was true. "It was just friendly."

"We are not friends." It was a statement of fact but the words fell between us like a challenge.

Derwent shifted his chair back a couple of inches and I thought he was going to walk off, but he stayed where he was. After a moment, he said, "Anyway. It was your fault for wearing that dress."

That made me look at him. "What did you say?"

"There wasn't much of it, was there?"

"Oh, I'm sorry. I didn't realize that gave you a license to grope me. What should I have been wearing? A suit like this, so you didn't accidentally forget I was your colleague?" I dropped the sugar-sweet sarcasm. "It was a wedding. A party. I wore a party dress. Maybe I should have got hold of a burqa since you find it so hard to control yourself when confronted by a fucking frock."

I had actually, genuinely, lost my temper. Before Derwent could answer me I stood up and stalked to the ladies, using it as a refuge for the second time that night. It took a full two minutes for my hands to stop shaking. I shook my head at my reflection as I ran water into the sink, annoyed with myself for letting Derwent get to me. There was a better-than-even chance he would punish me by leaving without me, and then I'd be stuck at this soulless, depressing rest stop for hours.

When I came out of the loo to find the teenager wiping the table we had used, my heart sank. Derwent had gone.

"Where is he?"

"He left." The teenager folded the cloth a couple of times. In a rush, as if he had to tell someone, he said, "He gave me twenty quid."

"Really?"

"Just now."

"Guilt," I explained. "Did he apologize for being rude?"

"He asked me if I knew what I wanted to do with my life. I said yeah, and he said if it didn't involve selling coffee I should quit and get a real job."

Of course he did. "I'm sorry."

"No, he's right. This is shit. The pay is

shit. I'm going to do it." He grinned at me. "Tell him I said thanks."

Instant Stockholm Syndrome. Derwent's magic touch struck again. Of course he couldn't do anything as straightforward as apologize for being an arse. And of course it worked.

I thanked the teenager and headed for the car park. I saw Derwent through the glass doors, sitting in the driver's seat, waiting. He was scrolling through messages on his phone when I got to the car, his expression forbidding.

"If you think you can buy me off with twenty quid and some career advice, you've got another think coming," I said. "I want a proper apology."

"Get stuffed." Derwent was still focused on his inbox.

"Right." I was looking at the cup holder by the handbrake. He'd rescued the coffee I hadn't been able to drink. A paper bag was propped against the cup. "What's this?"

He reversed out of the space and cut through the car park, ignoring the arrows for the one-way system. "Your usual. Bacon sandwich, extra lard."

"Why?"

"You need to eat something. You might

not feel like it now, but you'll be hungry later."

I was really trying to stay angry, but I couldn't quite manage it. "Thank you."

He glanced across at me. "I think it's stale. The kid gave it to me for free."

"Yeah, yeah." I shook my head. "You really are annoying, you know."

"If anyone is pissed off, it should be me. I was two inches away from getting into the bridesmaid's knickers when you did your coitus interruptus bit."

"Godley told me to find you."

"And Little Miss Nosey knew just where to look."

"You're predictable. But I'm sorry. How long did you need? Two, three minutes maybe?"

"Oh, ha ha." It was his I've-had-enough tone and I took the hint.

"Look, she's a friend of Christine's. You can get her number. I'm sure you can charm your way back into her pants in no time."

"No way."

"Why not?"

"We'd have to date, and that means talking to her. Listening to her talk, I should say. I can't be fucked with it. If I'd done her tonight, we could have met up again. You can always pretend you're too horny to eat, and then you can just shag. But if you haven't done the deed you have to start again and make small talk. And I hate small talk."

"Yes, I imagine there's nothing worse than getting to know the person you're about to stick your penis in." The sarcasm was, inevitably, lost on Derwent.

"It's so boring I would rather wank." A sidelong look. "I mean that."

"Can we go back to not talking?" I asked in a small voice.

"If you want." Derwent turned up the radio. He'd found the only station in the UK that still played Whitesnake, and it blasted through the car at a volume that vibrated in my bones. I wasn't all that familiar with the Whitesnake back catalog, but given the alternative, I was willing to be enlightened.

Chapter Three

The white gates of Richmond Park loomed out of the darkness, and not a second too soon. We had survived the stop–go suburban roads and made it through the dark heart of Kingston's one-way system but it had tested Derwent's patience to the point of failure. He was on edge anyway, as he always seemed to be at the start of a case. I recognized it as fear of failure. In Derwent, that fear was sublimated into aggression. Most of his emotions were.

"At last." He drove through the gates and stopped. "Which way?"

"Left." I'd been saving one nugget of information. Now, I judged, was the right time to use it to take the edge off Derwent's mood. "The GPS reference is near a place called Spankers Hill Wood."

Derwent's eyebrows shot up. "Is it, indeed?"

"Could I make up something like that?"

He laughed. "Spankers Hill. I wonder how it got that name."

"And I wonder why Terence Hammond decided to stop nearby."

Derwent's smile faded and he was silent for the next few minutes as I told him which of the winding roads to take, and watched for the small signposts that confirmed we were on the right track. The drive seemed endless and I was nervous, knowing that Derwent would lose his temper if I sent him the wrong way.

"There they are," I said, managing not to sound relieved.

A couple of police cars marked the checkpoint where we showed our ID to a square, red-faced PC in a high-visibility jacket. His breath misted as he directed Derwent to carry on and park on the left. "When you stop, don't try to pull off the road," he said. "There are posts in the grass to stop people parking along the verge and they'll do for your car. That's why we're leaving the right side of the road free for access."

Taillight reflectors gleamed red in our headlights as Derwent pulled in behind the last car in the line. He was out of the car quickly, leaving me to realize that the verge was too high to let me open the passenger door more than a couple of inches. I was damned if I'd ask him to move the car to let me get out. I climbed across into his seat, glad I was wearing trousers and grateful for long legs that made short work of clambering over the handbrake. Derwent, typically, didn't comment when I emerged from his side of the car. He was busy scanning the line of vehicles.

"The boss is here already," I said. The shiny black bodywork of the Mercedes gleamed a few cars ahead of us.

"He probably didn't stop. But we'll have beaten Chris and Tiny Dancer." Derwent was looking pleased with himself.

"His name is Dave, and he's nice."

"If you say so. I didn't think you went for the choirboy type."

"I don't have to go for his type to think he's nice. He's perfectly fine. He just looks young, that's all." I slid my jacket on, shivering. "I wonder how far it is to the scene."

"Come on. You'll feel better once you see the body. Get the smell of blood in your nostrils." He started walking. I really didn't want to walk down that dark road after him. It wasn't just that my stomach had clenched at the thought of a crime scene soaked in fresh blood. It wasn't just that I'd had more than enough of Derwent's company for one evening, or that I had better things to do with my time. It was simply that I didn't want to start investigating Terence Hammond's death. I had a strong urge to get back into the car and refuse to come out. I didn't believe in premonitions or fate, but I had a bad feeling I couldn't shake despite all of my faith in rational thought. And once or twice before, that bad feeling had saved my neck.

But since I could imagine how well that would go down with my inspector, I pulled my jacket tightly around me and hurried to catch up with him, walking fast until we got to a place where we could pause to take in the view.

The place where Terence Hammond had met his sudden end was on a side road that snaked up a hill and ended in a clump of trees. Impossible to imagine it without the scrum of police and forensic investigators, without the white tent screening the actual crime scene from view. Bright lights shone on whatever was inside the tent, and I thought it looked fake, as if it was staged. The figures around the tent moved like puppets in a show that was very definitely not suitable for children. Too much caffeine, too little sleep. That was why I couldn't shake the stifling feeling that I'd been here before. In a way, I had. There was a procedure in murder investigations, a well-worn path from body to interview room, from police cell to the dock. The familiarity of it all should have been comforting.

It felt suffocating.

"Kerrigan."

I turned and saw Derwent watching me. His face was shadowed, unreadable. "Sorry," I said.

"Why would you need to apologize?"

"I don't know. I thought you were annoyed."

"Why would I be annoyed? Feeling guilty about something?" He spoke softly, inviting me to trust him. *Never.*

"Of course not."

He tilted his head back, plainly not believing a word of it. I'd seen him do it to suspects time and again, and it worked more often than not. It almost worked on me.

"I'm just tired."

"No. That's not it." He took a step closer. "Lost your nerve, Kerrigan? Lost your edge?"

"Is this your version of mentoring? Because really, don't bother. You did your good deed for the night on the way here. That kid might have needed your advice but I don't need any help from you."

"Your heart isn't in this one."

It was like a punch to my stomach. "What makes you say that?"

"You were quiet at the briefing. You didn't talk about it in the car. You're not exactly hurrying to get up there."

All true. "I feel a bit off, that's all."

Derwent tucked an imaginary violin under his chin and played a few moping notes. "Stop sulking, Kerrigan. You don't want to be here. You'd rather be having fun. You and everyone else on this hill, including Terence Hammond, would rather be somewhere else. And his wife will wish things were different too, in about an hour, when Hammond's boss turns up at her front door. She'll know straightaway. Cops' wives always know. It's the thing she's dreaded since the first time he put on his uniform and went out on the street. And now it's happened. That's bad enough. Then she'll find out how it happened, and where, and the questions will start." He jabbed a finger in my direction. "You can help find some answers for her, or you can consider yourself too special to bother, and go back to neighborhoods. Spend your time on dog shit and parking. See how you like it."

My face was burning. "I never said I was too special for this."

"No, but you thought it." He leaned forward and tapped my forehead. "Turn this on, Kerrigan. Get interested or get a transfer, because I'm not dragging you around with a face like a smacked arse for however long it takes to find out who killed Terence Hammond."

He walked away, up the hill. Godley had emerged from behind the screens and Derwent made toward him. I hurried to follow him, trying to pull myself together. Every time I thought I was used to working with Derwent — every time I started to relax around him — he found some way of making me feel ill at ease. And it made it so much worse that I'd handed him the opportunity to make me prove myself yet again.

Godley came to meet us. "You made good time, Josh. Get caught by any speed cameras?"

"Not that I noticed. You?"

"Not this time."

Derwent was trying to smile but he obviously hated that he'd come second. "What was your average speed? One twenty? Did the wheels actually touch the ground?"

"The car likes to go fast," Godley said calmly. "And so do I."

"What's behind the screen?" I asked.

70

"The victim's car. He's still in it."

I tried to think of an appropriate response. "Oh good" didn't seem right. I settled for nodding.

"Why haven't they moved him?" Derwent asked. "Waiting for us?"

"Waiting for the forensics team to finish with the area around the car and the outside of the car itself. He was locked in. No keys in the ignition. No keys visible in the car." Godley shrugged. "They may be in his pocket or under him, but at the moment we can assume someone locked him in and took the keys away with them."

"Why would they do that?" I asked, puzzled.

"To annoy us." Derwent's voice was dust-dry and I couldn't tell if he was joking or if he meant it. "It slows us down. Gives the killer more of a head start."

"Maybe. It's his car, but it looks as if he wasn't driving. He's in the passenger seat." Godley checked the time. "No sign of Chris and Dave. You two might as well have a look at Mr. Hammond while he's still in the car. Pete Belcott is around there already with Colin. They've been working with the forensics team."

I bit back the swear word that I was thinking. I'd forgotten about Belcott, one of the other detective constables on the team. He'd been invited to the wedding like everyone else, but stayed in London, claiming to be too busy. Too lazy to travel to Somerset, I'd thought, and had been glad he wasn't there, with his damp hands and small, hostile eyes.

Derwent set off toward the screen. Rather than call after him and be ignored I ran and grabbed his arm. He swung around, ready for a fight.

"You'll need these." I held out some spare shoe covers and a pair of blue latex gloves.

A smirk. "I knew there was a reason I brought you along."

"Just take them."

He did as he was told, for once. The two of us passed inspection by a short, pretty SOCO who had pushed the hood back on her white boiler suit. Her hair was a shock of dark corkscrew curls. I wondered how she got it all to stay inside her hood when she was working.

Derwent smiled at her. "I like curly hair."

"Then why don't you get a perm?" the SOCO snapped.

"That's not what I meant." He watched her walk off, then turned to me. "That wasn't what I meant."

"She knows that."

"Does she? Then why can't she take a compliment?"

"Because she's working, not hanging out in a bar, and she doesn't need to deal with comments on her appearance while she's doing her job." If I explained it often enough, one day it might sink in. "Stop trying to distract yourself."

"I don't know what you're talking about."

"The flirting? It's your way of taking your mind off what you're about to see. Like the gum chewing and the car talk."

Derwent glowered. "Don't analyze me."

"I'm just saying what I see."

"Well, don't."

He headed past me through the screens that shielded the car from view. I followed, almost losing my balance as a couple of white-suited SOCOs brushed past me. It was quiet inside the tent, and hot from the lights that stood around the car. Colin Vale was deep in conversation with the crime-scene manager. The SOCOs had mostly finished with the car — a shattered Ford Mondeo — and its occupant, so we had it to ourselves. Derwent stalked toward the car, nodding to Pete Belcott, who stood to one side with his arms folded. I didn't even bother to acknowledge Belcott. He routinely ignored me, after all. Anyway, I had better things to do, like keeping up with Derwent. The animal side of his personality was in abeyance, temporarily, while the incisive investigator took control, and he'd expect me to be just as focused as he was. So I stopped looking at him and looked at the victim instead.

More precisely, I looked at what was left of him. He was a mess, slumped in the seat like a blood-soaked ragdoll, his arms limp by his sides. His face had slid down, unmoored by the damage to the top of his skull, and I couldn't actually tell how he would have looked in life. I could see he had been wearing a fleece over his uniform, as most uniformed officers did after a shift. Police officers weren't allowed to wander around in uniform off duty, but there was no point in changing out of it when you were going home to bed.

Bed. I imagined Hammond's wife, safe under the covers. She was probably asleep. She wouldn't have noticed yet that Hammond's side of the bed was empty, the sheets cold. She wouldn't know that he was never coming home. Once or twice, when Rob had been late home after a surveillance job had dragged on, I'd woken and wondered where he was, if he was alright. Worry had soured my relationships before now as boyfriends discovered I might not be on time, I might come home injured, or I might not come home at all. It was extremely unusual for police officers to die in the line of duty, but it happened. It was a possibility for all of us, all the time. And maybe that was why I had been hanging back. It was all too easy to see myself, or a friend — someone I loved — in the blood-soaked car. I felt the need to know kick in, like a long-suppressed craving. Finding out what had happened to Hammond suddenly seemed like the only thing that mattered.

"Two shots." It was the familiar corncrake voice of the pathologist, Glenn Hanshaw. His face was drawn in the bright lights that shone on the car. Tall and thin, he was never exactly robust, but he looked ill. Then again, no one looked their best at that time in the morning. "The weapon was probably a rifle, but ballistics will be able to tell you more about it. The first shot hit him in the chest. The other took the top of his head off, but he was already dead."

You didn't need a medical degree to know that the fist-sized hole in the man's chest would have been a fatal wound. I didn't say that, though. Dr. Hanshaw took himself too seriously for that.

"Overkill," Derwent said. "Maybe it's

personal."

He peered in through the shattered windscreen at the body slumped in the passenger seat. The second shot had effectively exploded Hammond's skull, showering the inside of the car with bone fragments and pink matter that had once been his brain — everything that had made him who he was. It made a fine old mess when it was splattered across glass and upholstery, all the same. I went to the driver's side where someone had left the door hanging open. I crouched down and played the beam of my torch over the seat, the steering wheel, the floor of the car. There was plenty to see and more to think about, and I stayed there for a couple of minutes before I became aware of movement behind me. I glanced around to see Godley, with Chris Pettifer and Dave Kemp standing beside him.

"Nice of you to join us," Derwent said, grinning at Pettifer. He looked deeply chagrined to be the last to get there.

"Some of us drive with due care and attention."

"Careful. The boss got here first. You don't want to accuse him of being a dangerous driver, do you?"

Pettifer squirmed. "Obviously not."

"Obviously," Derwent agreed.

We were gathered around the body of a dead police officer and maybe an outsider wouldn't have got it, but that made it more likely we would crack jokes, not less. The humor got you through when reality was hard to take.

Godley looked down at me. "What have you found, Maeve?"

"Nothing."

"Then why are you still down there?" Derwent was frowning.

"Knows her place," Belcott said under his breath, and caught a glare from Derwent for his trouble. It was fine for the inspector to be a misogynist prick toward me, I'd noticed, but he took offense on my behalf at the slightest provocation.

"There's nothing here, but it's interesting that there's nothing. There's a void here." I pointed with a gloved finger to the area of the car that had remained pristine. "Someone was in the driver's seat when he died."

"The SOCOs already said there was a void." Belcott sounded bored. "But look at the seat back. It's saturated. There wasn't anyone sitting there. More likely there was something on the seat. Whoever killed him took it before they locked the car."

"No," I said, keeping my voice level. "I

can see why you might think that, but I don't agree."

"Why, Maeve?" Godley leaned down to get a closer look.

"There's no blood on the front of the seat, or in the driver's foot well, or on the handbrake. There was someone in this seat, but they were leaning sideways when Hammond was shot. They were leaning toward him."

Derwent suddenly snapped his fingers. "I get it."

"I don't, I'm afraid." Godley looked at me expectantly. Beside him, Dave Kemp was frowning. Pettifer jangled the change in his pockets, his expression blank.

I was going to have to spell it out for them, I could see, and I wasn't going to get any help from a grinning Derwent. "Sergeant Hammond was in the front passenger seat, which is odd because it was his car. The person in the driver's seat was leaning across. I'd suggest that person had his or her head in the sergeant's lap, probably performing oral sex."

"The dirty so-and-so," Pettifer said.

"He was married." Dave Kemp looked around at us, wondering if he was pointing out the obvious. "It would have to be a woman."

"How little you know." Derwent's grin was even wider. "Go on, Kerrigan."

"They'd swapped seats because the steering wheel got in the way otherwise." I shone my torch into the back of the car, which was full of boxes, a ladder and some tins of paint. "Hammond seems to have been quite keen on DIY. No room to push the driver's seat back to allow for . . . access."

Belcott had his own torch out and he shone it on Hammond's crotch. "His trousers are done up."

I pointed. "Yes, and the area at the front of his trousers is clean. If they were undone, he'll have blood spatter inside them. The second shot would have done it, even if someone's head was in the way for the first shot."

"Check," Godley said, nodding to Dr. Hanshaw.

He leaned in and unzipped the trousers carefully, pulling the material instead of handling the zip, to preserve any microscopic traces of DNA we might recover. He spread them wide. On black material, the blood looked black too but it reflected a dull brown in the light of Belcott's torch.

Chris Pettifer shook his head. "Who would shoot a man on his way home from work, getting a quiet blowjob in a public park? That's just cruel."

"At least he died happy," Derwent said. "The lady — or gentleman — must have got a bit of a shock, though."

"Or she knew exactly what was going to happen." I stood up. "She took the keys, didn't she? Maybe she was driving when they parked here. Maybe she chose this spot because it was the right place for an ambush."

"Risky," Derwent commented. "She's relying on someone to be able to shoot straight. If I knew someone with a rifle was going to shoot at a car, I wouldn't want to be within twenty yards of the target."

"Maybe she didn't know how dangerous it was. I'm going to guess the reality of it was worse than she had expected. She must have been covered in blood, for one thing, and the noise would have been pretty disconcerting. I think that's why she took the keys with her. Dazed, shocked, in a hurry, she goes on autopilot. Grabs her stuff, grabs the keys, locks the car and runs for it."

"On the road we've all been tramping up and down all night." Derwent swore. "No chance of getting any evidence from it."

"We might get something from the nearest car park," I said. "She'd have had to have her own transport for a getaway. She couldn't have left the car on the road because you can't park on the verge. And she wouldn't have wanted to be too far from it because it wasn't that late and there might have been people around to hear the shot."

"We have some witnesses," Godley said. "The couple who reported the shooting. You can speak to them later, Josh. But from what I've heard, they didn't see anything conclusive."

"Sounds like a good way to waste our time when we should be chasing the lady who was sitting in the driver's seat," Belcott said.

"We do need to find her, but there is also the chance that she didn't know anything about it," I said quietly. "Running away doesn't prove anything. She might have been scared. She might have been afraid of being identified. Maybe she has a family too. She definitely shouldn't have been doing what she was doing with a happily married man. There are lots of reasons why she might have wanted to avoid talking to us."

"So we find her and find out what her problem was." Derwent turned and looked at the trees behind him. "Have they found where the shooter was waiting?"

"Not yet. But it's getting light. It should be easier in daylight." Godley's phone beeped and he checked it. "You'll have to excuse me. Hammond's superintendent is here. He's going to deliver the news to the family. I said I'd go along too."

Derwent pulled a face. "Rather you than me."

"It's never fun," Godley agreed. "Right. It seems to me we need to know if Terence Hammond was killed because of something he did or because of what he was. Because I'm not discounting the fact that he was a police officer yet. There are plenty of people who don't like us."

"But we're so lovable," Derwent murmured.

Godley ignored him. "Chris and Dave, I want you to talk to Hammond's colleagues. Find out if he was behaving oddly in recent times. Find out if there was any gossip about him sleeping with someone other than his wife. Find out if he'd had any threats made against him."

Pettifer looked mournful. "Boss, you know what you're asking us to do. The guy is dead. We're going to get punched. A lot."

"Stand behind Dave. He'll protect you." Godley turned to Colin Vale. "Feel like watching a few hundred hours of CCTV?"

"Can't wait."

"Try to get footage from near the gates of

the park so we can link any suspect vehicles back to this spot. We can be fairly accurate about timings because of the witnesses, so that should narrow it down for you."

"But there are five gates that allow vehicles out of this park and six pedestrian gates and it wasn't that late and . . . I'm going to be watching a lot of footage," Colin finished. He actually sounded happy about it.

Godley turned to Belcott. "Pete, I want you to dig into Hammond's past. See if there's any reason why someone would have a grudge against him. Check his personnel files, his old cases, any complaints made against him — the works."

"What about me and Kerrigan?" Derwent asked, as if we had to work together.

"I want Maeve to come with me."

Around the circle, I was aware of eyebrows going up, of meaningful looks being exchanged. I couldn't seem to kill the rumor that Godley and I were having a secret relationship. If only they knew the secret we shared, they would know there was nothing romantic about it. Godley had been passing information to a major criminal, John Skinner, for years. And I was the only one who knew about it. Derwent's expression was neutral, unreadable. He knew Godley better than most, and I thought he probably didn't believe there was anything going on between me and the superintendent, but I wasn't sure.

Apparently oblivious, Godley went on, "Josh, you stay here. Glenn's going to move the body soon and I want someone on the spot in case there are any surprises. Talk to the witnesses. Talk to the SOCOs. Get hold of the local Safer Neighborhoods Team and find out if this was a regular spot for couples. Maybe Hammond was a regular. I want you to concentrate on this end of the investigation, Josh. With your background in the army you know more than anyone else here about shooting."

"But Kerrigan knows more about giving blowjobs than anyone else."

It was a mutter but Derwent didn't miss it. He rounded on Belcott, who actually took a step back. "What did you say?"

"Nothing. Just a joke."

"And well up to your usual standards," I said, unruffled. There was very little Belcott could say that would genuinely annoy me. I had no need to impress him.

"Let's get moving." Godley headed off in the direction of his car. The others followed, Belcott glaring at me as he passed. I smiled sweetly until he turned away. I hung back for a moment, reluctant to walk down the hill with him.

Derwent came to stand beside me. "What did you ever do to Belcott?"

"Nothing at all. Except for being cleverer than him, and better at the job, and taller than he is, and whatever else it is that chafes his nuts."

"Whatever that may be." Derwent was smiling to himself. The smile died as he turned to look at the car, with its nightmarish passenger. The sky was starting to change color, the darkness lifting, the birds tuning up for dawn. It was cold and my spirits plummeted again. Around us, London would be starting to wake up on a clear Sunday morning. Terence Hammond's family would be waking up to a tragedy.

And nothing I could do would change that.

CHAPTER FOUR

When I got to his car, Godley was listening to the news, frowning.

". . . found dead in Richmond Park in southwest London. Police have not yet named him. There are unconfirmed reports that the man was a police officer, shot in his car in the early hours of this morning as he returned from work. Several roads are closed within the park and traffic in the area will be subject to diversions for the rest of the day." The calm, measured voice paused for a moment. "An eight-year-old boy has died in a house fire . . ."

Godley turned the radio off.

"They got hold of that quickly." I put on my seatbelt.

"They always do now. One of the witnesses tweeted about it." Godley shrugged. "Nothing we can do. As soon as it gets light there'll be a helicopter or two filming the scene."

A silver Volvo slid past us and Godley followed it. "That's Superintendent Lowry, Hammond's boss. He's got Hammond's inspector with him, Dan West. Do you know either of them?"

"No. Never met them."

"I don't know anything about West but don't judge John Lowry by this morning. He's not usually so tense. Hammond had two kids, apparently. Fourteen and sixteen. Tough age to lose a father."

"I'm not sure there's a right age for that to happen. It's good of Superintendent Lowry to break the news to Mrs. Hammond himself."

"I'd do the same. I've never had to, thank God." He looked sideways at me. "I've come close a couple of times, as you know."

I did know, since I'd been the one hovering between life and death on at least one occasion. It was a weird thing to be embarrassed about but I was embarrassed.

"No one ever thinks it will be them."

"The odds are against it," Godley agreed. He was staying close to Lowry's car, following him through the quiet streets. "It's still the sort of job that makes you a target. Like that PC in Lambeth a couple of weeks ago. What was his name?"

I knew who he meant. "Gregory. Philip or

Peter or something."

"Crossing the road, in uniform, on duty and he gets hit by a car. A walking target. He was lucky."

"He jumped," I said, remembering some of the details. "I think he broke an arm or a leg though. Did they get anyone for that?"

"They haven't even got a suspect. It was a residential street. No CCTV. No witnesses. He didn't get more than a quick look at the car himself and he was single-crewed." Godley shook his head. "I don't think they'll get whoever did it. My guess is that someone attacked the uniform, not the man. It was the day after Levon Cole was shot. You don't have to look too far for reasons for us to be unpopular at the moment."

Levon Cole was a teenager who had been shot by police officers in murky circumstances. It was just the latest reason for people not to love the Met. "Do you think Terence Hammond was killed because he was a cop?"

"It's possible."

"Maybe he was killed because he was having an affair."

"Also possible."

"So when do we ask the grieving widow about whether her husband was faithful to her?"

Godley's mouth twitched. "Derwent would ask her straightaway."

"Which is why he's hanging out with the dead man in Richmond Park."

"That's one reason."

"It's good enough."

"To answer your question about Mrs. Hammond, I'm not sure how I'm going to do this yet. I'm going to let Lowry take the lead with breaking the news and offering her whatever consolation he can. Then I'll talk to her. I haven't decided how I'm going to approach it. I want to wait until I see her. I'm assuming she'll want to find her husband's killer. If she's strong enough, she might want to talk about their ups and downs. If she falls apart we'll have to rely on friends and family to get a picture of how Hammond was at home."

"I have no sense of his personality at all," I said. "I couldn't even see what he looked like."

Still driving, Godley dug in his pocket and handed me his phone, tapping in the PIN code without looking down at the screen. "Check my e-mails. I got someone at Isleworth to send me an up-to-date picture of him."

I navigated to the e-mails, scrolling through many messages to find the right one. The picture was formal, a head-and-shoulders shot. Hammond had just missed out on being handsome, I thought. He looked like a rugby player, thick-necked and short-haired with a heavy jaw. Straight eyebrows. A nose too small for his face. I knew not to read too much into a single image — a formal picture at that — but I couldn't help trying to invest his face with character. There was something to the tilt of his head, the droop of his eyelids, that made me think he was arrogant. Maybe that was just because I knew he'd died with his flies open and some unknown person's face in his crotch. I flicked back to Godley's inbox.

"It's Sunday morning and you've had about twenty e-mails since the one with Terence Hammond's picture. How do you find the time to read all of these?"

"I don't."

"What if they're important?"

"They're never important."

"Seriously, though."

"Seriously, if it's important, I get a phone call. If it's rubbish, it comes as an e-mail. The ones with the Excel attachments are the ones I read last. If ever."

There was something giddy about Godley — as if he was excited but suppressing it.

Maybe it was because the end of his marriage spelled liberation. In almost three years of working for him I'd seen him angry a handful of times, serious most of the time, and light-hearted roughly never.

Covertly, I watched him as he drove. It had been a long night. The tiredness lurked in the corners of his mouth and around his eyes, where the lines were deeper and longer than usual. But he still looked as if something fundamental had changed and I wondered what it was.

"Sir —"

The phone vibrated in my hand. I'd forgotten I was still holding it. Automatically I glanced down to see the first few lines of the message flash up as a preview on the screen:

Make no mistake
you fucking cunt, you'd
better change your mind
or you know what will

I stared down at it for a few long seconds. The phone was on silent so Godley had no idea he had a new message. More importantly, he didn't know that I'd seen it. I turned the phone over so he couldn't see the screen and slid it on to the central console. It was none of my business.

I still couldn't stop thinking about it. I'd forgotten Terence Hammond. I'd forgotten why I was sitting in Godley's car and where we were going. *Change your mind. You know what will.* I could fill in the rest of that sentence without too much trouble. *You know what will happen.* Something to take the smile off Godley's face, I thought. Something terrible. The message was nothing to do with me but I was lightheaded with shock.

"This must be the place."

I looked up, surprised, as Godley pulled in behind Lowry's car. It had stopped outside a 1930s semi-detached house with an empty driveway. The curtains were closed. No one was up yet.

"I'll go in with Lowry and West," Godley said. "Make sure you stay close to me. I don't want you to get sidelined. I value your opinion." A sideways look. "That's why I wanted you to come with me, you know. You're good at people."

I dredged up a smile that felt stiff on my face. "Thanks." I did appreciate the compliment, even though I knew it was the one area where I had an advantage over my male colleagues. It was a widely held belief that female officers were useful to have around when people were likely to be upset. I wasn't so sure; I'd known more than a few who had no nurturing instincts at all.

"I want your impressions of the family. I want to know if you think Mrs. Hammond is surprised by the news about her husband."

"Are you thinking of her as a suspect?"

"Anything's possible. Especially given what Hammond was doing when he died. I doubt she pulled the trigger but she might have asked someone else to do it. Loving wives of unfaithful husbands make good suspects."

"Cynic," I said, smiling for real this time.

"You know the rules. Most murders occur for reasons that are close to home."

A bulky man was levering himself out of the driver's seat of the car in front. He was overweight, his jowls overlapping his collar, and his face was red. His blood pressure had to be through the roof. He gave Godley a sick look and nodded to the house.

"Right." Godley picked up his phone and slid it into his pocket without looking at the screen. "Time to go."

I hung back as he went to join Lowry and West on the pavement. The three of them conferred for a minute. West was a thin, wrinkled man whose skin was weathered to a shade that was almost the same light-brown as his fine hair. He kept passing a hand over the top of his head, smoothing his hair down. They walked up the drive together and Godley rang the doorbell.

It was a long time until someone responded. The light went on in the hall first, and then the door swung open to reveal a middle-aged woman. She was tying the belt on her dressing gown, but her attention was on us, her gaze flitting across our faces, trying to read our expressions. Her face was pale, sleep-saggy, wary. Her hair was short and streaked blond. At the moment it stood up like a cockatoo's crest.

"Mrs. Hammond?" Lowry began.

"Yes."

"I'm Superintendent John Lowry. Sorry to bother you so early. It's about Terence. I'm so sorry. May we come in?"

I saw the shock hit her. I watched her world fall apart.

And we hadn't even got around to breaking her heart yet.

The kitchen was dark, even with the lights on. It was in need of an update: at least two of the cupboard doors were hanging off their hinges and the tiles by the cooker had cracked. If it had been Hammond's intention to redo it, he'd missed his chance. I hunted for mugs and sugar, opening wobbly drawers in search of a teaspoon as the kettle boiled. I had one ear trained on the conversation in the living room between Mrs. Hammond and the three senior police officers. I didn't want to crash in at an awkward moment with my tea tray.

Tea, the answer for every problem. Burglary? Tea. Missing child? Tea. Dead husband? Tea. No one ever seemed to drink it. For us, the cups were a prop, something to do with your hands while gently delivering the bad news and easing yourself back out to the street. Nothing ever felt as good as the first breath of fresh air when you walked out of a house filled with grief.

And yet I felt as if I was in my natural environment. It was the wedding that felt unreal now. I'd already forgotten the details of the day, the dress, the conversations I had had. Now I was at work I focused on everything around me, my mind working to see significance in mundane details, even though I didn't expect to find anything of interest in Hammond's kitchen. I might never be in the Hammonds' house again but I would be able to close my eyes and say for certain which drawer had a loose handle or which cupboard door was chipped or where the floor was stained, by the bin.

The rest of the house was in a better state than the kitchen, but it was unwelcoming and unloved. I'd looked into a small dining room that was functioning as a junk room and study, piled with paperwork and boxes. The sitting room was furnished in a perfunctory way — two sofas facing each other across a wide coffee table and a single armchair facing the television. The carpet was gray, the curtains dark blue, and the effect dreary beyond belief.

The atmosphere in the sitting room wasn't helping much. There was a reason I was currently hiding in the kitchen. I'd made my escape thanks to foresight in standing near the door. Mrs. Hammond was not devastated by grief or silent with misery. She was angry, and she wanted us to know it. She had taken up a position on one sofa, her back ramrod-straight. She glared across at West and Lowry as if she held them personally responsible for what had happened to her husband. The air had fairly trembled with awkwardness.

"So you're saying he stopped on his way home. Why would he stop?"

Good question, lady.

West and Lowry fidgeted unhappily, and it was Godley who answered her.

"We're still trying to establish what happened in the last few hours. Anything that I could tell you now would be speculation. And I don't want to speculate. I'd ask you to wait until we're sure of the facts."

"The facts." Her voice was quiet. "I can tell you some facts if you like."

"Please do." Godley leaned in. I knew he was hoping she would bring up Terry's extramarital activities.

"It's a fact that I've got two kids. It's a fact that one of them has special needs. It's a fact that Terry's gone and I've got to try to look after them on my own." She laughed. "He was never bloody here in the first place; I don't know why I'm worrying."

"If we can alleviate that worry for you, there will be a pension." Lowry sounded relieved to have some good news to share. It didn't last long.

"It's not about *money,*" Mrs. Hammond said, her eyes as bright and unblinking as a snake's. "You don't have a clue. I earn more than Terry. I always have. Money isn't the problem. Money can't buy you someone to share the responsibility of having a son like Ben. Money doesn't help you make decisions about what's best for him. He's sixteen. When he's eighteen, he'll be finished at school. Done. Ready to go out into the world. Except that he hasn't learned anything in school, as far as I know. He doesn't talk. Can't write. He's not going to get a job, or a girlfriend. He's not going to move out. He's not going to lead anything like a normal life, and neither am I. And there's no one to help anymore. There's no one who understands what it's like. There's no one who's in exactly the same position as me."

"I'm sure there are support groups," West offered. I saw Godley flinch, but it was too late.

"Support groups," she repeated. "Oh, well, that makes everything all right then."

"Obviously not, but —"

"You have no idea what my life is like and you have no idea what it will be like. You come to my house to tell me my husband is dead and then you *patronize* me? How dare you?"

There was no easy answer to that. Her words hung in the air until Godley spoke again. "Can you think of anyone who would want to harm your husband, Mrs. Hammond?"

"No."

"Was he worried about anything recently? Did he seem distracted or unhappy?"

"He was just the same as usual."

"Was it normal for him to be late back from work?" Godley was sailing close to the wind.

"He came and went, you know. He worked shifts all the time, so some weeks he'd be here and other weeks I wouldn't see him at all. I didn't really keep track. I was busy. I work, as I said, and I look after Ben and Vanessa. That doesn't leave a lot of time for Terry." She stopped and corrected herself. "I mean it didn't leave a lot of time."

Happy families. I caught Godley's eye and slid out of the room. Now, on my own in the kitchen, I thought about the Hammonds and wondered if the marriage had been over in all but name. Maybe Mrs. Hammond knew about her husband's affair. Maybe not. It would take a braver police officer than me to raise it with her when she was in such a combative mood.

And that was something else worth noting. We'd been in the house for forty minutes and she hadn't shed a tear.

I'd been keeping in touch with the conversation in the living room as the senior officers stuttered through their script. Now the noise of the kettle drowned out everything else. I stood in the center of the room and stretched my arms over my head, fingers linked, arching my back to try to loosen out the kinks in my spine. Left to my own devices, I could feel fatigue creeping up on me. My eyes felt sore, my head heavy. I couldn't let myself relax yet, but I allowed myself a yawn that almost cracked my jaw.

The kettle clicked off and I swung my arms back down, sighing. Then I jumped about a mile in the air as someone spoke behind me.

"What are you doing? Who are you?"

I turned to see a girl who had to be Terence Hammond's daughter, a slight figure in oversized pajamas. She looked younger than fourteen. The button nose that had looked out of place on her father's face made sense here, giving her an elfin prettiness. Her hair was long and dark. It hung down over the left side of her face, shadowing one of her eyes. The one I could see was a striking shade of gray-green, as clear as well-water. I'd had a look through the noticeboard in the kitchen and knew more about her than her name and age. Vanessa played netball. Vanessa had a dentist's appointment on Thursday. Vanessa was going to Bordeaux on a school trip at half-term.

Vanessa was standing in the doorway to her kitchen, wearing pajamas and a huge woolly cardigan. It was ten to six on a Sunday morning and she had every right to look truculent.

"I'm Detective Constable Maeve Kerrigan."

"Do you work with my dad?" Her voice wasn't loud but it was clear, every word enunciated.

"I'm a Metropolitan police officer too."

"In Isleworth."

"In central London."

"Why are you in my house?" That question came with a childlike lift of her bottom lip; she was trying not to cry.

"I came with some senior colleagues to talk to your mum." *To tell her or not to tell her . . .* I'd waited too long to pour the water from the kettle. If I made the tea with water that had cooled, it would taste vile. I flicked the switch on again.

She raised her voice so I could hear her over the hiss from the kettle. "About what? About Dad?"

I concentrated on arranging the mugs, playing for time. "Would you like me to get your mum?"

"No, I would like you to tell me what's going on!" The kettle switched itself off halfway through and Vanessa's last five or six words sounded overloud in the small, shabby kitchen.

I heard an exclamation from the next

room, followed by soft, scuffing footsteps, and braced myself for Julie Hammond's arrival.

"What are you doing down here? Get back to bed." She sounded brisk rather than angry, and matter-of-fact rather than upset. I understood very well that she wanted to let her daughter have an hour or two more of normal life before she found out what had happened. I also understood that her daughter was having none of it.

Vanessa looked stubborn. "I heard people talking."

"They're talking to me. Now off you go."

"What's happening, Mum? Is it Dad?" The teenager's voice cracked.

The pause that followed told her everything. Mrs. Hammond watched her daughter's face crumple with a curious, detached expression on her own.

"I'm sorry, Vanessa. He's gone." A brief hug. I noticed the awkward contact between the two of them. You could see hugging wasn't something they did often. Julie Hammond stepped back. "I'll tell you more later."

"What? But —"

"Go back to your room now. Take a cup of tea with you."

"I want to stay here. I want to know what

happened."

There was an undertone of irritation in Mrs. Hammond's voice when she answered her. "I don't know what happened myself. That's what I'm trying to find out. That's why I need to talk to the police officers who are in the lounge."

"I can sit with you. I can help."

"No, you can't. You'll just get in the way."

That was temper, I thought, not no-nonsense parenting, and it hadn't taken long for it to flare up. Vanessa narrowed the one eye I could see.

"You can't keep me out of this. The police will want to talk to me."

"And I'll be present for that."

The girl looked at me. "Is that true?"

"Yes. Unless you want another responsible adult to be there," I added, and saw Julie Hammond's face darken.

"I'm her mother and I insist on being present when Vanessa speaks to the police."

"I don't want her there," Vanessa said to me.

"Vanessa!"

"Mum, I don't want you there."

"This is not the time to punish me for wanting to be a good parent." I could hear the strain in Julie Hammond's voice.

"It's not about that."

"Then what is it about?"

No answer from Vanessa. I watched the two of them face off. They were about the same height and Vanessa's slender frame was like her mother's, but the girl was prettier. At that moment, though, they looked just as stubborn as each other.

A movement in the hall caught my eye: Godley. He came forward, taking charge.

"This is a matter that can be resolved later. We won't be speaking to anyone in the family until tomorrow at the earliest."

Vanessa looked around at him. "Who are you?"

"Superintendent Charles Godley. I'm leading the investigation into your father's death."

"Why does there have to be an investigation?" She turned back to her mother. "What happened to him, Mum?"

"He was murdered."

"Murdered?" Even in the badly lit kitchen I could see the blood draining from Vanessa's face.

"Yes, murdered. Someone shot him on his way home from work."

Vanessa's lips moved as if she was trying to say something, but all that emerged was a sigh. I leaped forward to catch her as she slid to the ground but Godley was there before me, lifting her up and carrying her into the sitting room. He laid her on one of the sofas and put a hand to her neck to check her pulse. Almost as an afterthought he brushed her hair back off her face, so for the first time we could see her properly.

There were four police officers in the room and all of us went completely still. I don't think I was even breathing.

High on Vanessa's right temple was a bruise with a raised welt in the middle of it. The injury was a day or two old, so we were probably seeing it at its worst. It stood out on her pale skin like wine spilled on silk.

Godley stepped back and looked at Julie Hammond. "Did you know about this?"

"No."

"Do you know how she got hurt?

"I don't. You'll have to ask her."

"I will," Godley said, and I knew from his tone that he thought Julie Hammond was lying.

I was fairly sure he was right.

CHAPTER FIVE

"Where the hell have you been?"

Derwent was standing at the top of the hill, watching me as I climbed toward him. He had his hands shoved in his pockets and his feet braced a mile apart. He looked at ease with himself for once, and also disheveled.

"You know where. Breaking the news to Hammond's family," I said.

"Is that all? What took you so long?"

"Talking to the wife. Meeting the daughter." I checked the time. "We were only gone for a couple of hours."

"It felt like longer." Derwent was looking past me. "What's wrong with him?"

I knew who he meant without looking. Godley, who had hung back when I got out of the car because he wanted to make a phone call. "I don't know."

I did know. I could have told him the precise moment the superintendent had checked his phone and saw the abusive message. It was right before Godley began to extricate himself — and me — from the Hammonds' house. I'd taken a dazed Vanessa upstairs with her mother's help and watched as Julie put her to bed, and when I came down Godley was making a move to leave, in a hurry. He had promised that one or both of us would return to talk to the family, that day or the next. He had made arrangements for a family liaison officer to stay in the house, and for two community support officers to stand outside. The press were beginning to sniff out the details of the story; it was only a matter of time before tabloid journalists and news crews found the house. He had assured Mrs. Hammond that he would keep her informed, shaken hands with West and Lowry, and strode out of the house, leaving me to follow as quickly as I could. The car journey back to Richmond Park had been silent, for the most part. Godley was brooding and I was terrified he guessed I had seen the message. I made meaningless notes on what I had seen and done at the Hammonds' house, pretending to concentrate on what I was writing.

I'd been hoping our return to the crime scene would distract Godley from his woes, but the phone call didn't seem to have improved his mood. If anything the gloom was back with reinforcements. Derwent knew Godley all too well, unluckily for me.

"He's got a face like a wet weekend."

"I know."

"Did you two have a fight or something?"

"No. Of course not." I felt myself blush and knew it made me look as if I was lying. "It's nothing to do with me."

"What isn't?"

That thing I'm not supposed to know about. "Whatever's making the boss look grumpy."

Derwent was staring at me. I studiously refused to look back. He would lose interest. Or Godley would reach us and Derwent would have to talk to him instead of waiting for me to crack.

It took Godley a long time to walk up the hill to meet us, and Derwent didn't look away for a second.

"Josh, what have you got to tell me?" The superintendent was frowning. I could see the tension in his jaw. The corners of his mouth were turned down. The giddiness I'd seen in him earlier that day was gone, apparently for good.

With great reluctance, Derwent turned away from me to face Godley. "The body's gone. The postmortem will be this

108

afternoon, according to Hanshaw. Three o'clock, he said."

"I'll have to go." Godley took out his phone and made a note. "What else?"

"The car's been recovered. It's gone off for forensics to pull it apart." He meant that literally. The car would be stripped down to its chassis so every stray fiber, every hair, every drop of blood could be collected and analyzed. That might lead us to the person who'd been in the car with Hammond, or when we found them we'd be able to prove it. Either way, it was a gift that we knew there was someone with him when he died.

"Did you get to talk to the witnesses?"

"Not yet. They'd gone home. I've got their contact details."

"Make it a priority," Godley said and started to turn away.

"Hold on, you haven't heard the best bit yet." Derwent was like a puppy waiting to be praised. "We found where the sniper was waiting."

That got Godley's attention. "Really?"

"Yeah. The SOCOs have got it taped off at the moment but they should be finished soon."

"Anything useful at first glance?"

"Nothing obvious. They think they'll be able to estimate his height and weight though. They're in there measuring broken twigs and indentations in the ground as I speak. I'll show you later if you like but they don't want too many people tramping around at the moment. They'll be bringing in a dog to try and track the route the killer took. Not that it ever works. I guarantee you the dog will lead them to a rabbit hole."

"How did they find it?"

Derwent's chest swelled, visibly. "I found it."

"How did you manage that?" Godley asked.

"It was before they moved the body. I went for a wander through the woods."

Which explained the mud coating his trousers and his once-pristine shoes.

"How did you know you'd found the right spot?" I knew Derwent would be pleased to be asked to explain how clever he'd been but I genuinely wanted to know.

"It was where I would have waited. Bit of height. Good field of vision. Plenty of growth around it so he was protected from view. They'll get more information about the trajectory from the postmortem, once they've got a line on the wound tracks so the SOCOs have the angle, but it's the right place."

"When you say there was a good field of

vision, did it matter where the car stopped?"
I asked.

"Yeah. For accuracy. You don't want to leave anything up to chance if you can avoid it. He'd have planned it out beforehand as much as possible — the distances, the angles, the wind speed."

"So whoever was driving knew where to stop. It was an ambush. A trap. And whoever was in the car planned it along with the shooter."

"Looks like it," Derwent said. "Which means that person knew she was acting as the bait. I can't wait to meet her, if it is a her."

"She sounds like your type," I said, and got a glower for my trouble. Quickly, I went on, "They must have been here at least once before last night, then, to check it out. That might help. We can talk to the parks police — see if they came across a couple driving up this road or hacking through the undergrowth recently."

"It's the sort of thing that's worth a public appeal," Godley said. "I'll mention it at the press conference. I think we should try to get this on *Crimewatch* as well. Thousands of people use this park every day. We need to try to reach as many of them as possible."

"Look for someone who was here after

sunset. That might narrow it down." Derwent looked around. "He'd want to check the conditions at the time he was planning to do the shooting, not in the middle of the day. Place like this, it's going to be different in the dark. He'd have needed a night sight because there's fuck all street lighting around here, and that means he's using a modern rifle, not an old one, so that might help us. He'd have been prepared. And a bloody good shot, incidentally, because it was seventy meters from where he was lying to the target."

"Do you think ex-military?" Godley asked. "Should we talk to the army?"

"Maybe." Derwent rubbed a hand over his head, considering it. Being ex-army himself, he was in a better position to know than most. "The thing is, ex-military doesn't mean someone who was in the British army. We could be looking for someone who got experience as a sniper in the former Yugoslavia, or Syria, or in Africa. And you can't rule out terrorism at the moment." Terrorism was Derwent's pet subject. It was one of the few areas of policing that held his interest outside of homicide investigation.

"Terrorism." Godley didn't look convinced.

"We've imported plenty of them and we've grown our own. I'm surprised we haven't had a sniper attack before, to be honest. It's one of the skills they're teaching in the training camps in the Hindu Kush. They estimate hundreds of British Muslims have been through those camps in the last ten years. There's no shortage of potential shooters."

And if it was terrorism, the press were going to go insane. A police officer made a new kind of target, at least in Britain. The police in Northern Ireland and Afghanistan had known all about it for decades.

"They'd still need to practice, wouldn't they?" I said. "I don't imagine you can shoot a high-powered rifle in a suburban garden without the neighbors noticing. We could talk to the gun clubs around London."

"Not a bad idea." Derwent was nodding. I braced myself for a follow-up remark. He was never one to give a compliment without qualifying it. On this occasion, however, he let it stand. I found it more unsettling than being criticized, as I thought he probably knew.

"All right. This is what I want you to do next." Godley was fiddling with his phone again. He sounded distracted. It wasn't like him not to make eye contact with the people he was talking to, and Derwent's eyebrows twitched together as he looked from the boss to me and back again. "Maeve, stay with Josh. I've got somewhere else to be so I'm not going to wait until the SOCOs release the crime scene."

I was willing to bet Godley's "somewhere else to be" had something to do with the message he'd received. I hoped my face was safely neutral when he finally looked up.

"I'll do a press conference for the lunchtime news," Godley said. "I'll start off by giving some general information on the shooting and appeal for witnesses. We don't want to say too much at the moment about a possible terrorist connection, or anything else, so I'll keep it brief."

"Makes sense," Derwent said. "No point in causing a panic."

"Don't mention it to anyone else, either — not the SOCOs, not the local police, not the press."

"I wouldn't." Derwent sounded hurt at the very suggestion.

"I'm going to want to speak to everyone at six this evening in the office," Godley went on. "I'll let Chris and the others know about that. In the meantime find out what you can about the shooter, the gun, the ammunition — anything that might help us to come up with some suspects. At the moment, we've got nothing apart from a dead policeman and some broken twigs. We're not going to catch anyone with that."

"We're just getting started," Derwent pointed out, not unreasonably.

"I'm going to have the commissioner on the phone any minute to find out where we are with the investigation. I am not looking forward to telling him how little we know." The edge of irritation in Godley's voice was sharp enough to draw blood. "If you can spare the time, please talk to the witnesses before our conference this evening."

"I was going to."

"Well, make sure it happens."

"All right, calm down." Derwent rocked back on his heels. "It's not like you to let the pressure get to you, boss."

"The pressure is not getting to me. I'm asking you to do your job properly. That's all."

"And you know I always do."

Godley held Derwent's gaze for a couple of seconds before he nodded and turned and strode away. He didn't even say goodbye.

"That went well," I observed.

"Thanks for jumping in."

"I didn't."

"Exactly."

"Oh, come on. Like you need me to stand up for you."

"Obviously not. I can look after myself."

"Then you didn't need me to defend you," I said patiently.

Logic: not Derwent's strong point. He ignored me, though. He was brooding over Godley.

"What was his problem? He basically accused me of time-wasting. If anything, he's been wasting *my* time. I've been hanging around here for hours waiting to do something useful. I haven't even had a coffee."

"Poor you." I checked over my shoulder, seeing SOCOs in overalls bustling in and out of the woods like honeybees, every movement suggesting a strong sense of purpose. "They're still working. Let's go down the hill and see if we can find somewhere to have breakfast. I don't know if there's a cafe near here but there'll be a fast-food van in the car park at the very least."

"Where's the car park?"

I pointed. "Five minutes that way."

"You do have your uses." Derwent grinned at the expression on my face. "Too patronizing?"

"No more than usual."

"Over coffee," Derwent said, sliding off his jacket and hooking it over his shoulder, "you can explain to me what you did to piss the boss off."

"I told you, it was nothing to do with me."

"Yeah, and I don't believe you."

"I can't help that. It's the truth."

We walked down the hill in something approaching a companionable silence. The air was still and warming up nicely. It was a day for picnics in the park, not murder investigations. I should have been glad, I thought. More often than not outdoor crime scenes involved rain, or snow, or freezing winds. It was positively pleasant to be wandering through Richmond Park in the sunshine. If I could have forgotten that I was there because two teenagers had just lost their father, I'd have been happy.

We were getting close to the temporary barrier that blocked the road. One of the uniformed officers turned at the sound of our voices and leaned over it.

"Are you with the MIT team?"

"Yeah," Derwent said. "Why?"

"There's a young lady here who says she was here last night. She's been waiting to talk to you." He pointed and I saw a slender dark-haired girl sitting on the grass verge, her arms hugging her knees. She was watching us and as we came toward her she jumped up.

"Are you investigating that man's death?"

"Yeah. And you are?" Derwent sounded even more hostile than usual. I knew why. We were always on our guard for tabloid journalists pretending to be involved in a case so they could get the inside story on an investigation. There were plenty of young and pretty reporters angling for a big break who could convince you that black was white if you gave them the chance.

"I'm Megan O'Kane." She was pale, her expression worried. It was impossible to tell what she would look like when she was animated and happy.

"What's your address?" Derwent demanded, flicking through his notebook.

"Fifteen Sopworth Road, Richmond."

Derwent paused to read something, then looked up. "You're the one who found him."

"Yes. Well, I found the car. I didn't really look inside once I saw he was . . ."

"Dead."

"Yes."

"What are you doing here? We were going to come and see you later."

"I couldn't stay at home." She shivered. "My flatmate is there and she keeps telling me we should go for brunch and have a few drinks and forget about what happened last night. I couldn't stand it. I didn't mean to come back here but I couldn't think of anywhere better to be. I just wanted to know if you'd found out anything."

"We're making inquiries," I said, which was the standard line but true. "Why were you here last night, Megan?"

"Badger-watching. Well, it was supposed to be badger-watching. I didn't actually see anything."

"Why were you doing that?" Derwent sounded totally nonplussed.

"Do you know Hugh Johnson? He's on the television?" She looked from me to Derwent, not seeing any dawning recognition. *"Animal Neighborhood?"*

"Oh, I know," I said. I half-recalled the presenter, who was too old to be as boyish as he tried to be. " 'Look who you might meet at the bottom of your garden.' That kind of thing."

"Exactly. I met him in my local pub last week. He was asking the questions in a bonus round in the table quiz and my team won it. He sat with us afterward and we got talking about our favorite animals. I said I loved badgers and he asked if I'd ever seen a real one. I hadn't. He told me he knew where I would definitely see one and he said he'd show me and I was kind of flattered he was offering, so I said yes."

Derwent was shaking his head. "It's so easy if you're on the telly, isn't it?"

"What's easy?" Megan frowned at him.

I cut in quickly so Derwent didn't get a chance to explain what he'd meant. It would not have gone down well, I suspected. "What time did you get here?"

"He picked me up at my flat and drove to the car park near here. I suppose it must have been half past ten when we got here. Then we walked over to the place where he said the badgers were likely to be." She pointed to the hillside behind her, to the left of the road where Hammond's car had been parked. "That took another twenty minutes. Maybe longer."

"So would you say you were there at eleven p.m.?" I asked.

"Yes. Around then."

"And you were being pretty quiet, I assume."

"We couldn't move. Couldn't talk. Couldn't eat or drink anything." She shivered. "I was freezing. I got bored after half an hour when nothing happened but I didn't want be rude so I just stayed put."

"Did you see anything strange?" I asked.

"Or hear anything?"

"Not until I heard the shots," Megan said. "There was nothing to hear. I was trying to stay awake so I was trying to find anything to distract myself from how sleepy and cold I was."

"Is it possible that you fell asleep?" Derwent asked.

"No." She didn't sound sure, though, and I wasn't surprised when she qualified it. "Not for more than a second or two, if that. And Hugh didn't sleep at all. He didn't seem to mind the cold or how late it was or how long it took for something to happen. I suppose he's used to it. Anyway, he'd just seen a badger when we heard the shots, so we were both wide awake."

"How long was the gap between the shots?"

"Not long. A couple of seconds."

"First shot." Derwent mimed feeding a bullet into a rifle and held the imaginary weapon up to his cheek. "Second shot. That long?"

"About that long."

Derwent looked thoughtful. I took the lead again. "What about after the shots?

"Nothing for a bit. We argued about whether we'd heard shots and if it meant we were in danger. Hugh thought we should stay where we were and hide." Her voice dripped with disdain. "We didn't have mobile reception so we couldn't call the police. I wanted to move so we could call for help but Hugh was terrified."

"Why do I think he's unlikely to admit that when we interview him?" Derwent was grinning.

"He can say what he likes, but I know the truth. We'd still be up there if he'd got his way." She folded her arms, hugging herself. "Then a car drove by. It had the lights off, which was weird."

"What kind of car?" Derwent asked.

"I don't know."

"Anything at all. We don't need the make and model. Was it a saloon, hatchback, estate, sports car, people carrier —"

"I said I don't know." She could see from the looks on our faces that it was the wrong answer. "I'm sorry. It was dark and they didn't have the lights on. I thought it was medium-sized. Not a Mini or anything like that. Not a big car either. And the engine sounded rough. That's all I can tell you. I've tried to remember anything useful. I really have."

"I'm sure you have," I said soothingly. "Memory is a funny thing, though. We'll leave you our cards. If anything else comes back to you, you can let us know."

"I want to know his name."

"Who?" I asked, genuinely confused.

"The man who died."

"Oh." I glanced at Derwent, who shrugged, leaving it up to me to decide. I couldn't work out if I should tell her or not. If Derwent felt like it, I'd get in trouble for breaking the rules. "His name hasn't been released yet."

"I won't tell anyone." Tension was reverberating through her. "I just want to know who he was. Did he deserve to be shot?"

"No one deserves to be shot." Derwent looked at her for a moment, judging her. He looked severe, and no one was more surprised than me when he spoke again. "His name was Terence Hammond. He was a police officer. He had two kids and he used the park as a shortcut after his shifts. And none of that is to end up in the press."

"I won't say anything. I'm not doing any interviews. I don't care about that kind of stuff."

"What about your flatmate? She might fancy earning a couple of quid. Or your parents might tell their friends and neighbors. Things get out. So say nothing."

"Okay."

Someone behind us called, "Josh!"

It was the curly haired scene-of-crime officer, now liberated from her protective gear. Her top was tight, showing off some eye-catching curves, and she'd managed to get hold of some lip gloss before finding us.

"What can I do for you, Chloe?" Derwent asked. *Chloe.* So he'd made up for his earlier faux pas.

"We've released the scene. If you want to revisit it, go ahead. It's all yours."

"Thanks for letting me know."

"You're welcome." Chloe gave me a look that seemed to imply she'd noticed every single flaw in my physical appearance and wasn't impressed, then did the same in Megan's direction. To Derwent, she said, "I'll be here for another ten or fifteen minutes. If you have any questions, you know where to find me."

He moved across to get closer to her. "Did the dog find anything?"

"A squirrel."

"I told you," Derwent said to me, and I got another cool look from Chloe.

Derwent turned back to her and said something else that I couldn't catch. She lowered her voice to reply and the two of them talked for a couple of minutes before she walked away. He forgot himself enough to watch her go, staring for just a little bit too long. I cleared my throat.

"Was there anything else you wanted to ask Miss O'Kane, sir?"

"What? No. Not at the moment." He turned to Megan. "But we'll need you to give us a formal statement about what you saw and heard. My colleague here will write something up and you can amend it if necessary." He produced a business card at the same time. "Thanks again."

I handed her my card too and we left her gathering her things.

Derwent waited until we were more or less out of earshot.

"Fuck my luck. I'm not getting any breakfast, am I?"

"Not immediately. Let's have a quick look and then we can grab something to eat."

He made a noise deep in his throat that might even have been a growl. "The crime scene isn't going anywhere."

"You know better than that. We've been lucky so far with holding the press off. The minute we lose the cordon, they'll be in. I don't want to have to work around photographers and reporters, thanks."

"You look all right, actually." Derwent was regarding me critically. "Today might be a good day to be on camera."

"Oh, shut up. Sir," I added as an afterthought, just in case I got in trouble for not respecting his rank. "What did you think about Megan?"

"Not my type. Too intense."

Count to a million . . . "I meant about what she had to say."

"I thought Hugh needed to work on his game. 'Come and lie completely still on a cold hillside for a couple of hours while we wait to catch TB from some highly infectious badgers.' No thanks."

"Apart from dating tips, what else got your attention?"

He frowned. "She made me think we might not be dealing with a pro after all."

"Why not?"

"The second shot bothers me. There was no need for it. He should have known he'd got a kill with the first. And it was too quick. More like he wanted to shoot him than that he had to do it."

"Maybe he thought one shot wasn't enough to kill him."

Derwent shook his head, slowly. "Maybe one shot wasn't enough because he wanted him to die twice."

CHAPTER SIX

It was darker under the trees. I followed
Derwent, who seemed to know where he
was going. There was a path now, of sorts
— a trail of trampled undergrowth and bent
branches, where the forensics officers had
carried equipment through the trees to the
sniper's hideout. I wasn't sure that I'd have
been able to follow it on my own.

"Look out," Derwent said over his
shoulder. "This bit is muddy."

"Thanks." I picked a route through an
area of black ooze. "Any good for
footprints?"

"The SOCOs said it was too soft. Nothing identifiable." He paused to hold up a
branch so I could duck under it.

"Is it much further?"

"Not much." A flash of teeth. "This isn't
your natural habitat, is it? You're a proper
little Londoner. You probably can't imagine
a green space bigger than Richmond Park.

You probably can't imagine *anything* bigger than Richmond Park." He answered himself in a high-pitched voice that was nothing like mine. "But sir, Richmond Park is infinite."

"Don't try to pretend you spend your free time hiking through forests."

"True." Derwent sidestepped me so he was in front again. "But I did a shitload of training in the Brecon Beacons when I was in the army."

"I can't help noticing that you left the army."

"Best decision I ever made." He went silent, then, and there was something expressive about the line of his shoulders that told me not to push for any further details.

I wouldn't have admitted it to Derwent, but my sense of direction worked better on the street than in the trees, and I was struggling to work out where we were. I had a vague idea we had circled around from where we'd entered the woods. After I tripped on a root and almost fell I stopped thinking about where we were going and concentrated on where I was putting my feet, so much so that I collided with Derwent when he stopped.

"Steady."

"Sorry."

"This is it."

I looked over his shoulder and saw we had reached the edge of the trees. The area in front of us was taped off but I couldn't see much difference between it and the surrounding woods.

"How did you know this was the place?"

"Knowledge, Kerrigan." He pulled something out of his pocket and held it up. "This helped."

"What's that? A rifle sight?"

"Correct."

"Where did you get that?"

"I had it in the car."

"Why?"

"Essential bit of kit. You never know when it will come in handy. Like today."

"I've worked with you for what — two years? You've never used it before."

"Not that you noticed." He stepped over the tape and strolled into the middle of the area, looking around. "Probably wouldn't occur to you that it would be a good thing to carry around."

"Probably not." Because the majority of the cases we investigated didn't involve high-powered rifles, I managed not to point out. "I still don't know how you worked out this was the place."

"Experience and angles. Same as good

sex." He turned to check my reaction, which was a waste of time because I'd worked with him for long enough not to betray any emotion at all.

"So why here?"

"This is the best place to see the front of the car. Have a look." He handed me the sight. "You'll need to lie down, obviously, to see it as the shooter saw it. Just over here where the ground is lower. I'm not going to lie, it's a bit soft."

"That's fine." I knew Derwent was watching me for signs of reluctance to lie down in the dirt. I ignored him. I was actually too interested in seeing the sniper's line of sight to care about my clothes. I knelt, feeling the ground give slightly as moisture seeped through the fabric of my trousers. I stretched out so I was resting on my elbows and held the sight up to one eye. "Oh, I see."

"Do you?" He lay down beside me, his shoulder nudging mine. "What do you see?"

"Because of the way the earth is built up in front of here and the bushes around either side there's no way anyone would see him, but he has a good line on where the car was." The SOCOs had marked its location with white tape before the car was recovered and I had a clear view toward it.

"Know much about rifles, Kerrigan?"

"Not a thing."

"Well, the gun we're looking for will be an illegally held firearm. The only long-barrelled guns that are legal in this country are shotguns and .22 rifles. There's no way that was .22 ammunition. Terence Hammond was blown apart."

"So we're not going to be able to check the register of firearms licenses to find this weapon."

"Not as such. But it's not a bad place to start, and neither are the gun clubs. The thing is that people who like guns like all kinds of guns, legal and otherwise. They like other people who like guns. They like spending time with them at places like gun clubs, and they like to talk about their collections." Derwent took the sight out of my hand and peered through it. "Someone will know who owns the gun we're looking for. If we appeal for information, we'll get a call or two, I promise you."

"I didn't think people who liked guns necessarily liked us."

"They don't. But there are some who like to pretend they could be police, and there are others who don't like rule breakers. It spoils the fun for everyone."

"Fun?"

Derwent shrugged. "It's not your thing, but don't judge them. A lot of them take it seriously. There've been two big incidents that had legal repercussion for the firearms fans in this country. There was Hungerford in 1987, when sixteen people were shot dead in the streets, and Dunblane in 1996. Eighteen people died here, including the gunman."

Dunblane. The name made me shiver. Sixteen small children and their teacher had died at the hands of a middle-aged man armed with a collection of handguns, for no apparent reason. "I know handguns were made illegal after Dunblane."

"You're right. And Hungerford did for semi-automatic rifles. Every weapon Michael Ryan used in Hungerford was licensed and legally held by him. Thomas Hamilton was the same in Dunblane. The law-abiding gun lovers are scared of another incident, not that they have much left to lose. You know the politicians don't care about shooting as a sport. It's up there with hunting. They're happy to swap the chance of a few Olympic shooting medals for a public perception they've done something about mass murder."

"So bitter," I said.

"I'd ban the lot of them. I hate guns."

"But you liked shooting."

"I did." He slid the sight into his jacket pocket. "A bit too much."

Derwent never, ever talked about the army, or shooting, or anything else about his past unless he had no choice. I hesitated, wondering if I should ask him to explain what he'd meant, but before I could he had moved on.

"We think he had a groundsheet or something similar to lie on, from the way the mud is flattened."

"That seems sensible." I didn't want to think about how my clothes would look once we were finished in the woods.

"Makes me think he'd been here before to find this place, and that he was prepared to wait for a long time." Derwent rolled over and sat up, looking around. "I asked Chloe. The SOCOs weren't able to find a latrine, even with the dog. Either he buried it a long way down or he took it with him. No way he wasn't crapping himself with nerves."

"Lovely."

"It's all DNA. The cops in Perugia got Rudy Guede for Meredith Kercher's murder because he shat his guts out after killing her."

"I'm not sure that case is the best example of good forensic work," I said, standing up.

133

"Good point. You have to wonder if it would have turned out differently with someone like Chloe collecting the evidence."

"Yes, about her. When did the two of you make friends?"

"While you were off with the boss." He got to his feet, grinning. "I knew she wouldn't be able to resist me for long."

"For God's sake, are you on heat or something?"

"This is what it's like to be single, Kerrigan. You see opportunities and you take them."

"That's what it's like when *you're* single," I said. "Normal people can control themselves a bit better than that."

"You just don't remember what it's like. You're the type who goes from one big relationship to another. I bet you and the male model got together before you'd finished splitting up with your last bloke."

The male model being Rob, I guessed. Derwent had a million nicknames for him, mostly rude.

"I got together with Rob just after I broke up with Ian, but there was a gap." *Of about five minutes.* "I have been single in the past, though, and I don't remember trying to pull everyone that crossed my path."

"Then you were doing it wrong. If you ever need a few pointers, let me know." He winked. I knew it was designed to bother me but I couldn't let that go.

"I can't believe you just winked at me. Don't ever do that again."

"Protesting too much, Kerrigan."

"No, just the right amount." A glint in Derwent's eye could have been anger or amusement. Either way, I had probably said too much. "How far did you get with Chloe?"

"I got her number." He shrugged. "Don't know if I'll use it or not, but it's one for the shag bank."

"You'd have to take her out first. I thought you didn't believe in dating."

"Might be worth it, for her."

There was something in his voice that made me look at him, surprised. "Don't tell me you're smitten."

"Not smitten." The grin. "She looks properly dirty, though. Something about the way she walks. That look in her eye. You can't fake it."

I shook my head. "No matter how low I set my expectations, you always manage to get under them."

"And no matter how tight the knickers, I always get into them in the end." He

135

shrugged. "It's a gift."

I checked the time. "We'd better get going if you want to get something to eat. We still have to talk to Romeo himself, Hugh Johnson. Are you going to the postmortem?"

"Not likely. Not if the boss is going." He started back down the path. Over his shoulder, he said, "I've had enough of him for one day. He was a proper little ray of sunshine earlier."

"I've seen him in better moods," I said.

"Bet you have. You still haven't told me what you did to piss him off."

"I have told you, actually. Absolutely nothing. It's probably something to do with the divorce."

"Divorce?" Derwent stopped at that.

"Didn't you know? He and Serena have split."

"When? Why?"

"I don't know."

"Did she leave him or did he leave her?"

"I don't know that either."

"Like hell you don't." Derwent was frowning. "How did you find this out?"

"He told me. At the wedding. I didn't ask him," I felt compelled to add.

"What else did he say?"

"Not a lot. Look, I know you like to think the worst of people but it's nothing to do with me."

Derwent raised one eyebrow.

"Oh, come on. Not you too. I am not having a relationship with the boss. I've shared closer moments with you."

The other eyebrow went up.

"Seriously," I said.

"What about the boss's daughter? How's she taking it?"

"I didn't ask."

He looked thoughtful. "It might explain a few things, actually. Godley told me Isobel was applying to American universities. I thought it was strange that he'd let her go so far away, where he couldn't keep an eye on her. Maybe she was getting out of town because home was too miserable."

"Maybe he wanted her to go far away so she could have some freedom."

"No father wants his teenage daughter to have any freedom," Derwent said. "Believe me, I've known a few."

"If it was freedom to spend time with you, I completely understand."

Derwent shook his head. "I can't believe the boss is getting divorced. I'd never have picked them to break up, if I'm honest. Serena was the perfect woman. Beautiful, cultured, intelligent —"

"I didn't think intelligence mattered to

you. Or culture."

"No, but these things matter to the boss. She was incredibly understanding, too. Never seemed to mind when he was out all the time. Never complained about the job."

"That you know of. Maybe she got tired of coming second to his work."

"She knew what she was getting into. He was already a copper when she married him."

"It'll have got worse, though, since then. He's more important. He has more responsibilities. Maybe it was more than she bargained for."

Derwent pulled a face, brooding over it.

"You never really know what's going on in someone else's relationship," I said. "It might have looked good from the outside but something wasn't working."

"That's what you tell yourself so you can justify sleeping with him."

"I'm not sleeping with him!" I said it loudly enough that a couple of wood pigeons took fright and plunged away from us through the trees in a flurry of wings.

"No need to shout." Derwent seemed to feel he'd gone far enough. "Speaking of relationships, what did you make of Mrs. Hammond?"

I told him my impressions of her, and the

house, and what she'd said about their family. I saved the bit about Vanessa's black eye until we were eating our late breakfast by the burger van in the car park. The place was busy with families and dog walkers so I kept my voice low, a subtlety that was lost on Derwent.

"Bloody hell. What's going on there?"

"I don't know but I'd say it's a priority to find out."

"We should go through Vanessa's school. Find a responsible adult that way. Cut Mrs. Hammond out before she finds a way to keep us at arm's length."

"I'm sure the boss will support that."

Derwent hooked the meat out of the middle of his burger and wadded half of it into his mouth. With some difficulty, he said, "I don't like this, you know."

"What?"

"Poking around in this guy's life. I don't want to know why his daughter has a black eye. I don't want to pull his marriage apart. I just want him to be a hero. A copper gets killed and you want him to be a hero, not a prick. This Hammond is shaping up like a prick. Getting noshed off by some trollop on his way home from work sounds like fun but it's not what you want in the headlines, is it?"

A father pulled his small daughter out of our vicinity, glaring at us. Derwent was oblivious. I moved a bit further away from the burger van queue.

"He might have been a good cop even if his private life was messy."

"Yeah, maybe. Or maybe he brought all of this on himself." Derwent dumped the burger bun in the bin and wiped his fingers on a paper napkin. "You know how I told Megan no one deserved to be shot? I'm not so sure that's true."

"It's a good line, though."

"I thought so. And she did too, which is what matters." Derwent stretched. "Let's go and see what the badger-bothering television personality can tell us about what happened last night."

"Somehow I think his version won't be exactly the same as Megan's."

"Less perving, more heroics?"

"That sort of thing."

Derwent sighed. Under his breath, he said, "Can't wait."

CHAPTER SEVEN

I'd already formed an impression of what Hugh might be like from Megan's account of their evening together. It was generally unwise to bring any preconceptions to an interview, but Hugh conformed to type from the moment he answered the door. I recognized him from TV ads for his wildlife programs but he was smaller than I had expected, five foot six maybe. He had fair curly hair that he wore short, brushed back from a high forehead. He used his beard to define a jawline that was otherwise inclined to soften into his neck. I was sure his image was important to him: his eyebrows looked suspiciously well groomed and his teeth were capped to perfection. He was wearing a brown-and-green checked shirt and cords, country casual in the heart of London. He looked warily at us, half-hiding behind the door.

"Yes?"

"Police," Derwent said, his voice loud enough to be clearly audible to the neighbors. "Can we come in, Mr. Johnson?"

Hugh winced and hurried to stand back — anything to get us off the street and out of sight. As we came through the door, he snapped, "Shoes off, please."

It was a reasonable enough request. I might even have offered to take them off if he'd given me the chance, because the trudge through the woods had left its mark on me. Little flakes of dried mud drifted on to the floor as I pulled off my boots. For his part, Derwent glowered. He took his own sweet time about removing his shoes so I was on my own as I followed Hugh into the living room.

I could only imagine that Hugh had picked the basement flat in Fulham because of the posh postcode: inside it was low-ceilinged and dark. The living room was sparsely furnished, apparently at random. It looked dated and shabby.

"You can sit there." He pointed at a small sofa, taking a scuffed leather armchair for himself. He watched me as I sat down and I could practically hear him thinking, *too tall.* "Is this going to take long?"

"We just want to get a statement from you about what happened last night," I said.

"Sure. Yes. Of course." His eyes were fixed on mine, his stare so intense that I could see white around the irises. He had the air of a horse about to bolt. "I just wonder if I should have a solicitor present."

I blinked, wondering if I'd misheard. He looked completely serious. I gambled that he meant it. "That's up to you. But I don't think you need one."

"It's just, you know. In my position. As a public figure."

"A television presenter."

Hugh bristled. "My reputation is very important. Public perception matters. My livelihood depends on how popular I am."

"I understand that. But this statement is for use by the police and possibly the courts. It's not released to the press." *Even if they were interested . . .*

"What's the problem?" Derwent strolled into the room and started wandering around, picking up photographs and ornaments to inspect them. "I thought we'd be finished by now. Don't tell me you haven't even started."

"Mr. Johnson was wondering if he needed a lawyer."

"I'm just being wary," Hugh said, defensive immediately. "I know what can happen. Statements can be misconstrued.

143

Things can be taken out of context."

"By the police?" Derwent asked. His tone was deceptively innocent.

"Sometimes." He ran a hand through his hair, brushing it into place.

"You don't trust us."

"I didn't say that." The two men stared at one another in silence, until Hugh started to fidget. "I'm sure that won't be the case here."

"What exactly are you worrying about?" Derwent demanded. "That people might think it's a bit weird of you to use your reputation as a wildlife expert to convince pretty young girls to date you?"

"That sort of thing." Hugh tried for a smile. "You can see how it could be interpreted."

"I know how I've interpreted it."

"We've already got a statement from Megan," I said quickly, seeing the color rise in Hugh's cheeks. "So it's really just about confirming the details of what she told us, and checking whether you saw anything she didn't."

"You know, I want to cooperate. I'd assume I did see things she would have missed."

"Why's that?"

"I'm a trained observer. I notice the

details." He propped his elbows on the arms of the chair and laced his fingers in front of his chest. I could sense his confidence rising. "That environment is one I know particularly well. I'm used to being there."

"I'm sure you are." Derwent's voice was pitched low. I'd have known what he was saying even if I hadn't heard the words. To Hugh Johnson, he said, "How does that work, anyway? When do you make your move on them? Out in the open or back at the car, when they're grateful to be warm and dry again? Or maybe up against a tree on the way back. That would work, wouldn't it?"

"I don't know what you're talking about. I was simply responding to a fan's wish to see some beautiful animals in their proper environment."

"So it was *her* idea?" Derwent nodded. "I see."

I caught Derwent's eye and gave him a warning frown. To Hugh, I said, "What details did you notice?"

"The car. I'm pretty sure I got the color and maybe the make."

"Really? Because Megan seemed to think you wouldn't have seen much of anything." Derwent came to sit beside me, his knees so wide apart I had to turn sideways to make room for him.

"What's that supposed to mean?"

"She said you were terrified. You were busy hiding when the car went past." Not the most diplomatic way of raising that, but then Derwent wasn't the most diplomatic of men.

Hugh shifted in his seat again. "Why are you even here? If you're determined to discount everything I say —"

"We're not," I said, crossing my fingers that Derwent wouldn't contradict me. "We just want to be sure that what you tell us is the truth and not exaggerated. No one is blaming you if you didn't see anything. If you say you saw something and it later turns out that you were wrong, we could waste a lot of time looking for something or someone that doesn't exist."

"I would never do that." Hugh blinked at me, hurt.

"Just tell us what you remember about last night."

"Starting when?"

"When you met up with Megan," I suggested.

Frowning, Hugh began to describe where and when he and Megan had met. His account tallied with hers more or less exactly, right up until the moment after the second shot was fired. "I did lie down at that point, and stayed low. I was concerned for Megan's safety as well as my own. There are people who don't like what I do, and what I stand for. Just because I'm on television that doesn't mean I'm popular."

"Ever had death threats?" Derwent asked.

"None that I brought to the attention of the police."

"But you have had threats."

"Not in so many words." Hugh wriggled, put on the spot and not enjoying it. "Attention from the fans — it's nice, but it can be intense."

"So your first thought was that the shots had been fired by a fan," Derwent said slowly.

"Not my first thought. Not even my second." Hugh ran his hand through his hair again. "God. I don't know. I was in shock. I couldn't believe it was really happening. For the sake of being safe I got on the ground and I told Megan to do the same. I didn't want her to be endangered."

"Very chivalrous," Derwent commented.

"It's the truth."

"You were lying down. It was dark and the car didn't have lights on," I said. "How much could you see?"

"Quite a lot. I know it sounds unlikely but

I am used to spending hours in low-light areas, watching for small movements. A lot of animals only come out at night and they don't like artificial lights any more than murderers do. The car was quite a long way off but I'm long-sighted, as it happens."

"You said you thought you knew the color and make of the car."

"Yeah. I'd say you're looking for a Japanese car and not a recent model. It was boxy. I'd say it was a Toyota. Something like that. Color . . ." he pulled a face, thinking about it. "Dark, but not black. Call it gray. Maybe not gray but not black."

"Do you like cars?" Derwent asked.

"I watch *Top Gear* now and then." He laughed, obviously expecting us to join in. Derwent was stony-faced. I hadn't the heart to muster a smile.

"Anything else? What about the engine? Did it sound as if it was in good nick?" I asked.

"Not particularly. It was loud. Could have been a diesel."

Which fitted in with Megan's statement.

"Could you see the driver? Any passengers?" I asked.

"Someone in the back seat but I couldn't tell you anything about them except that they were there. I could see a figure but no detail. I can say more about the front of the car. I had longer to look at it. The driver was small — plenty of space in the car around him or her." He concentrated, staring at the carpet in front of him, and I thought he was telling the truth about what he'd seen. "I saw one hand on the steering wheel and either the driver was wearing light-colored gloves or they were white, because it was definitely pale. Stood out against the darker background."

"Could it have been a woman?" I asked.

"Yes." The answer was instant. "But I can't say it was — not definitely."

"Was there anything else you saw or heard that might be useful to us?"

"No. I've been trying to think. I just keep remembering seeing that car." Hugh put a hand to his eyes and shuddered. "It's not what you expect to see somewhere like Richmond Park. All the blood. And Meg went far closer than I thought she should have."

Derwent bristled. "She didn't do any harm. What if he'd been injured? She might have been able to help him."

"You know better than that. His brains were all over the back windscreen." Hugh's face had lost most of its color, but he was holding his own against Derwent. "He had

149

a hole in his chest the size of my fist. They don't teach you how to deal with that in first aid."

"You didn't know that twenty feet out."

"What do you think I should have done?" Hugh demanded. "What would you have done? Run down the hillside and stopped the car?"

Derwent laughed. "I wouldn't have been there in the first place, mate. I can think of a few better choices for a first date."

"Okay." Hugh nodded. "You've got a problem with me because I'm on TV. It happens."

"It's not because you're on TV. It's because —"

I cut in before Derwent could say something unforgivable and reportable. "I think we're finished. I'll write this up as a formal statement and get it to you for signature, okay?"

"Fine." Hugh stopped glaring at Derwent for a moment to smile at me. Derwent jumped up and padded out to the hall without a word to either of us.

"If you think of anything else or you want to amend anything you've told us, you can give me a call." I handed him a card and then started putting my notebook away.

"Is that your mobile number on the back?"

I glanced up, surprised at the question. "Yeah. Best way to get hold of me. This isn't a desk job and it's not nine to five either."

"I can imagine." He turned the card over and tapped the edge on his knee. "I thought you'd put it there for my benefit."

"Oh. You mean . . . no. That would be completely unprofessional." I tried to sound severe, even though I knew I was blushing. I hoped against hope that Derwent was too busy with his shoelaces to hear any of this.

"I don't suppose you'd like to go for a drink some time? Even though it would be unprofessional?" He waggled his perfectly manicured eyebrows at me.

"I have a boyfriend."

"Of course you do." He crossed his legs. "Can't blame me for trying."

"Er, right." So I wasn't too tall after all. I tried to feel lucky about that. Out of the corner of my eye I could see Derwent in the hall, arms folded, watching us. I stood up. "I don't think a drink is a good idea, Mr. Johnson."

"I see a girl like you, I have to ask." He gave me a rueful smile that made my skin crawl.

"You don't have to ask, actually. Not when she's just doing her job. She's working, not hanging out in a bar, and she doesn't need to deal with comments on her appearance." Derwent had come to lean against the doorframe. He was word-perfect after my lesson earlier, I noticed. And I'd thought he wasn't even listening.

"It's fine," I said.

"It's bloody not," Derwent said.

Hugh leaned forward, his eyes fixed on Derwent. "You know, you made a good point just then about Miss Kerrigan doing her job. Now I suggest you go and do yours and try to catch this guy before he kills someone else."

"What a great idea. I would never have thought of that." Before the situation could deteriorate even further, Derwent's phone started ringing and he took it out. "I have to take this."

"Don't let me keep you." Hugh was talking to thin air; Derwent had already gone through the hall and out the front door. To me, he said, "He'll be lucky if I don't make a formal complaint against him."

"Oh, he means well," I lied. "We've been up all night and this is a big case. He's under a lot of pressure. He's a good police officer."

"If you say so." Hugh sniffed. "If you need to come back, don't bring him with you."

"Definitely not." Although I would bring

someone, I thought. Preferably someone male and large. The more I saw of Hugh, the more I felt Megan had been lucky to stumble across a murder the previous night. I'd take a ringside seat at a violent death over a date with him any day.

I stumbled through a quick good-bye as I gathered my things and pulled on my boots, trying to be charming to make up for Derwent's demeanor. I really hoped Hugh would forget about his complaint. As I ran through the conversation in my mind, I couldn't think of anything that had been too awful. On the other hand, that might just have been because I was used to Derwent and I'd forgotten how normal people behaved.

I found him on the doorstep, ending his call.

"You got out all right, then."

"He'll hear you," I whispered.

"I don't care," Derwent whispered back.

"Who was on the phone?"

"Ballistics. I asked them to get in touch as soon as they had any information on the ammo."

"And?"

"Not a .22 or anything like it. American ammunition, illegally imported."

"As you thought."

"Yeah." His face was bleak, even though he'd been right. "He's got a good weapon, top-of-the-range ammunition, and the skill to use them. You'd have to hope this was personal so it's just a one-off. Make no mistake, Kerrigan, this guy was shooting to kill."

CHAPTER EIGHT

At five to six on a Sunday, the office was almost completely deserted. I threaded through the empty desks, heading for the conference room where a murmur of voices told me I would find my colleagues.

Godley looked up as I walked in, and frowned. "Where's Josh?"

"On his way." I slid into a seat and looked around. "What's new?"

"We're about to find out." Godley made a note on the pad in front of him. There was a grayish undertone to his skin, as if he was ill. The atmosphere in the room was funereal. While Godley wasn't looking I caught Colin Vale's eye and he shrugged, very slightly.

The outer door banged and quick, confident footsteps came toward the conference room. Derwent swung through the door. "Sorry I'm late."

"Just sit down." Again, there was that edge

to Godley's voice that was unfamiliar and unsettling. Derwent caught it immediately and did as he was told.

"Terence Hammond. Who wants to begin?"

"Me." Pettifer leaned over his notes. "Dave and I went to Isleworth and got a list of his colleagues. We've spoken to about half of them so far. We keep getting the same story. Decent bloke, good copper."

"Get the feeling that's true?"

"No." Dave Kemp sounded definite. "Not the whole story, anyway."

"Why's that?" Godley asked.

"A couple of things. The younger ones, the ones who hadn't worked with him for as long, they weren't all that keen. They said he was hard to get on with. He'd pick on small things and never let them forget it. Liked to put other people down. Inclined to lose the rag when provoked. Bit of a bastard."

"He's not the only sergeant to behave that way," I said. "I had one of those when I was in uniform."

Pettifer grunted. "There might be a bit more to it than him getting lairy because he's a sergeant. We spoke to one PC who told us, off the record, about a row one night with a lad they were nicking for fighting. He ended up in hospital with a fractured skull. They said he gave Hammond a lot of backchat when he was being arrested, and Hammond was the one who brought him in to custody. He was fine on the street — walking and talking. He'd collapsed by the time he got to the nick."

"Head injuries can be like that," Derwent commented.

"Or Hammond was teaching the boy a lesson. It got covered up. The boy didn't remember anything that had happened to him since the previous week and no one looked too hard to implicate Hammond."

"So he broke the rules at least once. Anyone know anything about a girlfriend?"

"It wasn't anyone from the team." Pettifer grinned. "Three female officers and all of them as butch as they come. I didn't even bother asking them."

"Too scared of getting beaten up," Dave Kemp said.

"Too right." Pettifer shook his head. "One of them was bigger than me."

It was a cheap laugh. I kept my expression neutral, but I was thinking about our colleague Liv, who was delicate and lovely and a committed lesbian. Pettifer still hadn't grasped that you couldn't define someone's sexuality just by looking at them. Nor did he understand that women didn't have to be pretty and feminine just because he preferred them that way.

"What about someone from a different team at Isleworth?" Godley asked.

"No one thought that was likely. And I think they'd have told us." Pettifer looked to Dave, who nodded.

"They told us what they did know, which wasn't much. He had two phones, one a cheapie pay-as-you-go job. He never let it out of his sight."

"Classic cheater's trick," I said. "A lot easier than trying to delete texts and messages you don't want your wife to see."

"Did we recover two phones?" Derwent asked.

"I don't think so." Godley flipped to the list of personal effects he'd received from the morgue. "One phone. It's gone off to the lab."

"If they download the address book for me I'll check the numbers," Colin Vale offered. "She might be in there under a different ID. I had one once who put his girlfriend in as Home Insurance Helpline, which was fine until the bathroom flooded and his wife tried to call an emergency plumber."

"Now that's bad luck," Derwent said, grinning.

"It got worse. They had a fight and she 'fell' down the stairs. Survived so she was able to give evidence against him at his trial for attempted murder. He's got another two years left before he can apply for early release."

"So the moral of the story is, always carry a second phone," Belcott said.

"Well, you'd need to have a bird to cheat on first, Pete, so in your case it's not strictly necessary." Pettifer beamed at him. I hid a smirk.

"We can assume the second phone is gone," Godley said. "We can try cell-site analysis and see if we can track all the phones in use in the area — there can't have been many."

"Not too many masts nearby," Colin Vale said, sounding dubious. "It'll be a big area to cover."

It was a good point. Cell-site analysis worked by collecting data from mobile phone masts and calculating the location of the phone according to which signal was strongest. In the sprawling wilderness of the park we would be lucky to narrow it down to a general area.

"If she was savvy enough to recover the

phone, she might have ditched it by now," I said. "No reason to keep it. In fact, every reason to get rid of it as quickly as possible."

Godley nodded. "I'll get a team of uniformed officers to search drains and bins near the park for the SIM card and the phone itself, or some bits of it anyway. It hasn't rained since Hammond died, so if we have any luck at all we'll find it where she left it. Colin, have you any idea which area we should be looking at? Any luck on the CCTV?"

"Yes and no. I've been trying to get hold of anything useful before it's deleted so I haven't had time to review much of the footage. The bad news is that quite a few of the cameras nearest the park weren't in use."

It was a perennial problem. The cameras themselves were the deterrent to crime — no one except the owners could tell if they were working or not. Repairing them was expensive. London was full of cameras, but that didn't help when they were out of action.

"What's the good news?" Godley asked.

"I've got three suspect vehicles coming out of the park just after the shooting, two using one gate in particular, one on its own. I'm going to need a bit more information about the car, if we can get it, to work out which is my favorite."

"What can you see on the footage?" Derwent asked.

"Not a great deal, unfortunately. The two cars were picked up by a camera on a house near the main gate. Right time of night, moving fast, looks to be a Ford Mondeo followed by a BMW coupe. The camera got the cars but not the occupants."

"Did they have their lights on?" I asked.

"Yes."

"Our witnesses said the lights on the suspect car were off."

"But that's going to draw more attention to you on the road. Easiest way in the world to get stopped," Belcott said.

"They also said it was one car that drove away from the area, not two," Derwent pointed out.

"They could have met up by the gate. One car for the shooter, one for the girl. And Pete's right." I hated to admit it, but it was true. "They wouldn't have wanted to get stopped. Even if they had a quick clean-up they'd have been covered in blood or mud. We should look for a car driving carefully. Slowly, even."

"Well, that fits in with the other car I've got on camera," Colin Vale said. "The only problem is that I can only see one wheel

161

and a bit of the front bumper. The footage is black and white. It's off a petrol station forecourt so the camera wasn't pointing at the road and it's just in one corner of the screen. Gives us something to work on — we've identified makes and models from less. But it's not as easy as checking a license plate this time."

"We've got two witnesses." Godley flipped through the notes, distracted. "Josh, did you get a description of the car from either of them?"

"Yep. For what it's worth."

"Not sure about it?" Godley rubbed a hand over his forehead. "Great."

"We just thought that one of the witnesses could have been overstating what he'd seen," Derwent said. "Maybe he did, maybe he didn't."

"I think he saw *something*." I was struggling to be fair. "I just think he wanted to tell us what we wanted to hear."

"He was trying to tell us things that made him look good. Attention-seeking little prick."

"Hugh Johnson." Colin was reading over Derwent's shoulder. "As in *Animal Neighborhood*?"

"One and the same."

"Wow. I love that program."

162

Derwent laughed. "I hate to break it to you, but Hugh Johnson is an arse."

"You think everyone is an arse." Colin looked at me. "What's he really like?"

"An arse," I confirmed. "Sorry, Colin. But I think it was still worth talking to him. The first witness didn't see a lot. He had picked up a lot more detail."

"Whether that's accurate or not is another question," Derwent said.

"There's no such thing as a reliable eyewitness," Godley said. "Maeve, how do the two accounts compare?"

"Megan O'Kane and Hugh Johnson were on the hillside to the left of the crime scene, too far away to be able to see it directly. Megan told us she saw a car with its lights off, shortly after the shooting. So did Hugh. Megan couldn't be specific about the color. Hugh thought it was dark gray. Megan said it had a noisy engine. Hugh thought it was a diesel, possibly Japanese, but couldn't give us an exact make. He thought it was an old Toyota. It was boxy, apparently. Megan couldn't see the driver or any passengers because it was so dark. Hugh said there was someone in the back seat. He said the driver was quite short and could have been a female."

"How did he see all this when she didn't?"

"Superior eyesight," Derwent said. "According to him."

"He's used to spending hours in the dark," I explained. "He can spot things that ordinary people might miss."

"Even though Megan said he had his head buried in the grass when the car went by, in case they shot him." Derwent rocked back on his chair at a dangerous angle, his hands in his pockets, unconsciously emphasizing the difference between himself and Hugh. Risk-taking for no apparent reason came easily to Derwent. Hugh was cautious to the point of immobility.

"It's a place to start," Godley said. "Colin, see if any of that helps you narrow down our suspect cars. What else did you find out, Josh?"

"I got a report on the ballistics. Still waiting for it to come through on e-mail but I'll send it round when it comes." Derwent gave the others the same lecture on illegal firearms and gun clubs that I'd had in Richmond Park.

"Right," Godley said when he'd finished. "Josh, you seem to be the best person to concentrate on the weapon. We need to make a list of gun clubs in the greater London area and the home counties."

"Done." I slid it out of the back of my

notebook. "We can expand the search if we don't turn up anything useful."

"Throw in a request for information on firearms at the next press conference, boss," Derwent said.

"I was going to." Godley leaned back in his chair. "What else? Pete?"

"I've put in a request for Hammond's personnel file but obviously it's going to take a while to get it. Before Isleworth he worked in southwest London and he started off in Bethnal Green as a probationer. I'm trying to get hold of people who knew him way back when." He looked around at all of us. "It's hard, on a Sunday. I keep hitting dead ends."

"You should make more progress tomorrow." Godley rubbed his eyes with the heels of his hands.

"So what do we think? Was this personal?" Derwent asked. "Or was it because he was a copper?"

When Godley replied, his voice had that edge to it I'd heard before. "It's far too early to say. We don't know anything about Hammond yet."

"We need to talk to the family again," I said. "Find out what Hammond was like behind closed doors, if we can."

"You handle that, Maeve. The wife is going to be tricky. Try to talk to the daughter without her."

"I'll find out when she's going back to school. I bet it's sooner rather than later. Somehow I don't think Mrs. Hammond is going to want to keep her nearest and dearest at home at this difficult time."

"You got that impression too, Maeve?" To the rest of the table, Godley explained, "Not a great mother–daughter relationship."

"That doesn't mean she won't keep us away from Vanessa. Especially if the family has something to hide."

"All families have something to hide." Godley's face was somber.

"Any surprises at the PM?" Derwent asked.

"No. Not about Hammond, anyway. He was fit and healthy until he was shot, and the injuries he sustained are consistent with the kind of ammunition you were talking about, Josh. Nothing we weren't expecting. But I've got some bad news. It's not really my news, but I have permission to share it with you." Godley took a moment before he went on. "I talked to Glenn Hanshaw at the PM. He's been diagnosed with cancer. They don't know where it started but he has secondary tumors on his spine and in his brain."

"That doesn't sound good," Pettifer said.

"It isn't. Six months."

There was a murmur around the table. Hanshaw wasn't the most popular person we worked with, or the easiest to get to know, but he was a brilliant pathologist. And what would it be like, I wondered, to work with death every day and know that your own time was coming? Maybe for Hanshaw there was no mystery to it, so there would be less fear. Or maybe it was worse that he knew what was in store for him.

"Is he going to keep working?"

"For the moment."

"I'd jack it in straightaway," Pettifer said. "Sorry, boss, but if I've got six months left I'm going to spend the time living, not working."

"That is life for Glenn. It's what he loves. When he can't do the job effectively any more, he'll stop, but until then it's business as usual." Godley's jaw was tight and I remembered that he and the pathologist were friends. Maybe this was why Godley was in such a rank mood. Maybe it had nothing to do with the text message I'd seen.

"Does he know we know?" Derwent asked.

"Yes. He wanted you to understand what was going on but he doesn't want to talk about it. Please, don't commiserate with him. Treat him as you would usually."

Which, as Godley knew, was far from easy. We all nodded, however, and Godley pushed his chair back.

"If that's everything, then, go home. Get some rest. Tomorrow is another day."

"But you're not going home." Derwent was watching Godley closely.

"I've got to organize the search teams for the area near the park and record another interview for the evening news. Bits and pieces. I won't be long."

There was a general upheaval as everyone else stood up and made for the door. I shuffled my notes together and followed more slowly. I knew better than to assume I'd be going home just because Godley had told us we were finished for the night. Derwent would find some reason to keep me at work if I looked as if I was keen to leave.

He himself seemed to be in no hurry. He was still watching Godley. "I'll wait for you."

"There's no need," Godley said shortly.

"It's no trouble."

"Josh, you don't need to stay. I'll see you tomorrow."

"I just thought we could go for a pint." Derwent was standing with his hands in his pockets, affecting to be relaxed, but I could tell he was tense. He'd have denied it to his dying breath but Derwent wasn't as tough as he pretended to be. For the very small number of people he cared about, Derwent would give his all. It made him vulnerable, and every now and then that vulnerability showed.

"I'm too busy." Godley took out his phone and stared at it again.

Derwent looked at me and tilted his head toward the door. *Get going.* I went, before he could change his mind. I knew he would persevere with Godley, and I knew Godley would keep saying no. I didn't want to hang around to deal with a disappointed Derwent. The fallout would be dreadful.

As I walked away from the office toward the Underground, I worried about Derwent. He worshipped Godley with a blind, unswerving loyalty, a loyalty Godley had earned when they worked together years before. I'd felt the same way, once upon a time. I hoped Derwent would never find out the truth. And if he did find out, I just hoped it wouldn't be through me, because I'd be lucky if shooting the messenger was all he did.

CHAPTER NINE

I was right about Julie Hammond not wanting to keep her daughter close to hand. It was only two days before Vanessa Hammond was sent back to her expensive private school, Uplands — two days Derwent and I filled with following up dead-end leads produced by Godley's appeals for information. The nutcases were out in force, and not just on the other end of the telephone or by e-mail. Because Hammond had been a police officer, the newspapers were full of speculation about who had killed him, and why. Godley had been careful to keep a lot of the details out of the press — there was no suggestion yet that he had been with anyone when he died. Lack of information didn't prevent conspiracy theories from blossoming. Endless, moralizing editorials suggested that the Metropolitan Police was unpopular because of institutional arrogance, racism, and being out of touch with the communities it was supposed to serve. The blame was placed squarely at our door. It was almost as if Hammond was a legitimate target.

"I'd like to see how they'd manage if we weren't doing our job." Derwent folded one of the more sanctimonious broadsheets and dumped it in the back seat of the car. We were sitting outside Vanessa Hammond's school, waiting for our scheduled time to interview her. "I'd like to see them deal with the shitbags who'd come out if we weren't keeping them under control."

"Levon Cole wasn't a shitbag," I pointed out, retrieving the newspaper and spreading it out so his photograph wasn't creased. "People are angry about what happened to him, and rightly so."

"Yeah, he should never have been shot and the armed officers should never have tried to cover it up, but the fact he was a good boy is irrelevant. We don't execute people, no matter what they've done. Not our job."

The photograph of the teenager took up a quarter of the page reporting on Hammond's death, far more space than Hammond himself had been allotted. Levon had been beautiful — high-cheekboned and doe-eyed, with dark skin and hair cut close to a finely shaped head. At sixteen he'd been growing into his features still, which gave him a fragility that was poignant once you knew what had happened to him. He looked like a rapper or a young actor, not a victim of mistaken identity. He'd bled to death in a grim stairwell, shot by police officers who'd tried to make it look as if it had been his own fault, not theirs. I wasn't one to think we were in the right, automatically, no matter what — it had been a mistake, and a bad one. The more right-wing media had gone to elaborate lengths to prove that he'd been a gangster, trouble personified, and had come up with nothing substantive. The truth was that his death had been a tragedy, pure and simple, and a stain on the Met's history.

"If I was Levon Cole's mother I'd be livid that his death was being brought up in connection with this killing. It's not relevant and everyone knows it. They're just using him to create a controversy."

"If I was Levon Cole's mother I don't know how I'd get out of bed in the morning. Mind you, I have a lot of time for her," Derwent said.

It wasn't all that often that Derwent succeeded in surprising me. "Why's that?"

"She's got dignity. She could be calling for people's heads. She's just asking for an independent inquiry. She wants to know the truth." Derwent shrugged. "I respect that."

"I understand why she wants an inquiry but nothing's going to bring him back. And his death is subject to an IPCC investigation anyway. There's no need for a separate inquiry."

"She doesn't believe that."

"The clue is in the name, though. Independent Police Complaints Commission. If there's a criminal case to answer it'll go to the CPS and they'll prosecute the hell out of the officers. You know that. No one is going to want to look as if they're not taking this seriously."

Derwent shook his head. "You're bringing logic to bear on this. That's not what Claudine Cole is looking for. This is about feeling someone is listening to you when you don't otherwise have a voice."

"It's not like you to out-empathize me."

"I've picked up the pieces a couple of times. Not in the police. In the army."

"Oh," I said, trying to adjust my opinion of Derwent to incorporate a new, compassionate side to his character. "What happened?"

"Never you mind," Derwent said. It was the usual thing: he hinted at his past but never actually told me the details. I thought it was a power trip, and I also thought it was annoying. "The main thing to focus on is that widows and mothers love me. These shoulders? Made for crying on."

"I'll keep it in mind." It made so much more sense for Derwent to use other people's grief to feed his ego, I didn't know why I was disappointed.

"Invitation only, Kerrigan. Don't go getting any ideas."

"You're the last person I'd ask for comfort," I said, truthfully. "Is it time to go in yet?"

"We're still a bit early."

"No harm in that, is there?"

Derwent grinned. "Teacher's pet."

"Amy Maynard is not a teacher."

"You're right. What bullshit title have they given her?"

"Student counselor, I believe."

"And that's a real job, is it?"

"Don't knock it," I warned. "She's the ideal person to be Vanessa's responsible adult, and she volunteered."

"Do-gooder."

"Yeah, and we're lucky she is a do-gooder. Without her we'd be stuck with Julie Hammond. Believe me, you don't want that."

"You probably didn't see Mrs. Hammond

at her best." Derwent smoothed the sides of his hair. "I bet I could charm her."

"I think you're sorely mistaken about that. Even the boss didn't make a dent."

At the reference to Godley, Derwent's face darkened. He opened the car door. "Let's go."

It answered the question I hadn't dared to ask. Godley was still keeping Derwent at arm's length, and Derwent was still upset about it. Titanically so, from the moody way he strode into the school's reception, flashed his warrant card, and demanded directions to Amy Maynard's office.

"I'll just give her a call and see if she's available," the receptionist said. She reached out to the phone in front of her. Derwent leaned over the desk and put one finger on the back of the receiver, holding it in place on its rest.

"She's expecting us."

"At eleven, I was told." The receptionist glanced at the clock near her desk. She was in her fifties and very tanned, with short dark hair and a lot of eye make-up. "It's only a quarter to."

"So we're early. We won't hurry." Derwent raised his eyebrows. "Seriously. There's no need to call her."

"Oh, all right, then." She took a

175

photocopied map off the reception desk and laid it in front of us with a flourish. "You need to go to Baker — that's this building here, two over from where you are now. Her office is on the ground floor. Go through the doors and straight down the corridor in front of you and it's on the left. You'll see the chairs outside it."

Derwent set off at a fast pace, and I had to hurry to catch up with him.

"What's the rush?"

Derwent checked the map. "You know what would have happened if I hadn't insisted on seeing her. 'Just take a seat for a few moments while you're waiting for Miss Maynard.' Half an hour later you're still sitting there and Vanessa Hammond is getting her story together, with the help of her devoted guidance counselor. No thanks."

"First of all, do you really think Vanessa has something to hide? And secondly, if she does do you think you're going to surprise her into telling us the truth just by turning up ten minutes early?"

"I will take any and every advantage I possibly can," Derwent said, opening the door to Baker Building and ushering me through with a flourish. "And I'm assuming nothing about Vanessa Hammond. She might be honest and open about how she got that bruise on her face. She might tell us all about her parents' marriage. She might even know who her dad was shagging on the side. But I bet we'll have to drag it out of her."

"I think you should let me do most of the talking."

"Why?"

"You can come across as slightly . . . intimidating."

"So?" Derwent's eyebrows were drawn together, his expression fierce.

"So maybe that's something to hold in reserve. If she doesn't seem to want to talk, you could give her a nudge. If I can gain her trust, don't interrupt. I met her at the house, remember. A familiar face might be reassuring for her."

There was a long pause before Derwent said, "Fine."

"Really?"

"Go for it." His expression had changed to studied neutrality and I wondered what he was really thinking as we walked down the echoing corridor toward a row of three metal-framed chairs, the seats wooden and chipped. They looked punishing.

"A. Maynard, Student Counselor," Derwent read off the door. "What do you think? Knock or wait?"

"Knock," I said, and did so.

There was a flurry of movement behind the door — a chair pushed back, a cascade of things that might have been books hitting the floor. Derwent raised his eyebrows at me and reached past me to knock again, more heavily this time.

"Coming!"

The voice sounded breathless and girlish, and when Amy Maynard opened the door her appearance matched it perfectly. She was petite, with shoulder-length brown hair and a nervous expression. There was no color in her face at all, which could have been shock or could have been normal for her; I couldn't tell. She looked from me to Derwent and back again, apparently at a loss. It didn't bring out Derwent's gentlemanly side.

"Detective Inspector Josh Derwent, Detective Constable Maeve Kerrigan, here to interview Vanessa Hammond. Or had you forgotten?"

"You're early."

"A bit." Derwent checked his watch. "A few minutes."

"I'm not ready. Vanessa's not here. I'm with another student, actually, so . . ."

"We'll wait." I pressed my elbow into Derwent's side, a movement too subtle for Amy to notice. He stood for a couple of seconds longer, staring at Amy, his expression forbidding. I felt like a dog owner tugging on a lead, in vain. Derwent's hackles were definitely up. It seemed like a long time before he turned away and sat down on the chair nearest the door, folding his arms. I smiled at Amy and got nothing in return except for a blank look and a door closed in my face.

I sat down beside Derwent who was glowering at the wall opposite us.

"Glad we're not sitting waiting in reception. You're right, this was a much better idea."

"Shut up, Kerrigan. It was worth a try."

"These chairs are much less comfortable than the ones in reception." I shifted on the hard wooden seat. "I bet the receptionist would have got us a cup of tea while we were waiting."

Derwent leaned toward me, lowering his voice. "Why do you think she volunteered for this job?"

"Who, Amy?" I shrugged. "Sense of duty? Curiosity?"

"She's shit-scared of us."

"Of you."

"Us."

"I don't think she's scared of me. I wasn't the one staring her out."

He grinned. "She didn't like that at all."

"Yeah, and I can understand why. What I can't understand is why you felt it was necessary to glare at the poor girl."

"To see what kind of reaction I'd get." He said it as if it was perfectly reasonable. "She was shitting bricks."

"Most people she interacts with are teenagers. They're not big on eye contact. She's probably never met a police officer before, let alone one who seems to think she's got something to hide."

"From the way she reacted she probably does have something to hide. It's just unlikely to be relevant to this inquiry."

Behind us, the door handle rattled. I leaned forward to see around Derwent. The two of us watched as a teenage boy walked out, turning left, away from us. He had a mane of curly fair hair, like a surfer. He didn't so much as glance in our direction. People who studiously avoided looking at police officers had raised a red flag when I was on the street.

Then again, he was a teenager. And one who had been having a quiet chat with the school's counselor when we knocked on the door. He was probably embarrassed. He had almost reached the double-doors at the end of the corridor when a sound from the other direction made me look round and I forgot about him. A girl was coming toward us, fast, her hair flying as she strode. She had her arms wrapped around herself. Her uniform jumper was huge, her skirt correspondingly brief. Black tights made her legs look spindly, especially since her shoes were thick-soled and heavy.

"Vanessa?" Derwent asked me. I nodded.

She stopped in front of us.

"Waiting for me?

Derwent stood up and held out his hand. "I'm Josh. And this is —"

"I know who she is." She didn't unfold her arms and after a second Derwent let his hand drop back to his side.

"How are you?" I asked.

"Fine." From her tone, she thought it was a stupid question, and it was, in a way. But I genuinely wanted to know. I wanted to know if she was coping all right, if she was ready to be back at school, if she was sleeping at night. It wasn't any of my business, really, but I couldn't turn off the part of me that wanted to make the world better.

I didn't hear her come out of her office, but suddenly I became aware that Amy Maynard was standing beside Derwent.

"If we're all here, we might as well get

181

started." She smiled at Vanessa. "Get it over with."

The girl nodded and followed her into her room. It was painted gray, with half-closed Venetian blinds at the window so the light was dimmer than I would have liked. A spindly plant was the only decoration. Most of the surfaces were piled with books, files, and photocopied pages. My desk was legendary for being untidy but this was in another class. Derwent, who couldn't stand mess in any shape or form, had to be hating it. Four low chairs surrounded a coffee table in front of the desk.

"Please. Take a seat. Does anyone need water? Or a cup of coffee?" In her own room, in charge, Amy seemed to be far more confident. She was wearing a fluffy green jumper that leached all the color from her skin and a long tweed skirt with boots. I could tell she had a good figure, even though her clothes hid it effectively. She moved with the precision and economy of movement of a dancer or a gymnast. She didn't have a scrap of makeup on, I noted. My mother would have been horrified, something that made me reassess my own reaction. Why did it bother me? Maybe it helped her to relate to the students.

No one wanted anything to drink. Amy

Maynard sat on the chair furthest from the door, and Vanessa took the one next to her. I sat opposite Amy. Derwent pushed his chair back a foot or two before he sat down, breaking the neat circle. I had no doubt that was deliberate.

"So, Vanessa, thank you for seeing us," I said. "We just have a few questions for you about your dad. I'm so sorry about what happened."

She nodded with a hint of impatience. "What do you want to know?"

"We're trying to understand your father's world. We want to find out what he was like."

"I wouldn't know."

"Why's that?"

"We never talked all that much. He wasn't around a lot."

"Because of work?"

"Yeah. Shifts. Even when he wasn't working, when he had some days off, he was always out. At least when Ben and I were at home."

"Where would he go?"

A shrug. "The gym. The pub. Hardware stores. Anywhere but where we were."

"Why?" I asked.

"He didn't like being at home with Ben. Or me. Mum and I fight. He didn't like that." She swallowed, hard. "You'd hear him pick his keys up and then he'd be gone. Phone off. It used to drive Mum mad."

"Do you think they had a good marriage?"

"No." The reply was instant. "If it wasn't for Ben they would have totally got a divorce years ago. Mum wouldn't let him walk out on his responsibilities that easily though."

I thought that phrase had come straight from Julie. "She couldn't have stopped him, could she?"

"She made him feel guilty enough about not doing much for Ben. Mum pays for our education. She runs the house. Dad was supposed to help. He always said he'd fix things around the place when they broke, but he never really got round to it. He was kind of useless." The last word cut through the air. Vanessa herself looked surprised to have said it. I thought it was long habit. I was starting to feel sorry for Terence Hammond.

"But your mum still wanted him to be there."

"Yeah." She used the cuff of her jumper to blot away some tears that were threatening to spill on to her cheeks. "She said it was better than being on her own. But I suppose she'll have to get used to it now."

"Vanessa, this is a hard question to ask,

but did you ever have any suspicions your father was in a relationship with someone else?"

Amy Maynard's eyebrows shot up. "Is that really an appropriate question?"

"It's one I have to ask," I said. "Vanessa?"

"I don't know. Maybe. Probably. I don't think he was getting much at home."

"*How* old are you?" Derwent asked.

"Fifteen, nearly." She looked at him, defiant. "Old enough to know about that sort of thing."

"If you say so."

"Vanessa, did you ever see your dad with anyone? Or hear him talking on his phone, maybe?"

"He used to go out to the car to make phone calls. He said the house was too noisy. Ben likes to listen to music in his room but he turns it up really loud. I usually have the TV on when I'm at home, too. I could kind of see his point."

I imagined Terence Hammond sitting in his car in the driveway of his house, planning his next meeting with his lover, while his children occupied themselves inside. I didn't feel all that sympathetic to him, on the whole.

"Did anyone ever threaten him? Was he scared of anyone?"

"He wasn't scared of anyone. He was really tough." She laughed suddenly. "Actually, that's not true. He was scared of Mum."

"Would you say it was a happy home?"

"No." She glanced at the guidance counselor, who smiled at her. "Pretty miserable."

"I'm sorry, I have to ask this too. Was your father abusive to you or anyone else?"

"What do you mean by abusive?"

"Verbal abuse, physical violence, sexual abuse."

"No way." Her face was red. "He was normal. He shouted at us sometimes. At me. He thought I needed to work harder at school. And he didn't like me having a boyfriend."

"Did he stop you from seeing him?" Derwent asked, brushing imaginary dust off his knee as if he wasn't really all that interested in the answer.

"During the week. And I wasn't allowed to go to his house. Dad was okay with him coming to our place. He liked to keep an eye on us."

"What's your boyfriend's name?" Derwent asked.

"We broke up."

"I still need his name."

"Jamie Driffield."

"Is he a student at this school?" I asked.

"He was. He's left. He's nineteen," she added, unable to keep the pride out of her voice.

"I can see why your dad wanted to keep an eye on you."

I shot Derwent a warning look, but it was too late. Vanessa was instantly livid. "Age doesn't mean anything. Maturity is different. I'm very mature for my age."

"I'm sure." Derwent didn't sound convinced.

I took over again. "So your father shouted at you. What about your mum?"

Her retreat was immediate. She sat back in her chair, slouching down, her hair falling forward over her face. "I don't want to talk about her. I don't see why you want to know about her."

"They're just all details of your father's life. We don't know if any of them are significant yet. They might be. They might lead us directly to his killer. At the moment we're just asking lots of nosy questions to try to get to know him and his world a bit better. And that means talking to you and asking you to answer questions that aren't necessarily very nice."

She nodded.

"What happened to your face, Vanessa?"

A hand went up to her hair. She looked up at me, wary. "How did you . . ."

"We saw it at your house on Sunday when you fainted."

"Oh." The sound was a breath. "Yeah. It was an accident."

"What kind of accident?"

"I was standing in the living room doorway and I didn't move in time. I wanted to talk . . . to Dad . . . and he was in a hurry, you see. I should have moved."

"Your father did it?"

"He didn't mean to. He just wanted to get out. He pushed me out of his way and —" she gestured at her head and shrugged.

"What were you trying to talk to him about?" Derwent asked.

"I wanted to know if he could come to the science fair at school next month. I've got a project for it. I really wanted him to see it."

"But he said no."

"He said he'd think about it." The corner of her mouth lifted, a movement too slight to be a smile. "He always said he'd think about it. He never came."

"It can be hard to manage that kind of thing, with shift work," I began, trying to find a way to blot the hurt out of her voice.

"That wasn't the problem. The problem was that they didn't have time for me. Ben takes up all their time and energy."

"From what your mum said about him, he needs a lot of care."

"What's wrong with him?" Derwent got two disapproving looks for that, one from me, one from Amy Maynard. Vanessa answered him though, her tone dispassionate.

"He was injured in a car accident when he was three. They thought he'd die. The surgeons had to dig bits of his skull out of his brain. He can't talk now. He walks with a limp."

"And mentally, is he . . . you know, all there?"

"No. Of course not." She was looking at Derwent as if he was distinctly lacking himself. "He does a lot of drawing and he likes listening to music but otherwise he doesn't do anything. And I get the pressure to be twice as good at everything because he isn't. I have to be twice as perfect. They don't know how lucky they are, you know. I could be really fucked up, with everything I've had to deal with. They don't appreciate me."

"I'm sure they do," I said.

"No. They only notice me when I'm doing something they don't approve of. But I'm not going to wreck my whole life just because they don't care about me. I don't need their attention anyway. I get to university and I'm gone. That's it." She stood up. "Are you finished?"

"For the moment," I said, with a glance in Derwent's direction. "We'll be in touch if we need to talk to you again. But if you think of anything you think we should know, get in touch."

She nodded. To Amy Maynard, she said, "Thanks, Miss."

"See you tomorrow."

"Yeah." She slipped through the door and closed it behind her.

"So you see a lot of her," I said.

The guidance counselor blushed. "At the moment . . . it's a safe place for her to come."

"Since her father died?"

"Mm. A little bit before that. I can't say any more, though. I'm sorry."

Derwent stood up, looking especially tall in the small office. "How do you get a job like this, anyway?"

"In this case I wrote to the school and offered my services. I'm the first person they've ever employed specifically for student welfare but it makes sense. It takes a burden off the teachers. You know, they get stuck with a lot of the pastoral stuff and they're not trained for it. I did a psychology degree, then I trained as a counselor. I've only been here since last year but I expect to be made a permanent member of staff soon."

"I wouldn't have thought they needed a permanent counselor on the staff," Derwent said.

"I help out in all sorts of areas. I have a special interest in helping children cope with family problems — deaths, divorce, siblings going through rebellious phases. It's not always the obvious kids who need support — the troublemakers. Sometimes it's the ones trying to hold everything together. I mean, Vanessa is a case in point."

"Because of her brother," I said.

"Yes. And —" She flushed and bit her lip. "I really don't want to say any more."

"Don't worry. We can fill in the blanks."

"I'm worried that you'll be wrong though." She crossed her legs, looking up at Derwent who was towering over her. "That wasn't the girl I usually see. She's very angry. She's lashing out. I'd never heard her say anything about her father having an affair or hitting her, and that's in the context of some very frank and open discussions.

Don't you think she's making it up to demonise him?"

"Why would she do that?" I asked.

"So she doesn't have to mourn him. She's pretending she didn't care and his death means nothing to her. It's a coping strategy."

"Or she was afraid to say what he was really like before," Derwent suggested. "Now he's dead, she's safe. She can say what she likes."

"Yes, even if it's a lie." Amy's neck was blotched with pink patches, I noticed. Temper. But she was standing up to Derwent, which I wouldn't have expected.

"Does Vanessa lie?" I asked her.

"When it suits her, probably."

"But you don't *know* that she lies."

"I know that I've heard two different versions of what her homelife was like. And I know which one rang true to me. It wasn't the one you just heard."

When we got to the car, Derwent stretched. "What do you think she would have said if we'd told her we were sure Terence Hammond was having an affair?"

"She'd probably have told us we were lying too." I flipped to a new page in my notebook. "Mrs. Hammond next?"

"Mrs. Hammond next. And let me tell you, I cannot wait to hear her version."

CHAPTER TEN

There was still a police constable posted outside the Hammonds' house. He looked as if he was bored rigid. He had to be straight out of Hendon: his uniform was immaculate, his face still babyish.

"Were we ever that young?" I asked Derwent as he stopped the car in front of the driveway. He ducked his head to look.

"Makes you feel every year, doesn't it? Jesus, at least I needed to shave before I joined up. He looks as if he's still waiting for puberty to hit."

The constable had noticed us and stood up a little straighter as we approached. "Can I help you?"

"It's all right. Police." Derwent held up his warrant card. "Is the lady of the house in?"

"I believe so, sir."

"Anything going on?"

"Nothing much, sir. Couple of reporters

— I turned them away — and a few flower deliveries."

"Visitors?"

"Not since I've been here. That's getting on for six hours."

"Good lad." Derwent thumped him on the arm. "You're doing a great job."

He gave a nervous laugh. "I'm just standing here, mainly."

"That's your job. Work hard at it and next week you might graduate to sitting."

The constable looked at him, trying to gauge whether or not Derwent was taking the piss. I took pity on him and rang the doorbell to remind Derwent why we were there in the first place.

As before, it took a couple of minutes for Mrs. Hammond to come to the door, though today she was dressed in a long gray cardigan cinched at the waist with a heavy black leather belt. She had a fitted black knee-length dress on underneath the cardigan. I noticed she was wearing subtle makeup — pale pink lipstick, and muted eye shadow. Her short fair hair was neatly brushed and the whole look was set off with pearl earrings. Not the disarray of grief, I thought, and tried not to judge her for it. Everyone had their own way of coping with loss. Looking as if she was in command of

the situation was probably important to Julie Hammond.

"Yes?"

I introduced Derwent and reminded her
who I was and that we had met before. "Is
now a good time to speak with you?"

"Not really." She pushed her sleeve back
to look at a narrow gold watch. "I've got a
conference call in twenty minutes."

"Twenty minutes should do us nicely."
Derwent would have said anything to get
his foot through the door. I knew he had no
intention of finishing up in twenty minutes
if he was getting somewhere with her.

Not that I thought that was likely. She had
given him a cursory glance without seeming
to be particularly impressed with what she
saw. She had been married to a police officer, after all. She was probably immune to
Derwent's laddish charm. And from the
look on her face, she was about to say no to
him.

"We've just been speaking to Vanessa," I
said. "At school. It would be very helpful if
we could follow up a couple of things with
you."

That got her attention. "You didn't waste
any time, did you?"

"This is an active murder investigation.
We are trying to avoid wasting time."

She stared at me for a moment and I thought she was going to slam the door in our faces. I had gambled that she would recognize I meant what I said, and appreciate the candor. Gambled, and won. The tension in her seemed to ease, just a little. "You'd better come in."

She left us to shut the front door and make our own way to the living room, where we found her hunched over a laptop that was open on the coffee table. She wrote an e-mail quickly and sent it before looking up.

"Sit down. I'm just trying to make some time. I've asked to push the call back ten minutes but that's all I can manage."

"Your work must be very important. I'm surprised you can't take some time off, given what's happened in your personal life." Derwent sounded as if he was impressed by her, when I knew he wasn't. I shot him a look and got wide-eyed innocence in return.

"I work in commercial property development. There's a lot of money invested in the projects I'm running at the moment. I can't afford to stop working just because my husband died. There are too many people depending on me." Her phone chimed softly and she checked the laptop screen. "Okay.

I've got about twenty-five minutes. Talk fast."

"Let's start with you," Derwent said. "Have you thought of any reasons why someone would want to kill your husband?"

"No. Next question."

"No enemies you can think of?"

"Not that I knew of."

"Yeah, and that's another question. Would you have known? You don't seem to have been very involved in your husband's life."

"What's that supposed to mean?"

Derwent shrugged. "Just what I said. You don't seem to have been very close."

"Based on what Vanessa told you?"

"Based on what I've heard about your marriage. He came and went, working his shifts. You didn't keep track of where he was and when he was supposed to be back. Not very wifely, is it?"

"Oh please, spare me whatever outdated idea of marriage you're imagining. He was a grown-up. I didn't need to be here when he got home from work to cook him a hot meal and tell him he was my hero. I saw him when our schedules allowed it and when we weren't out doing other things. We both worked. We took it in turns to go to parent–teacher meetings and take Vanessa to her various activities. We took it in turns to look after Ben. When we weren't working we pursued different interests. We didn't live in each other's pockets."

"Never sat down and watched the telly together? Or went out on dates?"

"I don't watch television. It's a waste of time." She looked at her watch. "And speaking of which, you need to move on."

"Did you ever think he might be having an affair?" Derwent asked.

"I thought it was possible." There wasn't the faintest crack in her composure. "Have you found out that he was?"

"It would seem he wasn't alone when he died."

Her knuckles went white as she clenched her hands on her lap, but it was the only outward sign of a reaction. "Who was she?"

"We don't know that yet."

"Did she kill him?"

"She was in the car. The person who shot him was some distance away."

"And what? She ran away? She didn't try to get help?"

"He was beyond help," Derwent said.

"She could still have called the police."

"Could have. Didn't."

"Maybe she's married too. Maybe she couldn't risk being found out."

"That's a possibility we're considering." I

was careful not to hint that the woman might have been involved in setting up Hammond's murder. "Do you have any idea who she might have been? Anyone your husband saw regularly?"

"I don't know. Someone at work?"

"We don't think so."

"Then I can't help you." She sounded almost relieved.

"Vanessa mentioned that he spent a lot of time out of the house. She said he went to the pub," I said. "Is it possible he met someone there?"

"Anything's possible. But I doubt it. He drank at the Duke of Gloucester on London Road. It's about five minutes away on foot. I can give you the details of the friends he usually met there. They might be able to help you. I think he went there to drink and spend time with his friends, not to pick up women — it's not really that sort of place."

"Where else did he spend time?"

"Driving Vanessa around. Going to things at school. He was always the one who went to the school plays and sports days. I just didn't have time to spare for it. I don't know how I'll manage now."

"That's not what Vanessa said." I flicked back through my notes to check. "She said the opposite."

"I don't know why she'd have said that." Julie's voice was flat.

I had one of those moments where I turned everything I'd known upside down and rearranged it in my head to make a completely different picture. It made sense in a way that the previous version hadn't.

Derwent was pursuing a different train of thought. "You don't seem very surprised by the idea that your husband was having an affair."

She laced her fingers around her knees. "You have to understand that Terence was always running away from reality. He always wanted to imagine that everything was going to be all right. He thought he could fix everything that was broken, and if he couldn't fix it he didn't want to know. He was like a kid. Impulsive. Emotional."

"So?"

"So he was always looking for alternatives to what was going on in his life, and that would have included looking for an alternative to me. He wanted reassurance that he was still attractive, even though he was middle-aged. He wanted to be someone's hero."

"And he wasn't yours," Derwent said.

"Far from it." She looked at him, defiant. "Someone had to be realistic in this family.

We have problems that are not going to go away. Terence thought he could ignore them forever. He was irresponsible, basically, and it became tiresome to me."

"You didn't have much respect for him, it seems."

"Respect has to be earned."

Derwent looked pained. "Did you ever love him?"

"That is none of your business. That is nothing to do with how he died or why." Her anger was white-hot. It came to me that anger was the only emotion I'd really seen from her. Irritating her was interesting but there was a very real possibility she would kick us out if she got cross enough.

"You might be right," I said. "We don't know yet why he died. But it sounds as if he was frustrated with life."

"You could say that."

"Frustrated enough to be violent?"

Her ice-blue gaze rested on my face for a moment. "Violent? No."

"Vanessa had a bruise —"

"She fell over and hit her head." Julie's tone was sharp. "Newsflash: teenagers wear ridiculous shoes."

"She told us it was Terence who injured her. But she said it was an accident."

"That's a complete lie."

201

"That it was him or that it was an accident?" Derwent asked.

"That it was anything to do with Terence. He wasn't even here."

"But you were," I said slowly. "You saw it happen. How exactly did she fall, Mrs. Hammond?"

"I don't remember."

"It would have been Friday, maybe? Thursday, at a stretch. You can't remember what happened last week?"

She pressed her lips together before she answered me. "I can't recall exactly how she tripped. I was moving past her at the time. She hit her face on the doorframe."

"Were you talking to her at the time? Arguing, maybe?"

"I don't think so."

"She wanted you to go to the school science fair next month and you said no."

"Is that what she told you?" She leaned back. "That was probably it. I don't remember exactly. I know I said I couldn't commit to going to the science fair. Vanessa has never appreciated that someone has to work to pay for all the things she takes for granted. She can't have everything."

"It seems as if you have quite a confrontational relationship with your daughter."

"Well, if you're going to take her word for it." She laughed, a brittle sound. "Show me the teenager who appreciates her parents and what they're trying to do for her. Please. I'd like to meet one."

"She said you imposed some very strict rules on her regarding her boyfriend."

"No, I didn't. Terence came up with the rules. I wanted to stop her from seeing Jamie altogether, but Terence said she'd be even more determined to spend time with him if we forbade it. I don't know if he was right about that, but they broke up in the end. Thank God. My biggest fear was that she'd get pregnant. I didn't want her to throw her life away on a pot-smoking unemployable idiot."

"He sounds like a catch," Derwent said.

"He was awful." She shuddered. "I knew Vanessa was only pretending to be in love with him because she knew it would annoy me, but it was still maddening to have to put up with him being in the house."

"We'd like to speak to him. Do you have an address for him? A telephone number?"

"Both, I think." She snatched up her BlackBerry and started tapping on it. "Here you go. He lives with his parents, you won't be surprised to hear. He's almost twenty, for God's sake." She handed me the phone and I wrote down the details.

I was just handing the phone back to her when a sudden blare of trumpets from upstairs made me jump.

"Oh, for crying out loud." She ran into the hall and yelled up the stairs. "Put your headphones back on, Ben. We don't want to listen to the music too."

There was no response. Her voice went up a notch in pitch and volume.

"Don't make me come up there or there'll be no more music today. Put your headphones back on now and plug them in or I will take your music away."

The trumpets blasted on. I heard her swearing as she started to run up the stairs, hitting each step hard. Before she had reached the half-way point the music stopped abruptly. She came back down more slowly. When she walked back into the room she looked upset.

"Is that your son?" Derwent asked. "I thought he'd be at school."

"So did I. He wouldn't go. His carer was here for an hour this morning, trying to persuade him to leave the house." Her mouth was a line. "It's annoying, but sometimes I have to give in. He's taller than me and much heavier. If I want to make him go somewhere, I need him to cooperate. Even if he doesn't actively resist us it's a nightmare trying to make him do something he doesn't want to do. He used to be normal. It was a car accident when he was three. Now it's like having a giant baby."

"Vanessa told us."

"He needs help with everything. Can't dress himself. Can't wash himself. It's too much for me on my own. That's why he has a carer."

"Was Terence good at dealing with Ben?" I asked.

"He was determined to treat Ben as if he was normal. He'd take him swimming. He took him to the cinema once but it wasn't a success." She smiled a little, remembering. "Mostly he'd just take Ben to the park. They went two or three times a week. Ben likes being outside. It was always a relief to have a break from having him here. He makes so much noise."

"Vanessa said he likes to listen to music," I said.

"He seems to find it comforting. I have to bribe him to use his headphones when I'm working here, so I can make phone calls in peace."

"Can we talk to him?" Derwent asked.

Julie went very still. "Why?"

"It's useful for us to talk to the whole family."

"Not Ben."

"Why not?"

"He doesn't talk. He won't understand the questions you're asking."

Derwent shrugged. "So maybe it will be a waste of time. I'd still like to try."

"You'll upset him for no reason."

"We'll try not to." Derwent leaned forward. "Look, I don't want to have to come back here and bother you again. But if I don't get to see Ben now, I'll have to."

"I don't want you to talk to him. He gets unsettled when he has to deal with strangers."

"Please, Mrs. Hammond. I have to be able to tell my boss I spoke to everyone. There's nothing I can do."

Her phone gave a short, imperious ring. She picked it up and stared at the screen. "I should take this."

Neither Derwent nor I spoke. I was holding my breath.

It rang again.

"He's not going to be able to help you," she said, her thumb hovering over the screen.

"We won't disturb him for long. Upstairs, is it?" Derwent was up and moving toward the door at speed.

"Straight ahead at the top of the stairs." She answered the call. "Hello? Mark. Yes, sorry. Go ahead."

I caught up with Derwent in the hall.

"Come on, before she changes her mind or follows us."

"I'm right behind you, but don't go too fast. You'll scare him. She said he doesn't like strangers."

"I don't either." Derwent took the stairs three at a time and I hurried after him. At the top of the stairs he knocked lightly on the door in front of him, which was not quite closed. There was no sound from inside so he pushed it open.

The boy had his back to us, his head down. He was bent over a large sheet of paper spread out on a desk. There was a row of cups in front of him, each filled with art supplies — pencils, paintbrushes, marker pens, and chalks. He wore big noise-canceling headphones and his body moved in time to the music we couldn't hear. He was tall, as his mother had said, and bulky. I really didn't want to surprise him and neither, it seemed, did Derwent. He leaned into the room, staring at the walls which were covered in pictures taped up in neat lines. There was nothing representational, nothing that could give us a clue as to what the boy was thinking. Loops and swirls passed from one picture to the next, a portrait of an empty mind.

Derwent had stepped back to the doorway, silent on the carpet, and now he tapped on the frame. Ben turned around, surprised. Once he was facing us I could see the pale scar on the right side of his head, running into his hair which was too long for me to see if the damage to his skull was still visible from the outside. One eye drooped and his face was as slack as if he was asleep.

"All right, mate? We just wanted to say hello. We're police officers, like your dad."

There was no flicker of recognition or understanding on the teenager's face. His eyes slid past mine to focus on the corner of the room, where they stayed.

Derwent tried again. "Is it all right if we have a word with you? Not for long."

Ben turned his back on us. He sat down at his desk and put the headphones back on, with decision. He picked up the pencils again and took out a new sheet of paper.

"No chance," I whispered to Derwent.

"Worth a try."

I turned to go back downstairs but Derwent hissed at me to wait, working his way around the landing to open every door and scan every room. It was habit, and I knew he'd probably done the same thing when he'd helped me move back to my parents' house a couple of years earlier. He didn't even know what he was looking for and I couldn't tell from his expression if he'd found anything when he turned back to follow me downstairs.

Julie had finished her phone call. She was walking into the hall as we came down the stairs.

"I told you."

"Yes, you did," Derwent said.

"Has Ben been upset about anything lately?" I asked. "Before his father died?"

"It's hard to tell with him."

"And we'll never know, is that right?"

Derwent turned round to look at me, surprised at the tone I'd used. I could feel myself losing my grip on my temper, and I couldn't stop myself. I didn't actually want to.

"You know, your daughter lied to us this morning. She told us that it was your husband who caused the injury to her face, although she said it was an accident. She told us it was because he was too busy to come to the school. I think Vanessa blamed him to protect you from getting in trouble with the likes of us."

209

Julie blushed, which didn't suit her. "It was an accident."

"Accidents happen," I said. "But so does child abuse."

She flinched. "That's not how it was."

"Maybe not. Maybe I'm right and that's exactly how it was. Things go on behind closed doors that no one would ever imagine." I took a step closer to her. "But your doors aren't closed any more. You don't have the luxury of privacy. We'll find out everything you think you can hide, one way or another."

"Is that a threat?"

"It's a warning. You have a think about what you haven't told us — any doubts, any suspicions, anything that made you wonder what was going on with your husband. When you're ready to tell us the truth, give us a call."

I left her in the hall and went out to the car, past the young police officer who was yawning and trying to hide it. I had to wait until Derwent unlocked the car door, which he was typically slow to do. It did nothing for my temper.

When Derwent had sauntered down the drive and slowly, fussily inserted himself into the car, he turned to raise his eyebrows at me. "Time of the month, Kerrigan?"

"She deserved that."

"And you're not regretting it already."

"A tiny bit," I admitted. "I just couldn't keep it back."

"Don't feel bad. You were right. I was about to say the same thing to her." He leaned a few inches closer. "I like it when you get all ferocious, though. I might start letting you be the bad cop for a change."

I gave him a withering look. "If you don't get back to your side of the car, you're going to see ferocious up close."

"Kerrigan." It was a warning in three syllables, and I knew why immediately.

"You're going to see ferocious up close, *sir.*"

"That's better."

Derwent was grinning to himself as he drove away.

CHAPTER ELEVEN

"These places are all the same."

It was only my third visit to a gun club but from what I had seen, Derwent was right. We had spent the previous two days asking questions at the gun clubs nearest Richmond Park, and had come up with nothing much. This time, we were genuinely in the middle of nowhere. We had driven up an unpaved road into featureless Surrey woodland, beyond the commuter-belt town of Leatherhead. It was a wealthy area, popular with the bankers and stockbrokers who filled the trains to the City every morning. White Valley Shooting Club didn't look all that luxurious, it had to be said, but the cars parked in front of the single-story clubhouse were mostly new. The building itself was painted cream. It was festooned with security lights, alarm equipment, and warning notices about trespassers, none of which was exactly surprising given that there was an armory on the premises.

There were plenty of free spaces in the car park but Derwent drove past them so he could park his Subaru in a crosshatched area close to the building.

"This isn't a space."

"It is now." He slapped the Police notice on the dashboard.

"You could at least straighten up." I popped open my door and checked. "Your wheels are over the line. Half the car is in a disabled space."

"Crips shouldn't be allowed to shoot."

"Oh God," I murmured, knowing there was nothing I could say to prevent him from going on.

"They're all depressed and angry. Why the fuck would you want to arm them?"

"That is a massive generalisation. There are lots of physically challenged people who have come to terms with their situation or never had a problem with it in the first place. They have just as much right to learn to shoot as you do."

"They're physically incapacitated. There's no point in teaching them to shoot. They'd be fuck all use in a war. Unless you stacked up their wheelchairs and used them as a barricade."

"I want to stay in the car," I said in a small voice.

"Come on." He hopped out and stretched. It was, presumably, why he'd left plenty of space between himself and the car next to him.

I got out and frowned at him across the roof of the car. "I really don't want to go in there with you."

"Imagine what I'll get up to if I don't have your restraining influence on me."

I shut my car door. "And you've convinced me."

We had phoned ahead to make an appointment to speak with the club's manager. He was waiting in the hall when we walked through the doors, his hands clasped in front of his crotch as if he was facing a penalty kick. He was wearing a blazer and a striped tie that probably marked him out as a member of some regiment or club or other, though I couldn't begin to guess which one. He was in his mid-fifties, with sparse reddish hair and a scattering of broken veins across his cheeks and nose.

"Andrew Hardy. You're very welcome to White Valley Shooting Club, although of course we would prefer you to be here in happier circumstances." He had a heavy way of speaking, pausing often as if he was considering the implications of what he was saying all the time.

Derwent nodded, impatient. "Not much call for us to turn up when the circumstances are happy."

"No, I imagine not. Would you like to have a look around the facilities? We've made considerable investment in the club in the last two years and I think it really compares very favorably to any others in the greater London area." He brightened as he talked about the club, more comfortable once he was launched on his usual spiel to visitors. "We're fully wheelchair-accessible now, with the ramp. You may have noticed it — I saw you parked very close to it."

I sensed that Derwent was about to snap and hurried to get in first. "We'd love to see the facilities but we need you to tell us about your current membership first."

"Why?"

"Because of the possibility that the killer we are looking for is a member."

Hardy looked appalled, as if he hadn't even considered that, or thought about what we would want to know from him. "You'd need to come into the office."

"That's fine," I said.

There was a moment where I thought Hardy was going to refuse to cooperate.

Then his shoulders sagged and he led us to an empty reception desk, where there was a clipboard with a sign-in sheet.

"Both of you need to sign this. Everyone who enters the club building has to sign in."

We did as we were told, then followed Hardy through a door marked "PRIVATE." His office was a glorified cubbyhole with an elderly computer squatting on the desk and two upright chairs squeezed in for visitors. We inserted ourselves and Hardy shut the door, looking up and down the corridor first for eavesdroppers.

"I doubt I'll be able to help you." He sat down and pinched the creases on the front of his trousers, running his fingers along them over and over again. "Our membership is exclusive. We really don't have the kind of people here who would do the things you're implying."

"We're not implying anything," Derwent said. "We have a dead police officer killed by someone who has experience and skill in shooting. We are starting by drawing up a list of people who possess those skills and the equipment to carry out such a shooting. What kind of guns do you shoot here?"

"Rifles mainly — .22 target rifles and sporting rifles. We also have some members who shoot muzzle-loading pistols and air

216

weapons of various sorts. Some clubs do clay-pigeon shooting and crossbow shooting and so forth but we don't." The curl of his lip showed me what he thought of that sort of diversification.

"I thought pistols were banned," I said, and got a weary look.

"Muzzle-loading pistols are perfectly legal. They're an old design but gun manufacturers are still making them. They're also called black powder pistols because you pour gunpowder into the barrel and push a lead ball in afterward. Think of duelling pistols."

"That's not what we're looking for," Derwent said to me.

Hardy brightened. "What kind of gun are you looking for?"

"A high-powered rifle capable of being fitted with a telescopic sight," Derwent said. "A sniper rifle."

"Those are illegal."

"Yes, we know that. That's why it isn't registered and we're chasing around the gun clubs trying to trace likely owners."

"You're in the wrong shop here." Hardy looked at the door, as if he was hoping to encourage us to leave.

"Is there a screening process for members? Do you even try to weed out the nutters?" Derwent asked.

"Of course. We're very particular about the people who use these facilities. Shooting is an Olympic sport, you know, and some of our members took part in the London games. It's all thoroughly respectable."

"Thoroughly," I agreed. "How many members do you have?"

"Just over two hundred. We have about fifty junior members as well. Obviously not all of the members would use the club regularly, but we have a close-knit group who come consistently. I get many requests to join the club every year but at the moment membership is closed. We simply can't accommodate everyone who wants to come and shoot here. Not that most of them would be able to join anyway."

"Why not?" I asked. "Is it expensive to join?"

"Not really. A couple of hundred pounds. It's just that you need a personal reference from another member to join. That's how our vetting system works. We vouch for each other."

Derwent was nodding. "It's the same with the police."

"Really?" Hardy asked.

"No." He moved on before Hardy's face had time to register disappointment. "How come it's so cheap?"

"We don't have big expenses. We own the club building. The refurbishment was carried out from donations and fundraising, not from membership fees, and any maintenance work is similarly funded as and when it's necessary to do so. I'm the only employee, and I'm part-time. The instructors are all volunteers. There's a cleaner once a week for the club but otherwise it's all down to the members."

"Starting with them, are there any who concern you?" Derwent asked.

"*Concern* me? I don't think —"

"Any who might own illegal weapons. Anyone who might be a little bit too much in love with shooting to be sensible."

Hardy leaned back in his chair and laughed awkwardly. "No, no. No one who would ever dream of killing someone."

Derwent pounced. "But there is someone who fits that description."

There was a long pause. "One person comes to mind. But he truly is harmless."

"What's his name?"

"Rex Gibney." He swiveled on his chair and pulled open a drawer of the filing cabinet behind him, flicking through folders until he found the right one. He peered into it, holding it up so we couldn't see what he was reading. "He's been a member here

219

for . . . thirty-two years, I see. Very dedicated. He worked as the club secretary at one time, although that was before I joined."

"Is he an older gentleman?"

"He retired a couple of years ago. He ran his own business. I think he leased equipment to the building industry."

"Successful?" Derwent asked.

"I would say so, yes. I don't think paying the membership subscription has ever been an issue for him. Beautiful house the other side of Guildford. He hosts a Christmas party every year for the club's members."

"I'm going to need the address," I said.

Hardy detached a piece of paper from the front of the file and handed it to me. I noted the address and phone number. No mobile, no e-mail address. The house was called Callancote and was located on Tigg's Lane, which sounded small and rural to me. There was no street number, but I guessed the place would be hard to miss from what Hardy had said about it. I handed the page back to Hardy, who spent a great deal of time reinserting it into the file.

"Rex Gibney may be old in years but he's young at heart. A true enthusiast. Not a great shot any more but he loves to encourage the young members. I know he's sponsored a few of the most talented youngsters to help them with getting better equipment. He covers their travel expenses and competition entry fees. He never looks for anything in return."

"Has he ever been CRB checked?" Derwent was permanently suspicious of anyone who volunteered to spend time with young people when they didn't have to.

"CRB? Oh — to see if he has a criminal record? No, no. Our instructors are all checked out, but Rex doesn't have any dealings with the young people on his own. He puts his hand in his pocket if we tell him he can help someone, but he doesn't see them much. In the club sometimes. He comes to watch them practice. He's a true enthusiast."

"He sounds like a useful person to have around," I said.

"He is. Very." Hardy tapped his fingers on the file. "In any other circumstances I wouldn't mention him to you. But I have my concerns about how closely he adheres to the law on firearms. In fact, I would go so far as to say that everyone at the club knows he owns a couple of guns that are not registered. I've never seen one, you understand, but I am aware that others have."

"Including these youngsters he encourages?" Derwent asked.

"Possibly." Hardy shook his head. "I can't imagine him doing anything wrong deliberately. I think he's just like a child. A little bit spoiled. He can't understand why he isn't allowed to own the guns he loves. He subscribes to magazines from America and of course they have so many really extraordinary weapons available to buy so easily."

"And he can afford to pay a premium to have them smuggled in," I said.

"I don't know how he acquired them and I don't want to know."

"What does he have?" Derwent asked.

"I have heard," Hardy said carefully, "that he has a Dragunov SVD Tigr and a ZVI Falcon. But I haven't seen them, as I said, and I have never asked him about them."

"Because you'd have a responsibility to report him."

"Yes."

"And he'd be very likely to leave your club and go somewhere else."

"Possibly."

"And you'd be responsible for killing the golden goose."

"I don't understand the reference," Hardy said stiffly.

"Did he make a contribution to developing the facilities here?" I asked. "A donation?"

"Yes. But he made the donation privately. No one knew, except for the club's financial committee and me. That's typical of the man, you see. He doesn't look for praise or thanks. He simply wants to use his wealth in good and useful ways."

"I can think of more useful ways to spend a fortune."

Hardy glared at me, the broken veins on his cheeks disappearing into an angry flush. "Of course, if you're not interested in shooting you might not see it as important. But shooting is worth £1.6 billion to the UK economy. It's not a minority interest at all."

"I'm sorry," I said. "It's just not my thing."

"What about you?" He turned to Derwent. "Do you want to try your hand at some shooting?"

"I could have a go," Derwent said, sounding uncharacteristically tentative. I looked sideways at him and got a flicker of the eyelids that told me to say nothing.

Hardy stood up, good humor restored. He ushered us out, locking the door to his tiny office after himself as if to demonstrate his commitment to security. It would have meant more to me if I hadn't noticed it was unlocked when we got there.

In the hallway, Hardy stopped. "This is the ammunition store."

It was a blank door to the left of the entrance; I hadn't even noticed it when we came in. There was an alarm keypad beside it, though, and Hardy keyed in the code, pressing very slightly too hard on the numbers. He opened the door and went in, choosing a box of .22 ammunition and making a note in the logbook by the door. Derwent leaned in, scanning the shelves, looking for the type of ammunition our killer had used. He straightened back up and gave the slightest shake of his head. Nothing there.

Or nothing there *now.*

"Does every member have access to this ammunition?" I asked.

"Only if they know the code for the door, and of course that's only passed on to our most highly trained members and those who work as instructors so it's completely secure."

"Four, three, nine, nine," I recited.

Derwent grinned at me. Hardy looked pained. "You looked over my shoulder."

"Sorry. It doesn't seem all that secure, though."

"It's police-checked and approved. All of

our security arrangements are monitored by the police. It's a Home Office regulation."

And there wasn't an alarm system in the world that could account for human error. I let it go, because there was no point in telling him that he had rendered his security arrangements worthless.

Hardy guided us through an empty club room, with chairs and tables stacked up against one wall. A small bar set into the wall was dark, with steel shutters padlocked in front of it. The room smelt of stale beer.

"This is where we have our socials. We have two or three a year. Great fun. And the bar is open on Saturdays and Mondays. All run by the members."

"I'm still not joining," I whispered to Derwent.

"This is the armory." It was another blank door, but this time it opened as we approached it and a man came out, carrying a rifle and an armful of equipment.

"Stuart, just the person I needed. Can you take this gentleman to the firing range and let him have a go at shooting?"

Stuart shook his head. "Not unless he's got a firearms certificate, Andrew. You know that."

"I'm a police officer," Derwent said. He was still uncharacteristically quiet. "I actually do have a firearms cert. I'm firearms qualified."

Stuart took a long look at him. He was younger than Hardy, with a shrewd demeanor. He hefted the rifle. "Ever fired one of these?"

"Not for years."

He held it out to Derwent, who took it and pointed it toward the ground. He pulled back the bolt and squinted down the barrel. Apparently satisfied, he pushed the bolt forward to close the breech and pulled the trigger. There was a click as the firing pin connected with nothing.

"You were in the services," Stuart said.

"The army."

Stuart nodded. "I'll take you out. Are you right-handed?"

"Yeah."

"You can use my kit, then. Here's the jacket. Might be a bit tight on you."

It was a special shooting jacket, with a leather patch at the shoulder and a strap that attached to the gun. Derwent shrugged it on while Stuart waited to hand him a single heavy glove.

"Stuart is one of our instructors," Hardy explained to me. "Stuart Pilgrew. Competed in the World Championships in 2004."

"It was 2005." Stuart flicked a look at me.

"And I didn't get anywhere."

"Still pretty impressive," I said, which was what Hardy had seemed to be expecting me to say. He turned back to Derwent and I wandered past him into the armory, expecting at any moment to be called back. It was a small room, lined with racks for rifles and a cupboard for pistols. There was a teenager in there, a rifle in pieces on a table in front of him as he cleaned it. It occurred to me he might be one of Gibney's protégés. He glanced up, his eyes wary. Brown hair, very short. His eyebrows were faint and almost invisible. It gave his face a vulnerable look.

"Hi," I said. "Don't worry. I'm a police officer. I'm just looking around."

He mumbled something and then stood up, knocking the table with one leg as he headed for the door. The rifle parts slid sideways and almost fell. He steadied the table and hurried out, his face bright red.

The horror of being a self-conscious teenager, I thought. "You don't have to go."

It was too late. By the time I got to the door he was walking across the club room, head down, making for the door with a sign for toilets.

"Jonny, where are you going?" It was Stuart who called out to him, his voice tight with irritation. The boy's shoulders hunched

227

up further around his ears and he disappeared through the door without breaking his stride.

"Is he yours?" I asked.

"So my wife says."

Derwent laughed. I didn't. I was thinking that a lot of teenage boys seemed to be running away from me these days. The fifteen-year-old me would have been heartbroken.

Hardy said, "Sorry, Stuart. I didn't know you were here with Jonny. If you need to go, I can find someone else to take DI Derwent to the shooting range."

"It's fine. We've only just got here. Jonny's making himself useful while I get some practice in. It'll be his turn in an hour."

"Does he come and watch you?" I asked.

"Not him. He used to. Now he thinks he knows it all." Stuart hefted a mat on to his shoulder. "Unfortunately for me, he shoots a lot better than I do. He shoots better than I ever did."

"That's annoying," Derwent said.

"Isn't it?"

The two of them went out together, ahead of me and Hardy, talking in low voices as they walked. There was a short path down to the range, which was essentially a long, low concrete shelter. Three others were shooting, though we'd arrived during a break. Hardy handed me a pair of ear defenders.

"Put them on, please. It gets loud down here."

Stuart went out to put up some new targets for Derwent. There were three, at intervals in front of us — 25 meters, 50 meters, and 100 meters. I stood at the back of the shelter, watching as Derwent settled himself on the ground and peered through the sights.

Stuart came back and lay down next to Derwent. He conferred with him, gesturing from the gun to the targets. Derwent nodded a couple of times, but not in his usual bored way. He was concentrating, for once. This mattered to him. He leaned in, his body completely still, his gloved hand supporting the weapon as he focused on the first target.

Even with the ear defenders, the sound of four rifles firing more or less in unison was shatteringly loud. My eyesight wasn't good enough to let me see how well Derwent was doing, but Hardy was watching through binoculars and he nodded a couple of times. I lost count of how many rounds they fired. Ejected casings rang and rattled as they fell on the concrete beside Derwent.

As the firing died away, the man in charge

of the range shouted, "Cease firing. Breeches open. Change targets."

Derwent did as he was told, then sat up, turning his back on the range, ripping his ear defenders off and letting them fall to the ground beside him. He leaned his elbows on his knees and stared into space with a concentrated expression. Stuart went out to collect the targets and I took my ear defenders off.

"Impressive," Hardy said. Derwent didn't answer. He stood up instead and slid off the jacket and glove. He gave them to me and went straight past me, up the path, heading for the car park.

"Is he all right?" Hardy asked.

"Usually," I said.

Stuart came back to us and took the equipment from me, giving me the targets instead. "That was good shooting. Very good. He said he hadn't used a rifle in years, but you'd never know from these."

"He should compete," Hardy said. "I could see about getting a recommendation for him from a member. Being a police officer I don't think we'd have any problem about admitting him."

"I'll let him know." I gave back the ear defenders and thanked them both, then followed Derwent's route back to the car.

I'd expected him to be waiting for me but I couldn't see him at first. Then I heard retching nearby. I went around the car and saw him leaning on the boot of the one parked next to us. As I approached he gave another heave and I heard the splatter of vomit on tarmac. I stood and waited until he seemed to have stopped. He was still bent over, but his breathing was returning to normal.

"Are you all right?"

"Fine." He straightened up and wiped his mouth.

"What happened?"

"Nothing." He wouldn't look me in the eye.

"You've just thrown up all over someone's car. That's not nothing."

He glanced at the car, which was a dusty green Nissan with a dent in one door. I was glad it wasn't one of the smarter models in the car park.

"It's just a few splashes. They won't notice."

"They might."

"Who cares," he said on an exhalation.

"They might," I said again.

"The rain will take care of it." His tone told me the subject was now closed. He unlocked the car and got in. I hurried around to my side and got in, looking across at him as I put on my seatbelt. He leaned across to get a stick of chewing gum from the glove box.

"Are you sure you're okay?"

"Yes."

"Did you want these?" I handed him the targets and he threw them into the back seat without looking at them. "They said you were good."

"Yeah, obviously."

"They said you should compete."

"Fuck, no." He drove out of the car park at speed. We bumped down the track toward the main road in silence, far too fast for comfort. I braced one hand on the dashboard, knowing that it would annoy him.

While we were stopped, waiting to pull out into traffic, Derwent said, "And don't ask about it any more."

"I wasn't going to."

"I don't want to talk about it."

"You're the one who brought it up."

"Don't mention it again. To anyone."

"Fine."

"I mean it."

"I understand."

"No," he said. "You don't. Now, where's this rich bloke's house?"

"Do you want to talk to him now?" I was scrabbling for the map and my notebook, trying to recall whether we needed to start by turning right or left and coming up blank.

He gave me a filthy look. "No, I suppose not. It's only a murder investigation. Only a dead copper. Nothing too urgent, is it? No need for a quick-time response."

"Right," I said under my breath. Because of course, for every revelation of weakness, there had to be an equal and opposite show of strength. I should have expected it. I knew to expect it. I concentrated on the map and told myself I didn't mind.

It almost worked.

CHAPTER TWELVE

Tigg's Lane was a devil to find, and by the time we located Callancote's high gates, Derwent was in a correspondingly demonic mood. I took on the job of dealing with the intercom, holding up my warrant card to the camera and hoping it was legible enough to get us in. The gates wheezed open eventually and Derwent drove in, leaving me to walk up the winding drive. I didn't mind. It gave me time to look at the well-kept gardens and the neat Georgian symmetry of the redbrick house.

The door was open when I reached the front steps, where Derwent was already deep in conversation with a small, plump man who looked as if his face was made for smiling. Currently, though, he wasn't.

Derwent gave me a warning look that had just a touch of pleading in it, and I braced myself without knowing what to expect. "This is Rex Gibney. Mr. Gibney, this is my colleague, DC Maeve Kerrigan."

Gibney's response told me exactly what I was dealing with: a good old-fashioned sexist. "The lady from the gate. I was just telling your pal here I wouldn't have let him in if he'd buzzed. Good thing he sent you to do it. I couldn't say no to a female in distress, could I?"

"I hope I didn't look as if I was in distress." I smiled at him. "It's good of you to see us, Mr. Gibney. I'm sorry to turn up without warning."

"Andrew Hardy rang me."

"Did he?" I shouldn't have been surprised. I hadn't told him not to warn Gibney that we were on our way. "What did he say?"

"That you had questions about the shooting in Richmond Park. I doubt I can help you." Behind small glasses, his eyes were as cold as glacier ice. "I don't know why Hardy thought I could."

"We asked him about people who were enthusiasts for guns and shooting and he gave us your name. We just have a few general questions." There was a timely gust of wind that carried a handful of rain and I didn't have to pretend to shiver. "If we could come inside for a few moments . . ."

"As I said, I doubt I can help." He stood there for a few seconds, not moving. We didn't move either. This was a world away from the warmth and generosity Hardy had described, and I thought two things: that most wealthy people didn't make their fortune by being nice, and that Gibney probably wasn't a big fan of the police if his interest in guns ran beyond what was legal.

Possibly it was the fact that my teeth were chattering that roused Gibney's conscience.

"Come in, if you must." He stood back and we piled into the marble-tiled hall without waiting for him to think again. It wasn't a large house but the proportions were lovely. I looked up at the ceiling. It was a riot of ornate plasterwork, an elaborate procession of sheaves of wheat and bunches of grapes and musical instruments.

"All original." Gibney sounded very slightly more friendly. "We had it restored when we moved in."

"It's amazing."

"You'd better come through to the study. It's the other side of the sitting room. These old houses, the rooms lead into one another. They didn't believe in corridors."

As Gibney turned to open a heavy mahogany door, Derwent applauded silently. I gathered I was being thanked for getting us out of the hall. I shook my head at him. I hadn't been faking an interest in the house, and if I had been pretending I thought Gibney would have noticed it. He was sharp, despite his age and cuddly appearance. Derwent needed to watch his step, and so did I.

There was a gray-haired woman in the sitting room with a Pomeranian perched on her lap. She looked up at us, surprised, but Gibney just waved at her and kept walking. No introductions, but this was Mrs. Gibney, I gathered. I smiled at her in what I hoped was a reassuring way. The room was warm and comfortable rather than formal, but the overall impression was of wealth and furniture chosen to be in keeping with the period of the house.

The study was small and not the book-lined room I'd been anticipating. There was one breakfront bookcase but the books in it looked as if they had been bought by the yard, matching sets jammed in tightly so you'd break the spine if you tried to pull one out. An ottoman in front of the fireplace had a stack of newspapers on it, and Gibney sat in a chair nearby with the air of a man coming home.

"I read the papers every day. Keep up with the news."

"And the crossword?" Derwent asked, sitting opposite him.

"No. Can't be bothered with that sort of thing. Pointless. Pat yourself on the back for being clever enough to work out something that thousands of people have guessed before you."

"Mr. Hardy told us you used to have a business hiring out equipment to builders," I said.

"We had everything. Cranes and cherry-pickers. The big stuff. If you wanted it there on time and in good working order, you called Gibney's. We guaranteed to supply what you needed when you needed it or you'd get what you wanted half-price. But we hardly ever had to do that."

"Looks as if it was a good line of work," Derwent commented.

"Because of this place?" Gibney chuckled. "Well, we're lucky. We're not short of cash, put it that way. But we bought this house in the eighties. The previous owners were direct descendants of the family who built it in the eighteenth century. I don't know how they'd hung on to it for so long; the last one who had any money was the one who built Callancote. I got it for next to nothing. They were desperate to sell and no one wanted to buy it. There was a recession on. Anyway, it wasn't a country estate. It was in the suburbs, according to the estate agent." He laughed again. "Nearest house is a mile and a half away but that's not far enough for some people."

"It feels as if we're in the middle of the country," I said, glancing out the window at the mature oak trees that ringed an immaculate lawn.

"Yes, but that's an illusion. We've no land. The previous owners had sold it off, bit by bit, to developers. There's a housing estate that way," he jerked his thumb over his shoulder, "and a garden center further down Tigg's Lane. A big one, too. Then there's a golf course on another few acres that used to belong to Callancote. Not that I mind. I can't see 'em or hear 'em and I never saw myself as a gentleman farmer anyway. Not a gentleman, for starters." He twinkled at me and I found myself smiling at him.

Derwent's next question put an end to the friendly demeanor. "So why the interest in guns?"

He shifted in his chair, at a loss. "I don't know. Why is anyone interested in anything? It could have been football but I prefer to do things than sit and watch someone else do it. I was all right at it. I started off and I was no good but I got better. I worked hard at it. I got a buzz out of it."

"You like the guns, don't you?"

"As machines? Of course. The design that goes into them. The thought." He shook his head admiringly. "They're effective and beautiful. What more could you want?"

"They're designed to kill," I said.

"They're designed to hit a target. What that target may be depends on the man shooting. People kill people, in lots of different ways. They just use guns to do it sometimes."

"And you don't have a problem with that," I said.

"I don't approve of murder, miss. But I don't make the mistake of blaming the instrument, any more than I'd blame the car manufacturers if my vehicle was hit by a drunk driver."

"Let's talk about your involvement with the gun club," Derwent said. "You're pretty hands-on, aren't you?"

"No. Not any more. Not in an official capacity."

"But you host a party for the members every year."

"Just a little get-together. The clubhouse isn't what you'd call glamorous, and we have the space. There's a drawing room on the other side of the hall that's four times

240

the size of the sitting room. We put a bar in the hall and give people a few canapés and mince pies. Simple, but it's nice for the wives to get dressed up."

"The wives? Aren't there any female members?" I had to ask.

"Oh, probably. I just assume they're interested because their husbands or boyfriends shoot. Or because they want to meet men."

Derwent's expression was pure glee. He cleared his throat though, and I got the message: *play nice.*

"Maybe so," I said, through gritted teeth.

"The party was supposed to be hosted by a different committee member each time, but I have this place and most people don't have a home big enough to accommodate everyone who wants to come. It just became my responsibility after a while. Not that I minded. I love a party."

"And you love the gun club."

"Yes." He glared at me, daring me to find it strange. "I like the people. I like the guns. I like shooting and watching other people shoot."

"And you like to help the younger club members."

"When I can. Financially, you know."

"Do you ever invite them to the house?"

"They're invited to the party along with their parents. It wouldn't be fair to exclude them. We make sure they don't get any alcohol," he added quickly.

"Don't worry. We're not going to nick you for facilitating underage drinking," Derwent drawled. "I'm more interested in knowing whether you ever spend any time with them alone."

Gibney went bright red. "What are you implying?"

"It's just a question."

"No. Never. If they come here for any reason it's in the company of their parents. I have little interest in getting to know them, you understand. I like to see the talented ones do well and I like them to tell me about the competitions they go to around the country and abroad. Sometimes I have them over for tea, if I've funded a trip. But there's nothing strange about it and I resent the suggestion that I am trying to get access to them for a sinister purpose."

Derwent smiled. "You know, I never said anything of the kind."

"I knew what you meant. Everyone has a filthy mind these days. Everyone expects the worst of people. Whatever happened to trust?"

"It was abused and children suffered."

Derwent's voice was crisp. "Ever been in trouble with the police?"

"No."

"Ever been run through the Criminal Records Bureau?"

"No."

"Did you deliberately avoid being CRB checked?"

"No, I did not." It was a shout, followed almost immediately by a gentle tap on the door. It opened a few inches and Gibney's wife put her head into the room.

"Is everything all right, dear?"

"It's fine. Go away, Evelyn."

She shut the door again, softly, as if that would make up for having disturbed us. Gibney sat in his chair, his fingers digging into the arms, his chest rising and falling quickly. I hoped he wasn't going to have a heart attack on us.

"We have to ask these things, Mr. Gibney," I said.

"I don't like the way you're talking to me."

"I'm sorry about that."

"I don't know where this is going. Why are you attacking me?" he asked Derwent, who shrugged.

"Because there's something strange about a grown man who likes playing with guns. I got talking to a few people at the club. Other members. People who said you had a stash of illegal weapons."

People named Andrew Hardy, I thought, but I appreciated Derwent's uncharacteristic subtlety.

"That's not true."

"A Dragunov and a Falcon, I heard."

"You are mistaken."

"Dangerous weapons, those."

"In the wrong hands," Gibney allowed.

"Do you know what the minimum sentence is if you're found to be in possession of a weapon such as either of those?"

Gibney went very still. Through stiff lips, he whispered, "No."

"Five years. That's the minimum. Five years. Not in a country club kind of prison either. You'd be in with the scum. Cat A, Cat B. No one you'd want to know. Not the kind of people who have country houses, with or without land. Even in the suburbs." Derwent laughed, even though Gibney was a long way from amused.

"I don't see how this is relevant to me."

"It isn't. Unless I get a search team in here and we take the place apart. Get some dogs in who can sniff out a gun a mile off. Check the attic. Under the bed. The garden shed."

There was a flicker behind Gibney's glasses at the mention of the garden. I saw it and Derwent saw it. His voice hardened.

"You see, you'd hide them somewhere clever. I'm not underestimating you. You wouldn't leave them lying around. But you'd want to look at them. You'd want to show them off to people who came to the house. Like-minded people, I mean. People who could be trusted not to talk." He leaned forward. "That's the thing, though. People always talk in the end. It's human nature. Like thinking the rules don't apply to you just because you're rich and ir-responsible."

"I'm not irresponsible."

"You own illegal weapons. You've caused them to be brought into this country, from what I hear. You're looking at a serious set of charges. Serious jail time. And you will be convicted, Rex. You needn't think you can buy a good QC and get off. Juries hate millionaires and they hate guns. Judges hate them more. The sentences are mandatory and they are long and you will loathe every minute of being inside, if you make it to the end of your sentence, which I doubt. What are you, seventy? There's not a lot of seventy-year-olds in jail. You don't get the healthcare, you see. Basic stuff, yes, but not the kind of tests and medications you'd be used to."

"What do you want?" Gibney ground out.

"World peace and a cottage by the sea." Derwent sat back. "But I'll settle for a trip to your gun stash."

"You must think I'm stupid, Inspector Derwent. If you saw that I had illegal guns you'd arrest me."

"Not if you told us someone had put them on your land unbeknownst to you. Not if I could recover them and hand them in to Surrey Police. Not if I got a personal, private assurance from you that you wouldn't dream of buying anything similar again. Not if Scotland Yard got an anonymous tip-off about the person who acts as your dealer in the UK and the route they used to get the guns into the country. Shop them, give me the guns, and save yourself a lot of trouble, Mr. Gibney."

He considered it for a full minute, his eyes locked on Derwent's face. I knew he was weighing up the risks, looking for something else to offer us, trying to see his way to making a better deal. But there was no better deal on offer, as he obviously deduced.

"I could promise you anything," he said at last. "Why would you believe me if I said I wouldn't buy an illegal weapon in the future?"

"Because once or twice a year the local

246

coppers are going to call on you. They're going to have a look around. And if they find so much as a bit of lead shot you shouldn't own, you're going to get done."

Gibney nodded. "You're a hard man, Inspector."

"Fair, Mr. Gibney. I want the guns. I don't care much about what happens to you. You've been stupid and self-indulgent and you've broken the law but I don't believe you meant to do any harm with your weapons. You just thought the laws didn't apply to you. Not my favorite attitude, but I'll give you a chance to change it."

Luck is a funny thing. We had been lucky in finding Rex Gibney, and Derwent had been lucky to break him so quickly. It was bad luck that the rain had settled down to a steady drizzle by the time Gibney took us out to the vegetable garden and pointed out a patch of ground near the marrows. It was worse luck that Gibney had buried the weapons there only a couple of months earlier, having decided their previous hiding place in a nice dry outbuilding was too risky. Even more unfortunate was that the weapons were buried deeper than Gibney had remembered, and that the soil was a particularly heavy, clinging clay that was a bugger to dig. Gibney had an umbrella but I didn't, and I couldn't exactly ask to borrow one. To give him his due, Derwent didn't complain about the miserable conditions. He handed me his coat and jacket, rolled up his shirtsleeves and dug until the spade hit something solid, by which time his hair was drenched and his shirt was so wet it was translucent. He worked around the package carefully, loosening the earth from the edges so he could lever it up. I helped him to pull it out of the soil and we laid it on the ground beside the hole. What he had uncovered was long and wrapped in plastic.

"That's the ZVI." Gibney pulled a penknife from his pocket and slit the plastic, revealing a hard plastic casing with the manufacturer's name stencilled on it. He opened it briefly, shielding the case with his umbrella so the rain didn't get on the parts of the gun as they nestled in the protective foam. "All there. The other one should be underneath it."

Derwent peered into the hole. "Beside it?"

"Underneath." Gibney sniffed. "I thought this was the first one in, actually, but it must have been second. Easy to get the two confused."

Derwent had jumped down into the hole

again and was poking around with the tip of the spade. "Nothing here, mate."

"There must be."

"No." He stuck the spade into the sides and bottom of the hole, pushing down with his foot to go as far as he could. "Nothing."

"That's impossible."

Derwent leaned on the spade. "Who knew the guns were here? Specifically in this place rather than the original hiding place?"

"Four or five people," Gibney admitted. "But reliable people."

"Four or five people who might have told a couple of people each." I looked at Derwent. "It's somewhere to start, though."

"Go back into the house and write a list," Derwent said to Gibney. "Names and addresses. I want to know who helped you put the weapons in the ground. I want to know who knew you owned them. I want to know the name of anyone who asked you about the weapons and their location, specifically. And I want to know how someone could have come and dug this gun up without you noticing."

"I can answer that one now," Gibney said. "We've just been away. A Scandinavian cruise. We were out of the house for three weeks."

"Who knew that?"

"Everyone at the club, I should think."

"Was it a last-minute holiday?"

"Booked since last April."

"And you talked about it."

"We were excited. I was looking forward to it."

So there had been plenty of time for someone to plan to use one of Gibney's weapons, if it was the gun that had killed Terence Hammond. And it needn't have been someone at the club, I thought. It could have been someone in the criminal underworld. Someone who was looking for a weapon and fetched up with Gibney's armorer. These guns weren't common. No one had one lying around to sell. But if you wanted it badly enough, and quickly, there was always a way. *There's this rich geezer out near Guildford has what you want, mate, but you'll have to get past his security gates. Course I can ask him where he keeps them, casual-like. No problem.*

As if he was reading my mind, Gibney said, "But you don't know if this gun was used on your policeman."

"Not until we find it," I said.

"What if you had bullets fired by that weapon? Could you compare them?"

"Yes," Derwent said. "Obviously."

"Then you'll need to go down to my

range. Or send your ballistics man, anyway. I collect the casings in a plastic bin and the projectiles should be still embedded in the earth behind the targets. Easy enough to recover. I've only shot five or six weapons there so they'll be able to work out which ones relate to the missing gun by a process of elimination. I'll hand over all the guns, of course. I'm cooperating fully with you."

Derwent was stuck on the first part. "You have your own range."

"It's just a makeshift affair. It's on the other side of the house, backing onto the garden center. I only use it when the garden center is closed," he said quickly, seeing our expressions. "But what's the point in having guns if you can't fire them now and then? And I couldn't take them to the club, could I?"

"Because they're illegal," I said.

"Exactly." Gibney looked at us from under the dripping brim of the umbrella, his expression a mixture of mischief and concern. I could see how Hardy could describe him as childish. This wasn't the millionaire businessman and property owner. This was a small boy trying to explain away bad behavior. "I'm not going to get in trouble for that too, am I? Because it's lucky for you I've got my own range, in the circumstances. It should help you rule the Dragunov out."

"Yeah." Derwent pushed his soaking hair back off his forehead with his wrist. He was still knee-deep in mud. Years of practicing high-level sarcasm ensured he achieved exactly the right tone when he added, "Lucky for us."

CHAPTER THIRTEEN

"You have to admit, though, you were lucky," Rob said.

I raised my head to give him an evil look. Our new flat was open plan, so Rob had been able to throw that remark at me from the kitchen, a safe distance away.

"That's what everyone says and it's bull."

"But it *was* just luck that you found Gibney."

"Don't you start. It was good old-fashioned legwork. That was the third gun club we'd been to ourselves, and other officers had been to check out the others around London. Godley had people looking into hundreds of leads. Statistically speaking, one of them was going to turn out to be worthwhile eventually."

"Yeah, but —"

I was ahead of him, talking fast. "Yes, it was lucky that Hardy gave us Gibney's name, but someone else would have given him up. Everyone who knew him knew about what he had in his secret stash. With all the public appeals, someone would have lifted the phone."

"But you got there before that happened." Rob padded toward the sofa, barefoot, looking like he'd stepped out of an ad for the jeans he was wearing. I thought of Derwent's crack about him being a male model and suppressed a smile.

"You're like a bloodhound."

"Excuse me?"

"Sorry. An Irish wolfhound."

"That's even worse." I threw a cushion at him, which involved getting it out from behind my head since I was lying down. It wasn't worth the effort. He batted it away without blinking and I went back to staring at the ceiling.

"It was the only useful thing I've done so far in this whole investigation and I didn't even do it. Derwent was the one who terrified Hardy into talking. He was the one who impressed the gun-club members with his shooting — they could not have been more helpful once the word got out. Every person on the list Gibney gave us had heard about it, and every one of them was happy to talk to us."

"He was good, was he?"

"Brilliant. Apparently." I shrugged. "I don't get the whole shooting thing, to be honest. I don't really know what he was trying to achieve. A bull's-eye, I suppose."

"Ask."

"I can't ask him. He won't talk about it. And I can't ask the gun-club people because they already think I'm a moron." I coughed. "I think I'm getting a cold."

"You've been doing too much talking. Too many interviews," he clarified as I raised my eyebrows at him.

"Most of which were a total waste of time. Except for the daughter's ex-boyfriend. That was absolutely worth the petrol."

"Was he helpful?"

"Not even a little bit. He has no experience of shooting and his hands shake anyway because he's permanently hungover. I don't think he'd have the nerve to kill anyone, or the skill to organize it. He was a total no-mark. No, it was just funny. Derwent hated him so much I thought he was going to lamp him. Instant dislike. Obviously the guy felt the same way. It was more of a slanging match than an interview."

"Derwent doesn't make a good first impression," Rob said, lifting my feet so he could sit down at the other end of the sofa. He put them back down on his lap and started rubbing them. "Or a good second impression."

"I think the boy reminded Derwent of himself when he was a teenager. He was a right little turd, apparently, and that's according to him. I can't imagine." I wriggled, trying to get comfortable. "You're tickling me."

"It's supposed to be relaxing."

"I don't really do relaxing."

"I had noticed." He stopped playing with my feet though, and stared into space, frowning a little. I watched him, endlessly fascinated by the line of his cheek and the cut of his jaw and the shape of his mouth. I could never get tired of looking at him, of learning him all over again every time I saw him. That was what I held on to when, as now, the conversation stuttered to a halt, or when a careless remark from either of us hit the wrong note. We were a little out of practice, that was all. Out of the habit of being together.

It wasn't for want of trying. Different shift patterns meant that I was often out when Rob was at home. A big case like a police shooting absorbed my time and energy. He was on the Flying Squad, dealing with commercial robberies. A big case for him meant endless hours in surveillance vans, clocking up the overtime. In between times, we were exhausted. That placed too much importance on an evening like this, when the rest of the world finally left us alone and we could turn around to one another and say what we really thought, like —

"Shall I put the news on?" He had the remote control in his hand already.

"Yeah, why not." I wasn't going to pick a fight with him for watching television. The news would be short, and then we could get back to talking. Or we could do something else. Something together. I had some ideas in mind.

I only half-listened to the headlines, which were mainly about politicians squabbling and unemployment rates rising. Terence Hammond had dropped off the news agenda days before. There was no new information that we could share with the public. We had no suspects for them to spot. Anything we'd turned up in evidence was too scientific to be of general interest or too important to the case to reveal it at this stage. But really, the trouble was that there were no dramatic revelations to show off. There was nothing but the slow chipping away at the mechanics of how Hammond had died. Ballistic tests on the expended rounds at Gibney's range had positively identified his gun as the murder weapon, although we hadn't traced the actual gun yet. We didn't know who had stolen it. We didn't know who had fired it. We didn't have a single suspect or a hint of a motive. We didn't know who Hammond had been with in the car.

Basically, we had nothing to shout about.

I watched the screen without seeing the images on it, thinking about our plans for the next day and the next round of interviews. The news rolled on, as teachers complaining about changes to the national curriculum gave way to a clampdown on benefits cheats. A shoe factory was to close down in Birmingham with the loss of 200 jobs. Personal tragedies. National problems. International catastrophes. The usual.

And then the newsreader frowned and put his finger to his ear, looking away from the camera briefly.

"If you'll bear with me for a moment, we have reports just coming in of a shooting in London." He hesitated as the graphic behind him disappeared and a Breaking News caption replaced it. "Initial reports say it is a police vehicle that has been shot at."

I dropped my feet to the floor, pivoting so I was sitting on the edge of the sofa. I was aware of Rob leaning forward, as I was, the two of us concentrating on the television.

"We don't have any confirmation of casualties at the moment, or a location." He looked down at the pages in front of him and shuffled them nervously, listening to whatever was coming through his earpiece. "It's a north London location, I'm told, but I can't be more specific than that. Obviously, we'll bring you more on that story as we get it. Now the sports, with Karen."

Karen launched into her intro and Rob muted the television just as a mobile phone started ringing in the flat.

"Yours or mine?" Rob asked as the two of us got up, fast.

"Mine." I hurried into the hall. My handbag was on the floor by the door and I wasted a couple of seconds rummaging through it before turning it upside down and tipping everything out on to the floor. I picked the phone off the top of the pile and checked it. Godley.

"Boss?"

"Have you heard?" His voice crackled a little; he was in his car.

"Another shooting?"

"Yes."

"It was on the news. Fatal?"

There was a tiny pause. "Yes."

"A police officer?"

"I'm not going to talk to you about it over an open line."

His tone had been faintly incredulous. I felt my face go warm. "Is it our guy?"

"I don't know yet. But in case it is I don't want local CID hoofing all over the crime scene, or anyone else except us. If we get this third hand or fourth hand, we've got no chance."

"Where am I going?"

"Tottenham. The location is one of the big housing estates, so watch your back. The residents are going to be difficult to handle."

"What's the address?"

"The Maudling Estate. Derwent is picking you up. He should be with you soon. I rang him first. Everyone else is coming too. Everyone I could get hold of, that is."

I registered that of all of us I was the last person he'd called, and tried not to mind. "Okay."

"I'll see you there." He cut the connection before I could say good-bye.

My pulse was fluttering. I took a couple of deep breaths, trying to calm myself enough to think about what I needed to take with me to the scene. I'd been off duty, my mind in neutral. I wasn't ready for this.

And I wasn't dressed for work either, I

thought, looking down at the skinny jeans and vintage Stone Roses sweatshirt that had been ideal for a night in. I pulled the sweatshirt off as I went into our bedroom and opened the wardrobe. It took me seconds to find a suit, still in its dry-cleaner's bag, and a crisp white top, and another minute to get out of the old clothes and into the new, including my freshly polished boots. Suited and booted. It was as if I had known I would need to make myself presentable at short notice. I tied my hair back, despairing of making it look neat otherwise. Small earrings. Minimal makeup.

In the mirror I looked tall, professional, a little severe. Worried, if you knew me. Tense, even if you didn't.

I went back to the sitting room, where Rob was frowning at his phone.

"What?"

"According to Twitter it was a van, on an estate in Tottenham."

"A borough van?"

He shook his head. "TSG."

I went cold. The TSG were the Territorial Support Group, a standing body within the Met who dealt with public-order offenses. They were the ones who took charge of marches and demonstrations, who were front line when it came to quelling riots and civil disobedience. They tended to be big, fit, male, and intimidating. When they didn't have a riot to deal with, they patrolled the places where trouble seemed likely to flare. A TSG van typically contained six officers and a sergeant and it made a very efficient deterrent if anyone was considering causing trouble. It also made a large target.

Rob glanced up, then looked me up and down. "Off out?"

"Godley wants us to be there."

Rob narrowed his eyes very slightly at that and I knew he was frustrated to be left behind. He'd left the team because of me, because Godley would not allow personal relationships between his officers. I felt the guilt hit and tried not to let it show on my face.

"Does he think it's connected to Hammond?"

"I suppose so, or we wouldn't be there. Not yet, anyway."

"But he didn't say specifically."

"He was in the car. He didn't say much about anything."

"According to the ever-reliable Twitter, it's multiple casualties."

"Seriously?" I went across to look over his shoulder. He scrolled up, pausing every so often to read a tweet that looked useful.

"It says here there's footage on Sky News now. Someone filmed it on a mobile phone."

"And they've got it already?"

He was changing the channel. "They pay big money for video. You know how it is. Pictures or it didn't happen. Oh, here we go."

The screen had a "breaking news" flash across the bottom, and a warning in the top right: GRAPHIC CONTENT. That always felt like advertising to me, not a warning. *Keep watching for the good stuff.*

It was poor-quality footage; that was obvious from the first few seconds we saw, which were jerky and difficult to interpret. A figure disappeared between two anonymous buildings, too far from the camera to be identifiable. The picture was orange-tinged because of the harsh security lights on the estate, and the video was shot from somewhere high up — a balcony, probably. The footage cut out in a couple of places. I couldn't tell if the news channel had edited it or if the camera itself had failed. They were playing the clip on a loop, though, so while we'd come in more than halfway through it wasn't long before it started again.

The camera was focused initially on the white TSG van as it turned into the car park of the estate. The driver was going slowly. It was all about showing we had a presence in the estates, proving that we weren't scared to go there and tackle whatever the residents could throw at us. Literally, in this case. Something flashed as it hit the windscreen of the van and the brake lights went on. Then the screen lit up as the object exploded.

"A firework," I said.

"Listen to the guy filming. He's laughing."

On screen the van door opened and two officers jumped out. They pounded across the car park, lit up by the ultra-bright alley light on the van. I couldn't see who they were chasing at first, but after a moment of darkness the film resumed with the two officers walking back toward the van, a small figure between them. He had a shambling, uncertain walk, and his head was down.

"A kid."

"Looks like it," Rob said.

The three of them stopped near the van, the two tall officers blocking the camera's view of the suspect they were questioning. Another officer got out of the vehicle. As his foot touched the tarmac of the car park there was a loud crack and he crumpled to the ground. The other two turned and went down in the same moment, both of them sprawling as they fell. I could hear nothing but swearing on the soundtrack.

"See that?" Rob pointed as the small suspect appeared in the top right of the screen, running fast, bent double. "He knew something was coming."

"It was a trap," I said.

"Who's this?" Rob leaned forward. "What's he up to?"

This figure was taller and moved with total confidence. He came from the bottom left of the screen and walked along the side of the van that was further from the camera. He didn't appear to be hurrying, and as he walked he fired through the windows, two shots each time, as the glass shivered to pieces and the camera jerked as if the man filming was having a fit. Tap-tap. Tap-tap.

The TSG didn't carry firearms. They would have had Tasers in the van, I thought, but they'd have been lucky to get one un-holstered. Certainly there was no time to use one. The whole attack lasted a few seconds. The police officers outside the van died before they knew enough to be scared. The ones inside would have known what was coming. They'd had nowhere to hide. I hoped for survivors but I couldn't imagine that implacable figure missing, or giving up, until every last one of them was dead.

The cameraman had ducked down when the shooting began. With a wobbly hand he tried to follow the shooter as he walked out of shot at the top right of the picture. The camera swung and shuddered before it settled on a gap between two buildings.

"That's where we started."

"Want to watch it again?" Rob was concentrating on the screen.

"Not really." I turned away, feeling sick. Anyway, I had seen enough. It had been a professional job. A set-up. The killer had known what he was doing.

We would analyze every frame of the footage, and any other material we could get our hands on, but I knew that we wouldn't be able to identify the shooter from what we had. He was a shape, no more than that. He was an emblem of hatred for the police and what we did. He was the embodiment of revenge, and we had zero chance of catching him from the footage alone.

With that cheerful thought, the embodiment of aggressive misogyny rang the buzzer from downstairs.

"That's Derwent. I've got to go."

"Good hunting." Rob leaned back to kiss me, then sat down on the sofa to watch the footage again.

"Don't stay there all night," I said as I headed to the door.

"I won't," he promised. I knew him too well to believe him.

CHAPTER FOURTEEN

It wasn't a long journey from Farringdon to the Maudling Estate. Derwent filled the time by complaining.

"And your old flat was easier to get into, as well as being closer to my place. Those gates are bloody annoying."

"I'm sorry. We should have kept that in mind when we moved."

"It's just inconvenient, that's all." Thirty seconds of silence. "It's a bit swank, isn't it? Especially for a couple of coppers."

I blushed because he was right: the flat was a conversion in an old warehouse and it was a definite step up from our last place. I loved the big windows, the wooden floors, the open-plan living area, and the incredibly high-end bathroom. I also loved the view: a brick wall. Not having to worry about being overlooked was worth any money. Ever since I'd acquired my very own stalker, a guy called Chris Swain who had an uncanny ability to find and scare me, privacy had taken on a new significance. He was a rapist and an all-round creep and I wasn't ashamed of being terrified of him when he'd proved himself to be a danger, time and time again. He'd also proved himself to be worryingly good at hiding from the police. I hadn't seen him for over a year and neither had anyone else involved in law enforcement. That didn't mean he wasn't out there. To Derwent, I said, "We got a good deal on the rent."

"I reckon you did."

"Rob negotiated it."

"Good for him." Derwent went silent again, anger billowing around him like smoke.

And it was nothing to do with me, or the flat, or the number of traffic lights in Farringdon (excessive, according to Derwent), or the other drivers on the road (morons, to a man). It was all about disguising the sharp anxiety that had him on edge. He carried his rage like a shield, hiding what he really felt, as if anyone would think less of him for being upset at what we were about to see.

I was dry-eyed even if I was dry-mouthed as we negotiated our way through the throng of journalists, camera crews, and hangers-on at the cordon outside the Maudling estate. It was chaotic, with reporters competing to do their pieces to camera, feet away from one another. Tempers flared as the cameramen fought to get the best angle, the clearest view, without having half their competition in the shot. Some of them had started filming one another.

We dropped straight into the scene I recognized from the footage on the news. Now the car park was an active crime scene, crammed with uniforms, police vehicles, ambulances, and plainclothes officers. The patrol cars of the borough's response officers were parked along the road outside. Armed response vehicles circled around the estate, which was big: eight tower blocks of varying heights, built in the 1960s when concrete was a glamorous choice of building material. The police helicopter chattered overhead, the noise of the rotors rebounding off the high-rise buildings. Everyone was looking everywhere but at the sheet-draped figures on the ground and in the van. There hadn't been time yet to move them, I knew, but I wished someone would take them away.

"I've never seen this many cops at a single incident."

"Incidents don't come bigger than this." Derwent stopped the car more or less at random, his attention focused on one particular person in front of us. "Fuck, who told her to come along?"

He was talking about Detective Chief Inspector Una Burt, Godley's second-in-command. She was front and center, peering into the van. Looking at her, without knowing anything about her, you would form two opinions: that she had a razor-sharp brain, and that she had got dressed by putting on the first three things she found in her wardrobe in no particular order.

"I assume Godley wanted her here. He wanted a strong response to this."

"He wants us to take over." Derwent pulled a face. "I can't imagine there'll be much competition. This job has grief written all over it. Why does he want it? We have enough trouble with Hammond."

"Where is the boss?"

"There." Derwent pointed. "Talking to one of the assistant commissioners. Lucky old him."

The assistant commissioner in question was Nigel Williams, a bulky, dark-haired man with a jutting jaw and heavy eyebrows. Nothing about his demeanor looked encouraging as Godley spoke to him, leaning forward, the words coming out fast.

Most unusually for the superintendent, he looked agitated, and not just because he was talking to one of the highest-ranked officers in the Met.

"Do you think he's all right?" I asked Derwent, forgetting that he and Godley had fallen out. His lips thinned to a line, but before he could answer, Una Burt turned around, her hands on her hips, and scanned the car park. She saw us almost immediately and beckoned with the bored impatience of a traffic officer.

"Oh, bollocks." Derwent put his head down on the steering wheel, just for a moment.

"Come on. Face the music."

He relieved his feelings by swearing under his breath as he got out of the car. We walked across to where the chief inspector was waiting, square and solid in pleated trousers and a boxy jacket.

"Ma'am." Derwent favored her with his sweetest smile. "What would you like us to do?"

"I'd have thought it was obvious. Investigate the case, Josh. You're not here to sightsee. We've got dead police officers here."

"How many?" I asked, knowing that Derwent was struggling to keep from snapping at her.

"Five."

"Only two survived?"

She nodded. "One who was outside the van, one other inside it. One was alive when the first responders got here but he died before they could get him into the back of an ambulance, let alone to hospital."

There were rubber gloves discarded on the ground, now that I looked, and swabs, and a mask that someone had forgotten in their haste. All the signs of a frantic scramble to save lives. Two out of seven. A bad result. I'd been expecting it and yet I couldn't quite get my head around it.

"Are the survivors talking?" Derwent asked.

"We haven't been allowed to interview them yet. One of them is in a bad way. The other one was lucky. Shot in the shoulder. He said they shot the driver first."

"Before they shot the guy by the van?" I was surprised. I hadn't noticed that on the film footage.

"So he couldn't drive away, you see."

"Yes, but I saw the film. The shooter came from this end." We were standing at the back of the van. "How did he shoot the driver from here?"

"He didn't."

"Two shooters," Derwent said.

"Exactly."

"Oh, marvelous. That is all we need."

I was looking at the bodies on the ground, each covered with a sheet to hide them from the residents of the estate. Most of them seemed to be out on their balconies filming what was going on below them. The sheets were thin enough that I could see the white square of the dead police officers' radio screens lighting up every time there was a transmission on the channel they'd been tuned to. The dark van glowed eerily as the radios inside flicked on and off in unison. The tinny sound of radio chatter filled the otherwise silent vehicle. The lights from our cars glinted off the shattered glass in the van windows and the glossy blood on the ground that was still wet.

"Can't they turn them off?" I said. "The radios?"

"The bodies need to be examined. You know that." DCI Burt sounded irritated.

I did know it. But I also hated the reminder that a couple of hours earlier these had been police officers out on a routine patrol, getting to the end of a late shift in the company of their friends. They couldn't have begun to imagine that all the radio traffic now would be about them, and finding their killers.

Raised voices behind Burt made us all look around.

"Oh Christ," Derwent said. "The boss."

It was so unusual for Godley to lose his temper in public that I couldn't recall the last time I'd seen him do it. He was venting his anger at a tall, gray-haired man I recognized as one of the most right-wing MPs in parliament. Geoff Armstrong was an ex-academic, an economist who'd abandoned university life for politics after appearing on television and radio criticizing the government for excessive public borrowing. He hated the NHS, the long-term unemployed, single-parent families, anyone who relied on benefits and anyone who allowed themselves to be poor. He was detested in places like the Maudling Estate at the best of times, which this was not.

"This isn't Geoff Armstrong's constituency. He's an MP for somewhere in Hampshire. So what's he doing here?"

"Making trouble." Derwent set off toward them, as if his presence would do anything but make things worse. I went after him, and Una Burt followed me. I saw Chris Pettifer hurrying over from the other direction, and Pete Belcott. It was only a matter of time before every team member in the post-code turned up. I reached the little group where Godley stood, to find him winding down from the pitch of annoyance that had made him shout. He was still a long way from calm, though.

"You are throwing baseless accusations around in order to get attention for yourself and you will positively harm this investigation if you do so on camera."

Armstrong laughed. "I can see you're scared to admit the truth, Superintendent Godley, but you can't change the history of this sorry affair. This estate has been a disaster waiting to happen ever since Levon Cole was killed. Your police officers have been too afraid of making a mistake to crack down on the drug dealers and gangsters who run this estate and anarchy is the result. They made themselves into targets and they were too cowardly to protect themselves."

"Are you actually saying that they deserved to die?" Godley snapped.

"I'm saying it was their fault all along the line. If they had done their jobs properly they would have been safe here. As it is, no one is safe here except the thugs who make a very nice living off the misery of others. And you're the very people who are supposed to be able to stop them. If you can't, there's something very wrong with the Metropolitan Police."

"Speculation is a dangerous thing without any evidence to back it up. You are a public person, Mr. Armstrong. If you make a connection between Levon Cole and what happened here, people will assume you know more than they do. Even if we discover that this is completely unrelated to the Cole shooting, the doubt will linger in people's minds."

Behind his rimless glasses, Armstrong's eyes were bright. "Are you trying to censor me?"

"No, I'm asking you to be responsible about the language you use and the assumptions you make about this situation. And frankly I resent having to waste my time on this futile conversation when I have five dead police officers lying over there and we haven't even begun to remove the bodies." Godley's voice had risen again. Above the collar of his crisp white shirt, the tendons in his neck were standing out.

Derwent cut in. "Here's an idea, Mr. Armstrong. Why don't you go back to Westminster and concentrate on your job instead of mucking around here trying to make ours more difficult."

"This is my job."

"This isn't even your constituency," Derwent said, appropriating what I'd said without a flicker.

"I represent the people of this country, not just the constituents who voted for me," Armstrong said loftily.

"Have you asked the people of this community if they want you to speak for them?" The assistant commissioner towered over Armstrong, who paled a little.

"I'm sure they're all aware of me and happy that I can give them a voice."

"I think you're underestimating them," Williams said. "They have the ability to speak for themselves, I can assure you."

"So where are they?" Armstrong looked up at the flats, eyeing the residents who were watching us. "Standing around on their balconies like animals in a zoo."

"We're keeping them out of the way at the moment because this is an active investigation and that is our crime scene." Godley pointed at the car park. "Let them wander around at will and they'll move through this area destroying any forensic evidence we might collect. It's our only chance to gather the evidence we need to catch and convict a killer."

Williams reached out and patted Godley's

shoulder. "Leave it, now." To Armstrong, he said, "You know that you can inflame this situation if you try to make us look bad."

"I don't have to try to make you look bad. You're managing that perfectly well on your own."

The assistant commissioner frowned. "Be that as it may, you have a responsibility not to make a bad situation worse. I understand that you wanted to come down here to see what happened at first hand. I am aware that you were allowed through the police cordon but that should never have happened." And someone's head was going to roll, I thought. Williams went on: "You are a civilian and you have no place here at this time. I'm going to have to ask you to leave."

"I'm not going anywhere. This is a free country and I'm not doing anything illegal. You do your job — properly, this time — and let me do mine."

"You know, the cameras are down there. That end of the street." Derwent pointed. "Isn't that where you want to be, really? On every news bulletin? In every front room across the country?"

Armstrong moistened his lips with his tongue. "I resent the implication."

"And I resent the way you're determined to make this about the police being

incompetent," Derwent said. "Those coppers were doing their jobs, and they got
killed. Don't try to put the boot in just
because they were paid for by taxpayers."

"Mr. Godley can handle this," Una Burt
said, her tone reproving.

"Mr. Godley has enough to be getting on
with." Derwent turned back to Godley and
the expression in his eyes was pure puppy-
dog, so hopeful I had to look away.

Godley ignored him. "Mr. Armstrong, I
consider this conversation to be at an end.
Now, I'm asking you to leave. If you refuse,
I will ask some of my officers to remove
you."

"Are you going to arrest me?"

"Only if there's a reason to do so. I don't
particularly want to tie up good police officers with pointless paperwork just because
you want to make yourself part of the story."

"That's an insult."

"File a complaint." There was something
in Godley's tone that made Armstrong take
a step back. I didn't blame him.

The acting commissioner flagged down a
couple of passing uniformed officers. "Mr.
Armstrong needs an escort back to the cordon. Make sure he doesn't get held up along
the way."

"I can manage by myself." Armstrong

looked left and right as the response officers took up positions on either side of them. They both happened to be big men, made more substantial by the stab vests they wore. I wouldn't have wanted to have a disagreement with either of them.

"It's no trouble," Williams said. "Thanks for your interest, though."

Armstrong moved away with enormous reluctance. Williams waited until he was out of earshot. "Charles, you need to be very careful with this. I appreciate that you're under pressure, but —"

"It's nothing to do with being under pressure, sir. It's the fact that I had to waste time dealing with him when there are more important issues at hand."

"I appreciate you feel strongly about investigating this, Charles. But I think we should allow the DPS boys to handle it, along with the local MIT team. You have enough to handle with the Terence Hammond case."

"Sir, this is my plan." Godley had pulled himself together — back to normal, I would have said, except that I thought it was taking a huge effort for him to maintain his composure. "My team and I are going to run this investigation alongside the Terence Hammond case, because there is a possibility that there may be a connection between them. The local MIT team doesn't want this one. I do. I want the local response officers to concentrate on keeping the residents out of our way. I want the SOCOs to report to me. I want Kev Cox to manage the scene. And I want Glenn Hanshaw to do the PMs."

"He's not answering his phone," Una Burt chipped in.

"Really?" Godley faltered for a moment, concern knocking him off balance. "Okay. Well, keep trying to get hold of him. In the meantime we need to get these men off the street. Find me a pathologist to sign off on moving the bodies and they can go to Glenn's hospital. It's not ideal but I want to get this tidied up, now."

"What else?" Williams asked.

"Talk to witnesses, collect evidence, analyze the evidence, find the killers. Sir."

"You make it sound so simple."

"It is. That doesn't mean it's going to be easy."

I could see Williams wavering. There was something very tempting about letting Godley take charge, especially since no one else would volunteer to take it on. "I'm not sure about this, Charles."

"I am."

And just like that, he had his permission

to proceed. Godley walked Williams away from us, toward his car, and Pettifer shook his head admiringly.

"Godley's a genius. He knows how to get what he wants, doesn't he?"

Derwent grunted. "I'd feel better about that if I thought he knew what was good for him."

"It's not your business to second-guess the superintendent," Una Burt said. Her eyes were cold. "And I thought your remarks to Geoff Armstrong were inappropriate. You inserted yourself into the conversation to insult him."

"I wanted to give the boss time to regroup. He was getting upset."

"He was in complete command of himself and the situation," Burt snapped.

Godley had many fans in the Met, but the biggest was almost certainly Una Burt. I thought it was because he had always treated her with respect instead of mocking her appearance and manner. If it was hard to be a woman in the Met, it was doubly hard to be a plain one. I could shrug off the comments about my looks and my sex life. They were irritating but I'd learned not to let them bother me. And they may have been unwanted but the comments I got were mostly positive. Una Burt came in for nothing but abuse.

Derwent looked singularly unimpressed. "You must have been listening to a different conversation then. I thought he was about to blow his stack."

"Whether he did or not was none of your business."

"He's my boss."

"And mine." Her voice was quivering. Derwent heard it too and went in for the kill.

"And where were you when he was facing up to that twat Armstrong? Listening to Glen Hanshaw's voicemail message?"

"I knew it wasn't my place to intervene."

"What exactly did you come over to do then? Stare at the boss adoringly while he shot himself in the career?"

"That's enough." Godley pushed into the circle that had formed around Derwent and Burt. "We had one dead police officer and now we have six. We are working in front of the borough's response teams, local CID, the TSG's superintendent and the world's media, and need I remind you, there are hundreds of residents watching you from the towers. They are waiting for us to do our jobs and frankly so am I. Watching the two of you bickering was deeply unimpressive — and I don't care to ask what you were arguing about, so don't tell me."

"A misunderstanding, sir." Derwent's back was ramrod straight, his arms by his sides. Some time I would laugh at him for standing to attention when he was in trouble. *Some time very far in the future,* I thought.

"DCI Burt was just explaining a few things to me. Very helpful," Derwent said through gritted teeth.

"I meant what I said, Josh. No details." Godley looked up at the towers, his face drawn and pale. "We need to get moving. We need witnesses and we need weapons. Una, you need to coordinate the door-to-door inquiries. Josh, find me the guns."

"They'll have taken them away with them," Belcott said.

"Maybe," Derwent said. "But if they're professionals they might dump them instead. It's bloody risky to carry them round if they don't have to." To Godley, he said, "A couple of dogs would help."

"You can have whatever you need." Godley turned, scanning our faces. "I want to get a result on this one, ladies and gentlemen. I want to find the kid who threw the firework, and the two shooters. I want to do it quickly. Start now. Stop when you get a result."

He turned and walked away, leaving a rising hum of conversation behind him. Una Burt's voice cut through it.

"Maeve, you'll be working on the door-to-door inquiries."

I knew I looked surprised. I had been expecting to work with Derwent. And Derwent had been expecting the same thing. His head snapped up. "I need her for the guns. She's good at searching."

"You heard Godley. You'll have dogs."

"Not the same."

"I should hope not." She smiled at me, but there was no warmth in it. I was a pawn to her and I knew it.

"This is stupid," Derwent said. "Kerrigan works with me."

"Not on this occasion."

"But —"

"Do you want me to remind you that I outrank you?"

That got his attention. "Is that what this is about? Is this supposed to make me respect you?"

"It's about effective deployment of resources. Maeve is going to be more useful to me than to you."

Derwent's eyes narrowed and he took a step closer to Una Burt. "You and I both know that's not true."

My face was flaming. Chris Pettifer cleared his throat. "There's a few others on the team. Kerrigan aside, what do you want us to do?"

Una Burt took charge instantly, issuing orders to six of us and leaving the remainder to Derwent. He was staring at the ground, refusing to look in my direction, more like a sulky teenager than a senior detective. I waited to catch his eye until it became apparent he was never going to look back at me.

"Why are you hanging about, Kerrigan?" Una Burt demanded. "Get a move on."

I did as I was told, walking across to the nearest tower block after the other team members. As I passed through the door Dave Kemp was holding open for me, I glanced back to see Derwent walking in the opposite direction, his hands jammed in his trouser pockets. Una Burt was watching him go. The expression on her face was pure malevolence and I felt a little jolt of unease for Derwent, and for myself. I knew she was a good police officer. I was increasingly convinced she would make a bad enemy.

CHAPTER FIFTEEN

Stop when you get a result.

It had not been a throwaway remark of Godley's. We spent the night knocking on doors, standing in echoing hallways asking the same questions over and over again.

Did you see the shooting?

Did you recognize the shooters?

Did you see the person apprehended by the police officers before they were shot?

Did you recognize him or her?

Can you name the person who threw the firework and caused the van to stop?

Did you see anything strange before the shooting?

Did you notice anything unusual after the shooting?

Did you hear anything about a threat to the police?

Why do you think this happened here? And now?

Is there anything else you'd like to tell us

about the shooting?

Is there anything else that you think might be useful for us to know?

The questions stayed the same and the answers, dispiritingly, likewise. "No" came in a variety of accents and languages, it being London, but it wasn't hard to understand anyone. They hadn't seen anything, even if they had seen it all. They wouldn't tell us anything useful, even if they could. Black, white, or any color in between, they didn't trust us and they didn't like us. Most importantly, they didn't want their neighbors to think they'd helped us. I spent a lot of time in drafty hallways, my feet aching from standing for hours. The only positive aspect of the situation was that we had plenty of officers to help us knock on every door in the estate. That meant it only took an eternity to get through them all. We worked through the night, ordered to knock on doors regardless of how late it got. No one in the estate was sleeping anyway. The night was alive with the sounds and lights of a major-incident investigation, with cars and heavy vehicles maneuvering in the car park and the occasional whoop of a siren or shout from below.

I took a break at six in the morning — not my first, but this one was long overdue.

I had wanted to finish the corridor I was on, although I had very little to show for my efforts. I walked back past the closed doors, smelling the peculiar blend of pot, urine, and bleach that I'd come to associate with the Maudling Estate. The stairwell at the end was made of concrete perforated at random to allow in light and air. I went down three steps to where there was a gap so I could see the car park. I stood huddled in my long camel coat, shivering, as the crippled van was hoisted on to the back of a flatbed truck. White-suited crime-scene technicians steadied it, lowering it with exquisite care to settle on the truck. It had been covered with plastic sheeting, disguising the full horror of what lay inside it, but I wouldn't be able to forget the blood smearing the upholstery and running in rivulets across the floor. I wouldn't forget the big men stiffening into their death poses, awkward and outraged. You could read in their expressions that they felt it wasn't how their stories were supposed to end.

A movement on the right caught my attention. Brooding, his head down, Derwent strode across the tarmac. He didn't acknowledge the SOCOs, shouldering past as if they were in his way. It was such a typically Derwent attitude, when he had deliberately chosen to walk through their crime scene. I watched until he passed out of sight, seeing frustration in the line of his shoulders and the angle of his head. No weapons, I deduced. No luck anywhere.

Every instinct told me not to go anywhere near Derwent. Experience had taught me I would get the abuse he wanted to direct at Una Burt. As he himself had put it, more than once, "Shit rolls downhill, Kerrigan." That didn't mean I had to stand in its way.

I waited until the truck had left with its sad burden, then trudged down the rest of the steps to the ground floor. Someone had propped open the door at the bottom and I was glad. It took the edge off the smell of old rubbish and wee that filled the hallway. I was just passing the lift when the doors rattled open. Una Burt was standing in it, alone. She looked out at me, showing absolutely no surprise at finding me there.

"Maeve. Any luck?"

"No, ma'am. Not as such. Did you do any better?"

"No." She came out of the lift and stood for a second as if she was trying to decide what to do next. "Where are you going?"

"I was just going to have a break."

"I'll come with you."

Please don't, I thought, aware that the one thing that would send Derwent completely over the edge was if I appeared to be enjoying the chief inspector's company. There was nothing I could do to shake her off, though: she kept pace with me across the tarmac, hurrying to keep up with my longer stride.

There were still plenty of officers hanging around. It was almost the only sign by now of what had happened, since the SOCOs had cleared away the blood and broken glass.

"Do you think there's anywhere around here to get a coffee?" Una Burt asked me, her tone abrupt rather than conversational.

"I was going to ask one of the local response officers."

She looked past me and her expression brightened. "Charlie will know."

"Charlie," or as I knew him, "Superintendent Godley." It was an excuse for the chief inspector to get to talk to him — that I saw straight away. He was standing by a police Land Rover, leaning over a large sheet of folded paper that was spread out across the bonnet. It looked like a plan or a map of some kind. A tired-looking man in uniform stood beside Godley, gesturing at whatever was written on it. Derwent was on the opposite side of the car, looking down at the paper. Even as I spotted him, his eyes flicked up and rested on me for an uncomfortable second before his attention switched to Una Burt. He gave her the briefest of inspections before looking back down at the bonnet of the Land Rover, concentrating as hard as if he had twenty minutes and no more to decipher the Rosetta Stone.

"Do you think the boss will have had time to find a place for coffee?" I asked. "I'd have thought he was too busy."

Burt's jaw jutted out. "He'll know. Look, he's got a cup."

He did, and I'd seen it already. I was trying to think of any reason not to go over to the little group around the Land Rover, though. No good could come of it.

"Maybe someone got it for him. More than likely he got someone to fetch it. I can just ask this sergeant." I started to move toward the officer in question, but Una Burt ignored me. She headed straight for Godley. I considered going the other way but curiosity won out. It always did, for me.

"What's going on?" She stopped between Godley and the uniformed man, who on closer inspection was a superintendent himself. I drifted up and looked over her shoulder. The paper on the bonnet of the car was a plan of the estate with all the drains and access points marked on it. Someone had inked in the location of the van, with an X for each body and a star for each of the two survivors. A line showed the path one of the shooters had taken through the estate to make his getaway. On either side of that line, every hole and corner on the plan had a pencil mark through the center. Derwent's work. Potential dump-sites investigated and found wanting.

"Una, this is Bryan Enderby," Godley said. "He's the superintendent who runs the TSG." It was no wonder he looked exhausted given that five of his men were on slabs in Dr. Hanshaw's morgue.

She shook hands with Enderby, murmuring condolences. I hung back, making sure it didn't look as if I was trying to be introduced to him.

"Thanks for all your work. I was just saying to Charles, it's a relief to me to know you're all working so hard on it. I was able to say as much to the families, which was a help." His voice made me think of seaside holidays and Blackpool illuminations: warm Lancashire tones.

"We haven't made much progress so far." Burt wheeled around and delivered a brief report to Godley, who didn't look surprised.

"We're not going to get a lot of co-operation here. We knew that coming in. It's still worth trying."

"Of course," Burt said. "Maybe if we're here for a while they'll get used to us. They might even start to trust us."

"Watch yourselves," Enderby said. "This is not a safe place for police officers at the moment, if it ever was. My men were never happy about this estate."

"Why was that?" Godley asked. "Intel or just a bad feeling?"

"Mainly the latter," Enderby admitted. "But you have to consider the history with the teenager who was shot. There's a lot of resentment in a place like this about that sort of thing, especially since he was only a kid. They want to feel his life had a value. There have been loads of rumors flying around that the police investigation is going to go nowhere and Cole is just going to be forgotten about. I don't think it's true, but it's all about what the community believes, isn't it? They already feel they're on a scrapheap. They want to remind the world that they still matter."

"And what better way than by lashing out at the police?" Burt said.

"It was always a possibility. My men felt

they were being pushed in here to keep the lid on the estate. They were never happy about patrolling this area. The sergeant, Mark Grayson, actually told me he felt like a target here."

"But they hadn't seen anything overt to make them think there might be a genuine threat," Godley said. "There was nothing in the files."

"Not anything worth reporting. Rumors and looks."

Derwent cleared his throat. "So what you're saying, if I'm right, is that your men were made to come in here to show the community the police were watching them. You were discouraging protests before they even began."

"That's essentially how it was."

"It wasn't that they had a remit to come into the estate and hassle people, then. It wasn't that they were supposed to find the troublemakers and provoke them into a public-order offense at the very least, so you could take them into custody and get them out of the community."

Enderby looked pained. "*Hassle* people? I don't think —"

"You provoked them. Lots of patrols. Lots of heavy-handed attention. You wanted to get a reaction. You bothered the residents and came down like a ton of bricks on any sign of dissent."

"Where did you get that idea?"

"It's obvious." Derwent's eyes were cold. "No one got out of the van until they absolutely had to. No one looked surprised about the firework hitting the van and from what I've heard it wasn't the first time. Your guys were unpopular and they behaved accordingly. Public-order arrests have been way above the London average on this estate in the last few months. I had a word with some of the local bobbies and they said it was typical TSG stuff — assault on an officer but the officer has a graze and the arrestee ends up in hospital."

"What's your point?" Enderby demanded.

"I don't have one. Except that you're making them out to be victims, and maybe they were, but you sent them here to do a particular job and they did it."

Enderby's expression darkened. "It's easy for you to come in here and judge them after the fact. Are you saying they deserved what happened here?"

"If I was saying that, I'd say it." Derwent had tilted his head back just a little, that extra inch that made the difference between neutral and arrogant. In his own way he was just as critical as Geoff Armstrong had been, but he wasn't angry with the dead men. He was livid about the superior officers who'd sent them into harm's way. The phrase "lions led by donkeys" came to mind. And Derwent was never one to hold back just because he was talking to someone who outranked him by a long way.

"I've spent the last few hours with the families of the officers who were killed here this evening," Enderby said. "You don't even know their names, do you?"

"Would their names help me find the weapons? No? Thought not."

"That's enough." Godley sounded drained. His voice had no force to it. "Josh, there's a time and a place for analyzing why this happened."

"That wasn't what I was trying to do." Derwent stuck his hands in his pockets. "This might be all about the teenager who got shot. It might be about something else completely. Too early to tell. What we can tell is that the community turned a blind eye to whoever was planning this, and make no mistake, it was planned. They may even have helped. That kid who threw the firework was local, I'll bet. Your policy here created an environment where it was possible to kill a handful of police officers in one go, and no one tried to stop them.

That's on your shoulders."

Enderby looked pinched. "I take responsibility for my men. I've been doing that all day."

"And you're still trying to sell the 'poor us' line when you talk about it."

Even if Derwent was right that the circumstances had been set up for a disaster, he was showing off and I didn't like it. I looked away, across the car park, and saw a small figure walking fast toward one of the tower blocks. His hood was up and his shoulders were hunched against the cold morning air. Something about his size and his wiry build reminded me of the fireworks thrower. He disappeared through a doorway before I got more than a glimpse of him. Without saying anything to anyone, I stepped away from the little group around the Land Rover and headed in the same direction.

I was expecting him to have disappeared before I got to the door of the tower, and so he had. The door was closed but the lock was broken and I was able to slip inside easily. The door shut behind me. Somewhere in the building another door closed, like an echo. I stood for a second, listening to the silence. The light was out in the hallway, a broken casing split and shattered on the floor. I moved forward, orientating myself. It was a twin of the tower I'd been working in, except a mirror-image, with the lift on my right instead of my left. The smell was the same. The doors looked the same. The paint was green instead of blue, but equally scratched and graffitied.

There was nothing to show me where the figure had gone. The lift stood empty; he had taken the stairs, if he'd gone up. I went to the end of the hallway and pushed through the door at the end to check the stairwell for any signs of life.

It was a mistake; I understood that straight away. There wasn't one figure in the stairwell. There were four. I had no sooner pushed the door ajar when one of them grabbed hold of it and slammed it back against the wall. I was still holding on to the handle so I fell against it, off balance. Another moved to block the open doorway and my line of escape. The remaining two came toward me, one sliding down the banisters and jumping off the end, the other low to the ground. They were teenagers, anonymous in hooded sports jackets, with scarves across their mouths and noses. Two black, two white. All male. Two lean and graceful, one bulky with muscle, one short. None was the person I'd seen outside. For the second time in a few hours, he'd done his job as bait and then faded away.

Because I wasn't under any illusions about what had happened. I had sprung a trap, and now I was well and truly caught.

One of them pulled me away from the door so the big one could close it. He leaned against it, massive and forbidding. I wasn't going that way, if I ran.

"Get her bag." The order came from the smallest one, who carried himself like a boxer and scared the life out of me. His eyes were blue and utterly without emotion. He looked me up and down as one of the black teenagers made a grab for my bag. "What's a nice girl like you doing in a place like this?"

I ignored him, pressing my bag against my side with my elbow so the teenager couldn't get a good grip on it. They were young. This didn't have to be serious. "You'd better step back, all of you. The only thing you're getting out of this is trouble."

There wasn't even a moment of doubt before they laughed.

"You're the one in trouble." The words came out muffled through the scarf, but their menace was undeniable. The short one stepped closer and used a finger to pull the neck of my coat apart. My stab vest was

301

tight and uncomfortable around my torso but I had never been happier to be wearing it. "What are you? A plainclothes cop?"

"A detective."

"What do you detect?"

"Murders," I said, refusing to act as if I was intimidated. Someone would notice I was gone. Someone would come and find me.

"So you've seen a lot of bodies." It was the muscled one who spoke, the one who was blocking the door.

"A fair few."

"What's the worst way to die?" the taller white one said. "In your opinion?"

"I know," the short one said before I could answer. "If you were raped first. A few times. And tortured. If you really suffered."

"That would be bad." Muscles.

"Terrible." The other white kid.

They were passing the idea around like a joint, high on the power they knew they had over me. I was scared, even if I wouldn't show it. I generally felt invincible on the street, but it was a fallacy. Being a police officer didn't make me invulnerable. In these circumstances, it made me a legitimate target.

"We could do that, you know. Rape you. Burn you. Cut you up." The short one blinked a couple of times as he spoke. He was getting excited and that was properly terrifying. He leaned in so he could get good and close for the next bit. "Cut your titties off. Slit your gash, end to end. Throw you off a balcony when we were done with you."

He dug his hand between my legs, his fingers probing, and I twisted to get away from him. I was backed up against the wall with nowhere to go. Instinctively I shoved him away. More by luck than skill I caught him off balance and he fell back.

"Fuck, man." The leaner of the two black teenagers shook his head. "This is sick."

"She's shitting herself."

"No," I said, proud that my voice was completely calm. "But I think I'm going to have to leave you gentlemen now."

"You're not going anywhere." The taller white boy yanked my bag away from me and started going through it. "Radio, Ste. —"

"No names." The short one took my radio and stared at it. "Looks like a shit phone."

"That's basically what it is." I sounded as if I was doing community outreach. Anything to drag the situation back from the edge of the unthinkable, where we seemed to be teetering. "It uses a mobile signal."

"What does this do?" His finger hovered

over the red button near the top, the one that overrode all other transmissions and acted as an immediate SOS for an officer in distress.

"Press it and see," I said.

He thought about it. He almost did it.

Almost.

He threw the radio down on the cement floor of the stairwell and I swallowed my disappointment, the crushing weight of abandoned hope making it hard to breathe.

"Ma— Meeve Care-again." The lanky one was reading my driver's license, slowly, with difficulty. "What kind of a name is that?"

"Mine." I pulled the card out of his hand and slid it into my pocket, then took hold of the bag and tugged it gently. He let go. So he wasn't committed, and neither was the lean and agile boy who was swinging one foot as if he'd rather be playing football. That left Muscles and the one I didn't want to think about, the terrifying one, the one who would, of course, be the leader. I didn't want to give him time to regroup.

"I don't suppose any of you saw who threw the firework at the police van, did you?"

Four heads shook in unison.

"You wouldn't know who did it."

"Nah." The short one reached out and

touched my cheek with a hot, damp finger. He was sweating under his sportswear and scarf, and he was excited. "Look at her, still trying to be police. Give it up, you cunt."

"Back off," I commanded. "Now."

"I'm going to enjoy fucking you. And when I'm done, I'm going to call up all my mates and they're going to fuck you too." He laughed. "Here, you'll know. Can you rape someone to death?"

I looked at him without seeing him for a moment, feeling total panic rush through my body. I couldn't imagine myself walking away from this. One wrong move would be enough to make him attack. A look, a word — it would only take a tiny mistake on my part and I would be taken away. Hundreds of coppers were outside the door and there was no way a scream would do anything but get me beaten, then dragged into the lift or carried up the stairs. They would move faster than my colleagues. They had worked out their route. They had planned this, or something like it. Even if they hadn't expected to get a woman, they'd wanted a police officer of their own to torture.

They were doing this because they felt deprived, I thought, and felt the analytical part of my brain switch on again.

"Did you feel left out?"

"Huh?"

"You weren't invited to the party, were you? You weren't allowed to help. Too young? Not important enough." I snapped my fingers. "Unreliable, maybe."

"What the fuck you on about?" Muscles demanded.

"I'm trying to work out why you're doing this. I think you're annoyed because no one told you about the attack on the cops until after it had happened. It wasn't someone on the estate who planned it, was it? This was just a good place to kill them."

"I don't know." The small one was looking confused.

"You should find out. Find out why you weren't included. It's disrespectful, isn't it? Like they don't think much of you and your mates."

His eyebrows drew together as he considered it.

"This has been a pleasure, but let's forget we ever had this conversation," I said, standing up straight, away from the wall. I put my bag on my shoulder, ready to leave. "Now, if you'll excuse me —"

A hand landed on my chest and shoved me back against the wall so hard the back of my head connected with the bricks. The short one wasn't giving up easily. "Not fucking likely, bitch."

"I'm going."

"Like fuck you are."

Three of them didn't know what to do. I gambled on that and elbowed the short one in the face, pushing him back into the arms of the slender black youth. I pivoted for the door and collided with Muscles. The impact sent me reeling against the tall thin one, who held on to my shoulders. I pulled away with enough force to rip open the buttons down the front of my coat, which was actually a blessing. Without even pausing to think I reached in to grab my extendable baton out of my inside pocket. There was no room to swing the Asp, or time to make room, so I had to use it as it was, folded up. I held it in my fist, my thumb on the end to stop it opening behind me as I brought it down hard. It connected with Muscles' chest high up, just over his heart, and I dragged the end of the Asp down his sternum, pressing it into his body as hard as I could. It was appallingly painful, I'd been told in training. Certainly, Muscles put up no fight whatsoever. He crumpled to the ground, wheezing, in agony.

Which was fine, except that he was blocking the door.

I turned back to the others and racked

the Asp so it shot out to its fullest extent. "Get your friend and get going."

They didn't move. I hit the end of the baton on the door, as hard as I could. The sound was deafening and the wood splintered.

"I said, get going."

They weren't going to move. I had gambled and lost. One of them would realize they could take the Asp out of my hand easily enough, and use it on me if they thought of that. My arm muscles were vibrating with tension. The tip of the Asp was wavering as if there was a high wind in the stairwell.

By my feet, Muscles moaned.

"We can't carry you, man." The lean black kid bent down and grabbed his shoulder. "Come on. You have to walk."

The tall white one went to help, propping Muscles up against the door. "Come on. Let's go."

Which left the short one. He had to salvage something. I got a finger in my face. "If you give the people round here any shit we will come after you."

I didn't say anything. I just looked at him, as if we were equals, as if we understood each other. He nodded, once, and then the four of them disappeared through the door, into the waiting lift. It clanked and creaked up, stopping every couple of floors so I couldn't tell where they'd got out.

I took a deep breath, for the first time in many long minutes. It was cold in the stairwell but I could feel sweat trickling down my back I bent to pick up the radio, wincing as my lovely, wonderful stab vest dug into me. Losing the radio would have been a bad mistake, especially when it was unlocked and in use. Small mercies. I closed my Asp, banging it on the floor until it retracted into its neat tube. I was fine. I'd done just fine.

And then my phone rang. I got a hand to my inside pocket and answered the call in the same movement, paranoid that the sound would bring the teenagers back. Derwent's voice was tinny but loud enough to be audible in the stairwell even before I lifted the phone to my ear.

"Where the hell are you?"

I saw the front of the building in my mind's eye, the name painted above the door. "Barber House. I'm coming out."

I disconnected without waiting for a reply and then made myself walk instead of run as I passed through the hall. I looked normal, I hoped — I was trying for normal.

Even so, the first breath of the morning air felt like being reborn.

CHAPTER SIXTEEN

He was right outside the door, of course. I almost walked into him.

"What happened to you?"

"Nothing." I'd made a split-second decision to say that, but it felt right to me. No investigation would find the four of them: they had melted away like snow. I couldn't describe any of them in any meaningful way. I couldn't identify them. I was sure, from the way the ringleader had reacted to me, that they hadn't been involved in the shooting of the police officers. That was, after all, the point of our presence on the Maudling Estate. I was very much not keen to provide a side attraction in the shape of one dizzy female detective who walked through the wrong door unaccompanied.

Derwent had stopped so close to me he had to lean back so he could get a proper look at me. "What happened? What were you doing in there?"

Sound normal. "I thought I saw the kid from the shooting. The one who they stopped. Our suspect for throwing the firework. When I got inside, he was long gone."

"That explains why you booted it across the car park. Doesn't explain why you were in there for so long."

"I was talking to some other kids. About the shooting. They didn't know anything useful," I added, anticipating that he would ask.

"I see. And did you get their names? Addresses? Any details?"

"No."

"That's not like you, Kerrigan."

I couldn't look at him. I stared over his shoulder, concentrating very hard on not crying. I was aware his expression was severe. He moved closer, effectively shielding me from everyone else in the car park. Slowly, one by one, he did up the buttons on my coat, as if I was a child.

"You lost one." He held on to the edge of the fabric halfway down, where a triangular tear showed the button had been ripped away.

"I didn't notice. It must have dropped off. The thread was loose, I think." Which was an obvious lie.

"The button was there when you walked across the car park before."

"Then I must have lost it in there." I jerked a thumb in the direction of the building behind me.

"Do you want to go and have a look?" Derwent's voice was silk-smooth.

Nothing was going to get me back into that building. I tried to smile. "I won't bother. There's a spare."

"I've got a better idea. I'll go." He started to walk away. "Where were you? Just here?"

"Try the stairwell."

He was gone for a few seconds, then came back with it on his palm. "Easy."

"Thanks." I took it from him and dropped it into my pocket. My skin felt seared where the cold metal of the shank touched it. It felt like bad luck. I wanted nothing that reminded me of how scared I had been, how fragile.

"Are you sure you're feeling all right?"

"I just need a break, that's all. I've been here for hours. I'm freezing."

"A break," Derwent said. "Not a bad idea. You should probably also brush the dirt off the back of your coat."

I swiped at it ineffectually. "Thanks."

"All part of the service." He took my arm. It was halfway between affection and custody. "So is breakfast."

"You don't have to do that. Take me to breakfast, I mean. I can get something on my own."

"I know. I'm hungry," he said simply.

Derwent had a police officer's nose for a good cafe. The one he'd found was two streets away from the Maudling Estate. It was charmless, with fixed tables and chairs and a 1980s pastel theme, but the smell of frying bacon was a compelling reason to take a seat. We threaded a path through tables full of scaffolders and builders loading up for a day of hard manual labor, finding a table at the back. Derwent ordered two full English breakfasts without asking me what I wanted.

"Tea or coffee?" the waitress asked. She was retirement age, with egg stains on her apron, and she had a truly world-weary air.

"Tea," Derwent said.

"Coffee."

"Coffee for you, love. Okay." She shuffled off toward the kitchen.

"The coffee," Derwent said, "will be shit."

"The tea will be stewed."

"What's wrong with that?"

I shook my head. "Awful."

"All right. See what you get, Miss Fancy-pants."

What I got was rich and dark, a proper Italian coffee made by an antique Gaggia machine that had been hidden behind the counter. The waitress put the cup down in front of me reverently, with wrapped sugar in the saucer and a little jug of hot milk.

"How did you know?" Derwent demanded.

"All the pictures on the walls are of Naples." They were greenish and blurred, the years not having been kind to the color reproduction of various tourist spots. "I thought the owners were probably Italians, once upon a time. Worth a gamble, anyway."

"I'd still have had tea." Derwent knocked back half of his in one long swallow. It was so strong it left a gauzy scum on the inside of the mug. I could taste a ghost of the tannin on my tongue, and sipped more coffee to take it away.

The food arrived then, on big oval platters. I stared at it, overwhelmed with nausea. The egg yolks seemed too bright, the whites wobbly and revolting. The beans looked dehydrated. I cut into one of the sausages and watched the shiny fat run out of it.

Across the table, Derwent was eating with single-minded efficiency. He didn't even glance in my direction while food remained on his plate. When there was nothing left but a few smears of ketchup and two despised, sagging tomatoes he put down his knife and fork and leaned back.

"That's better."

"Mm."

"How would you know? You've eaten nothing."

"I had some toast. And bacon." It was still wedged in my throat, somehow. I sat up a little bit straighter. "The coffee was what I really needed."

"Is that right?"

"Wide awake now."

"So I should hope."

The coffee was actually making me jittery. I assumed it was the coffee, anyway. The alternative was that it was the look Derwent was giving me that was making me fidget. He knew I was refusing to tell him something. With unusual delicacy he had let it go earlier. I knew him too well to think he'd forgotten about it. The best way to head him off, I judged, was to annoy him about something else.

"What were you doing, having a go at Superintendent Enderby?"

"Nothing, really. Just pointing out that it wasn't all that simple. I'd rather start off with the truth than make ourselves feel good by pretending everything was lovely here."

"He wasn't saying that. He said Sergeant Grayling told him he felt like a target on the estate."

"Grayson," Derwent corrected. "And he was leaving out why they were targets, wasn't he? Not just because they were job, whatever it says in this morning's papers."

"Be honest," I said, impulsively. "Were you showing off to impress Godley? Or were you making trouble to show Burt she needs to watch her step around you?"

"Neither." The corners of his mouth turned up. "Or maybe both."

"You need to leave her alone."

"She needs to leave me alone," Derwent countered.

"You've made yourself into a challenge. Not a good idea with DCI Burt. She doesn't like to be defeated and she won't let you win."

"We'll have to see about that."

"Fine. Do what you like. But next time you and DCI Burt want to have a pissing competition, don't involve me.

"It wasn't my idea to involve you, if you remember."

"No, but you went along with it and you embarrassed me."

"I'm surprised you found that embarrassing." He folded his arms. "I've done much more embarrassing things than that to you."

"And I'm sure you will again. But it was humiliating to have the two of you scrapping over me."

"You should have been flattered. We both wanted you on our team."

"You both wanted to win. I was just an excuse for the fight."

"That's not true. I could have done with your help."

"You had plenty of bodies for your search."

"Yes," Derwent said with barely suppressed impatience. "But I wanted you. You're good at finding things."

"I pray to Saint Anthony. He's the patron saint of lost things."

He looked delighted. "Really?"

"He really is. But I don't."

"Damn."

I grinned at him. "You believed me."

"Yeah, well, why wouldn't I? You know I love your peasant superstitions."

"You are far more superstitious than me."

"That's neither here nor there," he said loftily, knowing that it was true. "Look, I wanted you to be on my team and Twat-flaps Burt did not. I was never going to back down without a fight, but I didn't mean to upset you. That wasn't what I wanted. Not at all."

He looked sincere. I felt my eyes suddenly swim with tears, to my horror, just because Derwent was being nice. "Well, don't do it again."

"I promise."

"Just make sure you don't."

Derwent shifted in his chair, irritated. "I promised. That means something."

"It means you said you wouldn't. But we both know you're a liar."

His eyebrows went up. The temperature in the cafe suddenly seemed to drop twenty degrees. "Explain."

"You let Superintendent Enderby think you didn't know the names of the officers who died last night."

"So?"

"So that was a lie," I said patiently. "You know the names. You probably know more than that. You probably know all about them."

"What makes you say that?"

"I know."

"You know."

"Yes. I got the sergeant's name wrong just now and you corrected me as if it mattered to you. There's no way you didn't find out all you could about the men who died." I motioned encouragingly. "Come on. Let's hear them."

He didn't want to prove me right but he couldn't stop himself. "Mark Grayson, aged thirty-seven. Sergeant. Promoted six years ago. Two children. Martin Wade, thirty-one, separated from his wife, two kids. Adam Levington, thirty-five, married, first child on the way. Jordan Makepeace, twenty-eight. Not married. No kids. Stuart Broderick, twenty-nine. Not married. No kids."

"Wade was divorced, not separated. It came through last week. And Broderick's girlfriend is pregnant. Otherwise, word perfect."

"You knew them too," Derwent said accusingly.

"I didn't say I didn't."

"I've taught you well."

"I didn't need you to teach me compassion for the victims of violent crime. Knowing who died is sort of basic, for a murder investigation."

"Yes, it is, but you'd be surprised how many people working on this haven't bothered to find out anything about them."

"I wouldn't be surprised," I said. "Una Burt didn't ask any questions about them at all. She's not big on human emotions like grief and empathy."

"She's a lump of suet in a trouser suit."
Derwent checked the time. "We should go
back. Might as well waste the day on the
estate as anywhere else."

"You think it's a waste of time."

"I do. I don't know yet why those officers
were targeted but I bet the answer isn't on
the estate. It was someone from outside who
set them up because you don't bring that
kind of shit to your own front doorstep. If
this had originated on the Maudling Estate,
that's the last place the shooting would have
happened."

It was a good point and I thought about it
for a bit. "Is it connected to Hammond?"

"I don't know."

"We've been looking at Hammond as if it
was personal. We assumed it was something
he'd done that made him a victim. Maybe it
was just the fact that he was a police officer.
On duty, off duty, a legitimate target."

"That's a cheery thought."

"It would explain why we've made no
progress with the Hammond investigation."

Derwent pulled a face. "I still don't think
he was an innocent policeman going about
his business. Look what he was doing when
he died. Look at the comments from his
colleagues."

"There aren't that many people who could stand up to the kind of scrutiny we give murder victims," I pointed out. "Godley always says everyone has secrets."

"I just don't like Hammond."

"That's so strange. Usually you like everyone."

"It's his memorial service tonight. You can go."

"Can I? Thanks," I said, not bothering to disguise the sarcasm in my tone. It would be just exactly what I felt like doing after spending the day on door-to-door inquiries.

"You're welcome." Derwent smirked at me for a moment, then got serious again. "I think we need to stay on Hammond. The boss may be distracted currently but I don't want him turning round and asking us what we've been doing about him when the answer is nothing."

"And the two cases might be connected."

"They might," Derwent allowed. "Bit of a coincidence, having two people with a grudge against the police and heavy-duty weapons to hand at the same time. But they don't feel the same, to me."

"The boss seems convinced."

Derwent snorted. "The boss would say black was white if he wanted it to be. He was determined to run this case and I don't know why. This is not a career maker. He wanted to get stuck with it. Do you have any idea?"

"No." But I had been wondering about it myself. "He's not himself at the moment, is he?"

"You've noticed."

"Maybe it's the divorce."

Derwent raised his eyebrows. "You say it like you don't know."

"Because I don't."

"Are you sure? He seems to confide in you more than anyone."

"Really, don't start." I tipped back the last of my coffee and put the cup on the saucer with a clink. "We should go."

Derwent didn't move. "I know there's more going on between you and Godley than you're prepared to admit. I don't know what yet, but I will find out."

"You're wasting your time." I was never going to tell him what I knew about Godley — how he'd been on the take for years, how he and the crime lord John Skinner had been hand-in-glove since long before I'd known either Godley or Derwent. Derwent, who had been Godley's right-hand man when they were hunting Skinner, who worshipped Godley with a blind loyalty that I found touching and very slightly irritating, would be pole-axed by the betrayal.

"Am I?"

"You are." I put my coat on. "Anyway, you have more important things to worry about."

"Like what?"

"Like the fact that we've got six dead police officers to investigate and no leads."

"Oh, that."

"Yeah, that."

Derwent rubbed his eyes. "Do you know what I don't like about all of this? It makes us look vulnerable. It makes it look too easy to turn us over."

"We are vulnerable," I said. "We just look intimidating because there are lots of us and we generally win in a straight fight."

"It depends, though, doesn't it? Because if we're too nervous to patrol the way we usually do, the scumbags own the streets. That's what happened during the riots in 2011 after the Duggan shooting. We ran scared and they knew it."

"That won't happen this time," I said with more confidence than I felt. "The courts dished out decent sentences after the 2011 riots. People have more sense than to try anything like that again."

"There's a lot of resentment out there about us at the moment. And I spent a bit of time with the response officers today. They're not happy about the support they're getting from the bosses. They feel like they're on the front line with no backup. If they don't want to put themselves out there because they don't feel safe, we will have a big, big problem."

"We're not in that situation yet."

"Not yet," Derwent agreed. "But it wouldn't take much."

I had the uncomfortable and unfamiliar feeling that he was right.

We walked back to the Maudling Estate together in silence, each of us occupied with our own thoughts. I was concentrating on looking calm — in control rather than wild-eyed and traumatized. On the whole, I thought I was doing well. It was simply remarkable what good coffee could do to put you back on your feet.

As we crossed the road to walk into the estate, I saw Godley in front of a collection of journalists and cameramen, giving an ad hoc press conference. Microphones and digital recorders jostled for prime position under his chin. We stopped too far away to hear what he was saying, but every time he fell silent there was a cacophony of questions from the reporters.

"That's the bit I couldn't do." Derwent eyed them sourly. "All they want is something to fill their two-minute piece to camera or five hundred words. They don't care about what happened here."

"You don't know that. Anyway, they have their job to do, like us."

"They should get a real job. Something useful." He frowned. "Wait, what's this?"

He was looking at a small procession that had begun to issue from one of the towers: people carrying white and red tissue-paper roses. Right at the front was a woman I recognized. She was tall and elegant, the bags under her eyes the only sign of strain. Her hair was braided in hundreds of tiny plaits, a look that had become her signature.

"That's Claudine Cole, Levon's mum."

"What's she doing?"

"Making a statement," I said. "I hope that prick Geoff Armstrong is watching. There isn't much he can teach her about making a point, is there?"

The group was about thirty strong and mainly composed of middle-aged women. They all wore white and red scarves, or small roses pinned to their coats. They gathered in the middle of the car park and bowed their heads as Mrs. Cole made a short speech, or possibly a prayer. Then, at a word from her, they laid their flowers on the ground.

"What's the deal with the flowers?" Derwent asked.

"Haven't you seen them? It's the symbol of her campaign. It's on all the posters."

She walked away from them a few paces and stood waiting for the media to finish with Godley. Half of them had drifted toward her already, and the rest followed within a couple of minutes. She had a low, carrying voice, and I could hear her clearly as she began to speak. She had a sheet of paper in her hand but she didn't look down at it.

"I wanted to make a statement with regard to what happened here last night. This dreadful act — the murder of these policemen — is an outrage. Our community completely rejects this kind of violence, especially if it is in Levon's name. We don't want to see any more innocent blood shed on London's streets. We don't want to see any more lives lost. It's not what Levon would want, and it's not what we want."

"Do you think this was a reaction to what happened to Levon, Mrs. Cole?"

"Are you worried about further violence and protests against the police, Mrs. Cole?"

"Mrs. Cole, are you concerned about the

delay in publication of the report into your son's death?"

Instead of answering any of the journalists' questions, she said a quiet "Thank you." Then she walked back into the center of her group of friends. They gathered around her, forming a physical barrier between her and the shouted requests coming from the media.

"Well, it's not often I lose an audience that quickly." Godley had come to stand between us.

"She had the home advantage," Derwent said.

"It was all about reclaiming the initiative from opportunists like Armstrong who are blaming the campaigners for making the estate unsafe. And I applaud her for it." Godley narrowed his eyes as he watched the reporters mill around. "I wish they'd be more critical about the kind of rubbish he's peddling."

"Did he get an easy ride?" I asked. I hadn't seen any interviews with him yet.

"Very much so. He's making a lot out of it."

Still moving with tremendous dignity, Claudine Cole led her group of supporters back inside. They left the flowers scattered on the ground, where the van had been. A cameraman, walking away, kicked a couple to one side.

"It was a nice gesture from her, but I don't think it will have any affect. If people want to riot, they'll riot," I said.

"And there are plenty of people who want to complain about us." Derwent looked sideways at Godley. "Think it's significant that this shooting happened here? Where Cole died?"

"Maybe." Godley's jaw was tight. "Maybe not."

"Another coincidence?" I had made the remark without thinking Godley might interpret it. I saw him flinch and played it back, puzzled. What did he think I meant?

"We'll have to wait and see." Godley turned to walk away. Over his shoulder, as he went, he said, "I don't think you'll have to wait too long either."

Derwent looked baffled. "What's that supposed to mean?" he asked me.

"I have no idea," I said. "And honestly, I'm not sure I want to know either."

CHAPTER SEVENTEEN

The memorial service for Terence Hammond was short, which was a good thing for me. By the time I made it to Kingston and the small church where the service was taking place, I was so tired I could barely drag myself into a pew. As the sole representative of the investigation into Hammond's death I couldn't allow myself to be seen yawning, so I adopted a stern expression and sat bolt upright in my pew. The ceremony was just starting when I got there, and I had found a spot near the back. It was a good place to be: I had a view of the whole congregation. There were a couple of hundred people there and I recognized a handful of them: the family, of course, and Dan West, Hammond's inspector. The pews were full of uniforms, both police and school. Superintendent Lowry was listed as a reader. I was surprised Julie Hammond had agreed to let him be involved. Maybe she didn't care any more. She had aged, I thought. Her face was thin, her eyes hollow, her cheekbones pronounced. She sat between her children, but Vanessa had left a very distinct gap between them. There was no question of her mother hugging her. I'd seen strangers on the Tube share more personal space. Ben was twice his mother's size, his bulk meaning that he took up all of the space she'd allowed for him and then some. Their shoulders touched but she didn't have an arm around him. I found myself wondering if Julie Hammond was actually cold to the touch as well as by nature. It was cynical of me, the product of tiredness and stress. It wasn't up to me to tell her how to be around her children, or how to grieve for a husband who had been far from perfect.

The memorial service was standing in for the funeral they couldn't have until Glen Hanshaw released Hammond's body. I wondered why it hadn't happened already. It worried me that the pathologist was working while he was so unwell. He couldn't possibly be giving the cases his full attention. More than that, I wondered if he lacked the confidence in himself to sign off on his cases. He had to be afraid he would miss something. I'd never liked him but I had trusted him. I wondered if Godley would remain loyal to him for as long as he wanted to keep working or if he would gradually come to rely on the other pathologists who handled our cases. Godley was a professional to his fingertips, usually. I'd seen him put his personal friendship with Derwent aside more than once to do the right thing for an investigation. I thought I could trust him to do the same with Glen Hanshaw.

If I could trust him at all.

Without a casket there was no focus for the proceedings. The choir from Vanessa's school sang hymns, and Hammond's colleagues shared out the readings. Superintendent Lowry waddled up to the lectern, vast in his dress uniform. He read badly, breaking the lines in the wrong place a couple of times, paying little attention to the sense of the words. The vicar was a woman, a cheerful gray-haired person who spoke at some length about what a wonderful person Terence Hammond had been, and how accepting of his family's sometimes difficult situation. It was code, I gathered, for what had happened to Ben. I thought of Julie Hammond's insistence that he had been in denial. As so often, there were two ways to look at the same set of actions. Julie

Hammond had not been inclined to give her husband the benefit of the doubt. The vicar was far more generous.

The last person to speak was Dan West, who walked up on to the altar slowly, his shoulders rounded. I was struck again by his colorless quality. Charisma was not what had earned him promotion. He spoke without notes, and briefly.

"Terence Hammond was a good colleague. A friend. A father. A husband. A police officer. All of these things were important to him, and all of these things made him important to us. He leaves a big hole in our lives. It's no secret that his death was particularly sudden and shocking. It is my intention and my goal to achieve some measure of justice for Terence, and for his family. The person or persons who brought about his death can be sure they will be found and punished, as the law demands."

It was about as close to an Old Testament-style cry for justice as the Church of England could accommodate. The small group of journalists who had made it into the church for the service wrote it down. I thought it would play better in print than it had in person.

Once the service was over, the congregation divided into two groups. There were those determined to pay their respects to Julie in person, and they queued the length of the aisle. I estimated it would take an hour to get from where I was standing to the front of the church. The alternative was to go out and mingle with the second group, the people who had slipped out as soon as they could, for a cigarette or a gossip or a quick getaway. Vanessa had gone like a shadow, speeding down a side aisle with her head down. I was more interested in where she had been going than in commiserating with her mother, I decided, and I headed outside.

The evening air was clear and cold, the light fading. A hum of conversation rose from the crowd in front of me. I always thought the best parties were after funerals: the living reasserting themselves after mourning the dead. I paused on the church steps to orientate myself, sorting out the scene into its various narratives. Uniformed officers in high-vis jackets were dealing with a couple of photographers who had got too close to the mourners. A gang of teenage boys stood by the gates — Vanessa's classmates, I thought. One or two were smoking, the cigarettes hidden inside their hands, fooling precisely no one. I looked for Vanessa and found her surrounded by her friends. They were all smudged eyeliner and big hair, watching out of the corner of their eyes to see if anyone was paying them any attention. Vanessa had her arms wrapped around a tall, lanky guy with matted black hair and sky-high cheekbones — the ex-boyfriend, Jamie Driffield. An ex no longer, by the looks of things. I wondered if Julie Hammond knew he was back on the scene. He caught my eye and glared back at me defiantly. What he was defying, I didn't know. It was Derwent who had taken against him when we interviewed him, not me. I'd just tried not to laugh as Derwent took him apart.

Someone came out of the church behind me and collided with me. I turned, surprised, to see a man on crutches. He shook his head.

"Sorry. I'm clumsy with these things."

"I shouldn't really be standing here," I said. "It was at least half my fault."

"Nice of you to say so."

"Truthful." I looked down at the narrow steps. "Can I give you a hand?"

"Probably easier for me to manage by myself, to be honest." He smiled, making sure I wasn't offended. "I could take both of us out with one wrong move. You're safer to stand well back."

I did as I was told and watched him negotiate the steps. It wasn't difficult to see why he needed the crutches. His left leg was plaster to the top of the thigh. He was attractive, despite the fact that he was balding and at least fifteen years older than me. He had cut his remaining hair very short, and his head was a good shape, which helped. He was tanned, solid rather than overweight, and he had a winning smile. He also looked incredibly familiar.

"Have we met before?"

"I don't think so. I think I'd remember." The smile again, this time accompanied by a handshake. "Peter Gregory."

Something clicked in my mind. "The PC who got run over in Lambeth."

The smile tightened for a second. "That's me. Quite the claim to fame."

"Well, that's why I recognize you. How's the leg?"

He regarded it with a comically rueful expression. "It only hurts when I laugh."

"No sympathy, then. When are you going to be back at work?"

"Months, they think. It was a bad break. We'll have to see how I can manage when the plaster comes off." The humor faded. "I doubt I'll ever be the same, to be honest. Light duties forever."

"You'll do fine. I have a colleague who got shot in the leg last year and he's practically back to normal. He was obsessive about doing his physio." But then Derwent was obsessive about many things.

"Just give me the chance. I'll do whatever I have to." He took a second, thinking about what I'd said. "Are you in the job too?"

"Detective constable on a homicide team."

A whistle. "Get you."

I laughed a little, but warily. I was expecting the reaction that I got: he stood up a little straighter and he turned the friendliness right down. There was nothing wrong with being a career PC, but I had gone far and fast, and Gregory wouldn't be the first police officer to have a problem with that.

"Are you here on business?"

"I'm investigating Terence Hammond's murder, yes."

"Any suspects?"

"We're working on it," I said smoothly. "Why are you here? Did you know him?"

"A long time ago. A long, long time ago. We'd lost touch."

"Did you work together?"

"On response. We were on the same team. This would be going back twelve or thirteen years." He looked down, considering. "Thirteen. God. Where does the time go?"

"Were you friends?"

"Friendly. We only overlapped for a few months and we were never crewed together so I didn't know him all that well."

"It was good of you to come, then."

"What, here?" He shrugged. "It felt like the least I could do. I was sorry to hear he was dead, you know? And I wasn't doing anything else, being on sick leave. Maybe there was a bit of being glad it wasn't me after my close call. That's as close as I've ever got to dying."

I'd been close a couple of times myself, but I wasn't about to share that with Gregory then and there. I nodded. "You were lucky, by all accounts."

"Very."

"Have they made any progress with your case?"

"If they have, they haven't told me."

"I'm really surprised they haven't been able to trace the car."

"Me too. I gave them a pretty good description, I thought. Then again, it all happened so quickly." He started to laugh. "I sound like every witness I've ever hated."

"It's hard to remember the details, especially when you're shocked and in pain."

"I got a pretty good look at the car as it

came toward me, I thought. I have a very strong image in my mind, even now." He sighed. "You'd think I'd made it up, if it wasn't for the broken leg. They haven't even picked it up on CCTV."

"We have a CCTV wizard on our team. He'd have found it."

"But I would have had to be dead to qualify for his attentions." Gregory smiled. "I think I'll stick with the detectives I've got."

I was about to agree that his attitude seemed fair enough when I was jostled, again. This time, it was someone going into the church. It was the student counselor, Amy Maynard, today in dark gray and purple. This outfit was just as shapeless as the one she'd worn before. She turned to apologize, looked up at me, and gave a start.

"Oh, you're the police officer who came to the school."

"Maeve Kerrigan," I said. "How are you, Amy?"

"Fine. I mean, I'm okay. There's such a big crowd." She looked terrified, her eyes huge. "I wasn't expecting this. I thought I should come along to give Vanessa my support, but I didn't want to approach her in front of her friends and she seems very . . . involved."

I cast a glance over my shoulder, in time to see Vanessa kissing Jamie Driffield with abandon.

"There's a time and a place for that sort of thing," Gregory said, shaking his head.

"Sorry, I should introduce you. Amy Maynard, Peter Gregory. Peter's a police officer too."

She shook hands with him, doe-eyed. "Do you work together?"

"No. I'm not that glamorous," he said wryly. "I'm just an ordinary PC, not a murder-squad detective."

"There's very little glamor in it," I said quickly. "And very little sleep."

"Are you busy at the moment?" Amy asked.

I shrugged. "People keep dying."

"You're investigating Terence's death," Gregory said slowly, then snapped his fingers. "Are you investigating the officers who were shot last night?"

"For my sins."

Amy's mouth was a perfect O of horror. "That was so awful. I couldn't believe it had really happened."

"It was unusual," I said, wondering why I couldn't make myself be nicer to her.

"I'm actually surprised it doesn't happen more often," Gregory said. "We walk around, unarmed for the most part, with minimal body armor and equipment. We have to be out in the community to do the job but we're not really safe on the street. As you can see." He gestured to his leg, and laughed. "I used to think I was immortal. Not any more. Maybe a desk job wouldn't be so bad after all."

I knew what he meant. I had been feeling all too vulnerable since my experience in the stairwell. As a result, I probably sounded more forceful than normal when I replied. "You can't allow yourself to think that way. You can't be a good police officer if you're afraid."

"I don't know how you do it," Amy said, reverent. "I'd be terrified."

"It's vocational," I said. "Like your job. We do it because we love it."

"What do you do, Amy?" Gregory asked.

"I'm a student counselor. It's very rewarding."

Surely no one had ever been so earnest before. I tried, very hard, not to be irritated. Amy had such a little-girl manner, though, for a grown woman. She was practically playing with her hair.

"I'm sure it is," Gregory said. He caught my eye and smiled again, and I found myself liking him quite a bit more than I liked myself at that particular moment. It was just unpleasant of me to belittle Amy, even to myself, for being devoted to her job. I had spent too much time with Derwent lately, and not enough time with more pleasant human beings. To make amends for thinking evil thoughts I asked her what I thought was an uncontroversial question. "Did you know Terence Hammond?"

In the light spilling out of the church, her face was luminously pale. "Me?"

"I gather from Julie that he did most of the school-related stuff for Vanessa. I thought you might have got to know him."

"Yes. I mean, I did know him through that," she faltered. "Vanessa's on the netball team and I help out."

"Did you play?" Gregory asked.

"A bit. I wasn't any good. I don't coach them or anything. I just go along to matches and help with the equipment and stuff. It's a good way to get to know the students instead of just seeing them for appointments."

"And you got to know Terence on the sidelines."

"I suppose so. He gave me a lift to an away match once. My car was in for a service." She blushed as she said it and I had a moment of blinding insight: a young woman who seemed to be more innocent than most, who wasn't married, who had nothing better to do with her evenings and weekends than to help out with a netball team. A young woman who was in awe of police officers and the work they did. A young woman who went red to the roots of her hair at the memory of a trip taken to an away match, time spent in the close proximity of the car with a man she had undoubtedly worshipped. A young woman who had turned up at his memorial service for no good reason, except to say good-bye.

Ben Hammond emerged from the church, a middle-aged woman guiding him by the arm. His carer, I assumed. He looked at me, blank-faced, then saw Amy. He didn't smile, but he threw his arm up and waved at her. She waved back.

"Poor Ben. He'll be devastated. If he even knows, I mean. It's hard to tell what he can understand but he loved his dad."

I tried and failed to imagine Amy Maynard in the role of seductress. I couldn't see her going in for it, somehow. She was too demure. The woman who had been with Terence Hammond had been a risk taker. Sex acts in a public place were not romantic, especially if they involved a married man, and I would have put quite a lot of money on Amy Maynard being a romantic.

"So you were friends with Terence Hammond."

"N— no. Friendly. That's all." She blushed again. "I mean, he was nice to me." She paused for a second, struggling to explain. "He was kind."

It was the most heartfelt and sincere tribute to the man I'd heard that evening. From what I'd learned about him, Terence Hammond had been a deeply flawed individual, but Amy had seen the good in him and that only.

As epitaphs went, I'd heard worse.

CHAPTER EIGHTEEN

I could understand why security was tight at the hospital where the two surviving officers were patients, but I couldn't help sighing as we approached the third checkpoint on our way to interview Tom Fox. Derwent dumped the contents of his pockets in a small tray for inspection.

"Remind me to leave everything in the car next time we're here."

"You should get yourself a handbag," I said, putting mine on the table ready for the constable's attention.

"Don't be stupid." Derwent was not in the mood for levity, I gathered. "This is such a waste of time."

"They have to protect the officers."

"In case someone tries to finish them off? Hardly likely."

"We don't know why they were targeted," I pointed out. "You can't assume it was random. Maybe there was a reason for that

TSG team to get shot up. Maybe one of the survivors was supposed to die."

"Kerrigan," Derwent said in a pained whisper. "Not now."

I looked up to see an elderly patient staring at us, wide-eyed, his knuckles white on his walking frame. I smiled and held up my ID. "Police."

"Put it in the tray," the bigger constable said. I did as I was told.

"Anyway, I'd say this is mainly about keeping the press out," I went on. "You know they'd love to get hold of the families, even if they can't get an interview with the men themselves."

Derwent nodded. "I do know. Bill Stokes' fiancée was offered five thousand by the *Mail* for her story."

I stopped for a moment to wonder at Derwent's ability to get the inside track on these things. "Did she take it?"

"She's holding out for ten."

"Good for her, I suppose."

"I'd prefer a copper and his family to get it than some bloody no-mark celebrity selling copy about their latest divorce." Derwent had passed the inspection and was deftly restocking his pockets: phone, notebook, pens, gum, paperclips, change, a fold of notes — because like many police

346

officers he was paranoid about card fraud and used cash for preference.

"I'm not so sure." I took my bag back from the smaller constable. He'd done an absolutely terrible job of searching it but I wasn't about to point that out. At least he'd been quick. I picked up the leather wallet that contained my warrant card and frowned as something crinkled. I flipped it open and picked out the cellophane-wrapped lollipop that was caught inside it.

"Is this yours?"

"Thank you." Derwent whipped it out of my hand.

"I didn't think sugar was allowed on your diet."

"It's not a diet, it's a training regime." He tucked it into the top pocket of his jacket. "So you don't think the families should go for a quick buck from the press."

"If you take their money, they own you. I don't think there's any amount of money that would make up for the loss of privacy." I was thinking about how easy it had been to ignore the offers I'd received from various newspapers to tell my side of the story the previous year, when Derwent had been shot while being simultaneously brave and a dickhead.

For once, Derwent was thinking along the

same lines as me. "We both turned down a bit of money from them, didn't we?"

"You might have struggled more with the decision. I think you were offered more than I was."

"That's because I was the hero and you came along for the ride." Derwent whipped through a set of double doors before I could reply, letting them swing back in my face.

I was preparing a riposte as I followed him, but I didn't get to use it. A small boy was running toward us, laughing, pursued by a gray-haired man. Outpaced and winded, he called, "Kian, stop."

As the boy hurtled past him, Derwent put out a hand and fielded him. "Where are you running off to?"

"Nowhere."

Derwent squatted down to be at eye level with him. "Just running?"

The boy nodded. He'd gone from giddy to serious. I thought he was five or six — young enough to need to run around a lot just to stay sane. The elderly man reached us and took the boy's arm.

"He's bored, I'm afraid. He's been here all day yesterday and today. It's no place for a child but his mother won't let us take him home."

The boy looked up at us. He had a lot of

dark hair and an impish face. "I should be in school but Daddy's sick."

"Poor Daddy," Derwent said. He looked up at the man. "Is Daddy Tom Fox, by any chance?"

He nodded. "My son."

I showed my warrant card. "We're here to talk to him."

"I thought you might be. He's in room 412."

Derwent stood up. I hadn't seen him so much as move his hand toward his pocket, but when I glanced down at Kian the boy was holding the lollipop.

"Thank you," he whispered.

"Be good for your granddad." Derwent actually ruffled his hair. I raised my eyebrows as we walked away and got a very discouraging look: one more thing never to mention again, I gathered. Derwent was always most ashamed of what other people would consider his good points.

We passed an elderly woman who was sitting on a chair in the corridor, watching the boy and his grandfather. I assumed she was Tom Fox's mother. She looked exhausted, and worried, and more than a little fed up. I knew how she felt. I'd sat in enough hospitals waiting for something to happen to be very familiar with the combination of stress and boredom that made it a particularly torturous experience.

Derwent paused at the door of room 412, which was standing open, and rapped on it. "Sorry to bother you. Mind if we come in?"

"Depends on what you want." Tom Fox was lying back against a stack of pillows, his face gray and, at that moment, unwelcoming. A large bandage covered his shoulder. He looked too tall for the bed and too wide, his arms bulging with muscle. His wife was standing by the bed, worrying at her nail varnish. She looked fragile, with big shadows under her eyes. She was wearing high-heeled boots and pale pink skinny jeans with a low-cut cream jumper — very clinging and feminine. Her hair was elaborately curled. I guessed she was the kind of person who put on her makeup to put out the bins. The near-death of her husband was no reason to let her standards slip.

"DI Josh Derwent and DC Maeve Kerrigan. We're investigating the deaths of your colleagues."

Fox swallowed. "All right. Come in."

"Not for too long," his wife said sharply. "You don't want to get too tired, Tom."

"I'm not doing anything else."

"Talking is tiring." She put a hand out and

rested it on top of her husband's. He shook it off.

"Stop it, Kelly."

"Sorry." Her eyes welled up. "I'm only trying to look after you."

"I don't need you to do anything. Look, just go and have a coffee, okay? Or take Kian home. You don't have to be here."

"I want to be here."

"You're driving me mad." His jaw was clenched.

Derwent cleared his throat. "Mrs. Fox, I promise we won't keep your husband talking too long. We really need to talk to him about the shooting. We've tried to give you as long as possible."

"Not that long. He had an operation yesterday. A general anesthetic. He's still recovering."

"Kelly, for God's sake. I can talk for myself. I'm fine." To us, Fox said, "Before you ask your questions, tell me what's going on with Stokesy."

"William Stokes? He's still unconscious."

"Shit," Fox said. "That's not good."

"Don't read too much into it," I said. "They're keeping him under at the moment. They have to wait to see how he gets on in the next few days."

Fox shook his head. "I can't believe it. All

the guys. One minute everything was totally normal. Then I see Wadey's head snap back and I'm thinking to myself, that's a bit odd, and I haven't noticed the windscreen is shattered too because I'm so busy staring at Wadey and wondering why he isn't moving and why his head looks so strange. They blew his face off." He said it in a wondering tone, as if he still couldn't take it in.

"Martin Wade was driving," Derwent said.

"Yeah. He always drove. They did him first. Then Makers when he was jumping out to help Brods and Stokesy."

I was keeping track without too much difficulty. Makers, I had guessed was Jordan Makepeace. Brods was Stuart Broderick. And Stokesy was William Stokes. I would have bet a week's wages that Fox's own nickname among his colleague was Foxy.

"Then the shooter came up close to the van for the rest of us. He went along the side, shooting. He was so deliberate. No nerves. Professional." Fox was sweating now. He moved restlessly against the pillows, trying to get comfortable. "Makers was still alive for a while. He bled out. If I could have got to him I could have helped him. I could have saved him."

"No point thinking like that," Derwent said. "You'll drive yourself mental second-guessing what you did or didn't do."

"I can't help it."

"I know." Derwent waited for a moment, respectful. "You said the gunman came up close to the van. Did you get a look at him? Can you tell us anything at all about him?"

"I can't tell you his height. I was inside the van so I'd only be guessing."

"We can estimate that quite accurately from the mobile-phone footage someone took of the shooting," I said. "Our problem is the quality of the recording is bad. We can't see much more than his height and build. Did you notice anything else? His coloring, or his hair?"

"I didn't get long to look at him," Fox said, thinking about it. "He was white. He had a hat pulled down low so I couldn't really see anything but his eyebrows. They were light brown but they could be darker than his hair. He could be fair." He swallowed a couple of times. "Could I have some water?"

His wife held out a cup with a straw in it and he drank a little.

"Could you see his face clearly?" Derwent asked.

"He had his jacket zipped up all the way, to just under his mouth. I could see his mouth, nose, and eyes. No chin, no jaw-line."

"And did you get a good look at the features you could see?"

"Only for a second. Enough to recognize him again, I think."

"What about looking at some pictures for us?" Derwent nodded to me and I handed him a folder. He flipped it open to reveal a stack of mug shots.

"Have you got suspects? Already?" Fox asked.

"Not exactly," Derwent said. He was shuffling through the pile, discarding anyone who didn't fit the correct description.

"Who are they, then?" He stretched to pick up one of the pictures Derwent had taken out and stared at it.

"Gunmen. People who shoot people for a living. We're not looking for someone starting out, are we? This isn't the kind of thing you'd do unless you were pretty confident about your abilities. You said it yourself, the way he went through you was professional." Derwent began to lay out the pictures on the table, as if he was setting up for a game of solitaire.

Fox struggled to sit up. His wife bent to help him and he snapped, "Leave it. I'm fine."

His attention was on the pictures, so he didn't notice the look on his wife's face. It was anger more than upset. I had always found it harder to worry about someone in hospital than to be the patient myself, pain and frustration notwithstanding. Kelly Fox might have looked like sugar and spice with a French manicure but there was more to her than that.

"Not him. Not him." As Fox went through the pictures, Derwent slid them off the table and replaced them with another.

"He's a possible." Fox tapped one image. "That's quite like him."

Derwent went very still for a moment, his expression unreadable, even to me. "Okay. Keep looking."

"Not him. Not him. Not him." Fox went back to the one he'd indicated before and held it up in front of his face. He was frowning with concentration. "I really think this could be him. Who is he?"

"A guy called Tony Larch." Derwent was sounding deceptively calm. I looked sideways at him, noting the muscle that had gone tight in his jaw.

"Does he seem like the type?" Fox asked.

Derwent tried to smile. "Not a very nice person. It would certainly be well within his powers. And he shaves his head. That might explain why you didn't see his hair."

"Well, I don't think it's any of the others." Fox slumped back against the pillows. "That's all I can say."

"You've been a big help." Derwent shuffled all the pictures back into his folder and handed it back to me. "Look after yourself, mate. Try not to stress about what happened."

"I can't stop thinking about it."

"You'll get counseling." Derwent grinned. "Of course, that's generally a complete waste of time unless you get a good-looking woman counselor. At least then you can distract yourself. Let your mind wander."

Fox glanced sideways at his wife, pulling a naughty-boy face. She didn't look amused.

"Can I ask a question?"

"Of course, Mrs. Fox." Derwent put his hands behind his back, so polite it was almost a parody.

"These shootings are a big deal, aren't they?"

"Yes, very much so. They're getting all the resources we can throw at them."

"So how come you're the ones who are here to talk to Tommy? Why isn't anyone important here? Why hasn't that superintendent been here?"

Much more than sugar and spice. Pure

steel, when you got down to it. Derwent didn't answer her straightaway and she waited, hands on her hips, her expression a challenge.

Fox groaned. "Come off it, Kelly. It's not a big deal. He's busy."

"And you're the only witness who was anywhere near the gunman. I'd have thought it was worth his while to come and talk to you. Every time I switch the telly on he's there going on about finding the gunman and keeping London safe and he doesn't even have the courtesy to come and see you himself. I'm sorry, I don't mean to be rude, but I don't get it."

Derwent stood up a little straighter. "The superintendent is running the whole investigation, Mrs. Fox. He delegates the different jobs to people like me and her." He pointed at me. "That's how it works. He can't do everything himself or it would take too long."

"I understand that. I'm not stupid." She had gone pink. "But you pick and choose what you do, don't you? You prioritize the important things. Isn't Tommy important?"

"Of course he is," I said. "I know the superintendent will want to talk to him himself soon. But just at the moment —"

"I think I can live without seeing the great

Superintendent Godley in person," Fox said, rolling his eyes. "You just fancy him, Kelly."

"That's not true. That's not what I was saying." The tears that had filled her eyes started to overflow. She shoved her knuckles under her eyes, desperately trying to save her makeup. I hoped she'd had the foresight to use waterproof mascara.

"Thank you for your time, Mrs. Fox." Derwent held out his hand to her and after a moment she shook it. "I'll tell the boss he needs to get his arse in gear, all right?"

She gave a half-smile, reluctant to be charmed. "You tell him."

"It's a promise."

Derwent waited until we had gone past the two constables and were walking down the corridor. "Did you recognize the name?"

"Isn't Tony Larch one of John Skinner's men?"

"He sure is. Last time he was in London he was doing Skinner's dirty work for him. Remember the Lithuanians?"

I did remember them, and the small terraced property that had become a charnel house. I flashed on an image of a body on a kitchen floor, a naked young man sprawled on a bed, a giant of a thug with the back of his head blown off. "They would be hard to forget."

"Niele Adamkuté," Derwent said and sighed. "I still think about her sometimes."

"I bet you do. I don't want to know the details, though."

Derwent glowered. "Not like that. Anyway, I've had a grudge against Tony Larch ever since. Not that I could prove that he was the one who killed them. But if you want a gunman to do a big job, Tony is the first number you'd call."

"If you can get hold of him."

"Yeah. Well, we may not know where he is, but someone has his contact details. Dangerous little fucker that he is. I know of nine unsolved murders that I'd say are definitely his and another seven or eight that he could have done." Derwent unwrapped some chewing gum and stuck it into his cheek, chewing rapidly, more agitated than usual. "He's never been convicted of anything big. That picture is fifteen years old. He got picked up in a Flying Squad round-up after a big armed robbery. He wasn't actually involved in it and they couldn't hold him."

"But if the picture is old, Fox could be wrong."

"Yeah. He came back to it, though. He

didn't say it was definitely Tony Larch either, which I appreciate, because Larch would look different now. I'd have been worried if he'd been sure."

"You still seem worried."

"I am worried. John Skinner has a life sentence and he's not going to get out, ever, unless he gets cancer and gets out on compassionate grounds. Last I heard, his whole crooked business empire was in the shit. He's the last person who should be out there looking for trouble by killing coppers. When the boss hears about this he's going to do his nut. You know they go back a long way. A long, long way." Derwent was shaking his head.

I did know. I knew that Derwent had first worked with Godley on gang crime. I knew that Skinner had been unfinished business for both of them until his personal life unravelled and brought him back from voluntary exile in Spain. I knew that Skinner had no principles whatsoever. I knew that being in prison didn't stop him from being an active criminal.

And I knew what Derwent didn't: that Godley had been in Skinner's back pocket for years.

I was still walking, but on autopilot. For once, I wasn't listening to a word Derwent was saying. I was thinking about Godley sending us to the hospital to interview Tom Fox, when really Kelly was right and it should have been him who called to see him. I was thinking about the superintendent's mood, so brittle it splintered into anger at the slightest knock. I was thinking about the strain in his face and the black dog that was riding him.

I was thinking about a message I hadn't been meant to see.

A warning.

And I was thinking about six dead police officers.

I was miles away when Derwent grabbed my arm and swung me around to face him.

"What's up?"

"Nothing." I blinked at him, shaking myself free from my thoughts.

"It's not nothing. You've gone quiet."

"Sorry."

He waited, letting the silence lengthen. It was a trick I knew he used, and I didn't fall for it. When he was sure I wasn't going to speak, he started walking again. "It's unusual, that's all. Generally, all I get is chatter chatter chatter. Takes a lot to get you to shut up. If there's an off switch I want to know about it."

"Right."

"*Right.* Is that it? Is that all I get?"

"Sorry," I said again.

"Fuck's sake, Kerrigan, if that's the quality of repartee I'm getting I'm not going to bother either." He walked away, head down, the dark cloud over his head more obvious than usual.

I watched him go. I couldn't worry about Derwent being pissed off.

I had bigger problems than that.

CHAPTER NINETEEN

I didn't get a chance to challenge Godley about John Skinner and the message I'd seen on his phone over the next few days. In all honesty, I didn't try that hard to create an opportunity. I was heavy-eyed from lying awake wondering what I should do. Mealtimes passed me by. I couldn't eat for the knot in my throat that was tension and lingering anger about the teenagers' attack on me. I wanted to do something — anything — to make sense of the murders, but actually saying as much to Godley seemed impossible. All I had was an instinct that Godley was struggling with something more than the responsibility for investigating these crimes. That and a once-seen text message wouldn't convince any of the bigwigs that Godley was bent. Then there was the fact that he was my boss, and that I was a very junior member of his team. I'd worked hard to establish some kind of relationship with him that skirted around the reality of his lucrative sideline. I'd come very close to leaving his team a few times now, sometimes of my own volition — often because I felt he wanted me to go. Talking to him about Skinner was guaranteed to open old wounds. Tying it in with the deaths of six police officers would pour handfuls of salt on top.

But I didn't believe in coincidences. And when it came down to it, I'd rather be right than sensible. Good for my integrity.

Bad for my career.

Anyway, I had a cast-iron excuse for not confronting him: he was never in his office. He was fully occupied on the front line of a battle we looked like we were losing. The first night after the TSG unit were shot up, response officers across the Met reported sporadic incidents of violence. It was like the first hints of a forest fire in the making: dry tinder smoldering here and there, flaring into flames with the least provocation. Fed-up young people on miserable high-rise estates. Gangs who had something to prove to each other and themselves. High-flying rhetoric about the Met's institutional racism on the television and the radio and all over the newspapers. A sudden, unwelcome awareness on the part of our adversaries that behind the uniforms were people, and that people could be intimidated, or hurt, or sent running for cover.

The incidents were too scattered to amount to riots, or anything like the disorder that had spread across the country in 2011. But the first night, there were twenty or so assaults on police officers, trouble on a small scale. The second night, there were seventy-three. The third night, the Met control room logged over two hundred individual incidents and all leave was canceled.

"Get off my television, you ranting fuckstool." Derwent flicked a paperclip at the TV in the corner of the office, where Geoff Armstrong was holding forth from the safety of the Westminster studio.

"The commissioner has requested permission to use water cannon against the civilian population for the first time in British history —"

"Although it has been used in Northern Ireland," the interviewer chipped in.

"Yes, in very specific circumstances."

And who cares about the Paddies anyway? I filled in silently. As usual, what was perfectly acceptable in Belfast or Derry would be an outrage in Southwark.

Armstrong was still going on. "Water cannon have never been used on the mainland in a public-order situation and it's a sign that these communities are out of control. They are full of bored youths who have nothing better to do than get into trouble. They have no reason to work. We hand them whatever they want and then we're surprised when they feel they're entitled to take whatever they like."

"But the riots in 2011 caused two hundred million pounds worth of damage and harmed London's reputation worldwide. The protestors or rioters or whatever you want to call them disrupted people's businesses, their homes, their livelihoods — isn't the commissioner bound to try to avoid the same situation occurring again?"

"The commissioner is looking for a magic solution to a problem of his own making. His men are too scared to do their jobs because of politically correct nonsense about human rights. This all comes back to Levon Cole."

"Oh, here we go," Derwent said softly.

"Levon ran from the police. He didn't do what he was told. He behaved in a suspicious manner and he paid the price. Now, I am aware the matter is under investigation by various bodies so I shan't comment in detail, but I think it is common knowledge that if he had done as he was told he would still be alive. There have to be consequences for not obeying the police, or there's no point in having a police force and we should all be armed so we can defend ourselves."

The interviewer was struggling to keep up. "But — but Levon Cole was an innocent teenager. Even the Metropolitan Police have admitted his death was a mistake and a tragedy."

"You say innocent. I'm not so sure." Armstrong smiled, as if to imply he knew the truth about Levon Cole. The truth was that he *had* been innocent, but you couldn't slander the dead. Armstrong could say what he liked. "The fact is, this debate has been hijacked by Claudine Cole and her supporters who have their own agenda. We need to deal with the reality of the privileged poor who are costing hard-working taxpayers billions every year. We need to look at why they are choosing to engage in antisocial behavior. We need to talk about what they need rather than what they want."

The interviewer sounded shocked. "Claudine Cole is surely in a unique position to comment on this issue, though."

"She's personally involved. Do not imagine that Mrs. Cole can stand outside this situation as an impartial observer."

"Go back to university and concentrate on daydreaming about shagging your students, you prick." Belcott looked across at Derwent when he'd finished, transparently hoping for a nod of approval. He didn't get it, but that was more because Derwent was lost in a trance of rage than because he disagreed with what Belcott had said. He was shifting from foot to foot like a lion preparing to spring.

"I'm losing patience with this git."

Una Burt paused on her way through the office. "We should count ourselves lucky that you didn't hit him when you met him. That's your usual technique, isn't it?" It was a nasty little dig, a reference to Derwent punching an attention-seeking advocate for fathers' rights in front of television cameras.

"Only when I'm provoked." Derwent gave her a thin smile that I recognized as trouble.

"I'll keep that in mind."

"You're safe. I don't hit women." His attention was back on the screen.

There was a quick whisper followed by a stifled laugh. I didn't have to look at Belcott to know that he had been making a comment about Una Burt and her femininity to whoever was standing nearest him. She knew it too. She was outwardly serene but her ears betrayed her, turning scarlet as if

368

someone had poured boiling water over them.

"I didn't think that you'd be tempted to hit me, Josh. I like to think you have more sense than that."

"Do you?" He turned to look at her for a long moment, then laughed, with that sudden easy charm that could be so devastating. "I don't think I have much sense at the best of times, but I promise you, you're in no danger. I'm not so sure I can say the same for Armstrong if I ever run across him again."

"Then we'll have to try to keep you apart."

"Can we turn it off?" I slid off the desk where I'd been sitting. "Who's got the remote?"

"I do." Derwent unfolded his arms, revealing that he'd been holding it all along.

"Why are you torturing us like this?" I asked.

"Know your enemy." Derwent muted the volume but kept staring at the screen. "The best thing about Armstrong is that he's such a twat. No one could take him seriously. And the kind of things that are coming out of the woodwork to throw things at us don't give two shits for him and his rigorous intellectual debate. They only want to cause trouble."

"It's just a question of whether they outnumber us, isn't it?"

"Don't even say that." Derwent shook his head. "We've got to win, every time, or we lose the game forever. They have to stay scared, whatever it takes. If that's water cannon, so be it. Personally, I'd use flamethrowers, but that's why I'm not the commissioner."

"That's one reason." Godley had come in without me noticing. He didn't wait for Derwent to respond, but disappeared into his office and shut the door behind him. I went two steps after him and stopped. All of the very good reasons why I couldn't and shouldn't tackle him started spinning around my head. Now probably wasn't a good time. Besides, everyone was loitering in the office. They would see me knock on the door, and go in, and shut it behind me. There were enough rumors doing the rounds without me deliberately adding to them.

Eventually, I was going to have to acknowledge to myself that I was just being a big coward.

Armstrong disappeared from the screen, replaced with a shot of a boarded-up house streaked with smoke damage. Derwent turned away from the earnest reporter who was standing in front of it and walked over to look at the noticeboard that filled one wall of the room. I went to join him. He was staring at the pictures of the five policemen who had died. They were pinned up beside the map of the estate he had used to search for the guns, still covered with annotations and angry crosses. Tony Larch's picture was further along, with a couple of others that I'd dug out of the archives and a description. There was an alert out for him across the UK but so far we had no confirmed sightings. He had come out of the shadows to kill and then faded away.

"Frustrating, isn't it?"

"Yep." Derwent rubbed his chin absentmindedly. "The boss still isn't convinced we should be concentrating on Larch."

I tried to sound casual, although I felt my nerves begin to jangle. "Still? Why's that?"

"He doesn't see why Skinner would want to be involved in something like this."

"But Tom Fox identified Larch, and Larch only works for Skinner."

"He used to. John Skinner isn't the man he was, though. Plenty of people trying to take over his territory, and those people have money. Larch would murder his grandmother for money."

"Has anyone asked Skinner about it?"

"No. We don't want him to know that we know he's involved, if he *is* involved."

"Clear as mud," I said, and grinned at the look I got. "So what's the plan?

"We've got some intel sources down in HMP Lithlow where Skinner is banged up. They're trying to spot how Skinner is communicating with the outside world. It's clear he is getting messages in and out but no one knows exactly how. Now is a good time to watch him. He's got to be running this one himself if it is him. He's not the sort to delegate. And he's exactly the sort to get a kick out of murdering coppers."

"Even ones who had nothing to do with locking him up?"

"Easier that way, isn't it? We can take precautions if we know we're on his list. The whole of the Met can't run scared, though." Derwent shook his head. "I wish I knew what had given him the idea to start this now. Maybe it was just getting Larch back from wherever he was holed up. Maybe this has been his plan all along and he was waiting for the right moment to set it in motion. Revenge for getting banged up for life. Payback for us for not rescuing his daughter. I don't know. I'm not a criminal."

I had some ideas. Glad that Derwent wasn't a mind reader, I wandered down past the pages and pages of death threats and lists of those who had made aggressive comments about the police in the past. I wanted to look at Terence Hammond's picture. It was pinned a little way apart from the others, but on the same board. He looked doleful, in the image — all the way out the other side of serious to plaintive.

"What are you thinking?" Derwent was standing behind me.

"That he's been forgotten."

"I haven't forgotten him."

"Maybe not, but we're not doing very well, are we? We can't prove that his death was unconnected with the TSG shooting. We can't solve it, either. We're stuck."

"Poor old Terence. Shot twice and no one cares. Maybe he should have been nicer when he was alive."

"Amy Maynard said he was kind to her."

"Kind?"

"That was the word she used. She was at the memorial service."

Derwent tapped a finger on his mouth, brooding. "Why was that?"

"To support Vanessa, apparently."

"You don't sound convinced."

"I didn't actually see her speak to Vanessa. But then Vanessa was a bit busy."

"What was she doing?"

"Jamie Driffield was there."

Derwent actually growled, very low.

"Your favorite person," I said. "I didn't give him your love."

"I knew I should have gone."

"Oh, thank God you didn't. You might have made a scene."

"I would definitely have made a scene. Were they together?"

I nodded.

"Fuck. Driffield is such a little toe rag."

"You seem more concerned than Julie Hammond was."

"That wouldn't be hard. Julie has other problems." Derwent rocked back and forth, his hands in his pockets. "I looked up what happened to Ben."

"Did you?" I was surprised.

"Guess who was driving."

"Julie."

"Terence."

"Oh." I considered it. "So, he felt guilty?"

"Probably. And I don't think Julie is the comforting kind. Might explain why he was in denial about the extent of Ben's — shit, I don't know what we're allowed to call it now. Handicaps. Disabilities. Limitations." He snapped his fingers at me. "You get the idea."

"I do indeed. Is that a motive?"

"For whom? For Julie? The car accident was a while ago. I'd be surprised."

"If she knew he was having an affair, though."

"If she did. Which brings me back to Amy Maynard."

"No." I was shaking my head. "Definitely not."

"Do we think she was in love with him?"

"Yes. Emotionally involved, definitely. Remember how defensive she was about him? How he couldn't possibly have been sleeping around?"

"What if that was because he was shagging her?"

I leaned against the wall, my hands behind me. "You think you're a good judge of women. Do you really believe Amy Maynard would have been sleeping with a married man?"

"I *know* I am a good judge of women and honestly, I think she's a virgin."

"Typical."

"What's that supposed to mean?"

"It's always one or the other with you. Virgin or whore."

"I'm just basing my opinion on experience. I have a fair bit, as you probably know, Kerrigan."

"I keep hearing about it."

Unconsciously, Derwent assumed an alpha male power stance, feet wide apart, arms folded. "If I had to guess, I'd say Amy Maynard is asexual. No interest at all in doing the deed."

"Is this because she didn't fancy you?"

"She didn't even look, Kerrigan. And not in an I'm-too-shy-to-make-eye-contact-with-a-man way. No reaction at all."

"Yep. Definitely asexual," I said dryly.

"Then there's the way she dresses. Jesus, she looks like a nun having a weekend off."

"You're almost certainly underestimating her. Under the ankle-length skirts and the fluffy jumpers she's probably wearing hold-ups."

"Like you, you mean?"

I watched the slow grin spread across his face and thought, resignedly, that I deserved it.

He snapped back to business. "I'm going to have another word with Amy, I think. If she did have a crush on him, she'd have been watching him. She might have noticed him being a bit too friendly with a teacher or a parent at the school. We're pretty sure he wasn't shagging anyone at work. That leaves the pub and the school, from what Julie said. I've said all along, if we can find the woman, we can find Hammond's killer.

Cherchez la femme."

"You always do," I murmured. "Don't you think I should speak to her?"

"No. You've had two tries. My turn."

"I think you'll terrify her."

"I'll be nice," Derwent said with a glint in his eye that was nothing short of concerning.

I was about to argue the point when the door of Godley's office opened and swung back against the wall with a crash. The superintendent stood for a second on the threshold, scanning the room. "Josh."

Derwent was beside him in a second. "Sir."

"Where's Una?"

"Somewhere. What's wrong?"

Godley swallowed. He was ashen and his eyes looked sunken in his head. "Another police murder."

"Where? When?" Derwent closed his eyes for a second, getting a grip on himself. "What happened, boss?"

"A girl. Young. Twenty-two. Emma Wells. Just a PCSO." The information was coming in staccato bursts, as if Godley couldn't form a full sentence or organize it in his own head.

"A PCSO?" Derwent said. "Shit."

I felt a chill race over my skin. PCSOs

377

were the lowest form of police life, less useful even than the volunteer Specials, who at
least had the power to make arrests. Police
Community Support Officers dressed in
uniforms and high-vis jackets, but their role
was strictly pastoral. They existed to replace
the bobbies on the beat that the public
claimed they wanted — a presence in public,
armed with a radio and not much else.
Many of them were young, putting in time
and getting what experience they could
while they waited for recruitment to reopen
so they could apply for proper police training.

"Where was this?" Derwent asked.

"Leytonstone." It was east London, out in
the suburbs.

"What happened?" I asked, coming closer.
Behind me, I was aware of the team standing up, moving toward Godley. There was a
hush in the room that was unusual.

"I don't know yet. We need to get there.
Local CID are securing the scene for us at
the moment."

"Was she shot?" Derwent asked abruptly.

"What? No. No, she wasn't. Stabbed, I
think. She was lured to an empty house and
killed. The neighbors didn't hear anything."
Godley winced, as if he was in physical pain,
just thinking about it. "Her sergeant went

looking for her when she didn't respond over the radio."

"How did this happen?" Derwent asked.

"I don't know." Godley looked across the room to where Una Burt was stumping in. "Una, a word. Josh, get a team together. Six of you for starters. Anyone we can spare off the TSG investigation."

"Right you are."

Godley stood back to allow Una Burt into his office and shut the door behind her. I stood where I was for a moment, staring at the blank, smooth wood. I wasn't really capable of moving from that spot. Not while I was being buffeted with wave after wave of regret and guilt. If I'd said something to him. If I'd put my career to one side and concentrated on doing my job. If I'd run that particular hare to earth — even if it was only to prove to myself that I'd been wrong and Godley wasn't implicated in any way — I might have been able to set Godley's duplicity to one side. Then I might have been able to concentrate on the TSG shooting, or Terence Hammond's death. Then I might have traced Tony Larch. Then I might have been able to keep this nameless young PCSO from walking to her death.

"Wake up, Kerrigan." Derwent's voice was rough. "Do you want to come along or not?

Plenty of paperwork for you to get on with here."

I wanted to be anywhere but at another crime scene where the victim was a police officer.

"I'll come," I said.

CHAPTER TWENTY

I'd always heard you should buy the worst house in the best street you could afford. That, presumably, was what the estate agents who were selling 23 Rossetti Road were hoping, because it had zero curb appeal. Rossetti Road was a mixture of prewar terraces and postwar redevelopment. Whoever had built the bungalows had stopped at four. Two had been bought and refurbished extensively. One was dated but in good condition. One, number 23, was a wreck. It was the worst house on the road by a mile, even without the rake of emergency vehicles parked outside it. It was tiny, just one bedroom. It would have been a 1950s homeowner's modest dream, but it looked as if it had been unoccupied for a few years. The front garden was overgrown with weeds. Even they looked dispirited, as if the soil was too poor for dandelions and thistles to thrive. The window frames were rotten, the paint flaking and peeling. Gray net curtains hung in the windows, their edges tattered.

"How much do you reckon they want for it?" Derwent was looking at the estate agent's board outside, which was leaning at a drunken angle.

"Too much. But after this, I'd say they'd take an offer." I followed him up the path and through the front door. It led straight into a living room that had no furniture except for an abandoned chair with a cane seat that had fallen to pieces. It also contained a large number of police officers, SOCOs, and a woman who was talking to Una Burt and Godley.

"Who's she?"

"That's Dr. Early, the pathologist," I whispered, suppressing a shiver. The air in the house was cold and slightly damp. There was a sweetish, musty smell that made me think of mice. I hoped it was mice. Mice would be all right. Where you had mice you didn't have rats, I'd always heard.

Having tried and failed to place Dr. Early, Derwent shook his head.

"She did a case for us last year. A woman in the boot of a car. The doctor was pregnant," I prompted him. "You were rude to her." As if that was enough to remind him.

"Okay. It's coming back to me."

I couldn't tell if Derwent was humoring me or if he genuinely remembered, but he made his way over to Dr. Early and waved a gloved hand. Shaking hands at crime scenes was never a good idea.

"So, doctor, what have we got?"

"She's in the bedroom." The last time I'd seen Dr. Early she had been round and pink and more or less on the point of giving birth. In her nonpregnant state the doctor was pale and thin, with the fidgety movements of someone who burned a lot of calories without even trying to. She touched the back of her hand to her forehead. "I was just saying, I think it probably happened around eleven this morning."

"That's specific." Derwent sounded dubious and the pathologist colored.

"I'm basing it on what her colleague told me about when she came in here and the last communication he had with her. From my point of view there's nothing to suggest that she was here for long before she was killed. Everything is consistent with eleven as a time of death. This is an unoccupied building and it's cold in here. Colder than outside, in fact. Based on her internal temperature I'm fairly confident about the timings."

"Have you seen her yet?" Derwent asked Godley, who shook his head. "What are we waiting for?"

"Nothing. It's just a bit crowded in there at the moment." DCI Burt moved toward the door and I followed, seeing a corner of a postage-stamp-sized kitchen with a bathroom beyond.

"Where are the others?" Godley asked Derwent.

"I made them stay outside. No point in everyone coming in here."

I was one of the lucky ones, I gathered, and tried to feel lucky. I wasn't all that keen on going through to the bedroom. Una Burt was tapping her fingers against her legs, which for her counted as jumping up and down. After a minute she ran out of patience and leaned into the kitchen.

"Can you make some room in there, please? The superintendent would like to view the body."

The sound of shuffling feet and rustling paper suits filled the air. Four SOCOs edged into the living room, pulling down masks and pushing back hoods. One of them, his hair sleek with sweat, was Kev Cox, my favorite crime-scene manager. He was imperturbable usually, no matter how awful the state of the body. Today, he was grim-faced as he nodded to us.

"Cover up before you go in, please. Shoe covers and gloves. Maeve, you need to tie your hair back. Don't touch anything. Don't move anything."

"It's not our first crime scene," Burt said, flashing a tight smile that meant she was annoyed.

"A reminder before you wander in there is better than a compromised crime scene," Kev said solemnly.

"Of course."

I had been quietly getting ready while Burt was getting her lecture. Kev nodded to me to go ahead and I went in on my own, feeling self-conscious.

The kitchen was pale green and looked as if it had been installed when the house was built. It was all rounded edges and circular handles. Some of the drawers were hanging open. They had dusted for prints already, and a fine mist of black powder blurred the edges of the worktops and doors. I passed through without stopping, glancing into the dark bathroom as I went. It was dingy and dated, like the rest of the place, and the smell of rodents was stronger there. Beside it, I found the door into the bedroom. The

385

door was open already, a technician's bag holding it in place.

It wasn't a big room — about the size of the living room, maybe eleven feet by thirteen. There were built-in cupboards and a radiator, a single window and a bare light bulb in the ceiling. And there was a body on the floor, accounting for the reek of fresh blood and the big, spreading stain on the carpet.

I hadn't been expecting it to be anything but bad, given the circumstances. I just hadn't expected it to be as shocking as it was.

The first thing that occurred to me was how young Emma Wells was, and how pretty. Dark hair, tied back in a small bun. An oval face. Hazel eyes. She was still wearing makeup, bright on bloodless skin — pink lipstick, blusher, smudged mascara. Small hands and feet. She looked childish in her big high-vis jacket. She looked as if she had been playing dress-up when someone had come up behind her and slit her throat.

I crouched down near her head to look closer and jumped as a voice spoke behind me.

"You can see a mark on her jaw where he held her head." Dr. Early pointed a gloved finger at the shadow on the girl's face. "Very quick. No sign of a struggle."

Her hands were open and relaxed, I saw. "She didn't even know, did she?"

"I don't think so."

"God." Derwent had made it past Kev Cox's checkpoint. He leaned over me. "No messing."

"One cut," Dr. Early confirmed. "He knew what he was doing. Sharp blade. He didn't leave it for us, I'm afraid."

"Look at the size of her. It's not as if she was going to fight back. How old did you say she was?"

"Twenty-two," I said.

Derwent's face was hard with anger. "What a mess."

"How did they get her here?" I asked.

"We think she was flagged down on the street," Godley said. He was standing in the doorway, well back from the body. "She was walking around the area."

"On her own?" I asked.

"She'd just qualified for independent patrol. Her sergeant said he wanted her to get more confidence. She tended to hang back a bit. Let him take the lead." Godley's voice was strained.

"Is he here?" Derwent asked.

"Outside."

Derwent started toward the door and Godley put out a hand to stop him. "Don't be too hard on him, Josh. Imagine how he must feel."

"I want him to tell me that himself."

"Josh!"

Derwent had already gone, shouldering past Una Burt, who exclaimed in annoyance as she stepped out of his way.

"I'll go with him." I stood up.

"Don't let him hit anyone," Godley said.

"Oh, right. I'll just stop him, shall I?" Nine times out of ten, I managed to rein in the sarcasm when I was talking to my superior officers. This was definitely the tenth time, and from the look on Godley's face, he knew he deserved it. I softened, very slightly. "I'll do my best."

I found Derwent in a corner of the living room, standing over the sergeant. He was gray-haired and his face was lined. His hands shook as he turned his uniform cap over and over, mindlessly. The PCSOs were managed by regular police officers; this sergeant, at least, seemed to take the job seriously.

"So I sent Emma out for a bit of a walk around. We've got a drop-in session in the local library this afternoon, at three — or we did. One of the things our neighborhoods team is always asked is whether we get out on the beat enough. I try to get my PCSO team out every day, at least for a while."

"Yeah, but you sent her out on her own."

"I did. She wanted to go. She wanted to learn." The sergeant bit his lip. "You know the sort of criticism they get from people. That they're no use. That all they do is go round in pairs talking to each other. The chat-to-kill thing."

Derwent nodded. He'd been guilty of that particular line himself.

"I wanted to make sure my PCSOs looked professional and behaved like police officers, so people felt they could trust them. That's the whole point of them being here. They're supposed to be support for the real police, so we don't have to waste our time on stupid requests from the public."

"And yet so many get through anyway," Derwent said dryly. "Tell me about Emma. What was she supposed to be doing?"

"Walking around this area." He took out his phone and showed us a map. "These five streets. Then we were supposed to meet up. She got through three of them."

"Anything happen?"

"Not that I heard." He winced. "She didn't like being on the radio much. Got intimidated. She had a little voice, you know. She got teased when she was on the open channel."

I did know. I'd had to get over that myself. The temptation to become gruff or remain silent was overwhelming.

"So what happened? How did you know where she was?"

"She called my phone to say someone had flagged her down to tell her his aunt's house had been broken into, giving this address. She told me she was going to check it out."

"With him?"

"She said he'd driven off and she was on her own."

"And then?"

"Nothing. She didn't call back. I waited at the corner of Buckhold Street and Granger Lane, which was where we were supposed to meet. I checked with the control room after a while to see if she'd called it in and they hadn't heard from her. They couldn't raise her. I called her mobile a few times and there was no reply. I walked around here about half past eleven, I suppose."

"Was the front door open?" I asked.

"Yes, but pulled to. No one was here. No car outside. I went through to the bedroom just to make sure she wasn't here and I found her." He swallowed, hard. "She was a good girl, you know. She wasn't going to make a police officer but she knew that. She was talking about going into primary school teaching. She'd have made a lovely teacher. Brilliant with kids. They all loved her. I mean, we all did."

His eyes were liquid with tears, all of a sudden, and I felt my throat tighten in sympathy. Derwent swore, quietly, which was as good a way as any of relieving his feelings. I drew him away to the kitchen, where Godley and Burt were standing, talking.

"Well?" Godley said, and I told him what the sergeant had shared with us.

"Lamb to the slaughter." Derwent folded his arms. "What do we think? Random, copycat, or connected?"

"Random feels like too much of a co-incidence," I said. "We've got two men acting together, which is what happened with the TSG team. She was in uniform, going about her work. She was a soft target, admittedly, compared to the TSG team."

"But it's a better choice of victim," Burt remarked. "The death of a vulnerable young woman is going to make a big impact on the public. Bigger than a middle-aged

sergeant or even a lot of fit young policemen."

"A better choice," Derwent said with ill-
disguised distaste.

"For them, obviously." She had bristled
like a cross porcupine.

"Right," Godley said, wisely ignoring the
pair of them. "Josh, go and brief the others.
Get them started on door-to-door inquiries.
I want to know everything that happened
today. More than that, I want to know every
car that has parked along Rossetti Road in
the last three weeks. Anyone strange who
was here, anyone out of place."

"I'll get Colin Vale to check with the
council as well," Derwent said. "See if they
issued any parking tickets. It's all residents'
parking around here. Someone might have
got caught out."

"Good. What else?"

"It might be worth talking to the estate
agents," I said. "They might have shown the
property to someone recently, or they might
have had a phone inquiry about it. You'd
want to be sure it was empty before you set
up to wait for your victim."

"Good thinking. You can do that yourself,"
Godley said. "Josh, get a move on. We want
to cover this area as quickly as possible."

Derwent gave me a look as he left, which

I interpreted to be silent disapproval that I had found a way out of doing endless door-to-door inquiries. It would have been unfair had I not fully intended to spin out my estate-agent query for as long as possible.

Una Burt waited until he was gone. "Charlie, that man is intolerable."

"Josh? He's not so bad." Godley sounded absent-minded, as if this wasn't the first time he'd had this conversation so he didn't need to concentrate too hard.

"I cannot work with him. He's rude, he swears like a docker, and he has no respect for anyone."

"He's a good police officer."

It was faint enough praise, I thought, and couldn't help chiming in. "He's not so bad when you get to know him. I mean, he is just as bad as you'd think, but you get used to it."

"I don't see why I should have to get used to it." She turned back to Godley. "I really think he'd be happier doing something more muscular. He'd enjoy working with the Trident lot."

Trident investigated gang crime and homicides linked with gangs; Una Burt was right to suggest that it was a good fit with Derwent's skills. That wasn't why she was suggesting it, though.

"I think if he wanted to join Trident he'd have done it by now," I said.

"Maybe he needs a little push." Her eyes were cold.

I turned to Godley, waiting for him to tell Burt to get lost. He'd brought Derwent on to his team because he liked him and enjoyed working with him. He knew Derwent was an asset, even if he wasn't the sort of person you necessarily wanted to interact with the public.

Godley was staring at the floor, his mind obviously elsewhere. The silence made him look up.

"Una, I know you are more than capable of dealing with Josh and whatever he throws at you. I can have a word with him if you like."

"I don't need you to tell him to be nice to me but I would appreciate it if you'd point out his opportunities for career development are far greater elsewhere. Because I'm not going anywhere, no matter how hard he tries to make life uncomfortable for me."

And that was it in a nutshell, I realized. She thought Derwent was trying to get rid of her. In a way, she was right — he'd have thrown a party if she decided to leave. But he'd accepted he had risen as far as he was likely to in the police. He wasn't prepared to put in the time and effort to toady up to the bosses in the quest for a promotion. Una Burt was worried that Derwent had his eye on her job, but it was making her paranoid. She wasn't actually getting any special treatment from him.

"I'll try to find the time to talk to him," Godley said.

"You don't want him to leave, do you?" The question came out before I could stop it.

Godley shrugged, not meeting my eye. "It's about what's best for him and what's best for the team."

"But you can't think it would be better for Derwent to go?"

"I must have a word with Dr. Early before she leaves. Excuse me." Godley walked out past me.

He hadn't given me an answer, I thought, unsettled. I wasn't sure what he thought about Derwent. Maybe it was just that Godley was upset about Emma Wells's death. I was on the brink of tears again, I realized, and wasn't sure why, except that there was nothing right or fair about a young woman dying horribly in a miserable unoccupied house and there was nothing right or fair about Godley letting Burt put the boot into Derwent.

Una Burt was in a different frame of mind. She gave a sigh of pure pleasure. "I don't think we're going to have to cope with Josh Derwent for much longer."

I mastered my emotions to reply. "I don't mind working with him."

"You're too nice. I'm not." She gave me a narrow smile. "I'm not going to be treated like that and just put up with it."

"He's like that with everyone," I said. "It doesn't mean anything."

"That's not an acceptable excuse."

"Excuse us, ladies. We're going to need to move you." The men from the mortuary van had arrived, carrying a stretcher. The bungalow was so tiny, they needed the rooms to be empty so they could maneuver their way around the corners.

I took the opportunity to escape the conversation and the cold, dank atmosphere of the house. Outside, it was starting to rain. I looked for my colleagues and saw no one except Godley, who was leaning against his car, reading something on his phone.

Just like that, something snapped. I marched over to him.

"Can I have a word?"

"Of course." He slid the phone into his pocket and looked at me with a frowning, quizzical expression, as if to say *I have no idea what you could want with me but I'll listen politely anyway.*

"In private."

His eyebrows went up. "Really?"

"Yes. I don't think you want anyone else to hear this." Somewhere deep inside I was shaking, but there was no sign of it in my voice.

Wordlessly, Godley opened the passenger door of his car for me. I got in and he shut it, then went around to the other side and got in. "Will this do?"

"This is fine."

"If this is about Josh —"

"It isn't. Except that I think you would quite like him to leave the team so you didn't have to worry about him finding you out."

It was a guess, but I saw it hit home. "Maeve, that's not true."

"I don't think you've admitted it to yourself yet."

He shook his head, but there was no conviction in his expression and I knew I was right.

"I wanted to talk to you about what's been going on." I wanted nothing less than to talk to him about it but I made myself go on. "Terence Hammond, the attack on the TSG, and now Emma Wells. We've all been looking for a connection and not finding it. But the connection is you."

"What?" He laughed, but without humor. "This had better be good, Maeve."

"On the Sunday morning when Terence Hammond died, you gave me your phone to look at his picture. I was still holding it when you got a text message and I saw the preview of the first few lines." I closed my eyes and could see it without even trying. "It said, 'Make no mistake you fucking cunt, you'd better change your mind or —' "

"That's enough." He sounded calm but his fingers were tapping on the bottom of the steering wheel. "You're jumping to conclusions."

"You'd been happy before you got the message. You've been miserable ever since. John Skinner's pet assassin was tentatively identified by one of the victims in the Maudling shooting and you won't acknowledge that he might be involved because you know he is. Who else has the audacity to commission these killings? Who else wouldn't think twice about it? You took John Skinner apart when you were working on gang crime, making your reputation by smashing his organization. He's been obsessed with you ever since."

"This is preposterous."

"Is it? I think it's preposterous that a Met superintendent would allow himself to be used by a gangster for years without anyone suspecting a thing. I think it's strange that you get a threatening message just after a police officer gets shot. I don't think it's the only one you've received either. Are they turning up the heat?" I leaned toward him. "Did Emma Wells die because you pissed off John Skinner?"

"You have absolutely no evidence to support that allegation."

"I know. That's why I'm asking you if it's true."

"Jesus, Maeve, this is completely inappropriate. I can't imagine what you think you're doing."

"I'm trying to stop another police officer from dying. Or two. Or five." I was watching him closely and I saw the flicker that told me he was worried about exactly the same thing. "What do they want you to do?"

I thought he was going to go on denying all knowledge of Skinner and his blackmailing tactics, but fundamentally Godley was decent, and honorable. He hated lying even if he was good at it.

"I told him I didn't want to give him information any more."

"Why not?"

"Because he asked me to do something I wasn't prepared to do."

"What?"

Godley's face was drawn. "He wanted me to give him personal information on the team currently working on taking down his organization. He wanted to buy or blackmail or threaten his way into persuading them to leave him alone. And I'd had enough. I couldn't stand to be involved in putting someone else in my position. The lying. The fear of being caught. The fear of giving him too much information when I was trying to avoid telling him anything at all. The fear of what he'd do to me if I let him down. I couldn't do it any more."

"So what did you do? Give the money back?"

"It's never been money, Maeve. I told you that before. I couldn't say no to him because it was too risky for the people I loved."

"And it's no less risky now that you've lost your stomach for it." I thought for a second. "Is this why you're getting a divorce?"

"I have to try to keep Serena safe. I told him I wasn't in love with her any more so he couldn't use her to punish me. I told him he'd be doing me a favor if she died." Godley was sweating. He looked as if he was going to be sick.

"What about Isobel? Just because she's planning to study abroad, do you really think she'll be safe there?"

"I don't think she's safe anywhere. He told me he'd never harm Isobel because he had a daughter too. Then his daughter died, and Skinner blamed me for not saving her." Godley shook his head. "My job has threatened the safety of the people I love most in the world. All I could do was try to persuade him that I don't care about them any more so he couldn't use them against me."

"So he found a way to force your hand."

"Total strangers. Colleagues. People who were in the job. Anyone. Everyone. You're all at risk, because of me. And every time one of you dies, it weakens the very foundations of the Metropolitan Police. We cannot do our jobs if we are living in fear, and I can't do mine if I feel responsible for that."

I regarded him with horror. "What information have you been giving him that you're so important to him that he'd go on a killing spree just to keep you in line? It's massively risky."

"What can we do to him? He's never getting out of prison." Godley gave a brittle laugh. "He loves that he has me where he

401

wants me. He knows how much I hate this. He enjoys that he can manipulate me. He's an evil bastard and this situation can only be good for him. The weaker we are, the easier it is for him and his gang to do whatever the hell they like. The harder he pushes me, the happier he feels. He's sitting there in his prison cell pulling all the strings, making money, making a mockery of justice and of me."

"So what are you going to do?"

"I've been thinking about resigning."

"He'll kill you."

"There are worse things." Godley gave me a twisted little smile. "Standing in there looking at Emma Wells' body, I found myself thinking my own death would be quite bearable."

"If you make him angry," I said slowly, "what's to stop him from taking it out on us? The Met, I mean? That's the threat, isn't it? Do what he wants or he'll make you regret it."

"Yes."

"So can you take the risk? What if he doesn't go after you but he keeps killing, to punish you. It's working well so far. After this, no one is going to be able to do anything unsupervised. No single-crewed vehicles. Reduced night patrols. We're going to be running and hiding instead of doing our jobs."

"So what should I do? I can't keep helping him but I can't quit either." Suddenly he slammed the heel of his hand against the steering wheel. "It's so easy for you, isn't it? Right is right and wrong is wrong. I fell into this situation and I can't get out. What the fuck am I supposed to do now?"

"Stop shouting at me."

"Come on, Maeve. You've got all the answers. How do I get out of this one?"

"I can't tell you what to do, but I can tell you this: you need to do something. Buy him off. Tell him you've changed your mind. Even if you do the wrong thing, it's better than nothing. This is not going to stop just because you want it to."

"Are you finished?"

"Absolutely."

"Thanks for your advice." He didn't bother trying to sound grateful.

I got out of the car without waiting for him to say anything else and slammed the door as hard as I could, which was both childish and stupid because standing nearby, on the pavement, was Una Burt. Beyond her, a little way down the street, I saw Derwent. They were both watching. They had little enough in common, but at that moment they had precisely the same expression on their faces: curiosity, speculation, and disappointment. I knew what they were thinking, too: proof that there was something going on between me and the boss. I swallowed the unfairness of it and it sat in the pit of my stomach like a ball of hot metal.

As a rule, I had murder on my mind. That day, I had it in my heart.

CHAPTER TWENTY-ONE

If the killers of Emma Wells had intended to cause a massive reaction, they succeeded. The newspapers and television were full of wise-after-the-event talking heads holding forth about how vulnerable the PCSOs were, and what a waste of time and money it was to have them out patrolling in the first place. There were pictures of Emma everywhere, culled from her Facebook page. She was heartbreakingly pretty in every single one, whether it was a pouting selfie before a big night out or a holiday snap, grinning in a cowboy hat. The fact that she was pretty shouldn't have made a difference but of course it did. The comments on newspaper Web sites and social media said it all. "Such a waste." "She had her whole life ahead of her." "Her poor parents."

Far more important, though less visible, was the effect her death had on the Metropolitan Police. The statistics should have been reassuring — there were 31,000 full-time police officers and 2,600 PCSOs out there covering an area of 620 square miles that contained over 7 million people. There was no reason to fear that the next attack would be close to home, but for the first time none of us felt safe. There were just too many of us across too large an area for all of us to be kept out of harm's way. It was common knowledge across the service, though fortunately unreported, that officers in certain areas had refused to patrol. Everyone was jumpy. In the week after Emma died, there were four times as many incidences of officers deploying Tasers. The armed response crews were constantly busy, chasing shadows and rumors and finding nothing. Everyone was waiting for the next killing. Everyone knew it wasn't a matter of whether it happened, but when.

In the office, things went on much the same as usual. The team were slowly grinding through the tedious detail of a proper investigation: the phone records so we knew who was in a particular area and when, the CCTV footage so we could match a suspect with a vehicle and trace their journey via automatic number-plate recognition. Pete Belcott and Dave Kemp and a handful of the others spent hours running through the background of every police officer who had died, looking for connections. It was awkward and difficult and depressing. The victims' professional past was under scrutiny but so were their personal lives and it was hard not to say the wrong thing when you were dealing with damaged, grief-stricken wives and girlfriends. And it was futile, anyway, I thought. They'd been chosen at random. They'd been easily trapped and showily killed, and it was all about proving a point to Superintendent Charles "God" Godley, but of course no one else knew that and I couldn't prove it. It would be my word against Godley's. He was too clever to have left any evidence of what he'd been doing, and he was respected, liked, and admired throughout the Met. I was nobody. And a nobody who was widely assumed to be having an affair with the man I was accusing.

So my colleagues kept looking, gathering information and organizing it, plodding through paperwork. Racing against time. Waiting. And I hoped against hope that we'd find Tony Larch before anyone else had to die.

I concentrated on the gun that had killed Terence Hammond, trying to trace its journey from Rex Gibney's garden to Richmond Park. I worked through an endless list of interviews, talking to members of the gun club and their friends. It was tedious but somehow comforting because it was so specific. The gun had existed. It had been used to kill Terence Hammond. It had been in Gibney's possession before it was stolen. I was determined to follow it from the sticky soil of the vegetable garden to the hands of the person who killed Hammond.

For his part, Godley kept his own counsel. I stayed away from him — I'd said all I had to say. He shut himself in his office for long hours, reading reports. He looked thinner and grayer every day, with circles under his eyes. He was always composed and in command of himself, but the strain was obviously telling on him. I could see into his office from my desk if the blinds were open and I watched him from time to time. When he was on the phone he leaned right back in his chair, sometimes putting one hand over his eyes, as if the effort of sounding calm and confident took all of his energy. More than once I looked away from the window into his office only to meet Derwent's sharp gaze. Of course I blushed, every time. If there was a way to make myself look more guilty or to confirm Derwent's worst suspicions, I generally found it. Neither Una Burt nor Derwent had asked me what had happened in Leytonstone, which was a giveaway that they'd both made up their minds about it. I tried not to mind, but I did.

One week exactly after Emma Wells's murder I walked into the office, shaking the rain off my coat. The contrast between the chill of the evening air and the warmth of the office made my face glow. I put my notes on my desk and stood beside it, peeling off layers of damp clothes.

Colin Vale stopped beside me. "Where have you been?"

"Surrey. Chasing a gun."

"Find anything?"

I shook my head. "Any news?"

"Not so far."

I could have guessed that from the way people were behaving. It was quiet in the office aside from a few murmured conversations and the busy hum of a printer. All around the room, people had their heads down, concentrating, but not with the suppressed excitement I associated with a breaking case. It was the tense determination of prospectors panning for gold, despairing and hoping all at the same time.

I couldn't sit down among them to write up my latest series of futile interviews. It was altogether too depressing. My hands were freezing and I felt chilled to the core. *Tea,* I thought, and went out to the kitchen. While I was there, Chris Pettifer came in with one of the newer detectives on the team, Mal Upton. Chris sat down at the small table, his hands behind his head.

"Make us a cup, would you, love?"

"You'd be lucky," I said, stirring mine to get every possible bit of strength out of the pathetic teabags that were supplied as standard. The leaves looked and tasted like the sweepings off the factory floor.

"I am lucky. Notoriously so." He turned to Mal. "One for you, mate?"

"Yeah, don't mind if I do." Mal sat down on the other side of the table. "Two sugars, please. I like my tea as sweet as you are, Maeve."

I gave him a look for that and got one back that started out as a leer and ended up as panic that I'd think he was serious.

"All right. But no complaints that it's too strong."

"Make a proper Irish brew, go on." Chris was grinning.

I took down mugs from the cupboard and refilled the kettle. "English people don't know how to drink tea. My theory is that they don't actually like tea. They just like the taste of milk in hot water."

"Get her talking about this and she'll go on all night," Chris said to Mal.

"I was brought up to drink tea that tasted like tea, that's all." I dropped the bags in with a flourish. "You'll notice I never ask you to make me a cup of tea, Chris. Why do you think that is?"

"Because I make shit tea."

"I couldn't have put it better myself. You, Mal, I don't know about yet, but I'm guessing you make bad tea too."

"Why?" He looked wounded.

"Two sugars? You might as well have a Coke and have done with it."

Mal was new enough to the team that he wanted to get everything right, all the time, and apparently that extended to making hot drinks. "Give us a chance."

"I might. Maybe. Sometime."

"Rather you than me, mate," Chris said. "I wouldn't want the pressure."

"Oh, for God's sake, it's just a cup of tea," I said. "How difficult can it be?"

"Very, apparently." Mal was looking daunted.

"Don't intimidate the new boy, Maeve," Chris said. "Give him a chance to find his feet first."

"I'm not that intimidating," I said. "I'm not intimidating at all."

There was a short silence broken only by the kettle coming to the boil. I poured the water in and turned to face them. "Am I intimidating?"

Chris held up his finger and thumb an inch or so apart. "Little bit."

"I wouldn't have said so," Mal said quickly. "Impressive is the word I'd have used."

"Thanks, Mal."

"Smooth." Chris's expression was pure disgust.

"I'm just saying it as I see it."

Eventually I left them to their tea and bickering. I was still smiling when I went back into the office, carrying my mug. As I walked in, I saw Derwent leaning over Dave Kemp's desk, talking to him in a low voice. His forehead was creased with worry. He glanced up and saw me, then straightened up.

"Kerrigan."

"What's wrong?"

"Where's your bloke working at the moment?"

It wasn't what I'd been expecting. I blinked, trying to remember at the same time as I was wondering why he wanted to know. The handle of the mug slipped a little so my fingers touched the hot china and I twisted to put it down on the nearest desk.

"I don't know. Somewhere south of the river, I think. Bexley?"

Derwent didn't reply and I glanced up, surprised, to see from his face that it was the wrong answer. Before he could say anything, Godley hurried out of his office.

"Have we got confirmation?"

Kemp looked up. He had his phone clamped to his ear. "Just waiting to hear, boss."

Godley swore, and even though it was under his breath I was shocked.

"What's happened?" I asked Derwent.

"We don't know for sure yet."

"Well, what do we *think* has happened?"

"Just wait."

"Sir —"

Derwent stopped me with an impatient hand waved in my direction. He was focused on Dave Kemp's face, as was Godley, so I looked at Dave too. He was listening to something carefully, his pen racing across the paper in front of him as he took down the details.

"Right. Right. Okay. So that's confirmed. And do we know the identity of the victim?"

I looked back to Godley to see his shoulders slump. He leaned back against the doorframe behind him as if his legs wouldn't hold him up.

"Another one?" Chris Pettifer came to stand beside me, the good humor absolutely in abeyance as the police officer in him came to the fore.

"So it seems." I was back to feeling cold, in a way that had nothing to do with getting soaked while I was out. It was fear, I thought, with a kind of hazy detachment. My brain seemed to be working too slowly. Why had Derwent asked about Rob? Why had he looked so upset when I told him where he was working? I knew the answer and I didn't want to know it. I was running away from reaching a conclusion, and I would keep running until I had to stop, until reality crashed in and made me accept what had happened.

Dave hung up and turned around. "That's confirmed. One fatality. They're not releasing the ID yet. It was a Flying Squad surveillance operation. They were in a car, sitting outside a suspect's address. A motorbike drew up beside them and bam, took out the passenger, then made off. Whoever shot him made them as cops, which is embarrassing for starters."

He was talking about it as if it was just another murder, the way we all talked about murders, with that levity that makes the job bearable. Derwent leaned down, his face very close to Dave's.

"Shut up."

"What?"

"Kerrigan's boyfriend is on the Flying Squad."

And everyone looked at me.

I was standing completely still, like a puppet waiting for someone to make it move. I wondered how this could have happened, how I could have been laughing and giving a lecture on the art of tea-making at the same time as my world began to spin out of control. I swayed, just a little, and Pettifer put his arm around me.

"It's all right, lovely. He'll be all right."

I looked around, seeing the shock on almost every face. They all knew Rob, except for some of the newer detectives. Most of them had worked with him. Many of them had mildly resented me for bringing about his departure from the team as a result of our relationship. No one wanted to hear bad news about him.

Derwent moved, then, as if he couldn't stand doing nothing for a moment longer. He came toward me and picked up the phone from the desk where I'd abandoned my mug. "What's his number?"

I took the phone out of his hand, pulling

myself together. "It's okay. I'll call him myself."

I turned away as I dialed the number, although I knew everyone was still watching me. I couldn't stand to see the worry harden on their faces as the phone rang once, twice, three times . . .

"Voicemail." I had listened to his message before I said it, to his warm Manchester-inflected voice suggesting I left my number. It was impossible that I wouldn't hear it again, for real. I hung up and turned back, looking for Godley. "Sir, it could be a long time before we get a name —"

"I'll take you." Derwent was jangling his car keys. He had already picked up his coat, and mine. "You'll need to go down there to find out what's going on. No point in waiting for them to get around to calling us."

"Yes, Maeve, you must go," Godley said. "Get a head start on us."

I followed Derwent out through the crowded but silent office, not catching anyone's eye. I didn't want to see their pity.

I didn't want to deserve it.

Chapter Twenty-Two

Derwent was almost completely silent as he drove down to Bexley, which I appreciated. He indulged in very little of his usual showing off but the unmarked car was fitted with lights and a siren and he used them wherever he could, slipping down bus lanes and edging across junctions in the teeth of the heavy evening traffic.

The rain slowed us down, of course. The windscreen wipers seemed to be sawing across my nerves as they swept over the glass in front of my face. I sat holding my phone in both hands, biting my lip. Everything suddenly seemed clear. I loved Rob more than anything, including my job. Especially my job, which took me away from him all the time. I wanted to be with him forever. I wanted to have children with him. I'd never been sure it was possible, but of course it was. I could move to a different, less demanding area. Something with regular hours. Missing persons, maybe. Murder investigation was a quick way to burn out, and I'd had my fill of it. Work didn't matter. Work was much less important than life. If I had a choice to make I would choose him, every time. I just needed to be able to tell him that. If he was okay. But he would be okay. There was no need to worry.

It wasn't difficult to find the place where the shooting had happened when every blue light for five miles had congregated at that spot. Derwent parked and got out of the car without waiting for me, running to intercept a small blonde woman. I recognized her immediately.

Inspector Deborah Ormond.

Rob's boss.

I watched them talking, trying to read what they were saying and failing. Inspector Ormond's response to Derwent's questions was tight-lipped and she was turned a little away from me. I had to rely on Derwent's expression to guess what was going on. He was frowning, intent. Unreadable, at least to me.

It seemed like forever before Derwent looked back to where I was standing beside his car and gave me a thumbs-up. Not Rob.

The relief swept through me with a rush.

I leaned against the side of the car, feeling weak and oddly numb. I would have given the moon and stars to know that he was all right, and now I did know, and I was glad — of course I was glad. But I couldn't recover instantly from the fear that had gripped me.

Derwent was doing his best to deal with Debbie, who was not one of his admirers, probably because they had had a fling that ended badly. She looked a lot less glamorous than usual. Her hair was scraped back into a messy ponytail and her makeup had gone, washed off by the rain or tears or both. She looked much older, suddenly, and I felt sorry for her. Losing one of her team had to be painful. She had the ultimate responsibility for them, after all. Derwent finished off the conversation with an actual pat on her back, which didn't seem to impress her in the least, and jogged back to me.

"Right. Debs says it was a guy called Harry Cromer. He's been on her team for three years. Good bloke, she said. Forty last year."

"I've met him," I said, shocked all over again. I remembered him well. He had had big ears and a goofy smile, but you underestimated him at your peril. More than once, I'd seen him win an argument with a remark pointed enough to draw blood. I'd seen him be kind, too. "He was a really nice guy."

"Yeah, don't get me wrong, I'm glad it wasn't your boyfriend but Cromer sounds like the kind of cop we didn't want to lose."

"There aren't all that many I'd spare." I leaned around Derwent, trying to see behind him. "Did she say where Rob is?"

"Somewhere in that lot." Derwent jerked a thumb at the maelstrom of ambulances and police cars that was blocking the street. "She said she'd tell him you were here."

"I bet she will," I said. Deborah Ormond disliked me and liked Rob rather too much. The idea of her doing me a favor was unlikely.

"Now, now."

"You know what she's like."

"Better than you do." Derwent grinned.

"I always forget you two have history."

"No, you don't."

"No," I agreed. "But I try to. I don't want to call it *romantic* history . . ."

"Nothing romantic about it." The grin widened.

"Quite. How was your little reunion?"

"Awkward."

"I thought you were going to hug her. So

420

did she."

"Jesus, no." Derwent shuddered. "You don't want to get that close, believe me. Not twice. Not when you've escaped more or less intact the first time."

My mood was all over the place. I was on the verge of hysterical laughter, and I knew it was inappropriate. I also knew it was shock. It could just as easily have been anger, or tears. And Derwent was fully aware of how I was feeling, talking more or less at random, giving me the space and time to recover. I squared my shoulders.

"I should go and find Rob, and you probably need to get started on this shooting."

"Yeah. Hey, Kerrigan —" I had started to move past him but he grabbed my arm to keep me where I was. "It sounds as if your bloke is in a bit of a bad way. He was running the operation. He was coming round the corner when the shooting happened. He just missed seeing the bike, according to Debbie."

I felt the pit of my stomach drop. "Oh no. Poor Rob."

"He's going to feel pretty shitty about this, even though it's not his fault. He was the surveillance commander. He put the guys in the car. He picked the location for the stakeout. If they were made, it's his responsibility, or at least he'll take it that way."

I nodded, looking up at Derwent, who seemed to have something else to say though he was taking his time about it.

"Look, I know what I'm talking about, okay? He's going to struggle."

"Did you?"

The response was instant: shutdown. "We're not talking about me."

"But you're speaking from personal experience." I remembered what he'd said about wives and girlfriends crying on his shoulders; I hadn't really thought about why they might need to.

"As I said, we're not talking about me. Just — just look after him, okay?"

"Of course I will."

Derwent nodded, his eyes not meeting mine. "Go and find him and take him home as soon as they let him go. Don't let him hang around. Get a cab."

"I will," I said again. This time, when I walked away from Derwent, he let me go.

I found Rob sitting in an ambulance and my first reaction was pure, instinctive panic, even though I knew he was all right. His clothes were dark and sticky with blood. I ran up the steps.

"Are you okay? Are you hurt?"

He looked down at himself. "It's not my blood. Harry bled all over me."

I had a sudden, awful image in my mind of Rob hauling his friend out of the front of the car and trying to save him as he lay dying in the street. I swallowed and went to stand beside him, one hand on his back. "I didn't know who it was. I just knew it was one of your team. I couldn't get through on your phone —"

"I think I left it in the car. Or the street." His voice was flat. He sipped from the cup of water he was holding.

"We should try to get it back before we go home."

He made a noise that could have been agreement, or could have been *you'll be lucky,* or could even have been *I don't care.*

"Everyone at work was worried about you," I said, needing him to know. "I was, a bit. At least, I was a bit panicky."

"Sorry." That affectless tone again.

"Why are you sitting here? Do you need to get checked out?"

"No. They let me wait in here because of the rain and the people staring at me."

"Do you need to give a statement or anything?"

He shrugged. "I've spoken to a couple of people already. I didn't see anything useful.

I heard the shot and I heard the bike accelerate away but I was too late when I came round the corner. I saw nothing."

"Was Harry on his own in the van?"

"No. Richie Saunders was there too. He gave a statement. Didn't see a huge amount, understandably. There were two of them. The gunman was the pillion passenger, as you'd expect. They were wearing helmets and by the time they drove off he was too shocked to take much in. If you think I look bad you should see him."

I didn't know if it was better for Rob to talk about it or try not to think about it. I was a long way out of my depth. I clung to Derwent's advice like a life belt. "I'll see if you can go yet. I want to take you home."

His head snapped up and he looked at me for the first time. "I don't want to go."

"I'm not sure hanging around is such a good idea," I said hesitantly. "Derwent said—"

"I really don't care what he said."

"No, but you should. He's been in this situation before. I think. I mean, he seems to know all about it. From the army. You could talk to him about it. He might give you more of the details. I just got hints and dark muttering."

"I'm not talking to him about it." There

was a real edge to Rob's voice and I stepped back a little, faltering.

"He might be able to help."

"He's the last person I'd ask for help."

"I know. I would have said that too, but I really think —"

"Maeve. Drop it."

I dropped it. There was no point in arguing with him. I sat beside him as various people came to talk to him: Godley, who was charming and sympathetic and ignored me; a couple of officers from the Department of Professional Standards who were less charming, neutral on the sympathy front, and ignored me; Debbie Ormond, who was extremely charming and made a point of including me in the conversation, and an apologetic Kev Cox, who took Rob's clothes and bagged them up, giving him a spare paper suit to wear.

"Now you really need to go home," I said. "You can't wander around in the rain wearing that."

"It's treated," Kev said. "Should stand up to a bit of rain. I wouldn't wear one to Glastonbury but then I wouldn't go to Glastonbury in the first place."

I smiled politely. Rob was stony-faced.

"I'm not going."

"We should go soon."

"No."

I waited until Kev had packed up and left.

"We can't just sit here all night. What are you trying to achieve?"

"I don't know." Rob folded his arms, crinkling slightly. "I just don't feel I can go home. It doesn't seem right when Harry isn't going to go home again."

"Harry's not here any more," I said gently. "The mortuary men took him away hours ago."

"I know."

"Look, this isn't easy, but you are going to have to go home at some stage. You are going to need to eat, and sleep. You are going to need to go on living."

Rob closed his eyes. "Not now, Maeve."

"Now, Rob. Right now. You need to get away from here and sort your head out. There are plenty of people here working to make sure Harry gets justice. You aren't helping them and you're not helping yourself. You need to get some rest."

He squeezed his eyes tightly, fighting back tears.

"Come home with me," I said. "Please."

I knew he didn't want to, but in the end he agreed and I thought it was a victory.

I was wrong about a lot of things, and that was one of them.

■ ■ ■ ■

Rob had a shower when he got home, washing away the traces of Harry Cromer's blood that had soaked through his clothes, all the way to his skin. I understood why he locked the door, and why he stayed under the running water for a lot longer than usual. In a quiet, unobtrusive way he was as proud as Derwent and far tougher. He didn't want to let me see him suffer, and it didn't matter that I wanted to help — that it was my turn to support him, for once.

I couldn't make him lean on me, so I made dinner instead.

He came out of the bathroom in a T-shirt and tracksuit bottoms, his hair still spiky with water.

"Are you okay?"

"Yeah." A glance at the cooker where water was boiling, ready for the pasta to go in. "I'm not hungry."

"I thought I would do it anyway. You might feel like having some later."

"You sound like your mum."

"That's fighting talk," I said, nettled because it was true. I was starting to understand how she felt, though. It wasn't possible to make everything right again with

427

food and comfort, but if that was all you had, that was what you offered.

He sat on the sofa and put on the television, hunting for a news channel.

"Do you want anything else? Tea? A drink?"

"I'll get it myself." He came back to the kitchen and found a glass and an unopened bottle of whiskey, stepping around me. I stirred the pasta sauce I had made, wondering if I could be bothered to finish it.

In the end I turned off the heat under the two saucepans and went to sit beside Rob. He was leaning forward, staring at the news, and didn't look at me when I put a hand on his back. The news, of course, was all about what had happened in Bexley, and when they got tired of repeating the very small amount of information and footage they had managed to collect, they went back over the previous deaths, with accompanying graphs and maps. They were better resourced than we were, I thought, and wondered if we could borrow some of their material.

After a while, I said, "Are you sure you don't want to eat anything?"

"I'm fine." He was drinking steadily but slowly, and he wasn't one to drown his sorrows usually. He rarely got drunk, or anything like it. He would stop before he went too far, I thought.

"Do you want to talk about it?"

"No."

"Okay. Well, if you change your mind —"

"I won't."

I stood up, feeling a little dizzy from hunger. In the kitchen, the pasta sauce didn't look any more appetizing. I made a sandwich instead and ate it standing up, watching Rob. He was still focused on the television.

"You know, I understand why you're watching that, but I don't know if it's the best idea. It's just going over the same ground. It's not going to tell you anything you don't know."

That made him look at me. "Maeve, with the greatest respect, fuck off."

I was so shocked, I stepped back and collided with the kitchen cupboards. "I'm just —"

"Shut. The fuck. Up." He stared at me for a long, hostile moment, then turned back to the television.

"I'm sorry."

He didn't answer me.

Something close to panic welled up within me. I had thought everything was going to be all right because Rob wasn't hurt, but life wasn't that simple. People weren't that simple. I just didn't know where to start with making him feel better. This wasn't how our relationship usually worked. I was the one who generally needed rescuing from whatever disaster I'd plummeted into, and I didn't seem to be equipped to help him now. He was upset, of course, but I had expected that. I hadn't expected the anger. And he was the sort of person who didn't get angry easily, but stayed angry for a long, long time.

"I think I'm going to go to bed." I said it gently, making it clear that I wasn't going off in a huff. "Don't stay up too long."

"Okay."

I lay in bed and listened to the TV burbling. Rob had kept the volume low but I could guess what they were saying as the news cycle churned. Headlines, reports, interviews, sport, weather, repeat. I don't know how many times I heard the same portentous music. I couldn't sleep, knowing that he was sitting there, suffering. I heard his phone beep now and then as a new message came through and I tortured myself by wondering who was texting him and why.

Eventually the sound of the television cut out. I heard footsteps come toward the bedroom but at the last minute they veered away toward the front door. I was out of bed and into the hallway before he had finished putting on his jacket.

"Where are you going?"

"Out."

"I don't think that's a good idea."

"I don't want to be here." He was by no means drunk but his movements were a little larger and slower than usual. As he patted the pockets in his jacket I congratulated myself on having removed his car key, and the spare, before I went to bed. He frowned. "Shit."

"Look, there's no point in going out. Please, Rob. Stay here. Stay with me."

I coaxed and wheedled and begged him until he took off his coat and followed me into our room. He lay down on the bed and threw an arm over his eyes. I lay beside him, my hand just grazing his, to let him know that I was there if he needed me. He didn't move to hold it, but then he didn't move away either. It was small comfort, but comfort nonetheless. I listened to him breathing, wondering if he was asleep, and at some stage I must have drifted off myself.

I came awake knowing instinctively that it was the early hours, guessing that it was around two in the morning. I had enough experience of being roused from a deep sleep to be alert instantly, but I couldn't sit up. It was cold air on my skin that had woken me, and Rob's weight on top of me.

"Are you all right?" I asked, and got a noise in response that I translated for myself: *yes but stop talking.*

He kissed my neck, one hand squeezing my breast, and there was something desperate about it rather than passionate. After a few seconds I pushed him off so I could scramble out of my nightclothes, as if everything was normal. When I was ready I turned back to him, leaning toward him to kiss him. Instead he pushed me back down on the bed and carried on where he had left off. I knew he wanted to escape his thoughts for a while, but I was too preoccupied with worry to respond to him. This wasn't about me and him. It was functional and joyless. From what I could see in the dim light his expression was remote. Uninterested, almost. And Rob was the most attentive, generous lover usually. But now, it was like being with a stranger.

This was what I was supposed to do, I thought, panic and guilt swirling in a toxic haze. This was all I could offer him. He'd done so much for me and I loved him so much. I owed it to him to be willing but I wasn't ready; it wasn't right.

He leaned on me then, crushing me. He

caught both of my wrists and held them above my head as with his free hand he pushed my knees apart. I felt panic flare inside me as he touched me and couldn't think why until my mind flashed up an image: the stairwell in the Maudling Estate. I could smell it, all of a sudden, and taste the coppery fear I thought I'd left behind there. The probing fingers felt the same: intrusive. Unwanted. I had made myself forget about it and told myself I didn't care but now it seeped back through my mind and body like oil spreading through a puddle. There it was, the feeling that I was powerless. I tried to move and couldn't and felt helpless, vulnerable. Violated.

"Wait."

He didn't listen. He was focused on himself, not on me. I winced as he moved over me. He was leaning on my hair. His arm was pinning mine to the bed, which was agonizing. The way he touched me was rough, not tender or even passionate. I caught my breath and he didn't seem to notice.

"Rob, wait." I turned my head, trying to make eye contact with him, but he wasn't looking at me and my heart just about broke. His face dissolved in a blur of tears as he pushed himself into me with a sharp, stinging pain. "Rob, please, stop. Just stop."

I don't know if it was the word or the note of panic in my voice but he pulled away and sat back, staring down at me. He looked angry, and hurt, and confused.

"What's wrong?"

I couldn't answer him. I put my hands over my face and cried, close to being hysterical. I couldn't seem to stop, or speak. I was aware of him sitting down on the edge of the bed, his head in his hands. Eventually I got it together enough to say, "I'm sorry."

"What's the problem?"

I wondered where he had been for the previous few minutes and how he could have missed it. He was waiting for an answer, though.

"I just wasn't ready."

It was the best I could do. I hadn't told him about the Maudling Estate, about being cornered and threatened. I hadn't wanted to hear about how stupid I'd been. Now didn't seem like the right time to bring it up. "I'm sorry. I feel as if I've let you down. I'm so sorry."

"Stop apologizing." He got up without even looking at me and started to pull his clothes on.

"What are you doing? Why are you getting dressed?"

No answer. He was the quickest person in the world at getting ready anyway, and by the time I'd sat up and focused on what he was doing he was halfway out the door. I went after him, throwing on a T-shirt of his that he'd left on a chair.

"Where are you going?"

"I can't do this now. I can't be here."

"It's the middle of the night."

"I know."

"Stay here. Stay with me." I rubbed the back of my hand across my cheeks, smearing the tears away.

He shrugged his coat back on, picked up his phone, and went out, shutting the door behind him.

I let him go. I had to. There was nothing I could say or do to keep him, no matter how much I wished there was.

CHAPTER TWENTY-THREE

"Where are we going?"

"You'll see." Derwent hummed happily to himself, driving his car, in control. I sat in the passenger seat and seethed. It was two days since Rob had left, two endless days, and if anything my mood had worsened over time.

"I don't like magical mystery tours."

"Tough."

I wasn't quite at the level of a black-cab driver but my mental map of London was pretty good after years of criss-crossing it to do my job. I guessed where we were heading as Derwent headed southwest.

"Richmond Park?"

"Got it in one."

"Why?"

"Wait and see." The humming got louder. It was his way of forestalling conversation, and a bloody irritating way it was too. I gritted my teeth and tried not to listen, which was difficult in a small space. It was even more difficult when you were trying not to think about a really substantial number of things, so you couldn't even drift off into your own thoughts.

An eternity later, Derwent pulled into the Pen Ponds car park and stopped the car and the humming simultaneously.

"Why are we here?"

"I'm not telling you yet. Come on."

With bad grace I followed him up to the side road to where Terence Hammond's car had been parked. The sunshine was watery, Turner-quality, and there was no heat in it. Fortunately, Derwent set a cracking pace so I was warm and out of breath by the time we got to the scene.

"So?"

"Come on." Instead of stopping he struck off through the woods, toward the sniper's site. I thought evil things about footwear, adequate warnings, and dry-cleaning bills as I picked my way after him, trying not to get left behind.

I caught up with him in the little clearing he'd found. He was leaning against a tree, his expression giving nothing away.

"Can we stop walking now?" I asked.

"Yeah."

I took a minute to get my breathing under

control. "Right. What are we doing here?"

"Two reasons," Derwent said. "I wanted to talk to you."

"Your desk is three feet away from mine."

"Not in the office."

"Why not?"

"Because I won't get anything out of you in the office."

I frowned at him. "What do you mean?"

"You've been a zombie for the past two days. I want to know what's going on."

"Ugh." I turned and started to walk away.

"Kerrigan, you'll get lost."

"I don't care."

"Come back and face the music. I am going to have this conversation with you sooner or later." His voice got louder as I got further away. "It's a long walk back to the office."

And he wouldn't drive me there unless I cooperated. *Shit.* I trudged back. "You've basically kidnapped me to make me talk to you."

He shrugged. "The end justifies the means. What's going on?"

"Remind me why you care?"

"Because you've been going through the motions and that doesn't work in this job. Emma Wells doesn't deserve it, does she? She should be getting the best investigation we can manage, not you being half-hearted and snappy."

He always knew how to get me. "So?" I said, but the fight had gone out of me and he knew it.

"So talk. Tell me what's going on."

I sighed. "Why would I confide in you?"

"You don't have anyone else to talk to. You're missing Liv."

"I have other friends," I pointed out.

"And you'd have spoken to them by now if you thought they could help. Either you did speak to them and they didn't help, or you need someone who understands your world. Someone who does the job."

He was right, annoyingly enough. I kicked at a fallen log, considering my lack of options. Obviously I preferred to keep Derwent at arm's length. Even more obviously, this was a delicate conversation about matters that were highly personal. But Derwent had been open with me in the past when he needed to be. He hadn't held back. And with his background — his experience of being the one responsible for a dead colleague in the army, his years in the police, and his slightly disturbing familiarity with the ins and outs of my private life — he was just about the best person I could talk to. I knew what my friends would say; they would be solidly on my side, even before I'd finished telling them what had happened. Derwent wouldn't hold back. He'd tell me what he really thought.

Derwent fidgeted, impatient. "Think of it as going to confession."

"Okay, definitely not. I can't believe I was even contemplating it."

"I'll absolve you of your sins."

"What makes you think I have sins?"

"Just a guess. You're usually harder on yourself than on anyone else. If someone had done something to you, you'd have shrugged it off by now. You haven't got over it. You feel guilty about something."

"You are making some pretty big assumptions."

"Come on, Kerrigan." Derwent's voice softened. "Talk to me."

I would regret it, I thought. I should run as far and as fast as I could.

"This doesn't go any further," I said.

"Cross my heart."

"And I don't really want to talk to you about it so don't push me, okay? None of your interview tricks."

"Would I?"

"Yes, you would." I took a deep breath. "Right. The thing is, I think Rob and I have broken up."

"You think."

"Yes."

"You don't know."

"I don't know."

He folded his arms and settled himself against the tree trunk, getting comfortable. "This is interesting. Go on."

"Yesterday morning, before work, I went around to Deborah Ormond's flat."

His eyebrows shot up. "How did you know the address?"

"I am a detective," I said loftily. "Rob walked out in the middle of the night. At that hour there was no public transport to speak of and I had his car keys so I knew he'd have to walk to wherever he was going, or get a cab. I went to our local cab office and made some inquiries. They told me where they'd taken him. I actually got the same driver so he was able to show me exactly where Rob had gone."

"Did you tell them you were a cop? Did they think you were asking for work?"

"Of course. They wouldn't have done it otherwise."

Derwent shook his head admiringly. "I wouldn't have thought you'd do that, Kerrigan."

"Well, I did. I didn't know it was Debbie's flat, obviously, but I wasn't surprised." I felt the slow swell of nausea that had been affecting me since the previous morning and tried to suppress it. I hadn't eaten anything. I couldn't.

"Did she let you in?"

"Of course. She was delighted. She couldn't have been more welcoming. She was very keen for me to see Rob sleeping in her bed."

"Whoa."

"Exactly."

"Sleeping, though. That doesn't mean shagging. You've slept in my bed."

"I wasn't naked and you didn't sleep in the same bed with me," I pointed out. *Thank God.* "It was completely obvious what they'd been doing. I'm not an idiot. I'm not jumping to conclusions."

"Are you sure?"

"Positive. She admitted it. I barely had to ask before she told me."

"What did he say?"

"I left before he woke up."

Derwent whistled soundlessly. "Does he know you know?"

"If she told him. I haven't heard from him."

"Fuck."

"That is a really helpful comment. Thanks for getting me through this difficult time." I started back toward the path again.

"No, come back. You're not finished."

"I think I am."

Derwent was too shrewd for that. "You've left out a big chunk of the story. The last time I saw you, you were on cloud nine because he wasn't dead. You were going to take him home and look after him. You're in love with him and he's mad about you. How did he end up in Debbie's bed a few hours later?"

"Don't ask," I said, using my I-mean-it tone of voice, which, of course, didn't work on Derwent.

"I just don't believe it. I don't know why you'd take Debbie's word for it. She's lied about it before. Maybe it was all innocent."

I shook my head, annoyed at the tightening in my throat that told me I was getting close to crying, again. I wasn't going to tell Derwent about the way the flat had smelled of stale sweat and wine dregs, or the condom wrappers on the bedside table, or the scrapes on Rob's back from Debbie's long nails.

"So now you hate him, is that it?"

"No. I want him to come back. I don't blame him. They'd had most of three bottles of wine, by the looks of things. She got him drunk and took advantage of him. I know

443

he was upset when he left our flat. He wasn't thinking straight."

"Why did he leave?"

I looked at Derwent with pure loathing. "You came back to that one."

"Trained interrogator. I can't switch it off."

"Try."

No chance. "Why did he leave? Did you have a fight?"

"No." I hesitated, trying to find a neutral way to put it. "I let him down."

He tilted his head to one side, intrigued. "How?"

"I can't talk to you about this," I said flatly. "There's no way."

"Who else are you going to talk to? Come on, this is the thing that bothers you. You talked about Rob shagging Debbie like it was nothing and now you've clammed up again. Get it out."

I walked around in a tiny circle, feeling trapped.

"Whatever it is, it's not as bad as you think it is."

"You don't know that," I said.

"You hold yourself to a high standard, which is something I happen to appreciate in a woman. I'm interested to hear what counts as letting your boyfriend down."

"Stop joking about it," I said hopelessly. I turned my face away so I could blot the tears away against the back of my hand. When I turned back again, it was as if I'd flipped a switch. Derwent had been relaxed, leaning back, amused and curious and infinitely mocking. Now he had straightened up and he was watching me with the focus of a hunter.

"Tell me."

"I don't want anyone to know what happened."

"Why not?"

"I think people might misinterpret what happened and it wouldn't be fair."

"Fair to whom?" Derwent's patience never lasted all that long. "For God's sake, Kerrigan, I'd get straighter answers from a Jesuit. Just tell me what happened."

I wavered. On the one hand, hideous embarrassment. On the other, getting a man's perspective might not be such a bad idea. Derwent was nothing if not experienced, after all, and brutally frank. He would tell me what he thought without sparing my feelings.

I sat down on a tree stump, folded the skirt of my coat around my knees and told him everything, without looking at him once. In short terse sentences I described how Rob had been that night, and how I had tried to do and say the right thing, and how I had failed. Then I told him what had happened in the middle of the night.

"And I got upset. It wasn't . . . It wasn't what I wanted, or how I wanted it."

"Did he rape you?" he asked. It was a policeman's question, trying to define what had happened in a technical, legal sense. There was no outrage in his voice and that made it easier, somehow, to answer the question I'd asked myself.

"No. Definitely not. He'd been drinking a lot and he was really upset. He wasn't being rough with me deliberately. He stopped the second I told him to. It was just bad." I went back to looking at the leaves in front of me. "It was my fault. I wasn't in the right frame of mind. I got panicked. I felt trapped."

"Why would you panic? You said he stopped when you told him to. You must have known he would."

"Yes, I knew he would, but I still felt like I was depending on him to do what I asked. There was nothing I could do if he didn't. I just got into a state." My heart was thumping as if I'd been running. I only seemed to be able to take shallow, gulping breaths that didn't give me enough air. Back to feeling trapped. Back to feeling vulnerable and pathetic.

"That's not like you, Kerrigan."

"I know. I — I had a bad experience." Why was this harder to talk about than how my relationship had fallen apart?

"Recently?" Derwent suggested.

"On the Maudling Estate."

"I knew it." Pure triumph. For Derwent, there was nothing better than the high of being right. He'd waited for this, like the cat by the mouse hole.

"Of course you knew," I snapped. "I didn't want to talk about it then, and I don't want to talk about it now. I'm just explaining the context, that's all."

"Did some little shitbag try it on with you?"

I shook my head. Then, because he wouldn't have let it drop, "Four of them."

"In the stairwell, where I found your button."

"Yes."

Derwent's face darkened. "What happened?"

"They cornered me and threatened me with various horrible things. I scared them off. The end. I just wanted to forget about it afterward and I thought I had, but it just — came back."

"Trauma is like that."

"Let's not overstate it. I was fine."

"Bullshit." Just for a second I caught a flash of the blazing anger inside Derwent. "You walked out of there looking like a ghost. I should have made you tell me what happened. I should have insisted."

"I wouldn't have told you. It was over. I dealt with it. I got myself into trouble and I got myself out of it."

"And now you're completely fine," he said softly. "You didn't think it should be investigated?"

"I thought it would waste time and divert resources that were needed elsewhere."

"You didn't think you needed counseling?"

I laughed. "*You* think I should have had counseling? Is this the devil quoting scripture? You think it's bollocks."

"It doesn't work for me. It might work for you. I can arrange it for you, if you like."

"No."

"Kerrigan, when are you going to learn that it's okay to ask for help? You can't always deal with things on your own."

"You are a fine one to talk."

He took a step toward me, jabbing a finger for emphasis. "When I was in real trouble, I came to you."

"You used me to get the inside track on

an investigation you should have known nothing about."

"Yeah, all right, but that was still me asking you for help." The anger faded out of his face, replaced by something that looked a lot like affection. "And you did help me, and I was grateful."

I was increasingly immune to the shouting and the sarcasm. It was always, always when Derwent was nice to me that it got under my defenses. I put my hand over my eyes so I didn't have to look at him as I cried. They were proper, heaving sobs, the kind you can't hide, the kind that generate torrents of snot and end up in red-nosed hiccups. I had tissues in my pocket, thankfully, so I wasn't reduced to wiping my nose on my sleeve. That was as close as I got to keeping my dignity.

When I finally got control of myself and dared to look at Derwent again, he was staring into the middle distance, rocking back and forth on the balls of his feet.

"Sorry, am I boring you?"

"A bit," he admitted. "Finished?"

"For now." I blew my nose. "If this is you being a shoulder to cry on, I'm not sure you're all that effective."

You criticized Derwent at your peril. The result was instant belligerence. "What do you want me to do? Do you want a hug?"

The way he said it was awfully close to *do you want a fight?* I didn't hesitate. "Absolutely not."

"Well, what would make you feel better?"

I cleared my throat, afraid to look at him again. At least he would tell me the truth. "Do you think — in your view — was it my fault?"

"You are so thick sometimes," Derwent said. "Why should you take responsibility for something you didn't do? Why can't you admit it's Rob's fault?"

"It wasn't his fault. He didn't know about the Maudling Estate. He was confused and drunk and hurt, probably."

Derwent frowned at me, interested. "Why didn't you tell him?"

I shook my head slightly.

"The same reason you didn't tell me? Because you didn't want a fuss?"

"I suppose."

"It's a quick way to fuck things up. Keeping secrets," he clarified. "The trust isn't there any more, if it ever was."

"I trust him," I said, needled.

"Not enough to tell him the truth."

"He didn't need to know."

"He absolutely did. If you were my girlfriend I'd dump you for that."

"Very comforting. Are you finished?"

"No, not yet. Why aren't you angry with him for sleeping with Debbie? Don't you care?"

"Of course I do."

"Well, then."

I sighed. "I could murder him for it but I know why it happened and I know what state he was in. He made a mistake."

"It's a pretty big mistake."

"It happens. I've been tempted."

"Have you?" Derwent was delighted.

Not by you not by you not by you.

"Of course. Monogamy is difficult." I could feel myself blushing at the memory of Ben Dornton's wedding and hoped Derwent wouldn't notice. Even if he was a trained interrogator, I would never tell him about my moment of weakness. I would die first. Or kill him, alternatively. That option had its attractions. I went on, "If it had been me, I would want him to forgive me. I'll forgive him if I ever get the chance."

"Do you think he'd forgive you for cheating on him?" Derwent's tone made it clear that he wouldn't.

"He's a better person than I am."

"If you believe that —" Derwent broke off, shaking his head. "You'll never have a proper relationship with him if you spend your time being grateful to him for loving you."

"But I let him down. I —"

"Now I am bored." The expression on his face was tender, though. "Look, you didn't do anything wrong, except for not telling people what was going on when you should have."

"Oh." I swallowed. "And do you think he'll come back?"

"He's a twat, but he's not an idiot. He'd be an idiot not to come back to you. Whether you should welcome him back is another question. I wouldn't, but that's up to you. Does that make you feel better?"

It actually did. I nodded.

"Told you it was worth your while to talk to me." He grinned, then got serious again. "Let's deal with the practical side. Do you want me to book you in for counseling? No one has to know about it and no one has to know why."

"Not at the moment. I'll ask if I think I need it."

"See that you do. Now, according to you, what happened between you and Rob definitely wasn't a sexual assault, so I don't have to go and get him picked up."

"Oh God, no. Would you?"

"Of course," he said, in a matter-of-fact

way. "Do you want me to go and beat him up for shagging around with Debbie Ormond?"

"Definitely not."

He looked hurt. "It's a genuine offer."

"I know," I said, trying to keep a straight face. So that was where we were in our relationship. Derwent's scale ran all the way from wouldn't piss-on-you-if-you-were-on-fire to would-kill-for-you-no-need-to-ask-twice. I was quite glad to be somewhere near the middle. "I appreciate it. No."

"Do you want me to go and find those four cuntbubbles on the estate and deal with them?"

Deal with, not *arrest.* Derwent was looking incredibly dangerous and not at all as if he was going to do things by the book. I shook my head. "You have enough to do. Anyway, you'd never find them."

"I'm highly motivated."

"I don't doubt you. But no."

"All right. In that case, stop being such a drip. Pull yourself together and let's get on with the job."

I stood up, feeling physically lighter for having unburdened myself. I wiped my eyes again. "I can't believe you made me cry."

"It wasn't difficult."

"I never cry at work if I can help it."

"Why not?"

"I don't want to be that girl — you know, upset about everything. Attention seeking. People would not be nice."

Derwent shrugged. "It's what birds do, though, isn't it?"

"I'm not a bird, I'm a police officer. At work, anyway. You can't imagine Chris Pettifer sobbing his heart out, can you?"

"Only every time Arsenal loses."

We walked back out of the woods together. I stopped when we got to the crime scene.

"What was the other reason for coming here?"

"Huh?"

"You said you had two reasons. One was to talk to me. What was the other?"

"I thought it might help to come back." Derwent looked around, restless again. "This is where it all started. After everything that's happened I thought it might help to go back to the beginning. Get some perspective."

"And did it help?"

He pulled a face. "One out of two isn't bad."

CHAPTER TWENTY-FOUR

Derwent and I arrived back into the office in time to intercept a glower from DCI Burt.

"Where have you been?" She looked accusingly at the mud on our shoes and the general post-weeping dishevelment I hadn't been able to fix in the car.

"The Hammond crime scene for a quick reminder," Derwent said. "Did we miss anything?"

"Probably. I'm sure you have work to do." She turned her attention to me and I cleared my mind of Rob, and everything to do with him. *Concentrate.* "Maeve, did we ever get an answer from the estate agents about the Leytonstone property?"

"The killer or an associate of his made a phone call to see if the place was still available and if it was currently unoccupied. A man's voice — nothing distinctive about it according to the girl who spoke to him. He was polite, she said, but brief, which she was glad about. She was busy."

"She didn't think it was strange he wanted to know if it was empty?" Una Burt snorted. "What if he'd been a squatter? Or a scrap metal thief planning to strip it?"

"He rang on the Saturday so all the agents were out on showings, which was clever of him. She was just a temp, answering the phones, taking messages, and registering new clients. I think she's about eighteen."

"No excuse."

"She was a bright girl," I protested. "He just had a good line. She said he wanted to know if the place was habitable or if it would need building work first to make it safe. He said it didn't look occupied from the pictures on the Web site. She'd heard two of the agents saying it was hard to sell it because the place was so cold and unwelcoming, so she just confirmed that it was empty but as far as they knew, sound. Buyer beware, obviously."

"Buyer beware of being completely mental. Her first clue that something was off should have been that he sounded normal and wanted to know about that house," Derwent said.

"She was rushed off her feet that day. I don't think she was thinking about whether there was anything strange about him. She left a message on the relevant agent's desk saying that there had been an inquiry but the caller hadn't left a name or a number."

"If she noted the time of the call we can pick it up off their phone records and get the number," Una Burt said. "I know these guys treat mobile phones as if they're disposable but they're still unlikely to have dumped it until after the killing. We could get a location for where they were staying and that should help us trace a car, and —"

I was shaking my head.

"What?"

"I got the time of the call off the message slip and we pulled up the number. It was a payphone about a quarter of a mile away, near the cemetery. No shops or businesses nearby so it was out of range of CCTV or anything helpful like that."

Burt regarded me for a moment, her pale eyes bulging slightly as she considered the implications of it: another dead end. "Golly, how disappointing."

"Isn't it?" I said, trying not to look in Derwent's direction. He was grinning widely. In Burt's place he would have been howling with rage and punching something — an inanimate object if we were lucky. Una Burt's mastery of her emotions counted as a sign of weakness to him, which was one of

457

his many illogical prejudices.

Burt had moved on to a different issue: my shortcomings. "When did you find out all of this? Why isn't it on the board?"

"We only got the confirmation of the phone box this morning. I just haven't had time to write it up." I absolutely refused to be ruffled. Derwent had hauled me away from my work and he was two ranks above me. It wasn't my fault and I wouldn't pretend that it was.

"Well, next time you leave the office when you're in possession of an important piece of information, I suggest you tell someone first. We could have wasted a lot of time on that."

"Colin Vale knew," I said, looking across to where he was working, head down in a sea of paper. "He's the one with contacts at BT. He sorted out the phone records and we looked at them together."

"Well, I didn't know that. This is why the board is so important." She looked over at it proudly, which seemed strange to me. It was nothing more, currently, than a long stretch of failure. "It's our collective brain, our memory, our understanding of this case. Too often you go on a solo run, Maeve, and you don't tell anyone what you're doing. You need to communicate better. Talk to your superior officers. Keep everyone informed."

"I was just telling her the same thing," Derwent chipped in.

Burt glowered at him. "Were you involved in the estate agent inquiry?"

"Not me."

"Then why are you still involved in this conversation?"

"The same reason you are. I wanted to know what she'd found out. And now I do."

"Get on with something useful," Burt said scornfully, and turned on her heel. I watched her stump across the room and execute a textbook knock-and-enter on Godley's office. I heard her laugh loudly as she closed the door.

"Look at that," I said. "She didn't even give him a chance to hide. The blinds were closed and everything. He could have been changing."

"He could have been having a wank." It was a half-hearted effort for Derwent — automatic, almost.

"What's wrong?" I asked.

"Why was she picking on you?"

"She doesn't like me."

"She loves you. She wants to mold you in her image."

"No thanks," I said. "I'll stick with my own."

"What did you do to piss her off?"

"I threw in my lot with you and I will never be forgiven. But if you could stop actively annoying her, it would probably make my life a lot easier."

"I can't help it."

"You could try harder. You could try at all."

"All right, Goody Two-shoes." He patted my shoulder. "Well done for knowing everything there was to know about the estate agents. I do love to see her disappointed."

"I love doing my job." I watched him walk off. "Where are you going?"

He swiped a newspaper off someone's desk and kept going. "For a shit."

It was my own fault for asking, I thought, sitting down and trying to remember where I'd left off. I should get the phone stuff on the board now, while Burt was occupied, and then I could get on with —

The door to Godley's office opened and he came out. He looked over at my desk in a way that was more than a casual glance, but as soon as he saw me watching him, he looked away again and picked up his pace. He looked dreadful — pale, ill, tired, and thin. His suit was roomy on him, the shirt collar too loose and, most unusually, grimy. He disappeared through the double doors to the hall, a set expression on his face.

Strange, I thought. Why had he looked to see if I was there? Checking up on me? Had Una Burt been complaining about me?

But he hadn't looked as if he was angry with me. I tried to think what it reminded me of. An old black-and-white film on Channel 4 on a dull Saturday afternoon, with the rain streaking the windows and my father entranced before the only television in the house. Declan and I had watched it with him because there was nothing else to do. Dirk Bogarde looking noble in heavy makeup. *It is a far, far better thing I do than I have ever done.*

I got up without really knowing why and went to the door of Godley's office. Una Burt was still in there, reading a report and eating a biscuit. She looked up.

"What is it?" The question came with a shower of crumbs, and a frown.

"Where did the boss go?"

"He said he was going down to the basement."

The basement was home to a couple of changing rooms with showers. It was possible Godley had been going to freshen up.

Possible, but somehow not likely.

"This might sound a bit odd, but can I ask what he was doing when you came in here?"

The frown deepened. "You're right, it does sound odd. And impertinent, if I'm honest."

"Please," I said. "It might not matter. But — you laughed. What was he doing?"

"He had dropped his fountain pen and it rolled under something. He was on the floor looking to see where it had gone. When I came in he popped up from behind his desk like a meerkat." She gave a little chuckle, then went serious again. "Is that all?"

"Did he find it?"

She thought about it. "No. He didn't."

"Okay. Thank you." I started to turn away, then stopped. The look on his face. The crumpled, dirty suit. Looking for something but abandoning the search once he was interrupted. Leaving Una Burt unattended in his office. Secrets. Lies. Red flags. *Did you notice anything different about his behavior? Did he seem to be himself?* I'd asked those questions too many times in the aftermath of a tragedy.

I bent down and started peering under the desk.

Burt was watching me with frank disgust. "Is this really what you do for him? Pick up after him?"

"It's just one of the things I do for him." Without straightening up, I gave Burt a look that implied all of her worst fears about Godley and me were true. She threw the report down on his desk and walked out, muttering to herself.

Which was exactly what I had wanted. I pushed the door closed and lay down on the floor, checking under every item of furniture in the room. It wasn't a big space but it was cluttered with things: a small round table with three chairs, the desk, Godley's chair, filing cabinets, a leaning rubber plant that had seen better days, a ton of cabling. I was looking for something small, I thought. Something he had been desperate to find, but something he had to lie about. Una Burt was a good police officer but she hadn't spotted, as I had, the distinctive white top of Godley's Mont Blanc pen under a hastily flipped stack of papers.

I was lucky that what I was hunting turned out to be shiny. It was a gleam from the metal that caught my attention, between the desk leg and the bin. I reached it with the end of a pencil and knocked it out into the open, where I could see it.

"Oh *shit.*"

I picked it up and darted out of the room in search of Burt. She was standing in front of the board, staring at it.

"Did the boss say what he was going to do in the basement?"

There must have been something in my voice that persuaded her not to make me wait. "He wanted to check something in the property store." The property store, where we kept evidence for upcoming trials.

"Right. Of course. Thank you." I walked away quickly, not running, a little fake smile on my face as if I was really enjoying today, thanks, but just a bit busy and not able to chat.

I cannoned into Derwent in the doorway and pushed him back into the hall.

"Watch it, lady," he said, annoyed.

"Come with me."

"What's wrong?"

Instead of answering I opened my hand and showed him the bullet on my palm.

"Where did you get that?"

"The boss's office."

"What —"

"I don't have time to explain. Just come." I didn't wait to see if he was following me as I hurled myself down the stairs. I was trying to think how big a head start Godley had on us. Too long. But he wouldn't be in a hurry. He'd be thinking it through, one last time.

The property store was a big room in the basement of the building, accessed via a gate beside a desk. You had to sign in; you couldn't just walk in and start opening evidence bags.

Derwent was right behind me as I came off the last step of the stairs. I managed a smile for the civilian who manned the desk, who was fiftyish and fleshy. I was breathless from running, my chest heaving. I leaned on the desk, squeezing my elbows in for maximum cleavage and said, very softly, "Hi, Neil. Did my boss come down here?"

"Signed in a few minutes ago."

"Can I pop in and see him?"

He turned the clipboard round and pointed at the line below Godley's signature. "You know the rules, Maeve."

I took the pen and signed, leaving the rest of the columns blank. My attention was on the details Godley had filled in, which might of course have been fake. But I knew the case name he had written down, and the details of the case were consistent with what he needed. "I'll fill the rest in later, is that okay? It's just I really have to speak to him. It's very important. Please, just bend the rules for me. I'm not breaking them, I promise. You won't get in trouble." I was gabbling.

He shook his head. "How can I say no to a request made so beautifully?"

Now is not the time for speeches, creep. Write it in a Valentine's card I can throw away. I smiled at him as if he had made my day. "Let me in?"

"Go on." He buzzed me through. Derwent tried to crowd after me. "Ah-ah. Not you, sir. Come back and do it properly please."

Derwent had never been nice to him, ever, not once, I guessed, hurrying through the shelves. This was Neil's chance to give a little of it back. Knowing that Derwent deserved it didn't make me feel any better.

I couldn't hear anything except my heart hammering and the hum of the air-conditioning. I was holding my breath so I didn't make too much noise. If Godley had been telling the truth, he'd be near the back on the right. I jogged down the central aisle, checking left and right in case I went past him. It was a small storage facility for current cases only. The main Met storage places were vast warehouses on anonymous sites around London, filled with the evidence from cases long solved or still open. We kept what we needed in our building, no more. And the case Godley had mentioned was coming up for trial.

I was almost on top of him before I heard him, and even then it was just a small click, but it had a terrifying implication. I flung myself around the corner, all thought of finesse or stealth gone.

"Stop. Don't."

He was standing at the very end of the bay, as far away from the central aisle as he could get, which put him about twelve feet from me. His suit was buttoned, his tie straight. The gun in his right hand was pointing at the floor, his finger pointing down instead of curled around the trigger. That gun was a Glock 9mm. It had been recovered from a loft in Poplar, where it had been hidden, wrapped in the T-shirt worn by the owner when he shot his ex-girlfriend dead on her doorstep. The thing that had caused him to snap, I recalled, was that she had put a picture on Facebook of her with another man. The guy hadn't recognized that the "George" of "Me and George!!!" in the caption was the singer George Michael, lightly disguised with a full beard, a flat cap, and sunglasses. Stupid and tragic, my least favorite kind of murder.

"Maeve." Godley tried to smile. The light shining above him caught his cheekbones and made hollows of his eyes. He was a death's head already. "How did you know?"

I showed him the bullet I had retrieved from his floor.

"I was looking for that. I decided three would do."

"Una Burt told me."

He shook his head, very slightly. "She didn't know."

"No, but I did."

"Yes. You always see more than you should. You were one of my mistakes."

I would like to say that I was far more concerned with Godley's personal safety than bothered by any criticism of my work or of me personally, but I flinched and he saw it.

"I mean that I underestimated you, Maeve. You were better than I ever expected. You'll go far, if you want to."

He raised his left hand in a kind of benediction that was actually intended to distract me from what he was doing with his right hand. It worked; I didn't notice him nudge the safety catch off until he had done it. He pointed the gun at the underside of his chin and I cried out.

"Please, don't. This isn't the way to deal with it. It's not the answer."

"Tell them it was an accident. Tell them I didn't know it was loaded. For me, Maeve."

It would have to be an accident, I understood. An accident would mean no big inquiry into why a superintendent with a glorious career would kill himself. No demolition of Godley's reputation. No rewriting of all the records of his undoubted achievements to take away the shining brilliance and replace it with the tarnished gilt of a bent copper.

"Wait! What do you want me to tell Serena? And Isobel?"

His finger was around the trigger now, but loosely. "What?"

"You won't have written to them. If it's an accident, no suicide note, am I right? So they won't know what you want to say to them. I know you wouldn't want to leave them without saying good-bye."

"That'll do. Tell them I love them. Tell Isobel I'm proud of the woman she's becoming. I know she'll achieve her dreams." In the dark wells of his eye sockets the tears caught the light, glittering. He was trembling, I noticed.

"And Serena?" I took a couple of steps toward him as if I was just desperate to hear every word. He was still too far away. I could maybe get a bit closer if I kept him talking, but . . .

"Tell her I never stopped loving her. Not

being with her is the hardest thing in all of this. I promised her, you see. I promised she'd get me back when I retired."

"That's not for ages," I said, as if he wasn't preparing to put an end to his life. "She must be very patient."

"She's . . . extraordinary." He took a deep breath and braced himself.

"But you can't leave her like this," I said, edging closer. "It's not fair. She'll know this wasn't an accident."

"She hates me anyway."

"Because you were divorcing her."

"I just wanted to keep her safe."

"You should tell her that. Now, I mean. Explain. Call her." *Better yet, go and see her. And leave the gun behind.*

"I can't." He looked thoroughly wretched. "I can't tell her I'm not who she thought I was."

"The man she knows you are would never kill himself."

"I don't have any choice. It's the only way to stop this."

"You're wrong," I said. "Please. No one has to know about this. I promise you, I won't say anything. Come out of here with me and we'll talk it out. We'll work something out."

"I have thought about it quite a lot," God-

470

ley said with a gleam of his usual understated irony. "I think if there was an alternative solution I would have found it."

"People keep telling me I can't do things on my own," I said, slightly desperately. "You don't even know what you haven't thought of."

He lowered the gun. "I know you want to help, Maeve, but you can't. I'm far beyond that point."

"Just don't do this now. Give me a couple of days, sir, please." *Anything.*

"A couple of days. That seems like too long to me, when every minute another innocent police officer could die. Have you been playing the game too, Maeve? Who's it going to be this time? A diplomatic protection officer? A dog handler? A soft target or the bloody commissioner?" He laughed but I could see it was tearing him apart. "They've proved they can reach anyone. They can kill anyone they like and we can't stop them." He paused. "Well, I can."

I took another step toward him.

"Stop."

I did, obedient to the note of command in his voice.

"You're not going to get there in time, you know. Even if you run." He managed a smile. "Come on, Maeve. You don't want to see this. Just go. You don't have to watch."

He was right. I didn't want to see it. But I couldn't walk away either. "I can't just leave you."

"Then don't. But you can't stop me."

I had tried everything — every appeal. Every way I could think to reach him. All that I had left was anger and it came rushing to the surface.

"This is a coward's way out, sir, and you have never been a coward. You made mistakes and you have to deal with that, but you can't just run away now, after everything. Die the way you lived. Not like this."

"I can't —"

"Yes, you can. You said it was easy for me. Right is right and wrong is wrong, you said. Is this right or wrong?"

He closed his eyes. His whole body was trembling.

"If you can honestly tell me you think it's the right thing to do," I said, "I'll walk away and leave you here and tell everyone who asks it was an accident, nothing more."

He shook his head.

"Put the gun down," I said. "You don't deserve this. If you do this, Skinner wins. If you live, you have a chance to make things right."

"I don't see how."

"No. That's why you're standing in an property store preparing to shoot yourself." I was close to tears myself. "Please, be the person I always admired. Be the real you. Hasn't Skinner taken enough from you already? Do you have to give him your life as well?"

Slowly — infinitely slowly — Godley lowered the gun. He put the safety catch back on and stood there, his head hanging down. He looked defeated.

And Derwent strolled around the corner, his hands in his pockets. He went straight past me and stood right in front of Godley, looking down at the gun. "You want to unload that and put it back in the evidence container where you found it."

"It's not what you think," Godley said.

"You don't know what I think. Now stop wasting time. That tool on the desk is going to wonder what he's missing and I don't want him coming down here and getting the wrong idea."

Derwent's bracing practicality seemed to get through to Godley. He shook the bullets out into Derwent's palm. Without looking, Derwent held his hand out to me.

"Stick them in your bra, Kerrigan. Bringing ammo in here is a big no-no. We could all get in trouble."

There were four bullets including the one I'd found. I ignored Derwent's suggestion and dropped them into my boot instead. If Neil ran true to his usual practice he'd be staring at my bra and its contents with X-ray intensity.

"Come on. Put the gun away," Derwent said.

Godley did as he was told. He was sweating, a world away from the icy calm he'd maintained when he was set on suicide.

Derwent dropped an arm around his shoulders. "Time to go home."

He started to walk out, supporting Godley. The superintendent was clearly struggling to put one foot in front of the other. Derwent looked back to make sure I was following.

"Talk us out of here, Kerrigan."

I went past them and out to the desk, where I chatted inanely and brightly to Neil as I filled in the form properly. Everything he said was hilarious. I enjoyed talking to him so much, I hadn't even noticed that two of the buttons on my shirt had come undone. Neil did notice since he looked nowhere else the entire time, but he didn't mention it.

I was aware of the other two coming out and going past, heading for the stairs. I leaned forward, dropping my voice.

"That's so typical of Derwent. Just leaving me to sign them out. Like I'm his secretary or something."

"He probably imagines you are. A sexy secretary. Take some dictation, please." Neil was wheezing with excitement.

"Cheeky," I said, wondering if I should wink. A wink was probably going too far.

As if to settle the question, Neil winked at me. Definitely going too far.

"Thank you for everything. You're a sweetheart." I fled before he had time to think of a reply, taking the stairs two at a time. The bullets were digging into me, which was reassuring rather than annoying. I got to the foyer and found it deserted, then saw Derwent standing beside a black cab in the street. I ran out.

"What took you so long?" he demanded.

"You can't rush these things."

"Get in."

"I don't have my coat — my bag —" I patted my pockets and found my phone but no wallet.

"In," Derwent said firmly, more or less pushing me into the cab. He got in after me and slammed the door. He must have given the address already because the driver started immediately. I collapsed on to the bench seat, fumbling for a seatbelt as I eyed Godley. He was huddled on the other side of the cab, not talking or making eye contact. I looked back to Derwent, who had taken the fold-down seat opposite me.

"Is he all right?"

"Not really."

We were three streets away from the office, moving fast. I shivered. "I don't even have my suit jacket. It would have taken two minutes to go and get my things."

"Two minutes was too long," Derwent said. "I didn't want anyone to see us." Then a long, slow grin spread across his face. "You might not be so cold if you do up all your buttons."

Too late I remembered the Neil-distracting view I had created. I did as he suggested, my face flaming. Derwent watched, of course, but then he looked back to Godley and his smile faded. He looked worried, because he was.

He had every reason to be.

Chapter Twenty-Five

I'd never been to Godley's house before. It was big, a classic Victorian terraced property with a tiled porch and elaborate stained glass in the front door. Everything about it, from the light above the door to the bay trees flanking the steps, showed good taste and money.

Derwent had frisked Godley for his keys and unlocked the door. He was more or less holding Godley up at the same time. "Upstairs," he said over his shoulder, and started to haul the superintendent up one step at a time.

I followed, as I was supposed to, but looked around as I went. Unopened post and junk mail lay in a drift behind the door. The beautiful furniture was dim with dust, the mirrors smeary. No one was looking after the house. The air was bone-chilling, as if no one was living there. I wondered if Godley had been sleeping in the office. He'd done it before.

The two men had made it to the first floor. Derwent manhandled Godley along to the bedroom at the front of the house. The curtains were drawn already and I switched on a lamp so we could see. It was a big room, with pretty bow-fronted chests of drawers flanking the fireplace and a small sofa at the end of the antique bed, which was unmade and rumpled. A silver-framed picture of Serena and a girl who could only be Isobel stood on one bedside table.

"Sit down." Derwent pushed Godley on to the bed and knelt to take off his shoes. "Jacket off. Tie too."

Godley did as he was told. He looked exhausted, I thought, as if he was beyond making any decisions. He just needed sleep.

Derwent collected up the shoes, jacket, and tie and thrust them at me. "Take them downstairs."

I went. I hung the jacket on the end of the stairs, looped the tie around the newel post and left the shoes on the bottom step. For want of anything more useful to do I sat on the floor and sorted the post. Looking at the postmarks, it was a couple of months since anyone had done the same. I ended up with a small stack of bills and letters that went on the hall table, and a heap of junk mail.

The kitchen was at the back of the house, down a flight of steps. I put the lights on and whistled. It was huge, impeccably fitted, expensively done. A marble floor, black granite worktops, designer lighting. There was no fruit in the bowls, though, or flowers in the vases. Again I had the sense that Godley hadn't been living here, even if he'd slept in his bed now and then. I dumped the junk in a bin that seemed to be recycling and prowled, checking the fridge and the cupboards. There was almost nothing to eat in the house.

"Hungry?"

I whirled around, my heart thumping. "You scared the shit out of me."

"Sorry."

"How is he?"

"Asleep." Derwent was carrying an armful of ties, which he tipped on to the table.

"What are those for?"

"In case he tries to hang himself when my back is turned."

"He won't."

"He might." Derwent looked at me and I caught my breath at the sheer depth of loathing he managed to convey. "I didn't think I'd find him trying to shoot himself in our property store, but there he was. You can't blame me for not wanting to take any chances."

"He could use anything to hang himself. This is what — a four-story house? He could throw himself out of a window. You can't keep him safe here if he really wants to kill himself. But I don't think he really does."

"What was that back at the office, a cry for help? It looked to me like he meant it."

"He did."

Derwent stared at me for a long time, then seemed to make up his mind. "Right." He went and got a chair from the table and slammed it down in the middle of the floor. "Sit there."

I did as I was told. He got another one for himself and put it in front of me, uncomfortably close. We were knee to knee when he sat down. An interrogation. Just what I needed. He leaned in, his face inches from mine.

"No messing. No lies. No bullshit. What do you know that I don't about the boss? What did you do to him?"

"It wasn't me," I said quickly, understanding why he was so angry. "It's nothing to do with me. I just happened to find out about it."

"Find out about what?"

There was no way around it. "Godley's been working for John Skinner. For years."

He leaned all the way back in his chair, tilting on the back legs. "Fuck off."

I should have been getting used to that: first Rob, now Derwent. "It's absolutely true. He told me himself."

"Pillow talk, was it?"

"Of course not," I snapped. "He took me to see Skinner in Wandsworth nick after that horrible shooting in Brixton three years ago–the three lads in the Range Rover. Skinner's gang was knocking holes in the opposition and Godley wanted him to stop it. I was supposed to be the chaperone, so Godley didn't have to worry someone would guess he and Skinner were communicating privately. He didn't think I'd work out what they were talking about, but I did. Godley even said he'd underestimated me. That's why he's been off with me. It's not personal. He just can't stand that I know the truth about him."

Derwent regarded me with total disgust. "You will say literally anything rather than admit you've been shagging him."

"I haven't been shagging him. That's not even the issue. Didn't you hear what I said?"

"It's not true."

"It is. Why do you think Skinner stayed one step ahead of you the whole time you were hunting him, back when you were working on gang crime? Godley was tipping him off every time you got close."

"No."

"Yes," I insisted. "You couldn't get him or his main lieutenants. You tried everything but they were always too quick, or too lucky. But it wasn't luck. Then Skinner ran away to Spain out of your reach and kept things going by proxy and everything was fine for him until his daughter disappeared and he came back. He was too worried to be careful when he went on his little rampage, trying to find her. There was nothing Godley could do to get him out once we arrested him so Skinner made the best of it, pleaded guilty, and set up again from inside. He never let go of Godley. The best the boss could do was to give him as little information as possible without pissing him off. He tried to be unhelpful without giving away that he wasn't trying. It was a tough thing to do for so long."

"Why the fuck would the boss want to help a scumbag like Skinner at all? He doesn't need the money. Look at this place. His wife is loaded and he's not short of a few bob either. That's not from Skinner."

"He was blackmailed. They threatened Serena. He was worried for her safety, and for Isobel. You know they'll always find something they can use against you. Everyone has a weak point. Skinner found Godley's. I think he loved getting to make use of him because he knew Godley loathed it. He's a manipulative prick, as you know."

"That's about all I know." Derwent jumped up and started to pace up and down, beside himself. "How did I not notice any of this?"

"Because you love and respect Godley and you wouldn't have believed it even if you noticed it."

"I know him better than anyone."

"You know the best version of him. He wouldn't have wanted you to know about Skinner. The worst thing for him, I think, was thinking how people would change toward him once they knew. He couldn't stand to lose their respect."

"But it wasn't his fault."

"He doesn't see it that way. He thinks he should have taken the risk."

"Not with someone else's life," Derwent said. "Not Serena's."

"He adores her. I don't know how much you heard in the property store but he worships her. The whole divorce thing was his way of saving her. He must have made her move out of the house so Skinner didn't know where to find her."

"Why now?" Derwent asked.

"Because Skinner pushed him too far and he'd had enough. Godley told Skinner he was stopping. Don't you remember how happy he was up to Dornton's wedding? And then after we'd been to see Julie Hammond he was doom in a suit?"

"Yeah."

"Skinner sent him a message to tell him that he wasn't allowed to quit. I actually saw it but I didn't know what it meant until later. Hammond was the first murdered policeman. Then the rest."

"All to put pressure on the boss?"

I nodded. "And he'd had enough. He decided to put an end to himself rather than go on."

"He should have talked to me."

"You are the last person he'd have told."

"*You* should have talked to me."

He was still angry with me. "I wanted to. I didn't know what to do, though."

"You should have reported him."

I jerked my head back in surprise. "I'd have destroyed him."

"You stupid tart," Derwent said coldly. "What he did was so illegal — so wrong —

that you don't want to be standing near him when he gets found out, let alone complicit in it." He leaned on the kitchen worktop, his hands over his eyes, and groaned.

"That's not fair," I said, angry now. "You know what would have happened if I'd turned whistleblower. I'd have been screwed. My reputation would have been damaged by association anyway. No one likes a grass, do they?"

A glint from Derwent. "That's surprisingly selfish. I'd have seen you as the martyr type, willing to die for what was right."

"It wasn't just about me. Godley's career would have been over too. He's a good police officer — the best I've ever worked with. He was doing so much that was right, I didn't want to be the one to point out what was wrong."

Derwent covered his eyes again. "Just shut up. I'm trying to think. I have to sort this out and I don't want to throw either of you out of the lifeboat. Although don't think I'm not tempted."

The minutes wore by. I managed not to make any smart remarks about how hard it was to think when you weren't used to it. Eventually Derwent straightened up and took out his phone.

"This is what should have happened the

minute you found out about Skinner." He gave me a filthy look as he scrolled through the contacts. "You think you know everything, Kerrigan, but you have a lot to learn."

I stayed silent, afraid to move off my chair.

It was Serena's number he was looking for, it transpired, and he got hold of her immediately. His voice softened as he spoke to her.

"I'm at your house. I'm sorry, I don't have time to explain what's happening, but Charlie needs you."

There was a short pause.

"No, I promise you, that's not true. I can't tell you what's been happening but he does love you. He never stopped. He was trying to keep you safe."

Another pause.

"Serena — Serena, just come, all right? I want you to be here when he wakes up. No, he's not okay, but he's not injured. He just needs you. Okay. See you soon." He hung up. "She'll be here in twenty minutes."

"Right," I said, watching him choosing another number. "Who are you calling now?"

"Never you mind." He walked out of the kitchen, shutting the door behind him. I stayed where I was, feeling small and stupid and wronged. I hadn't asked to be let into

Godley's secret. I hadn't wanted the responsibility. I hadn't known what to do with it, either, once I had it, but that was the burden I'd carried. It was easier to be blind, I thought. Easier to believe the best of people, and not ask the questions that had uncomfortable answers. I wished with all my heart I was capable of not caring. Life would have been so much easier if I could have just stayed out of other people's business. Doing that, though, would kill off something so fundamental to me that I wouldn't be me any more. Was that what Derwent would prefer?

I was shivering by now. All the marble in the kitchen made it as cold as an ice rink. I got up and hunted for the boiler or a control pad for the central heating. It had to be somewhere but I couldn't find it. I walked around, hugging my arms around myself to ward off the cold. I took out my phone and looked at it. I could call Rob . . .

I shouldn't.

I should tell him what was going on.

He should call me to apologize.

I could text him.

That was essentially the same as calling him. And I wasn't calling him.

Eventually I made a pot of coffee and drank two cups too quickly, and wondered if I was developing cardiac arrhythmia from the combination of stress and caffeine.

Derwent came back in, still on the phone. He liked to wander when he was talking. I couldn't guess from the monosyllables he was uttering what the conversation was about, or who was on the other end of the line. He did one circuit of the kitchen island and looked at me, his head on one side. *What's wrong?*

I rubbed my arms and mouthed, "Cold."

"Of course," he said into the phone, shrugging his jacket off. "I'd have thought so." He came over and slung the jacket over my shoulders, not even looking at me. He drifted out again, rolling up his sleeves as he went. I wrapped myself up in the jacket, wondering if I should get him to have a go at sorting out global warming while he was in problem-solving mode.

My own phone buzzed. I hooked it out of my back pocket. DCI BURT flashed on the screen.

"Oh, hell no." I muted it and watched until the call went to voicemail. Derwent came back in while I was listening to her message.

"Who are you calling?"

"No one. Burt called me."

"What did she want?"

"To know what's going on." I weighed my phone in my hand. "What do I do?"

"Call her back."

"What?"

"Tell her the boss was taken ill. He asked me to take him home and you came along to help nurse him."

"I'm not saying that. She thinks I'm sleeping with him too."

"Unsurprisingly," Derwent said, as if I had deliberately misled them and only had myself to blame.

"I'll say I came along to help you. That's true, basically."

"Tell her it's flu or exhaustion or something but we don't want to leave him. Tell her we'll be back in the office in two hours after the doctor has seen him."

"Will we be back then?"

Derwent shrugged. "I don't care. I just don't want her turning up here. Go on. Call her back."

I did as I was told, focusing on an empty fruit bowl so Derwent didn't put me off while I was talking to her. I more or less gave the impression that I was with Godley and therefore couldn't speak for long, or very loudly. The second time she said, "But I don't understand why you couldn't come back upstairs before you left to tell me what was going on," I told her I had to go. I hung up before she could protest.

"Good work," Derwent said.

"I don't think she believed me."

"She definitely doesn't trust you, and why would she? You're the skinny whore who's sleeping with the boss."

A noise from the doorway made us both jump. Serena had let herself in without us hearing her. She looked fragile in a huge jumper and narrow jeans, and she was much thinner than the last time I'd seen her. She was still utterly ravishing — delicate features, huge blue eyes, immaculate fair hair.

"Serena." Derwent went over to her and put his arms around her. She clung on to him, her face anxious.

"What's happening, Josh? What's going on?"

"Charlie's not doing so well. He's been working hard and — well, someone's been threatening him. The stress has really got to him. He had a bit of a breakdown at work. We're sorting it out, so please don't worry, but I think he needs you."

"Who is she?" Serena was staring at me.

"A colleague. Detective Constable Kerrigan."

"We've met before." But that was at a

Christmas party and I'd been a lot less disheveled. There was no hint of recognition on Serena's face.

"She managed to stop Charlie doing something very stupid today," Derwent said. "We're lucky she was there."

Serena was still glaring at me and I played back the bit of conversation she'd overheard. The direct approach seemed necessary.

"Sir, would you mind explaining to Mrs. Godley that you were joking about me sleeping with the boss?"

"Oh, shit. Yes. It was just a joke." Derwent gave Serena a little shake. "He's been missing you something chronic."

"Really?" She looked as if she was on the verge of tears.

"Truly. I've been getting shit from him pretty much every day. Thank God you're back."

"I don't know. I have to see Charlie. I'm not back really." She drifted into the kitchen and started putting on lamps, pulling a face as she looked into the sink. "God, how has he been living?"

"Not well," Derwent said. "He needs you."

"Oh . . ." She even cried beautifully, I noted. "If you're right and he wants me back, of course I'll come. I never wanted to go in the first place."

"Do you want to go upstairs? He's asleep at the moment, but —"

"I want to be with him." She headed back into the hall where she paused for a second to open a cupboard I hadn't noticed. A hum filled the air.

"Is that the central heating coming on?" I asked Derwent.

"Sounds like it."

"Thank God."

"I see. My jacket's not good enough for you."

"It's not keeping my nose warm," I said. "Or my ears."

Derwent laughed. "Well, keep it anyway. I don't need it." He was keyed up, moving around all the time as if he couldn't keep still. He kept checking his watch.

"What's up? What are you waiting for?"

He tapped his nose instead of telling me and went out again. I waited a couple of minutes and went after him, not as scared of his rage as I had been. He was putting on lights in the big reception room that ran the length of the house. It was beautifully arranged with small sofas and antique chairs and a huge marble fireplace in each half of the room.

"Expecting company?" As I said it the doorbell rang.

I fully expected Derwent to send me to answer it but he didn't. He hared past me, giving me a pat on the bottom as he went. "Showtime."

I hesitated, wondering if I was supposed to go back to the kitchen or if I could stay. I found a chair near the back of the room, beside a radiator that was lukewarm but better than nothing. If Derwent wanted me gone, I would be kicked out quickly. If not, I wanted to know what was going on.

The door opened to admit two anonymous men, blank-faced and gray-suited, who nevertheless intimidated the life out of me as they walked into the sitting room. Behind them came a man I did recognize: Nigel Williams, the Met assistant commissioner who I'd last seen in the Maudling Estate. Derwent brought up the rear and shut the door. I got a glance from him and a look that I couldn't interpret, but he didn't tell me to leave.

"This is highly irregular." One of the gray men had settled himself in an armchair by the fireplace. He slung a foot over the opposite knee. "I hope there's a good explanation."

"The explanation is that Charles Godley is in a bad situation," Derwent said. "Not his fault, and not the point of what we're doing here."

"What are we doing here?" Nigel Williams demanded.

"Gentlemen, we have a unique opportunity. We can use it, or lose a good police officer forever."

"An opportunity?" Gray man two had a surprisingly deep voice. "Tell me what that may be."

Rapidly, Derwent sketched in the background: how Godley had been passing information to Skinner, and why, and for how long.

"So Skinner trusts him. He believes in him. He does what the boss tells him to do. That gives us the edge on him, doesn't it? We can nudge him in certain directions. We can find out more about how he operates and who works for him. And in the end, we can defeat him."

"He'll spot it a mile off," Williams said.

"No. He's too pleased with himself. He believes he has Godley over a barrel." Derwent was still standing, leaning against the fireplace. "He hates him with a passion and he loves to use the information Godley gives him. Godley is our best asset."

"He's a bent police officer," the first gray man said. "Not the sort of person we want to protect. We need to make an example of him."

"No. Definitely not. That's what Skinner would love. It won't stop him recruiting someone else. It won't help the Met. It will be embarrassing and public and wrong."

"I don't like the thought of publicizing that a superintendent has been passing information to the other side," Williams said. "It makes us look very bad. But these police killings — we need to hold someone accountable for them."

"That's why you're here instead of your boss. The commissioner can't know anything about any of this. But you three can organize it between you." Derwent shifted his weight from foot to foot, obviously frustrated that they weren't falling in line with his plan. "You want to hold someone accountable. I understand that. But not Godley. It's not his fault. This is on Skinner. We can't destroy him from the outside — God knows, we've tried. We need him to destroy himself. And this is how."

The two gray men were shaking their heads. It wasn't going to work, I thought, despairing. Derwent had overreached himself again.

"We need to make an arrest. We have too many dead police officers to let this go," the first gray man said.

"That's the beauty of it," Derwent said. "The price Godley will demand for coming back into Skinner's fold is Tony Larch and his accomplice."

"Why would he do that? He's got Godley where he wants him. He needs Larch on the outside doing his business," the second man rumbled.

"Skinner has never liked anyone being more powerful than he is. Larch walked when Skinner didn't. He's always been lucky and he has a huge reputation in the criminal world. He's a real super-villain. Also, he costs Skinner a fortune from what we hear. Give Skinner a chance to saw him off at the knees and I reckon he'll take it."

"We haven't even seen Larch, and we've been looking," Redfern said. "How's Skinner going to find him?"

Derwent shrugged. "Not my problem. He can get hold of him when he needs to. I know John Skinner. I know what he's like. It will put him back on top again and that's where he needs to be. He'll never be happy while he's stuck in prison and Tony Larch is out having fun, carving a reputation at Skinner's expense."

"We need to talk to Charles about this. Where is he?"

"Upstairs. But he's not well enough to talk to anyone."

"What's wrong with him?"

Derwent looked to me. I understood that he didn't want to tell them what had happened in the property store.

"He's suffering from mental exhaustion. He's been under tremendous strain. He needs medical attention," I said. "He needs some time off."

"And you are?" the first gray man asked.

"Not important," Derwent said smoothly. "She's useful." To me, he said, "Go and check on the boss. See how he's doing."

I went. I didn't want them to focus on me any more than Derwent did. I ran up the stairs and tiptoed to the door of Godley's room, which was ajar. I wondered about knocking and didn't, in the end, leaning around the door to see if the silence from inside was a good thing or a bad one. They were both asleep, their arms wrapped around one another. Serena was behind Godley, curved around him protectively. I withdrew as quietly as I could, holding my breath. I didn't want to disturb them.

Nor did I want to return to the sitting room. I sat down on the top step of the stairs and waited, fidgeting a little, until the door opened and the four men emerged.

Derwent shook hands with each of them and ushered them out of the front door. When he'd closed it, he turned and looked up to where I was lurking.

"Everything all right up there?"

I'd been sure I was out of sight. I got up and ran down the stairs, keeping my voice low as I said, "They're asleep. Did you sort it all out?"

"More or less. They were happy to agree to it. Anything to hide the fact that Godley's been corrupt for years and no one knew about it."

"Won't they punish him?"

"I don't think so. Not if he cooperates now. He's stored up a lot of goodwill over the years. And you said he tried not to help Skinner too much. If he gives them the details of what he told him and when, they'll be happy."

"You actually did it. Why do you think Godley didn't come up with this himself?"

"He's too proud. He was ashamed to be caught up in Skinner's games and he wanted a way out. The trouble is, there isn't one. I don't care about being good. I don't care how we get results. I'm not bothered about being irreproachable."

"Poor Godley," I said.

"He'll be all right. They won't be telling

anyone about any of this. We don't do deals with criminals, officially, but when we do we get our money's worth, so the bosses are happy. Godley will still be doing the job and he won't have to look over his shoulder any more. Win, win, win."

It seemed too good to be true. "There's got to be a catch, though. Is there a catch?"

Derwent's face darkened. "Did you have to remind me?"

"What is it?" I was instantly on edge, expecting the worst.

He shook his head, steeling himself before he could say it. "The boss is on leave for the foreseeable."

"Of course."

"Who could possibly step in to run the team at short notice? What beautiful lady of our acquaintance knows the cases and the staff and would be prepared to take charge at a moment's notice?"

"Not Una Burt," I said.

"Got it in one."

I assessed the implications for me and came up with nothing good. "Oh, *fuck.*"

"I think you mean 'Oh gosh.' " Derwent heaved a sigh. "Come on. Back to the office. If we're in luck she won't have heard yet and I won't have to congratulate her."

CHAPTER TWENTY-SIX

They found Tony Larch at a spa hotel near Bath three days later. He was having a massage when a team of burly policemen kicked the door in and arrested him. The pictures of him — naked, strategically pixelated, furious, gleaming with essential oils, his arm muscles impressively defined as he fought against the cuffs — quickly went viral. His accomplice, Michael Knaggs, was not at the hotel. He had been picked up seven hours earlier at a strip club in Soho, where he was watching a performance so filthy that the coppers who came to arrest him blushed when they talked about it, and they were not the blushing kind. There were no pictures of that one, at least officially.

Knaggs was twenty years younger than Larch and a novice at the killing game. He'd been a junior motorbike champion, though, and grew up on a farm in Norfolk, where he learned to shoot. Unlike Larch, he had no idea how he'd been found. Larch knew Skinner had given him up. That was why he was so angry.

I had little sympathy.

Neither of them was talking but that didn't matter. We had taken the contents of Larch's suitcase and emptied out most of Knaggs's flat, so we had enough material to piece together a timeline for them. We had evidence, and we would be able to gather more. We would make a case against them easily enough.

"Are you coming out tonight, Maeve?"

I looked up to see Mal Upton standing by my desk. "I don't know yet. Maybe."

I did know. I wouldn't be going. It was a celebration of our tremendous success in locating Larch and Knaggs and I couldn't quite bring myself to take pleasure in it. Not since I knew the price we'd paid for the information.

But you couldn't say that kind of thing to Mal, who was standing there looking hopeful and shaggy, his hair untidy, his shirt pulling out from his trousers on one side.

"I'll try to make it."

"If you do, I'll buy you a drink. I owe you one and I don't want to risk making you a cup of tea in case I get it wrong."

"Did I really scare you?" I asked.

"Not really."

"I must be losing my touch." I went back to the report I was writing. I knew Derwent was sitting at his desk and I had a feeling he was grinning, but I wouldn't give him the satisfaction of looking. He had the courtesy to wait until Mal had gone out of the room.

"Velcro Kerrigan strikes again."

"Stop talking now," I said.

"Does he know you're single?"

I glowered.

"Sorry, that you might be single. Have you heard from the wandering boyfriend?"

"Nope." I tried to sound carefree, as if I didn't mind and it didn't matter, when really I did mind, a lot, and it was mostly what I thought about when I wasn't thinking about work. Not a text message, nor an e-mail, nor a voicemail. Nothing at all. I was worried about Rob, and angry with him, and still cross with myself, no matter what Derwent had said about it not being my fault. I just couldn't bring myself to get in touch with him, or — worse — Deborah Ormond.

Derwent looked as if he was about to say something but, most rarely for him, didn't. He kicked his desk a couple of times instead. "So, you're single. Should I tell him?"

"You shouldn't speak to him. About

anything. He's a sweet boy and you'll corrupt him with your dirty mind."

"Interesting. I would not have said he was your type."

"He isn't."

"You can't be that desperate yet."

"I am desperate for you to stop talking to me about this." I sat back in my chair. "Terence Hammond."

"No." Derwent shook his head. "Don't even think about it."

"But —"

"Tony Larch and Michael Knaggs are in custody. We have a backlog of work that will take me until March to get through, because very inconsiderate people kept killing one another while we were worrying about getting shot ourselves. Don't say Terence Hammond to me."

"I'm just not sure."

"I hate you."

"I know." I tapped the end of my pen on my notebook, thinking. "It's the woman that bothers me. Larch and Knaggs are good at what they do, but where did they get a woman who was prepared to help?"

"I don't know. Maybe they hired her. I don't want to shock you but there are women who will do that kind of thing for money."

"Conspire to kill people?"

"Get them off in parked cars. You know, Knaggs was a regular at that club in Soho." Derwent snapped his fingers. "You are a genius. I've got a reason to go and I'm going."

"It won't be open now."

"What time, do you think?" He checked his watch. "Soon?"

"I wouldn't know." I went back to work, still thinking, and after a few minutes of fidgeting Derwent threw down the file he was reading.

"You are ruining my life."

"Why?"

"I'm finished with this case. Hammond is over. Done and dusted." He took his notes out of the folder and spread them across his desk according to his own arcane system. It was eerily close to tarot, as I'd told him before. "One last look."

I left him chewing it over and went to an interminable meeting chaired by Una Burt, who liked to read things out loud, at length. She was not a good reader and I spent my time fantasizing about screaming, throwing my papers in the air, and walking out. Something was bothering me. Something Derwent had said. He said so much, though, and most of it was troubling one way or another.

I came out of the meeting room with a suggestion for him but he wasn't at his desk. The tarot layout was gone, the file closed with a stapler resting on top of it like a cross on a vampire's grave. *Do not open.* He really wasn't interested any more, and that was fine, but I couldn't let it drop, even if it meant doing something I found repugnant. Like talking to Peter Belcott. I went across the room to the big noticeboard which Belcott was stripping of its photographs and notes.

"Tidying up?"

"What does it look like?" He was stacking the information neatly on the desk beside him.

I pointed at the stack. "Do you mind if I have a look through this?"

"Why?"

"I want to see if there's anything about Terence Hammond's career. Complaints or inquiries." I was shuffling through it as I spoke. Belcott's hand slammed down on top of the pile.

"You're making a mess. Anyway, it's not there."

"Oh. Does that mean there wasn't anything?"

"No, there was. I just didn't put it up. By

the time I got hold of it, the Maudling Estate shooting had happened and it didn't seem important." He dropped a couple of tacks into a box and went over to his desk, where he unearthed a thin cardboard folder. "There you go. Knock yourself out."

"Thanks, Pete." There were three pages in the file and I was skimming through them already. As I turned the first page a name jumped out at me. I hadn't been consciously expecting to see it but I wasn't surprised, all the same. I sat down at my desk and read through the file properly, a few times, until I was sure I'd taken it all in, and then I lifted the phone.

"Coming." The voice came from quite a long way back inside the flat. "I'll be there in a second."

I waited on the doorstep, thinking that there was no need to hurry. I wasn't going anywhere.

After a great deal of unlocking, Philip Gregory opened the door and hopped backward a little. "Sorry, it's the crutches. They slow me down. What can I do for you, Maeve Kerrigan?"

"You remembered my name."

"I never forget a good one. I recognized you as soon as I saw you on that thing." He pointed at the intercom, which had a tiny camera for checking who was at the door. "This is going to sound rude but why are you here?"

"I wondered if I could have a word with you about Terence."

He gave me a puzzled smile. "I think I said at the church that I wasn't in touch with him. I really don't have any information that would be useful for you. And I thought you'd got the guys anyway."

"We have two in custody," I said. "You know what it's like. I'm just chasing up some loose ends."

"And I'm a loose end, am I?" He smiled again. "Honored. It's cold out here. Do you want to come in?"

"Thanks."

It was a small flat and Gregory obviously lived in it alone. He dragged a basket full of ironing off one of the armchairs.

"Sorry about the state of the place. I wasn't expecting a visitor."

"Don't worry. I'm always surprising people. At least you were dressed."

"There is that." He lowered himself into his chair and slotted the crutches underneath it.

"How are you managing with those? Getting used to them?"

"Not so you'd notice." Again the likeable smile. "I'll get the hang of them about a day before the plaster comes off."

He was being very friendly but I thought he was nervous all the same.

"Right. The reason I've come is because I wanted to clarify a couple of things that were bothering me."

"Sounds ominous," he said with an edgy little laugh.

"Probably not. It was just that one of my colleagues took me back to the crime scene in Richmond Park a while ago because he said that was where it all started, with Terence's death. And it made me think that he was wrong. It wasn't where it started." I was watching him closely. "It started with you."

He pulled a face. "Glad I was the dress rehearsal, in that case. They didn't have their hand in yet."

"It definitely didn't work out the way they intended."

"Look, I know what you're saying but it doesn't seem likely, does it? Someone had a grudge against the police, saw me crossing the road like an idiot, saw red, hit the gas. I didn't jump far enough out of the way and I got a broken leg. They drove off. The end. That's not the same as Terence being shot,

508

or the PCSO having her throat cut. It's not skillful."

"No, it's not." I leaned forward. "Why did you lie about it?"

"What?"

"You said you'd given them a pretty good description of the car but they didn't pick it up anywhere on CCTV — there was no car matching that description in the area at the time you were attacked."

"The guys were professionals. They must have dodged the cameras."

"No. You sent the cops looking for the wrong vehicle. You didn't want to find the person who attacked you."

"That's just stupid," he said forcefully. "Why on earth would I want to avoid it?"

"That's what I was wondering. Then I re-alized you'd lied to me too."

"No."

"Small tip." I took the folder out of my bag. "Don't lie to a police officer, especially about something that's easy to check and even more especially if you don't have to."

"What are you talking about?" There was a sheen of sweat across his scalp.

"You said you'd never been crewed with Terence Hammond when you worked in the same team. You said you weren't even friends. I spent quite a bit of time today on the phone talking to people, including your old boss. You and Hammond always worked together and you were thick as thieves. Now, why would you lie about that unless you were trying to hide something?"

"Like what?"

I tapped the folder. "This is a report into an investigation carried out by the DPS in 2001. You and Terence Hammond got in serious trouble, didn't you?"

Gregory swallowed. "Everyone's forgotten about that."

"You haven't. Tell me about Annabel Strake."

"I can't."

"I know she was fifteen. I know she had problems with depression and alcohol abuse and that she'd attempted suicide twice. I know she'd gone missing from her home and you and Hammond were supposed to find her."

"We did find her. We had a hunch she might be hiding out in an abandoned factory because it was raining and that was where the local kids tended to go."

"What happened?"

Gregory took a moment to answer, reliving it. "Nothing. We found her. Terence found her, actually. We took her home."

"What happened before you took her home?"

"Nothing happened. But that's not what she said."

"She said you sexually assaulted her."

"Not me. I didn't do anything."

"But Terence?" I let the question hang in the air as Gregory struggled with his conscience.

"He was exonerated by the DPS. Annabel Strake was using us to get out of trouble with her parents. They were older, very strict, thought she was the devil incarnate for getting into a bit of trouble here and there. And she was an old fifteen, let me tell you. You'd never have guessed she was a child."

"No one believed Annabel, did they? You gave evidence that contradicted her statement. Were you telling the truth or was she?"

He didn't answer.

"Terence is dead," I said. "Tell me what really happened in the factory."

"We split up. Terence went up to the top floor where there were offices. I stayed down on the ground floor. It was dark, and cold. The place was condemned. Full of rubble and pigeon shit." He shivered, remembering. "I wandered around for a bit. I thought Terence was taking ages to search the place.

Then I heard them coming back. He'd found her on the top floor."

"And?"

"He'd had sex with her. It was her idea."

"Is that what he told you?"

Gregory shrugged. "It's what I believed. Terence was having real trouble at home. He and his wife weren't sleeping together — she wouldn't, after the car accident that injured Ben. Terence was frustrated, and Annabel was a little slut. She told him to shag her and he went for it."

"Do you really believe that?"

"She was laughing when she came down. I mean, she was off her face. We found a couple of joints on her, and some pills, and she'd been drinking."

"And she was *fifteen.*"

"Like I said, you'd never have known." Gregory glared at me. "Don't make this my fault. I didn't know anything. I wasn't even involved in what happened. I got in trouble then but I'm not going to get in trouble now."

"Even though you lied to the DPS."

Gregory put a hand down, dropping it casually on to the crutch that was under his chair. He was tense, the adrenalin running high. I watched him.

"I don't know what you're planning to do

with that, but people know where I am and why."

"I wasn't planning anything." He drew his hand away, though, and let his head fall back against the chair, defeated.

"So Annabel complained about Terence Hammond's conduct and you protected him. What happened to her?"

"She died. She went back to the factory about three weeks later and jumped off the roof. It was nothing to do with Terence though. She was a very mixed-up kid."

Anger was making my hands shake but you would never have known I was anything but detached. My voice was calm. I was all-seeing, all-knowing. He needed to think that he couldn't lie to me, that there was no point in trying.

"Has someone been threatening you?"

"Why would you think that anyone would threaten me?"

"Because you stopped working with Terence, changed jobs, and lost touch with him soon after all this happened, even though you were friends. Because you deliberately misled the police investigating an attempt on your life, as if you didn't want anyone to find out why you might be a target. Because you came to his memorial service and you spent your time looking over your shoulder for anyone you recognized. Because you have serious locks on your front door and a video-based intercom for a flat which, let's be honest, is not a burglar's dream. You live like you're scared. Why are you scared?"

Gregory closed his eyes. "Leave it alone. It was a long time ago."

"I need to know. And you need to tell me. Did you think the attack on you was related to Annabel?"

"Of course. I've been waiting for it for a long time. Always looking over my shoulder. Always being afraid someone would catch up with me. Keeping a low profile, not looking for promotion." He took a deep breath. "I made a mistake a long time ago. I trusted Terence and he fucked up. It wasn't my idea, and it wasn't my plan, but I take responsibility for not admitting what had happened. We should have told the truth." He gestured to his leg. "And then this happened and I was scared it was the beginning of the end. I lied to the detectives who interviewed me, just in case there was a connection. Either it was random or it was aimed at me. I couldn't tell which until Terence died. Then it seemed even more important not to talk about Annabel."

I stood up and gave him a notebook and a pen. "Write me a statement. Start with

Annabel and make it the real story, please, not the invention that you've stuck with for twelve years. And give me a proper description of the car that hit you. We're probably too late to recover most of the CCTV but we might be lucky."

"Are you going to look for them?"

I looked down at him. "They tried to kill you and shot Terence Hammond. I think I should try, don't you?"

CHAPTER TWENTY-SEVEN

Mindful of Derwent's dislike of being left out, I rang him as soon as I left Philip Gregory's flat. No answer. I called the office instead and left a message on his voicemail. I was heading back there anyway, but I wanted him to get a head start on explaining to Una Burt why we were reopening a bit of the nightmare case we'd just resolved to everyone's satisfaction.

He wasn't at his desk, though, when I walked in, and his coat was missing from the back of his chair.

"Where did Derwent go?" I asked Colin Vale, who frowned.

"I'm not sure. He left about an hour ago."

I checked the time: a quarter to three. Still too early for the strip club, probably. "Did he look as if he was going out drinking or for work?"

"Work. He made a call, got his things together, and went."

"Thanks, Colin." He started to walk away and I called him back. "Mobile or landline, did you happen to notice?"

"The call? Landline."

"Thank you. I'm going to have some CCTV for you to look at in a while, by the way."

"Can't wait," he said, which would have been sarcasm from anyone else, but not from him. He genuinely loved it.

I tried Derwent's mobile again. This time it was switched off. I frowned at my own phone, wondering what was going on. It was beyond unusual for him to switch his phone off. In fact, I couldn't remember him ever doing it before. I always felt slightly nervous when I called him in case he was in the middle of having sex or in the bathroom or something. I had listened to him weeing countless times while he issued me with new instructions and it never got any less revolting.

I went and sat down in Derwent's chair, resisting the urge to spin round. It was strange, seeing the room from his perspective. He had an altogether too good a view of my computer screen, I thought, making a mental note to change my desk around when I got the chance. I picked up the desk phone and hit redial.

"Uplands School, Pamela speaking, how may I help you?"

I remembered the receptionist instantly: fifties, glamorous. "Oh, Pamela, it's Detective Constable Maeve Kerrigan here. I'm hunting my colleague, DI Derwent. I just wondered if he'd been in touch."

"He rang to speak to Miss Maynard," she said. "He's got a lovely manner, hasn't he?"

"Mm," I said, not actually able to agree even for the sake of being polite. "Is Miss Maynard there?"

"No, she doesn't work on Wednesday afternoons." The receptionist said it as if it was a basic truth like water is wet and fire is hot and I should really have known better than to ask. "Shall I tell her you rang?"

"No, there's no need. Unless — you couldn't let me have a number for her, could you? And a home address?"

"I can't give out any information about staff or students, I'm afraid."

"Even to a police officer?"

"Sorry." She sounded implacable. "I can give her your number but not the other way round. That's what I did with DI Derwent."

"Don't worry about it," I said. "I'll catch up with her somehow."

I had an idea about how, too. I had just noticed Derwent's jotter was still on his desk. He was fastidious about writing on a new sheet of paper every time, so I hooked out the bin and checked through it. Telephone numbers, notes, a doodle that looked vaguely, disturbingly sexual. Not the thing I was looking for.

I sat back in Derwent's chair, staring at his desk. The light from his desk lamp slanted across the jotter, across the white, uninformative page. I could imagine him getting the details of where Amy Maynard lived, arranging to meet her there. He would have written it down — in the correct place, not on a scrap of paper, because his orderly mind wouldn't allow for scraps of paper — and then he would have removed the top sheet of the jotter, folding it into his pocket so he could consult it when he needed the address.

Which meant that I was looking at the next sheet down, more than likely. A SOCO would have used an electrostatic detection device to reveal the indentations. I had a pencil. I picked it up and ran the side of the lead, very lightly, over the page. White lines jumped out of the gray straightaway: Derwent's writing. He pressed down hard when he wrote, like a small boy, and the words were more or less legible: 24 Braemar Road, Norbiton. I stared at it for a second, amazed that it had worked. Sometimes the old tricks were the best.

It was the work of moments to ring the DVLA and check if there were any driving licenses registered to that address. Amy Maynard. Bingo. It wasn't far from Hammond's address, and I wanted to go back and speak to Julie, to find out whether Terence had ever told her anything about Annabel Strake. I just didn't want to go on my own. I would swing by Amy's house and check for Derwent's car, and if I still couldn't find him I would get someone to meet me at the Hammonds' place. I found Julie difficult to like, and a little intimidating, though I would never have admitted it. She had the cold blue gaze of a zealot. I tried to imagine her commissioning someone to kill her unfaithful, careless husband, dressing it up as vengeance for Annabel Strake's death, and found it believable. Worth putting to her? Not yet, I thought, but I wanted to see her face when I said Annabel's name.

Burt was shut in Godley's office, having a meeting with a senior officer I didn't know. I wasn't going to barge in there to tell her I was going out in search of Derwent — I wouldn't have anyway, but the senior officer was a decent excuse. If she minded, I'd apologize when I got back. I grabbed my coat and went.

Naturally, there was no sign of the Subaru on Braemar Road. I cruised up and down it and did a little tour of the streets that ran parallel to it, but there was nothing. Derwent was in the wind. I rang his mobile again.

"The mobile phone you are trying to contact has been switched off," the voice said brightly. "Please try again later."

I stopped outside number 24, looking up at it. Pebble-dashed, painted beams, bay windows: 1930s semidetached living with a wooden garage to one side and a small garden in front. It was a big family home, a strange place for a twenty-something professional woman to live. The curtains in the windows looked old-fashioned and fussy, as if it had been redecorated in the 1980s and never since. If she was in, it occurred to me, Amy would at least be able to tell me whether Derwent had been there already, and if he had mentioned where he was going next. I could wait for him if he hadn't arrived there yet. I rang the bell and waited, for ages, until a shape appeared behind the glass and started unlocking the door.

Subconsciously I had been convinced I

might have the wrong address, but no, there Amy was. An ankle-length tartan skirt, a mustard-colored jumper, a little frilled collar. She had to be shopping in charity shops, I thought. I couldn't imagine where else you would find clothes like that.

She gave me a beatific smile. "Detective Constable Kerrigan."

"Call me Maeve," I said. "I'm just looking for Inspector Derwent. I had some idea he was coming here but there's no sign of him."

"He's coming tomorrow," she said, looking a little nervous at the thought. "I'm not really sure why. He rang me and asked if he could speak to me about Mr. Hammond. I did say on the phone I didn't think I knew anything helpful, but he wouldn't really take no for an answer."

"I know how he can be," I said, distracted by the smell of smoke. A blue haze was filling the back of the hall. "Is something burning?"

"Oh!" She ran down to the kitchen. I stepped into the hall and shut the door after me. It wasn't just nosiness. If I spoke to her Derwent wouldn't need to call on her and I could save her from his attentions. I wasn't a huge fan of the student counselor but she didn't deserve whatever test of her modesty Derwent was planning, to prove she had to be a freak if she wasn't attracted to him.

The house was stuffy, as if the windows were never opened. I glanced into the living room, seeing elaborately ugly ornaments, pearlised wallpaper, a gray carpet with puffy pile that looked like clouds. It was decorated exactly as I'd expected it would be from the outside of the house. The next room was a dining room, pristine but unwelcoming, with a shiny mahogany table and matching chairs. It looked as if no one ever ate in there, or used it for any purpose at all.

I found her in the kitchen, mourning over a heavy cast-iron saucepan. "It was supposed to be soup. Now I've burned the onions."

"I don't think I've ever made soup."

She dumped the saucepan in the sink and turned on the tap. "I'll start again. At least I hadn't got too far."

The kitchen was painted green and yellow. The Aga in the corner made it warm, and the room was noisy, with the dryer and the washing machine both churning and the radio blasting out an opera that was heavy on shrieking. It was cluttered, the walls hung with ornamental bits of earthenware and wooden hearts and copper molds for making jellies. She switched off the tap and the sound of running water continued, thundering through the pipes.

"Where's that coming from?" I asked, pitching my voice a lot louder than I usually did.

"Oh, it's the washing machine, I think. The plumbing in this house is very strange. Every time I get someone to look at it, they just say it's a big job and too much for them. I think they don't want the work."

"Maybe not." I was looking around, in vain, for signs of anyone else living there. "Are you the only one who lives here?"

"It was my parents' house."

"And they gave it to you?"

"They died."

"I'm sorry."

She tilted her head to one side, looking, if anything, amused by my sympathy. "Don't worry. It was a while ago. And it was expected in both cases. I miss them but they were glad when it was their time to go."

There were no bowls on the floor. "No pets."

A laugh. "Nope. Just the mice."

"Don't you get lonely in such a big house by yourself?"

"Everyone asks that. I like my own company. I get a lot of people talking to me at school — parents, teachers, the students, of course. Then I come home and just want silence. Well, music. But not talking."

I nodded. "I can understand that."

"Can you? I think most people think I'm strange. That's why I like the students so much. They don't really know what to make of me so they've just allowed me to be myself."

"I don't think you're strange." *Not* very, *anyway.* "I'm sure your friends don't think you're strange either."

"I don't have many friends."

I tried to look surprised. "Well, you must have some. Terence Hammond was a friend, wasn't he?"

"I thought of him that way. I don't think he really knew I existed." Amy gave a little breathless laugh, as if she was embarrassed to recall it.

"You must have seen a lot of him, though. Ben knew you, at the memorial service. He waved."

"I'd met him a couple of times."

"You obviously made a big impression on him."

For some reason, that struck her as enormously funny. She had taken out a chopping board and started working through a bag of onions, half-laughing, half-crying. The smell made my nose tingle. All at once I was tired of talking to her. Derwent could have a crack if he liked, but all I got from her was crazy. I made a mental note to warn him about flirting with her, just in case.

"I suppose I'd better be going. Good luck with the soup."

"Thank you." She picked up a tea towel to wipe her hands. "I'll let you out."

I followed her through the hall, relieved to be out of the noisy kitchen. There was a board hung with keys near the door.

"You should be careful about that," I said.

She turned, fast. "What?"

"The keys. Having them out in the open like that. You'd be surprised how many burglaries begin with a fishing expedition through the letter box." I was scanning the board as I spoke, out of habit.

"You're right. I should put them away."

"Especially the car keys."

She laughed. "No one would want my car."

"Why do you say that?"

"It's ancient. A little Nissan. I don't care. I love it and I'm not a great driver. There's no point in buying an expensive car for myself. I'd just wreck it." She had come to stand close behind me, looking over my shoulder.

"My first car was a Nissan," I said, and

swung an elbow back to hit her just under the chin, so hard that I heard her teeth click together. I turned and made a grab for her wrist in the same movement: I had no idea which hand had the knife, and the tea towel was in the way so I couldn't see. I caught the blade through the fabric as it flew toward me and felt a sharp sting on my palm but I ignored it, holding on for dear life. The material slipped, the blade sliding free no matter how hard I tried to grip it. I let go and caught her hand instead, squeezing hard. My free hand went for her face, shoving her nose back, reaching for her eyes with my fingers. Anything to distract her from my main objective, which was getting her to drop the knife. I was scared, though I couldn't allow myself to admit it. I flashed back to Liv lying in hospital, to the stitches that crawled across her abdomen from the surgery she'd had after getting stabbed. She had almost died. She still wasn't herself.

I didn't like knives. Not one bit.

Amy was a fighter, lashing out in a flurry of kicking and punching and biting. I was taller than her and heavier, and I had been trained in unarmed combat so I should have had the advantage, but she was hellishly strong. Somehow she got a hand up and raked her nails across my cheek, grabbing at my mouth and clawing my skin. I kicked her legs out and fell on top of her, pinning her to the floor. The knife was somewhere between us and we both reached for it, all elbows and cursing and a good hard knock to my nose that made the world flare white, then dark. I shook the pain off, desperate to get control. She was trying to move me off her and I leaned as hard as I could, not giving her enough space to get her hand around the knife, let alone bring it up. I got hold of her wrist again and dug my fingers in so she hissed in pain. More by luck than skill I managed to knock the knife away so it rattled into the corner, out of reach of either of us.

"Listen to me." I sniffed, feeling warm liquid gush out of my nose, tasting hot metal from the blood that was filling my sinuses. "I know what you did."

"Get off me."

"No chance."

My blood dripped on to her jumper in coin-sized splashes. She squirmed beneath me, trying to bite my hand as I searched her. I had jammed her up against the bottom step of the stairs so she didn't have anywhere to go.

"Stop that," I said. "Don't make me angry."

She twisted to lie on her front so I had to pull hard to get one of her arms out from under her.

"You can't do this."

"It's my job." I clicked my handcuffs on to one of Amy's wrists, got up with some difficulty and hauled her to her feet with my fingers hooked in the other cuff, to cause her maximum discomfort.

"You're insane," she said.

"I don't think so."

"You attacked me for no reason."

I hauled her over to the keys. "Tell me about the car keys on the bottom row, Amy. The ones with the Ford logo and the Metropolitan Police fob. Terence Hammond's keys went missing — did you know that? I've got a funny feeling they're the ones we've been looking for. You must have taken them with you when you got out of his car. Habit is a funny thing. You put them on the board because that's where keys go."

She twisted and spat in my face.

"That's not nice." I wiped the saliva off with my sleeve, then pulled her down to the kitchen, holding her arms behind her, and stood her next to the Aga. I slid the solid bar of the cuffs behind the long rail that ran along the front of it, and clicked the open cuff shut on her other wrist. She could run away if she liked, but she'd have to take five hundred kilos of cast iron with her.

"You can't do this."

"I'm going to go and look at your car. Then I'm going to call the police," I said, examining the palm of my hand, which had a two-inch gouge across it that was seeping blood at a worrying rate. I picked up the abandoned tea towel and used it as an impromptu bandage, blotting my nose with it once my hand was wrapped up. "I'm going to arrest you for murdering Terence Hammond."

She started to cry. "It's not true."

"It is true, and I will prove it. I will admit that I didn't think you were the type to have sex with married men in public places, but I was wrong." Irritated by the heavyweight duet that was wailing out of the radio, I switched it off. "That's better."

Her face was white, her eyes huge. "Switch it back on."

"Definitely not."

"Please."

"Why would you even ask —" I stopped. "What was that?"

"What?"

"I thought I heard something strange."

"It's an old house. It makes noises." She

rattled the cuffs. "Please let me go. I'm sorry I hit you but you scared me."

I listened again; heard nothing. I went around the kitchen switching off everything I could find that was on. The washing machine was running through its cycle with an empty drum. I raised my eyebrows at her.

"I was cleaning it. You're supposed to run it empty every so often."

"And the dryer?" It was empty too.

"I must have forgotten I'd emptied it. I put it on automatically."

While I'd been standing outside the front door waiting for her to answer it. I frowned, trying to work out why. The water was still thundering down and rattling out into a drain outside the back door.

"Where's that coming from?"

"I told you."

"Tell me again."

"It's just the plumbing." Her face was streaked with tears now. "I don't know what you're doing. Why are you so angry with me? The things you're saying about Mr. Hammond are insane."

"You tried to stab me."

"*You* attacked *me.* And those keys belong to my brother. I have a spare set for him in case he loses his or locks them in the car."

She started sobbing loudly. "You're being horrible to me and I don't understand why. I haven't done anything to you."

"Shut up." I headed for the door.

"The cuffs are too tight. I can't move my hands."

"I find that very unlikely. I didn't sever your spine," I snapped.

She wailed even louder.

"Don't leave me here like this. Please. Come back. Come *back*. You're crazy. I didn't do anything. You can't prove anything. You're just trying to make me look guilty."

I went outside, stopping to pick up the keys to the garage. I levered the door up. Two cars stood there, one covered in a dust sheet. The other was a small green Nissan. I stared at it, knowing I'd seen it somewhere before. Not at the school. I closed my eyes and remembered: Derwent leaning forward, vomiting his guts up at the firing range. I dropped to my knees by the boot and shone my torch on the paintwork, seeing the small splashes that were fogged with dirt now. If we dusted it for prints, we'd find his palm print on the boot, where he'd leaned. It put her car at the gun club. The gun club was where she had found the weapon. It would be where she had recruited her shooter.

Slowly but surely, the evidence was stacking up.

I took out my phone to call for backup. And stopped, halfway through putting in the code to unlock it. I was looking down at the car next to the Nissan, at the logo on the hubcap. It was horribly familiar.

Moving fast because I was scared of what I would find, I dragged the dustsheet off the car and stared at Derwent's Subaru, sitting there with its keys in the ignition. I ripped open the door and took them out, checking the front, the back, the boot for signs of life.

But no Derwent.

Just a young woman who liked killing coppers, and a house full of places to hide a body.

Chapter Twenty-Eight

I ran back into the kitchen to find Amy Maynard dry-eyed, tugging at the cuffs with all her might. I took hold of a handful of her hair. "What have you done with him? Where is he?"

"I don't know what you're talking about."

"Is he still alive?"

"I really couldn't say."

I pulled on her hair, hard, and she grinned as if it tickled her. "Tell me."

"I don't know," she said. "I'm serious. You might be in time. You might not."

I was shaking with fear and rage and the terrible, agonizing worry that I was much too late already. I flipped up the hotplate cover on top of the Aga and put a hand out to feel the heat radiating from it. "Think. Where is he?"

"I don't know."

I bent her over the top of the Aga and pressed her down so her cheek was an inch away from the plate. "Tell me."

"You wouldn't."

I thought about Derwent, and what he would do for me in the same circumstances. He wouldn't hesitate.

But I wasn't him, and I couldn't do it.

That didn't mean I couldn't fool Amy Maynard into thinking I would.

I leaned on her, just a little bit, and felt her suck in her breath just before her face touched the hot metal.

"Stop."

"Where?"

"Bitch," she spat and I made to lean on her again. "No, stop. Upstairs."

"Where?"

"The bathroom at the top of the stairs." She started to laugh again. "He won't have gone anywhere."

The temptation to jam her head down on the plate for the sake of it was overwhelming. I left her cackling there and hared back out, up the stairs, on the edge of tears. If he was dead, I thought, I would never forgive myself for not working it out sooner. The terrible, tearing anxiety made my legs weak as I pulled a wheelchair out of my way and hurled myself at the door at the back of the hallway, the only one that was closed. The sound of running water was louder here, and there was another sound too, a weak kind of knocking that I'd half-heard in the kitchen and wondered about. I'd been distracted. I hadn't known I should have been paying attention. It was no consolation.

The door, of course, was locked. I looked for a key and found nothing: spinning around I saw only doorways to rooms I didn't have time to search. I ran back down to the kitchen. Amy was sitting on the floor with her arms stretched up, still cuffed around the bar.

"This is very uncomfortable."

"Where's the key to the bathroom door?"

"Lost it."

I didn't have the time or the heart to hurt her until she told me where it was. I ran out to the garage and hunted until I found a crowbar. Back at the bathroom door I stuck the end of it into the gap between the door and the frame and began to work it back and forth, sobbing under my breath, until finally I'd got it in far enough that I could lever the door open, the lock breaking through the flimsy wood of the door frame, leaving it splintered.

The door swung open and I understood what she had meant about him being where she'd left him, and why she'd found it funny, though I couldn't laugh. He was chained to a hook that was set into the ceiling. It had originally been fitted to accommodate the invalid hoist that swung over the bath. His feet were high up, his legs straight. He was resting on his shoulders, his hips suspended so he couldn't get any purchase to sit up. That meant his head was lower than the level of the water that was filling the bath, and filling it, and filling it, from the taps that were turned on full. His hands were chained behind him so he couldn't use them to lift himself either. Somehow, he had managed to turn sideways and get an elbow under him, raising him far enough that by making a huge effort he could stretch his face above the surface of the water to snatch some air for a second or two, but he couldn't do that indefinitely. When he was too weak to fight any more, he would drown. When he gave up, he would die.

Derwent was not the sort of person to give up easily, but he wasn't moving.

He wasn't moving at all.

I had a second of pure panic before my brain came back to life.

The first thing to do was to turn off the taps that were keeping the bath full, despite the water spilling down through the overflow. Frantic to get Derwent out from under the water, I pulled the plug, then put a hand under his head to lift him up. He broke the surface with a noise like a gasp crossed with a groan, dragging air back into his lungs. He didn't speak — couldn't, I think. His chest was heaving, his eyelids fluttering, and although my arms were breaking from the weight of him I couldn't let go of him again. I couldn't let him sink back into the water that had almost killed him. I knelt beside the bath, cradling him, the water soaking through my clothes. He felt amazingly alive in my arms, warm and vital, and I could have wept over him if I hadn't been so annoyed that he'd got himself into such trouble in the first place.

Gradually, the bath drained enough that I could lay him back down without endangering him. His eyes flicked open and stayed open.

"What are you doing?" It came out shouted, but coherent.

"I have to work out how to get you out." I looked at the chains. They were padlocked in three different places, and the chain itself was a heavy gauge. No keys anywhere in the bathroom.

"Always the fucking keys with this one," I said, mainly to myself.

"What?" Derwent said, still groggy.

"Nothing. Stay there." I didn't really think about whether he had any choice about that.

"Maeve." The desperation in his voice was as close to begging as Derwent could get.

"I won't be long, I promise."

I started looking into rooms, finding a master bedroom that smelt of greasy hair and old clothes. No one was using it currently. The bed was stripped back, revealing a stained mattress and yellowed pillows. A few family photographs stood on top of a chest of drawers. I took two seconds to peer at a smudgy wedding picture from the early eighties of a couple who looked middle-aged and unglamorous. The woman was giving a lopsided smile, not looking at the camera. She had sloping shoulders and a heavy bosom that her wedding dress didn't flatter. The man was small and neat, with graying hair. There was something reminiscent of a rodent in the way his features were laid out. I could see a likeness to Amy in them, although she'd got the best of what was on offer from both of them.

Next to it there was a holiday snap of two children and two adults, all wearing thick glasses and unflattering clothes: the wedding couple ten years on as his hair receded and her chest sagged a little further. Amy was giving the camera a gappy grin, her shorts pulled up too high and her T-shirt a horrible shade of blue. The girl beside her was sullen. Not a picture I would have framed, personally, but it was the whole family, I guessed. No bother, obviously. The last was a school photograph of the older girl, fair-haired, with a wide, sensitive mouth and vulnerable eyes.

What I didn't see were any keys.

The next bedroom was draped in sheeting, a room full of ghosts. I looked under a couple of them: a chest of drawers covered in old make-up and jewelry. A single bed, again stripped. Occupying one corner of the room, a screen.

"Holy shit." The screen was in three parts, dedicated to two different things: the attack on Philip Gregory and the shooting of Terence Hammond. It was disconcertingly similar to our noticeboard, with one major difference: most of it was devoted to planning rather than reconstructing what had happened. This was Amy Maynard's command center. I skim-read the information she had collected on Gregory and Hammond, reading e-mail chains between Gregory and "Laura" from LonelyHeart SeeksAnother.com, a dating Web site. He'd given her his place of work, his neighborhood, his date of birth — everything she had needed to track him down. For Hammond, the rules of netball and information about gun competitions. A map of Richmond Park spread over two panels of the screen, with a route marked on it and a star sketched where the murder had taken place. There was nothing about an accomplice, from a first look at it. She would give him up, though, I thought. She would give us anything to save herself.

The third room had a double bed in it. I assumed it was hers, from the clothes and shoes that lay around the place. I saw the hideous green jumper she'd worn in school. She wasn't tidy at home any more than in her office, but that wasn't the main problem with the room. The bedclothes were in a chaotic state, as if it had been the scene of a struggle. Blood spattered the carpet and a broken lamp lay close by. Derwent's clothes were in a crumpled heap by the bed. His mobile was on top of the pile, switched off.

I went back to the bathroom. "Did she whack you over the head?"

"She must have. It hurts."

I leaned to look. The water had washed the blood away so I hadn't noticed it at first, but through his hair I could see a nasty gash above his left ear and it was still seeping all along its length. "That'll need stitches. What were you doing in her bedroom?"

"What do you think?" He sounded very irritated now, and he was starting to shiver. It wasn't all that surprising when he was only wearing a very soggy pair of pants. They had a clinging quality that I was trying very hard not to notice.

"So she wasn't asexual, but she was a homicidal maniac. Does that make her better or worse, in your view?"

"Kerrigan, I don't mean to complain, but could you find the mother-fucking keys and get me out of here? It's actually less pleasant now that there's no water in the bath. I think my shoulder is breaking."

"Right. On it."

I went down to the kitchen. "Padlock keys."

She was sitting where I'd left her. She must have known that Derwent was alive, and that the house was full of evidence that would be difficult if not downright impossible to explain in court. Somehow, she smirked. "I don't know what you mean."

"You're just wasting everyone's time. I've turned the water off. He's not dying. He was fine." Stretching a point, perhaps, but I wanted her to stop grinning at me.

"He's a prick. He thought he could walk

in here and click his fingers and I'd be happy to fuck him while he was on duty. As if it was his right. As if I would have enjoyed it."

"Did you enjoy fucking Terence Hammond?"

"Of course not."

"Did you fuck him when he was on duty?"

"He liked anything that made him feel like he was being bad. On duty. Behind his wife's back. In the back seat of the car with his vegetable of a kid in the front. He liked to come on my tits, or on my face. Up my arse. He liked to hit me. Swear at me. Anything, as long as it was degrading for me and fun for him."

"You knew what he wanted. You had him hooked."

"It wasn't difficult. Just like it wasn't difficult with the one upstairs. They're all the same. Fucking pigs." She spat at me again, the gobbet of saliva landing just by my foot. "Keep looking, bitch."

Back out to the garage, to find some bolt cutters that were covered in cobwebs and tarnished with patches of rust. They still seemed viable. I ran back in and up the stairs and got a lecture the entire time I was wrestling with cutting through the links, until I stopped and told him I would leave him there for the fire brigade to rescue if he liked. That bought me enough silence to finish the job. The last bit of metal gave way and the chain slithered into the bath with a rattling thud.

"Do you need any help?"

"I can manage." Derwent levered himself up and fell over the side of the bath, landing facedown on the mat. "Ow."

"Ow," I agreed, sitting down beside him and taking out my phone. My nose hurt. My hand hurt. I seemed to have torn something crucial in my shoulder at some stage, though I couldn't remember what or when. I was covered in cobwebs and blood, and my clothes were cold and damp.

"Who are you calling?" Derwent asked.

"Someone to come and take Amy Maynard away."

"Where is she?"

"I handcuffed her to the Aga."

"Seriously?"

I nodded, then concentrated on getting through to the control room and giving the details of where to find us. Derwent eased himself into a sitting position, wincing.

"You look like shit. Did the two of you have a fight?" he asked when I hung up.

"We might have. I won, obviously."

"I can't believe I missed it." He sounded

genuinely regretful.

"You were tied up."

"No, no." He wagged a finger at me. "None of that. Don't even start."

"You were hanging around up here."

"I'm warning you, Kerrigan."

"Don't get me wrong, I'm glad she didn't just kill you, but why did she do this?" I gestured at the bath.

"She really hates coppers." Derwent stretched, wincing. "She wanted me to die slowly. She said that was the problem with just shooting Hammond. He hadn't known what was coming. She wanted my death to be my fault, because I was too weak to live."

"But you survived."

"She picked the wrong guy," Derwent said, conveniently ignoring the fact that it was only because I'd happened to find him that he hadn't drowned.

I eyed him. "Do you want to put some clothes on before the cavalry arrive, or are you planning to greet them in a state of nature? And if so, what are you going to tell them about why you're wandering around the house naked in the middle of the working day? You'll get in serious trouble if anyone finds out you were planning to shag a witness at all, let alone while you were on duty."

"I know. I'll get dressed, if I can find my clothes." He got to his feet slowly, wincing. "Bloody women."

"Don't blame women," I said, following him into Amy's bedroom. "Blame yourself. If you'd just stop thinking with your dick, *sir,* this kind of thing wouldn't happen to you."

For an answer, he stepped out of his pants and held them out to me.

I put my hands over my eyes instead. "Excuse me, what are you doing?"

"I can't wear them. They're soaking."

"Well, *I* don't want them. And put some clothes on, for the love of God."

He dropped the pants with a wet slap and groaned as he bent to pick up his trousers. "I may need some help."

"You're on your own." I slid past him and ran down to the kitchen to tell Amy the good news that she'd be taking a little trip to the police station. I stopped dead in the doorway.

"Oh, *fuck.*"

I went back to Derwent. "Did you have your cuffs on you?"

"In the car. Why?"

"Where was the key?"

"With them."

"Fuck," I said again. Handcuff keys were

tiny. Easy to lose. Easy, unfortunately, to hide. "She must really like keys."

"What?" He was knotting his tie. "What are you talking about?"

"I don't think DCI Burt is going to be very pleased with us."

"Why not? We just caught her a killer."

"That very much depends on how you define 'caught.'" I held up my unlocked handcuffs and shrugged.

In the distance, a siren whooped.

"If we ran too," Derwent said, quite seriously, "how far do you think we would get?"

CHAPTER TWENTY-NINE

"Just tell me what happened again. One more time." Una Burt was walking up and down in front of us, her hands behind her back. If she wasn't careful, she would wear a path in the carpet and it wasn't her office. I was missing Godley more than I could say.

I stood up a little bit straighter, not feeling in the least like laughing at Derwent for standing to attention now. It was stressful, reciting the same half-truths over and over again. It was all too easy to slip up on a detail. No wonder it was one of our interrogators' favorite techniques. My hand throbbed where the doctors had glued it together. My shoulder ached. *Concentrate.*

"I arrived and saw no sign of DI Derwent at the premises. I interviewed Amy Maynard to find out if she had seen him, and to establish her relationship with Terence Hammond, which was what DI Derwent had been intending to ask her. I noticed a set of keys for a Ford Mondeo hanging on the board in the hall and I asked Amy what car she drove. She said it was an old Nissan. That fitted with Hugh Johnson's account of what he saw at the time of the shooting, and with Philip Gregory's revised description of the car that drove at him. And Terence Hammond drove a Mondeo. We hadn't found the keys and our theory was that the woman in his car had taken them away with her after the shooting. I felt it all fitted together and pointed to Amy Maynard as a credible suspect."

"So you attacked her. You were taking a pretty big risk given that all you had was a feeling that it fitted together and two sets of car keys. I call that jumping to conclusions."

"Well," I said, trying to hold on to my temper. "It was more than a feeling. A lot of things fell into place when I saw the keys. And anyway, I was right."

"Yes, you were. Go on."

"She was holding a knife. I restrained her and disarmed her. I handcuffed her to an immovable object and went in search of DI Derwent."

"Why didn't you call for backup immediately?"

"I didn't want to wait. I thought Amy was trying to keep me talking. I thought it might

549

be time-sensitive. And it was."

"So you found him chained up and in danger of drowning."

"Yes."

"And you untied him."

"Yes. I had to look for the keys, and then a bolt-cutter when the keys didn't turn up. It took a while."

"Did you search Amy Maynard at any point?"

"I did."

"But you missed the keys."

"I must have."

"And you missed the handcuff key she had hidden somewhere on her person."

"Yes."

"So she was able to free herself."

"Yes." All the wriggling and complaining had been very convincing, I didn't add. Amy had fooled me comprehensively.

"And you, Josh. How do you explain what happened?"

"I had a short conversation with Amy Maynard. She seemed very defensive about her relationship with Terence Hammond. I had wanted to speak to her because I thought she had a crush on him and that she might have identified his girlfriend, the lady we still hadn't been able to trace. During the course of our conversation, I became suspicious of her and I asked to use the bathroom. I took the opportunity to look into the bedrooms upstairs and while I was looking around Miss Maynard's room, she hit me over the head with a lamp. When I came to, I was suspended above the bath in danger of drowning."

"How did she manage to move you from the bedroom to the bathroom and lift you into the bath? You must weigh twice what she does."

"She used a wheelchair to move him," I said. "The bath was equipped with a hoist. According to the neighbors, her mother nursed her father in the house before she became too feeble to cope and they both went into a home. The house was equipped for moving heavy individuals."

"Okay." Burt was frowning. "But why would she just attack you?"

"She doesn't like police officers," Derwent said. "Or men." It was the understatement of the year, and close enough to the real reason to sound true. Especially if you didn't think about it for too long.

"Her sister was Annabel Strake, who died in 2001," I said, judging it was time to distract from what Derwent might or might not have done in the house to incur Amy's wrath. "Amy changed her name to Maynard after her parents died."

"And she blamed Terence Hammond and Phil Gregory for what happened to her sister," Una Burt said.

"Rightly, I think. She killed herself because no one believed her. Terence Hammond took advantage of her."

"Why would he do something like that? He was an experienced police officer."

"He was under tremendous pressure. He'd had a car accident the year before that caused a catastrophic injury to his son. His marriage was in trouble as a result. He had two small children and an angry wife who wasn't providing him with — um — his conjugal rights. Annabel Strake was young, high, and an easy target."

"Have you told the DPS Gregory lied to them?"

"With great pleasure," I said. "I think they'll be interviewing him again soon."

"How did Amy Maynard find Gregory and Hammond?"

"By chance, and then by design," I said. "She trained as a counselor because she genuinely wanted to help young people, I think. Annabel had problems with depression and alcohol abuse. Amy grew up around that. She had real empathy with teenagers, especially ones who were coping with family problems. Being a counselor was actually quite a good career for her. Then she came across Hammond. She had a printout on the screen that was a report from a local paper, about two years ago. It mentioned him by name."

"And she decided to get close to him by going through his kids."

"She offered to work at his daughter's school and they accepted because she was willing to work for a pitiful salary. According to the headmistress, she said she wanted to get some experience for her CV. She spent a lot of time getting to know Vanessa, gaining her trust, being the alternative to the very difficult Julie Hammond. Vanessa liked her, Ben liked her — Terence liked her. He liked her a lot. He was reckless around her. He liked the crazy things she suggested they do, like meeting in Richmond Park after his shift for illicit sex in a public place."

"He must have thought he'd won the lottery," Derwent commented. "Young, pretty, absolutely filthy, and interested in him."

"Yeah. How could he say no?" I managed not to give Derwent a meaningful look because Burt was watching for it, but that was the only reason I didn't.

"He was someone she hated. How could

she bear to let him touch her?" Burt mused.

"To get what she wanted. She was quite single-minded about it," I said. "She had a plan to execute. And she would have loved the thrill of it. She basically made an excuse to talk to me at Hammond's funeral service. I was with Gregory. He might have made a connection between her and Annabel. They looked very similar, even though Amy dressed so modestly."

"Why take the risk?" Burt asked.

"I think she wanted to know what he was doing there, and she wanted to talk to him face to face. She'd found Gregory on the Internet too, in his case on a dating site. She e-mailed him from a few different profiles, getting to know as much about him as she could. He was forthcoming. He made it easy for her to find him. The only thing she couldn't control was how quick his re-actions were when she tried to run him down."

"Good for him," Derwent said.

"She liked talking to me about the investigation at the funeral. It gave her a kick to fool us."

"Then she must be loving this," Una Burt said, her voice very dry. "No sign of her. The dog didn't track her further than the end of the road. She must have been ready to run."

"I'm sure she's good at improvising," I said. "She's clever. She can't have known she was going to need the handcuff key but she had it on her. Mind you, she likes keys. That's why she kept Hammond's."

"We know she's got an accomplice out there somewhere," Derwent pointed out. "She didn't shoot Hammond. She just made it possible for someone else to do it. That means she has someone to call on for help. Someone who has an interest in keeping her out of prison."

"So what do we do now? Wait?" Burt was back to pacing. "I don't like that approach."

I cleared my throat. "Without wishing to jump to any conclusions, I think I have an idea."

This time, I found Andrew Hardy in his office at the White Valley Shooting Club, rather than standing in reception. He hadn't known I was coming and his expression when he saw me was pure dread.

"What can I do for you, Miss Kerrigan? Do you need to speak to more of our members? I'm fairly sure you've seen them all by now."

"I just need to look at a few files," I said. "It won't take long."

"What sort of files?"

"When we came to see you originally, you made us sign in. Do you keep the sign-in sheets?"

"We do. It helps us to keep track of who is using the facilities and what our busy times are." He took down a lever-arch file that was fat with yellowing paper. "They're all in here."

I leafed through, looking for the day we'd visited. I didn't expect to find Amy Maynard's name in the book, and nor did I. She wouldn't have been an official visitor. I doubted she'd even been in the clubhouse. She was there to meet her fellow murderer, someone who was probably a member of the club, someone whose name appeared on the list Rex Gibney had given us of people who knew about the gun. Probably someone I'd spoken to already.

There were about twenty names on the sheet when I found it. I scanned through it. "Can I see the files on everyone here?"

"Why do you need them?"

"Just checking."

Hardy went through his filing cabinets methodically, taking out the files and setting them on his desk. The office was so small that he ceded it to me rather than try to work around me.

I was halfway down the list when I opened Jonny Pilgrew's file and the obvious answer hit me between the eyes. Under "other gun-club membership," in a straggling, unformed hand, Jonny had written: "Uplands School."

Jonny, Stuart Pilgrew's son. The boy with light eyebrows and short dark hair. The boy who'd walked away from me without even knowing who I was or what I wanted with him. The boy who'd known very well who I was because he'd seen me at his school a few days earlier.

He'd cut and dyed his hair since I'd seen him leave the student counselor's office, where he'd been with Amy Maynard. He'd done what he could to change his appearance. What he couldn't hide was his fear, and now it made sense to me.

It was a nice house, not large but detached. Cream-painted, like its neighbors. Two cars in the driveway. Lights on in the living room and a bedroom upstairs.

I rang the doorbell and waited, Derwent beside me.

"Yes?" Stuart Pilgrew stood in the doorway, obviously not long home from work. He had shed his tie and his jacket, and he was wearing socks with a hole over

one toe, but he looked more like a successful businessman than he had at the gun
club. He frowned at me, not knowing who I
was, then spotted Derwent. His face
transformed itself into a welcoming smile.
"All right, mate?"

"Not bad, thanks. Do you mind if we
come in for a minute?"

"Of course, of course." Pilgrew let us into
the hall and directed us to the living room,
which was comfortable and untidy. A young
teenage girl unwound herself from the sofa
and disappeared silently. There was a smell
of roasting meat and an occasional clatter
from the kitchen. I heard a woman's voice
asking a brief question that got an even
briefer answer from the girl.

"Sorry for disturbing you. We'll try not to
stay too long," I said.

"What can I do for you? I thought I'd seen
the last of you after you ran out on us at the
club."

"I had somewhere to be," Derwent said.

"In quite a hurry." Pilgrew was affecting
good humor and friendliness, but there was
a shrewd look in his eyes that told me he
was frantically trying to work out what we
wanted. "Is this about the gun?"

"What gun?" I asked.

"The one you've been asking everyone in

the club about. Rex Gibney's gun."

"Did you know about it?"

"Yes. I saw it."

"Did you?" I was genuinely surprised that he was volunteering that information.

"He showed me and Jonny when we were at his house once. He let Jonny actually fire it."

"Jonny, your son."

"So my wife tells me."

"That's the second time you've made that joke," I said coldly. "You need some new material."

He was watching me, definitely wary now. "What do you want?"

"I want to know why you've just told us Jonny fired the gun. It makes me think you're trying to muddy the waters. Because if we find it and there's forensic evidence linking Jonny to the gun, you've already said he handled it and fired it, haven't you?"

Pilgrew shrugged. "It's the truth."

"Can we have a word with Jonny? Please?" Derwent waited for a moment. "I'd rather talk to him here than at the station, but I will take him in for formal questioning if you prefer."

"No. Definitely not." Pilgrew was jittery with tension. He got up and went into the hall. "Jonny? Get down here. Now."

Now took a minute or two. We sat in silence, staring at Pilgrew, while he stared back. He was squeezing his hands together, over and over again. Not happy. Not at ease.

He knew, I thought.

Jonny Pilgrew walked into the room looking as if he was going to the scaffold. He was white with fear and looked very young in his wine-colored school jumper and dark gray trousers, a uniform I recognized instantly.

"I see you go to Uplands School," Derwent observed. "Are you in Vanessa Hammond's year?"

"No. The year above." His voice was hoarse and almost inaudible.

"Do you know her?" I asked and got a definite headshake in response.

"Do you know Amy Maynard?"

The boy flinched, visibly. "Yes."

"Do you know that we're looking for her?"

He stared at me dumbly. I thought he was going to cry.

"Who's Amy Maynard?" Pilgrew demanded.

"The student counselor at Uplands," Derwent said. "And chief suspect in the murder of Terence Hammond."

Jonny was so pale I thought he was going to faint.

"When we saw you at White Valley," I said, "we didn't know that Amy Maynard was there too. But her car was in the car park. Was she there to see you?"

"No."

"Why was she there?"

"I don't know. I didn't see her."

"Were you expecting to see her?"

"No. I don't know."

"Why did you cut your hair, Jonny?"

He put a hand up to touch it, uncertain.

"I don't know why he did, but it was a good thing. He looked ridiculous with it long." Pilgrew's eyes were switching back and forth from me to Derwent, considering what we were saying.

"Why did you dye it?" The roots were starting to show already, a line of paler hair that told its own story.

"I wanted a change."

"When did you decide to do it?"

"A while ago."

"After we saw you at the school coming out of Miss Maynard's room."

He nodded.

Pilgrew rounded on his son. "Why were you having counseling? You're not gay, are you?"

"No! Dad, come on." Jonny tried to laugh, but he was shaking. "Leave it out."

"I just don't understand why you were going for counseling."

"Miss Maynard suggested it. She spoke to the sports department about talented people. She thought she could help us. She did hypnosis and stuff. Gave me advice on focusing when I was shooting. She'd read books on sports psychology."

Which qualified her to teach him precisely fuck all. She'd heard about his talent for shooting and decided she could use him.

"What a waste of time," Pilgrew said dismissively.

Jonny flushed. "She was really good."

"You like her, don't you?" Derwent smiled. "I can see why. She's pretty."

The boy was scarlet.

"Did you fancy her?"

"I don't know."

"Did she fancy you?"

"He's just a kid," Pilgrew said.

Derwent gave him a thin smile. "He's a teenager who will be tried as an adult when he is charged with murder. He'll be looking at a life sentence."

"What? What are you talking about?"

Instead of answering, Derwent said, "Jonathan Pilgrew, I am arresting you for the murder of Terence Hammond. You do not have to say anything but it may harm your defense if you do not mention when questioned something which you later rely on in court. Anything you do say may be given in evidence."

Jonny sat down on the edge of the sofa and dropped his head into his hands.

"What the hell's going on?" Pilgrew thundered.

"This is what we think happened," I said. "Amy Maynard got close to Jonny. She persuaded him to help her. She arranged for him to steal Rex Gibney's gun and he used it to shoot Terence Hammond, at her request."

"Is this true?" Pilgrew asked his son.

"He was a bad person. A killer. He'd abused vulnerable kids. He maimed his own son." Jonny sounded as if he still couldn't fathom how evil Terence Hammond had been. I marveled at the half-truths, the compromised facts that Amy had used to construct her trap. "He raped Miss Maynard. She was so brave. She lured him back to the place where it happened and made him think she wanted to be with him again."

"And what did you do?" I asked.

"I did what she asked me to."

"Which was what?"

"I shot him."

"Stop talking," Pilgrew said. "He needs a solicitor."

"No, I don't."

"We need to find the gun. We have a search warrant." I showed it to Pilgrew who read through it carefully, then handed it back to me.

"It's under my mattress," Jonny volunteered. "In pieces."

"I told you to shut up," Pilgrew yelled.

"What's the point? I did it. They knew it. They were going to find the gun anyway." Jonny's eyes were wet. "She asked me to do it and I didn't want to but I had to. It was different from shooting at a target. A lot different. I didn't think I could do it — but he was so gross. All over her. Touching her. Pushing her head down so she could —" He broke off, swallowed, regrouped. "The world would be better without him, she said. So I did it. I didn't want to let her down." He stared around at us, moving from one face to another like a lost dog seeking reassurance. He looked very young indeed.

"It's all right," Derwent said. "I understand."

"She loves me and I love her."

"Has she been in touch with you, Jonny?" Derwent's voice was quiet, in contrast to

564

the boy's father. "Do you know where she is?"

"No." But he put a hand up to rub his upper lip just after he said it, and we all saw the panic in his eyes. Not a practiced liar. Not a good one. But very useful to us indeed.

"Do you think she's going to show?"

"She has to. She needs the money." I watched the crowds milling around the shops, fast-food stands, and entertainment arcades that filled the Trocadero. It was one of the busiest places in London, just off Shaftesbury Avenue, and Amy Maynard couldn't really have picked a more difficult place for surveillance. There were too many exits and too many places to hide. The only good thing about it was that the undercover officers who were loitering in key locations had plenty of cover. No one would have noticed twenty extra people standing around, not doing much. Even if they were on edge, as Amy presumably would be.

We were standing opposite the escalators that led up to the cinema complex on the second floor. It was where Amy had suggested Jonny could meet her, to hand over the £1,200 in cash he'd taken out of his bank account over the previous few days.

"Do you think she'll be on time?" I asked.

"He's her lifeline. I'd imagine so."

"Do you think she'll show herself if she doesn't see him?"

Derwent scowled. "She'd better. I still think it's bollocks that we weren't allowed to use him."

"He's a child."

"Old enough to kill. Old enough to be tried as an adult."

I scanned the scene in front of me, trying to see if the undercover officers stood out. A male and female officer were having a deeply intimate conversation while looking over each other's shoulders. Another, a tall black guy, was talking on his phone. Two bulky men in bomber jackets strolled across the concourse holding cups of coffee. To me, they were obviously police. But in the milling crowds we might just get away with it.

Derwent was scanning the scene too. "Where is she?"

"I don't know." A few minutes passed as we watched and waited, the tension twisting in my gut. I couldn't help expecting to see the Amy Maynard I'd met before, the girl in colorful, unflattering clothes. I'd warned the surveillance teams that she might be dressed differently but it still took me a second to appreciate that the woman walking out of the cinema complex was Amy herself. It was only her walk that gave her away; it was hard to disguise the way she moved. Her hair was cropped and blond, her jeans skin-tight, her top fitted enough to show, very clearly, that she wore no bra. She was attracting plenty of attention, but not from the undercover teams.

"There," I said.

"Where?" Derwent was trying to see where I was pointing. I didn't wait. I was gone already, moving fast to get to her before she had time to run. In my earpiece, Derwent was relaying a description to the undercover officers over the radio, his voice tense. One by one I saw them focus on her and head toward her, iron filings to a magnet.

And Amy looked straight at me. It took her no longer than a second to realize she was in trouble and to start running. It wasn't her fault that a second wasn't long enough.

I collided with her when she was about ten feet away from the escalators. I sent her sprawling to the floor and landed on top of her.

"Let's try this again, shall we?" I pulled her hands out and the black undercover officer cuffed her with her wrists behind her.

Amy was kicking the floor, overwhelmed with rage. "Stupid fucking cretin. Dickhead. Twat."

"Who's that, then?" the other officer asked.

"Jonny. He must have told you where to find me."

"He didn't have much choice," I said. "He's under arrest too."

"Fucking *fuck.*"

"Amy, Amy. That's no way to talk," I said.

Derwent crouched down beside her head. "You look good, Amy," he whispered. "That's a nice look on you."

"Get stuffed."

A crowd was gathering. Amy looked around, then started to hit her face on the floor. I caught her head.

"None of that. Everyone can see you. Half of the people here are filming this. No one is going to believe you when you say it was police brutality."

"I hate you," she hissed.

"You're just angry. Whereas I have never been happier." I leaned in. "Terence Hammond wasn't a great person. He wasn't a good police officer. He was a lazy husband, and a poor enough father. He was inadequate and stupid. But you still shouldn't have killed him."

"I didn't kill him."

"It was your plan. Your idea. Jonny pulled the trigger but you set Hammond up."

"I didn't know what Jonny was going to do. He's obsessed with me. He was stalking me. He —"

"Stop," I said, very softly. "Save it for your lawyer. You pretend to care about young people but all you care about is yourself. Nothing justifies the fact that Jonny Pilgrew is going to get landed with a life sentence for murder."

"That's not my problem."

"It is your fault and I will make it your problem." I leaned even closer. "This is it, Amy. This is your life. I hope you enjoyed it, because you're not getting out of prison for a very long time."

CHAPTER THIRTY

When I got to my desk, my phone was ringing. I stared at it, feeling a strange reluctance to answer it. Whatever it was, it didn't feel like good news. I let it ring for longer than I should have, and then broke at the last possible minute before it switched to voicemail.

"Hello?"

"Is that Maeve Kerrigan?"

I recognized the honeyed voice, given an edge by the slight huskiness of the heavy drinker the morning after. "DI Ormond."

"Deborah, please."

I said absolutely nothing in response. Hell would freeze and the demons would skate before I called her Deborah.

"What do you want?"

"Have you heard from Rob?" The question burst out of her as if she'd been holding it in.

"Haven't you?" I asked, suspicious.

"No. All I've had is a notification that he's

been put on leave indefinitely, at his own request. And of course the request was granted, I mean, half of my team is off sick because of seeing Harry bleed out and I don't blame them but I don't understand how Rob could just *disappear.*"

"When did you see him last?"

"The morning you came round." She sounded sulky. So it had been a one-night stand and no more. I jabbed my pen into my desk, feeling glad and angry and unsettled.

"I haven't seen him."

"Has he spoken to you?"

"No," I said truthfully, and hung up on her. I didn't tell her about going home the previous night, though. I didn't tell her about walking in and knowing, absolutely knowing, that Rob was back. There had been a change in the order of atoms in the flat, somehow, an energy that had been missing from my world. I hurried into the living area and found it deserted. Back to the bedroom. The bathroom. The small room that was supposed to be for guests and had ended up as a dumping ground for things I didn't want to throw out and Rob didn't want to own.

The smile on my face had faded along with the hope.

In the bedroom I opened the wardrobe and saw air: empty hangers. Empty drawers by the bed. I'd been right; he had been there. And now he was gone. I had wanted to howl then and I wanted to howl now.

In the kitchen, second time round, I'd spotted it: the note. One sheet of paper, folded over. I opened it with a sense of tremendous despair.

Maeve,

I am going to spend some time away from work and London and, I'm sorry to say, you. I need to get my head together. I'm sorry for everything that's happened. I can't tell you how sorry I am.

The rent — don't worry about it. Stay for as long as you like. Stay until I come back, preferably. I bought the flat a few years ago, so I'm the evil landlord, and I'm giving you a rent reduction. I can cover the mortgage so don't worry about it. (I had been meaning to tell you this for a while. One more thing I got wrong.)

I love you.

R
X

"You bastard," I'd said, on an exhalation. I'd been holding my breath as I read it, I realized. I spent a lot of time that evening reading it, and then reading it again. By the way, I'm rich, which I kept pretty quiet. By the way, I'm sorry. By the way, I'm leaving and I'm not saying when I'm coming back. Oh, and you don't get to talk to me about it, or anything else.

You don't even get to say you forgive me.

I rang my mother, in the end, who knew us both, and told her an edited version of what had happened, including Debbie Ormond's role but leaving out the Maudling Estate stairwell. I wasn't really expecting her to be able to help. I just wanted to talk to someone who was solidly, definitely on my side.

"I mind much more about the flat than about him sleeping with someone else. Is that strange?"

"I don't know. I don't know how you young people behave these days, sleeping around. Things are acceptable now that never were in my day."

I rolled my eyes. This had been a mistake.

She went on. "You're funny about money, though. You like to be equal with people. You don't like feeling as if you're worth less than anyone else. That was the big problem between you and Ian."

"That was *one* of the problems between me and Ian."

Which Rob had known.

I was starting to see why he hadn't wanted to tell me he was loaded.

I paced around the flat. "But it's such a big lie. And for years, Mum. I remember talking to him about whether we could afford this place — really worrying about how we could manage. And then he negotiated a good deal for the rent — with himself — so it was all fine. He lied and lied and I had no idea."

"As I said, you're funny about it."

"Did you know about it?" I asked, suddenly suspicious.

A pause. "We had some idea."

"What? You said 'we.' You *and* Dad?" The scale of the betrayal amazed me.

"He told us about the flats some time when we were asking about his plans for the future."

When we were interrogating him about how suitable he was for our daughter.

"Flats? You mean there are more?"

"I think he has six altogether."

"Mum!"

"They're worth millions. It just shows what you can achieve."

"But where did he get the money?"

"His parents are very wealthy. Didn't you know?"

"No, I didn't. I really didn't." I'd never met them. They were divorced, for one thing, and lived outside Manchester, far enough away that dropping in wasn't an option. Rob had been happy to go to my parents for Christmas and Easter and many occasions in between. I'd never insisted on visiting them instead. I'd thought it looked too pushy. I was starting to regret it.

"Your father and I thought he was sensible to invest in property the way prices are going. You know I've always worried you're getting left behind. You'll never be able to afford anything the way you're going."

"Not this again. Not now," I said sharply.

She'd taken the hint and fallen silent while I worked out how I felt about all of it. The lies. The cheating. The fear I had that he'd never really trusted me. I couldn't forget what Derwent had said. No trust, no relationship.

"Do you know what the worst thing is?" I paced up and down. "I don't actually care that he cheated on me. I don't even care that he lied to me. I know I should be furious with him and with you two for knowing what was going on and not saying, but I just want him back. I'd forgive him in a second if I could just talk to him."

"That's the trouble, isn't it. He doesn't want to be forgiven."

"But why not?"

"Sometimes the hardest thing is admitting you were wrong. It's hard to say you need to be forgiven."

I thought about that.

"You had him up on a pedestal, Maeve. You always thought he was perfect, but he's just human. That's hard for him to admit. Let him go. He'll come back to you when the time is right."

"I don't have much choice," I pointed out. And that hurt so much. I'd always assumed I'd be the one to ruin everything. I'd thought I would have a moment of madness, like doing something unthinkable with Derwent at the wedding. I'd thought I'd lost Rob in Bexley. Then I'd thought it was my fault he'd left me. I hadn't realized I could lose him again, and for good, without doing anything more than love him.

"If you don't have any choice you have to put up with it. And don't do anything stupid like leaving the flat. Save some money while you can. You'll need a good bit of money for a deposit with an income like yours. Your father says —"

"Thank you, Mum." I'd meant it, though, and she knew it.

"Come home and see us this weekend. I've forgotten what you look like."

I'd promised to try. And I would, too. I would steel myself for criticism of whatever I was wearing and how my hair looked and everything I'd ever done or was planning to do. It was worth it, sometimes, just to be looked after.

Someone had left a newspaper on the desk next to mine. I became aware that I was staring at it, at the picture of Amy Maynard that took up a quarter of the front page. I reached over and got it, flipping it open to read the headline. It was a broadsheet, but they'd gone for an emotional angle. "Face of an Angel, Heart of a Killer." There was nothing angelic about Amy, I thought. We'd found where she hid her keys, but it had taken a strip search. They had been inside her.

"Nature's pocket," Derwent had said, grinning happily. But then, he hadn't had to supervise the search and watch as each key was retrieved by the doctor on duty.

"Maeve." For once, Una Burt was a welcome distraction. I folded the paper.

"Ma'am."

"Come in here, please."

I went, feeling wary. There was something in the very casual, cheerful way she spoke that made me suspicious. She was up to something.

"How are things?"

"Fine."

"I hear you're going to see Charlie later."

"Yes, I am." It wasn't a secret that I was visiting Godley; I hadn't been planning to hide it from her. I still felt unease prickle in my fingertips.

"It's going to take him a long time to get back to where he was. We all have to support him in the meantime, but we shouldn't encourage him to take on too much too soon."

Translation: I am *loving* having the top job and I'm not giving it up any time soon.

"Maeve, I'm making a few changes to the team." She hadn't sat down. Sitting down wasn't her style. Pacing back and forth, however, was, and she indulged herself for a few seconds while I stood and waited to hear her plans. I was genuinely convinced she was going to get rid of me. I should have known she had a bigger target in her sights.

"You did a good job on the Hammond case. I think you'd have done a better one if you hadn't had Josh Derwent to hold you back."

"He was really good," I said, surprised.

"You get stuck with minding him, time and time again. You're better than that."

"Really, I think we work well together."

"He's a distraction."

"Sometimes," I admitted. "But sometimes he makes me think again about what I'm doing. He challenges me. That has to be a good thing."

"I think you would work better if you weren't working with him." She stretched. "So you won't have to worry about it for much longer. DI Derwent is being transferred."

"What? Why?"

"Because I'm in charge now." She smirked at me, enjoying the moment. "I get to decide who stays and who goes. I don't want troublemakers and I don't want people on my team who make good detectives do stupid things."

"When Godley gets back —"

"*If* Godley comes back."

"He'll be fine," I said. "He's going to get better."

"We'll see. Even if he does get better, a stressful environment like this isn't the right place for him."

"But —"

"Your trouble, Maeve, is that you think

you're unique. You're just a detective. Rank and file. People keep telling you you're something remarkable and senior officers — male senior officers — seem to want to work with you. I wonder why that might be."

It struck me as very unfair that I was getting this sexist crap from another woman. I swallowed, trying to clear whatever was blocking my throat.

She went on, "You've been singled out for special treatment time and time again while good detectives — talented people — are sidelined. That's all going to change. No more Derwent. No more headline cases. You are going to go back to the beginning and put in some hard work on the boring, tedious cases that you've been able to dodge."

"I've never dodged anything. I do my share."

"I know what you've been doing. I've been watching you. And I'm telling you, it's all change from here." Her chest swelled with pride, putting the buttons on her blouse under serious strain. "A new broom sweeps clean, and I am that broom."

I walked out of Una Burt's office — because it was hers now, not Godley's — and straight through the team's room to the hall. I couldn't go any further. I was shaking, my stomach a tight knot, my brain stalled. I took stock of the things I had lost: no Rob. No Godley, who had given me opportunity after opportunity. No prospects. I marveled that I was still able to stand up.

Worst of all, somehow, was the thought of no Derwent. It was the thing that should have mattered least, but it hurt the most. Not sparring with him. Not cutting corners on his instructions. Not relying on him for the honest answer, even if I didn't want to hear it. Not leaning on him when I needed to. Not hauling him out of trouble by the scruff of his neck. No eye to catch when Una Burt was droning on. No one in my corner, most of the time.

Someone was running up the stairs, two at a time. I knew who it was going to be before Derwent came round the corner, heading for the office. He reached out to tip up my chin as he went by.

"Head up, princess. Your tiara is slipping."

I'd been holding it together until that moment, and I managed not to cry until the door had closed behind him. Then the sob I'd been suppressing fought its way up, and out. I put one hand over my eyes, as if that would let me hide from my colleagues or random passers-by.

I heard the door open again, and footsteps coming back toward me, slower this time. He must have stopped and turned around more or less as soon as the door closed behind him. Trust him not to miss the state I was in.

"What's up?"

I shook my head, turning away.

"Stop crying." He leaned in and said it again, quite loudly. "Stop."

"I can't."

"You don't cry at work. Don't be that girl who cries at work. You've worked too hard to be that girl. You don't want to be her."

I sniffed, wiping away tears with the back of my hand. "Stop being mean."

"Stop being pathetic."

"A normal person would give me a hug."

"And they'd get snot on their suit." He looked up and down the corridor. "Look, this isn't the place for this, unless you want an audience. Come on." He took my arm and marched me down the corridor until he found an empty meeting room. He pushed me through the door. "Stay there. I'll be back."

I didn't know where he'd gone and I didn't really care. I sat down at the table and leaned my elbows on it, burying my head in my hands. I had no fight left in me anymore.

He came back in balancing a glass of water on top of a box of tissues. He dumped them on the table. "Have at them."

I did as I was told, wondering where he'd got the tissues. Someone's desk, probably. It would have to be a woman, because the men never bothered with that kind of thing. I really hoped he hadn't stolen Una Burt's tissues. Fuel for the fire.

Derwent sat down on the other side of the table and watched me, frowning a little. When I'd recovered enough to talk, he tilted back on his chair. "What's this about? The absent boyfriend?"

"No. A bit," I said. "Not really, though. More about work."

He looked surprised. "Work is good."

"No," I said, blowing my nose. "It's not. DCI Burt."

That got his attention. He went very still. "What about her?"

"She's not going to let me work with you anymore. She's waiting to talk to you when you get in. She's going to get you transferred."

"Like fuck she is."

"That's what she told me. She seemed pretty sure of herself." I wiped my eyes.

"She's getting rid of you and I'm going to be made to shovel shit until I've earned the right to do my job again."

To my surprise, Derwent laughed. "Oh, good. I'm going to enjoy this."

"What?"

He stood up. "Burt doesn't get to make decisions about who stays on the team and who goes. She's strictly caretaking until the boss gets back, and he will be back — don't worry about that."

"But she's in charge."

"She thinks she's in charge. That doesn't mean she can do what she wants, as I'm about to tell her. It was one of the things the assistant commissioner made very clear to me."

"Are you sure?"

"No hiring and firing. No major changes. She's stuck with me, because I'm not going anywhere. And that means you work with me."

"But she outranks you. If she gives me stuff to do, I have to do it."

He shrugged, uncompromising as ever. "You'll just have to work harder and do both. I'm not going to let her take you away from me. I've put a lot of work into you, Kerrigan, and I'm not going to let someone else get the benefit."

I prickled with annoyance. "You didn't make me a good detective. I did that myself."

"Better," he said. "More anger, fewer tears. Stand up for yourself."

"I can't stand up to her. I'm too junior."

"That's what I'm for." He frowned at me. "Are you okay?"

I nodded.

"In that case, it's time to face the troll. Wish me luck." He leaned across the table and patted my hand. "Don't worry. I'll sort it out. Everything's going to be all right."

There was nothing Derwent liked more than an argument. He bounded out of the room in high good humor, looking for Burt. I stayed where I was, praying to Saint Jude. Desperate cases and lost causes were his area of expertise. It would have delighted Derwent if he'd known. The stakes were too high for me to enjoy the thought of him blasting Burt out of her complacency. He could argue all he liked, but that didn't mean he would win.

I could have been amused that of all the things I'd lost, Derwent assumed he was the most important. I'd never have admitted it to him, but he wasn't altogether wrong. He was tied in with work, with my confidence in myself, with everything that mattered to me. My personal life was way out of my control; all I had left was my job, and Derwent made it what it was.

So out of everything that had gone, if Derwent was the one thing I got back, I would accept it and be glad.

CHAPTER THIRTY-ONE

The hospital wasn't what I had expected. It was in an old country house for starters, with massive grounds that stretched down to a lake. A few people — I assumed patients — sat on benches or walked along gravel paths. They wore ordinary clothes. They looked normal. They probably were normal, I reminded myself. Mental illness affected a lot of people. Addiction would account for a few more. I wasn't there to judge.

Actually, I had no idea why I was there. I was nervous as I walked up the stairs. I didn't know what to expect, or how to be.

I knocked on the door and waited until I heard a familiar voice say, "Come in."

Godley was standing by the window, his arms folded. He was wearing a jumper and jeans, which was unsettling for starters. He was made for immaculate tailoring, silk ties, crisp shirts. I didn't know how to be around an off-duty Godley.

He had been staring out the window, but when I didn't say anything he glanced at me.

"Maeve." A genuine smile spread across his face. "I thought you were a nurse or an orderly. I get nothing but interruptions."

"I thought you were here for peace and quiet." I crossed the room and then stopped, feeling awkward. What I wanted was to hug him, but he was still the boss. "It's good to see you."

"And you. Thank you for coming. Sit down."

He had a big room with a sofa and armchair as well as a bed. More than ever, I felt as if I was in a luxury hotel, not a hospital. Obediently, I sat on the sofa. He took the chair.

"How long do you think you're going to be here?" I asked.

"I don't know. Weeks. Maybe months."

"All paid for by the job?"

"One of the perks," he said dryly. "You wouldn't believe the fun we have in here. It's like a country club."

"Not really."

"Not at all." He stretched. "I can't wait to get back."

"You have to take it slowly."

"That's what everyone says."

"Everyone didn't see you pointing a gun at your head."

He flinched. "Maeve."

"I'm sorry, sir. I can't pretend everything is normal. You almost killed yourself." I felt my throat tighten. "I thought I wasn't going to be able to stop you."

"I know." He looked down at his hands. "That's why I asked you to come here. I wanted to thank you for that. And for saving my job."

"That was Derwent's idea."

"I know. I saw him already."

"What did he say?" I asked.

"That I should get my arse in gear and get back to work, pronto. And that I was an idiot for keeping it a secret. And that he missed me."

"He loves you."

"I know. You're going to have a tough time with him."

"Why?"

"You have to keep him out of trouble. Una is going to be watching him, all the time."

"She wants to get rid of him."

"Yes, she does. And it will burn her that she hasn't managed it yet."

"He told her she can't make him leave."

"And he was right about that."

"But she could make him want to leave."

Godley shook his head. "Josh is too stubborn for that. He'll hang on. But if he gives her any opportunity to make him look bad, she'll take it."

"Are you going to go along with Derwent's plan? Fooling Skinner?"

"I don't really have any choice." He sighed. "It would be nice to get something out of all this. If I can make that happen I'll feel I've made myself useful."

"I don't think you have much to prove to anyone. Everyone just wants you to come back."

"Including you?"

I leaned back, startled. "Of course including me."

"The last time I saw you, you were very angry with me."

"For giving in. For giving up. For not doing anything to help yourself. But I know you were trying. I don't know what I would have done in the same circumstances. I hope I'll never know." I hesitated, wondering whether to go on, and decided it wasn't worth keeping quiet when I'd already said so much. "You always thought I was judging you but you were much harder on yourself than I ever was."

"I hated myself."

"I know. But I never felt that way about

you. I've always loved working for you and I will work for you for as long as you want me to."

"Thank you, Maeve."

I took it as a dismissal and stood up to go.

"Well done on the Amy Maynard arrest. I saw the footage."

I blushed. "Everyone has a camera these days." Forunately no one had been close enough to pick up our voices.

"You did a good job."

"Thank you, sir." I edged toward the door. "I should go."

He frowned at me. "Tell me to piss off if you like, but are you all right?"

"Why?"

"You look tired. Upset. Not yourself."

"I'm fine," I lied. Aside from the not sleeping and not eating. Aside from the ache in my chest that plagued me all day and woke me up at night. I hadn't known until now that heartbreak was a physical thing.

"You told me you were learning to ask for help when you needed it. Don't end up somewhere like this."

"It's not like that," I said.

"Talk to Rob," Godley said. "He's a good man. He'll look after you. I should have leaned on Serena instead of pushing her away. Don't make the same mistakes I did."

"I'll try not to." I made an attempt at a smile and said good-bye.

"Come back and see me soon."

"I will."

"Any time, Maeve."

"I promise."

I trudged back down the stairs with a heavy heart.

Talk to Rob.

If only.

I walked through the gardens to the car park, which was full of whirling beech leaves from the hedges that surrounded it. My coat snapped and billowed in the wind like a sail. The wind had a razor-sharp edge to it and I hurried, head down, to get into the car. I was about to drive away when I saw the envelope stuck under the windscreen wiper. I hopped out and retrieved it, wondering slightly at getting junk mail here, in the middle of the country, and at a hospital at that.

Heavy paper. A lined envelope.

My name on the front in the difficult, crabbed handwriting I knew to fear.

I ducked down to check there was no one in the back seat of the car, then popped the boot to make sure there was no one lurking inside it, then looked behind the hedges and in the other cars and everywhere and anywhere that the bogeyman could hide. I got down and checked under the car, looking for wires or bugs or anything that shouldn't be there. My mind was running through every single possible threat, every way that I could be harmed, even though I knew that Chris Swain had only wanted me to be scared, again. I sat back into the driver's seat. My heart was thudding and my hands were wet with sweat as I struggled into blue evidence gloves. The one thing I didn't feel was surprise. Of course he had found me. He always found me.

I opened the envelope. It wasn't sealed. There was just a single sheet of paper inside.

I saw you on television. You looked beautiful. But you seemed lonely. Everyone leaves you, don't they? But don't worry, Maeve. I'll never abandon you. I'll always be here.

Watching.

Waiting.

Drive carefully. It's a long way back to Farringdon.

See you soon.

Chris

I put down the letter and stared out through the windscreen at the trees, where Swain was probably lurking. He would want to see me scared. He lived for that.

And I had had enough of it. I was tired of being frightened. I was tired of running away.

One way or another, I was going to end this.

ACKNOWLEDGMENTS

My thanks to all at Ebury, especially Gillian Green, Emily Yau, Louise Jones, Amelia Harvell, Helen Arnold, Martin Higgins, Guy Lloyd, Jake Lingwood, and Fiona Mac-Intyre. Their tremendous support, guidance, and encouragement are what turned an idea into an actual book.

I am always grateful to everyone at United Agents for their faith in me, and in Maeve. Special, heartfelt thanks to my wonderful agent, Ariella Feiner, for making all sorts of dreams come true.

James Norman provided me with many insights, a detailed explanation of cell-site analysis that I completely failed to understand the first five times, advice, help, encouragement, access to police officers and their knowledge, and, most importantly, time. Nothing at all would happen without him.

The following people helped

tremendously, whether they knew it or not, sometimes just by saying the right thing at the right time: Liz Barnsley, William Ham Bevan, Peggy Breckin, Fergus Brennan, Lauren Buckland, Declan Burke, Frank and Alison Casey, Philippa Charles, Brian Cliff, John Connolly, Rhian Davies, Mili Doshi, Fred, Alan Glynn, Lesley Harrison, Amy Herron, Anne Marie and Aidan Herron, Kerry Holland, Áine Holland, Catherine Kelly, Erin Kelly, Frank and Rosie Kenny, Paul and Ann Kenny, Pat and Kathy Kenny, Barbara Mahon, James McConnachie, Claire McGowan, Edward and Patrick Norman, Bridget and Michael Norman, Katherine O'Callaghan, Helen Gleed O'Connor, Vanessa Fox O'Loughlin, William Ryan, Stav Sherez, Jeanette Slinger, Ann Sloane, Abby Stern, Nick Sweeney, and, last but not least, Mary Brennan, who is so generous with her time and praise. This book is dedicated to her.

ABOUT THE AUTHOR

Jane Casey was born and raised in Dublin. A graduate of Oxford with a master's of philosophy from Trinity College, Dublin, she lives in London, where she works as an editor. *The Kill* is her fifth novel in the Maeve Kerrigan series.

The employees of Thorndike Press hope you have enjoyed this Large Print book. All our Thorndike, Wheeler, and Kennebec Large Print titles are designed for easy reading, and all our books are made to last. Other Thorndike Press Large Print books are available at your library, through selected bookstores, or directly from us.

For information about titles, please call:
   (800) 223-1244

or visit our Web site at:
   http://gale.cengage.com/thorndike

To share your comments, please write:
Publisher
Thorndike Press
10 Water St., Suite 310
Waterville, ME 04901